Spiegel & Grau

New York

2008

SAHER
ALAM

The

Groom

to Have

Been

PUBLISHED BY SPIEGEL & GRAU

Published in the United States by Spiegel & Grau, an imprint of The Doubleday Publishing Group, a division of Random House, Inc., New York.
www.spiegelandgrau.com

SPIEGEL & GRAU is a trademark of Random House, Inc.

Book design by Terry Karydes

Library of Congress Cataloging-in-Publication Data
Alam, Saher, 1973–
   The groom to have been : a novel / Saher Alam. — 1st ed.
      p.   cm.
      1. East Indians—Canada—Social life and customs—Fiction.
   2. Arranged marriage—Fiction. 3. East Indians—Marriage customs and rites—Fiction. 4. Domestic fiction. I. Title.
   PS3601.L326G76 2008
   813'.6—dc22
   2007049047

ISBN 978-0-385-52460-5

PRINTED IN THE UNITED STATES OF AMERICA

10 9 8 7 6 5 4 3 2 1

FIRST EDITION

for Marshall

"I want—I want somehow to get away with you into a world where words like that—categories like that—won't exist. Where we shall be simply two human beings who love each other, who are the whole of life to each other; and nothing else on earth will matter."

She drew a deep sigh that ended in another laugh. "Oh, my dear—where is that country? Have you ever been there?"

—The Age of Innocence,
   EDITH WHARTON

No compulsion is there in religion.
Rectitude has become clear from error.

—QUR'AN

The

Groom

to Have

Been

BOOK
one

PART *one*

1

The engagement had been announced before the terrible thing happened. Sometimes it was hard to remember that. And at other times, when one was deep in the midst of choosing table linens and centerpieces, it became possible not to think about the terribleness at all, to let it drift into a distant corner of one's mind as if it had happened in a distant corner of the world. Even so, there were some on Nasr's side who, as late as November, suggested that postponing the wedding (perhaps even indefinitely) would not, under the circumstances, be an unreasonable request to make of the bride's family. Eventually, it was the "perhaps even indefinitely" part that would catch Nasr's attention—what, exactly, had that meant? But at the time he was simply annoyed. He wondered how long he and Farah were expected to accommodate world events. And he knew that the people who had made such remarks were letting themselves see bad omens and connectivity even though one thing had been set in motion before the other.

But before all that, in August at the engagement party, there had been a sharp, satisfying little gasp from the crowd when Nasr pulled open the blue clamshell box containing the ring he had secretly purchased. Sitting beside him, Farah had drawn back, too. Her face was concealed behind a filmy green rupatta, so Nasr couldn't tell by her eyes whether her slim shoulders had reacted to the flash of the carats or to the sound of their reception. He paused to wait for an instruction from one of his elders on how to proceed. He didn't mind extending these little courtesies; to him, they were not acts of blind deference but facets of a sensitivity to the benefits of accommodation that he had long cultivated in himself. A pinch of patience cost the younger generation so little and meant so much to the older set.

Hosted by Nasr's mother, the party was originally meant to be a small affair, as the proposing and accepting had already happened twice, first in July, over the phone, with Nasr in New York and Farah back here in Canada. When he called to deliver the happy news to his mother, she'd exclaimed, "Arré, but Hamid Uncle hasn't even met them yet," which was her way of reminding him that she herself, by an albeit unexpected turn, had yet to meet Farah or the other Ansaris. To banish entirely the notion that Nasr and Farah had acted of their own accord, the two families convened a few days later for the presentation of a peghaam, a formal proposal written and recited by Hamid Uncle, who was a close friend of Nasr's family.

This party in August was, therefore, the third marking of Farah's acceptance, and although Mrs. Ansari had originally wanted to serve as hostess, when the guest list swelled to fifty she conceded that the Ansaris' tiny bungalow plus basement wouldn't suffice. Instead, the Siddiquis' living-room furniture was pushed to the walls, white sheets were laid over the carpet, and heavy, log-shaped cushions were strewn about. A low sofa was put out in the center of the room, where the bride and groom accepted blessings and were subjected to all manner of related but unsolicited attention: chin-squeezing and cheek-pinching. But the crowd now looming above Nasr and Farah, though several bodies thick in every direction (the closest layer being all ladies: mothers and aunts, brightly dressed and elaborately bejeweled), was watchful and strangely unassertive. Also strange was that Nasr didn't recognize many of the faces before him, even though it was his own side that had run up the numbers, while Farah's had arrived in only three minivans.

Eventually, one of Farah's aunties stepped forward and thrust a palm under his nose. She wore a shalwar kameez of a shiny peacock blue that Nasr's mother would have deemed inappropriate for the woman's age, and her wispy gray hair had mostly escaped from the rupatta tied about her head. She wasn't smiling, but her teeth were somehow visible, unevenly spaced and stained red from paan. Nasr could guess what the old woman wanted—under the pretense of preserving the bride's modesty, she was demanding to have the honor of putting the ring on Farah's finger herself. Had she been sent by the Ansaris, he wondered, or his mother? Where, come to think of it, was his mother? While prying the ring out of its tight velvet casing, Nasr made the mistake of looking up and found himself exchanging awkward smiles with yet another unfamiliar woman. She had been craning her neck, as though viewing an exhibit at the zoo, but then seemed surprised, even dismayed, when the main attraction stared back.

Much of the evening had turned out like this: fretful speculations—*Who ought to be assigned to greet the guests? When should the giving of the blessing be scheduled? Who is deciding whether the bride and groom should be allowed to face each other?*—followed by elaborate, well-intentioned stagings that begat mixed signals and improvisations. Nasr supposed he shouldn't have been surprised. Although an Indian wedding usually involved a number of ceremonies, the engagement party was a relatively recent addition to the sequence, an attempt to harmonize with the traditions of Western society. But even now that it had become decidedly fashionable to hold such an event, there was still uncertainty about what, exactly, was being celebrated—no actual marriage, after all, just a promise. And not even a promise that held any religious import. The Ansaris were initially resistant to the idea, and then wanted to keep the event dinner-party-size (a proposition Nasr had heartily seconded), but Nasr's mother had strong ideas about the duties required of families like theirs—to not fall behind trends, to establish standards, to lead by good taste—and she was keen on doing all that was expected. After a few slips, she was careful to extend the "theirs" to include the Ansaris.

"Perhaps it is a good sign the boy is having so much trouble managing ladies' jewelry," said Farah's aunt. Impatient fingers brushed against Nasr's cheek. At this, he plunged his arm into the heavy, brocaded folds of fabric in Farah's lap and drew out a soft cold hand.

There was another gasp from the crowd. Nasr caught a glimpse of Farah's chin, a blade of nearly white skin dipping out from below her rupatta. The band was too big—the thick platinum slid easily over the knuckles—but the fingers Nasr held curled around and tugged slightly against his own, and the lips above the finely pointed chin were red and smiling before they slipped out of sight again.

A round of cautious applause followed, and a few uncles came forward to shake Nasr's hand and deliver congratulatory pats on his back. But when he glanced in Farah's direction she was turned away from him even more than before, and her aunt's head was bent over hers in deep consultation. He was glad he'd thought to buy the ring and keep it a surprise (even if this Western touch made the party more redundant than it already was), and he knew, of course, that Farah would never actually look at him, not with all these people expecting to see a classic Indian bride. But a man didn't give a woman a diamond only to stare at the back of her covered head for the rest of the evening. He stole another glance, hoping she'd make her profile available. Later, Nasr would wonder how he could have thought a piece of jewelry would instantly cleave a daughter from familial duty and allow her to favor her fiancé with anything more than a smile on a half-hidden face. How could a mere diamond (even one whose carat size alone was proof that he hadn't entered the engagement lightly) procure for him the privileges that many husbands enjoyed only tentatively? But for the moment Nasr indulged a pleasant reverie. Perhaps that first and unmistakably spontaneous smile meant that Farah had come to the same realization he had when she saw the ring on her finger: that the two of them had crossed a threshold, and from now on they would no longer need go-betweens.

More guests began streaming by, and as the wall of people shifted and cracked Nasr finally spotted his mother, smiling in that proud but embarrassed way she had when accepting compliments she more or less expected. At all such events in their community, the older generation's measure of success was tied to the question of what had been lost in the transplantation of old customs into new soil. Nasr's mother and Hamid Uncle, especially, were experts in identifying which silly concessions (pizza ordered for the children who had declared that they didn't eat Indian food) corrupted the authenticity or solemnity of an occasion and which substitutions were so imprecise (plastic garlands instead of those made from fresh flowers) that they ought to have been left out altogether. Nasr was satisfied that Farah was a person who would, like him, recognize that, despite a few moments of indecisiveness and vague orchestration, tonight's event had struck the right note. The congratulations he accepted

7

now were as much for his engaged status as they were for the gleaming and immaculate Siddiqui home, the sleeves of jewelry his mother had gifted the Ansaris, and even the way her three days of cooking lingered lightly in the air without giving the impression that the whole place had been fried in oil. But Nasr still wished he could have seen Farah's expression when he grabbed her hand. Had she really been surprised? And if so, what had that surprise looked like on her features, lit by that moment?

"Found it!" said Farah's aunt, cackling victoriously. Standing over the bridal couple, she held up a white box and pulled it open to reveal a silver watch. Farah's palm was outstretched but waiting too modestly to be noticed. After circling the box in the air for display and collecting a murmur of approval, the woman turned, made a rough grab for Nasr's arm, and slipped the watch on his wrist with a toothy, triumphant smile.

Just as a round of polite cheers subsided, Hamid Uncle's daughter, Jameela, said above the din: "I hope this doesn't mean, Auntie, that he's half engaged to Farah and half to you."

Jameela was always making jokes. She was a tall, angularly framed girl with dark curly hair (the color of which was constantly being adjusted), a permanently wry mouth, and a flat, amused voice that seemed to reside somewhere in the back of her throat but could spring into an exasperated or persuasive pitch with sudden energy. She wasn't pretty, exactly. There was always something distracting about her person—a strangely ornate nose ring, ill-fitting or floppy fabrics, an oddly boyish haircut, a dramatic use of makeup—that promoted her looks to striking or eye-catching, but probably nothing could bring them all the way to beautiful.

This latest joke of Jameela's, launched from somewhere deep in the back of the living room, inspired an eruption of laughter and applause that was, to Nasr's ear, the first genuinely comfortable moment of the evening. As though released from a semi-frozen state, the guests finally began embracing and calling out hearty mubaraks. The noise of their chatter gathered high above Nasr's head, as if it were happening at the mouth of a well, at the bottom of which he sat with his fiancée, whose hands were again buried in her lap. Nasr couldn't imagine what Farah thought of Jameela's comment; he could envision neither the arrangement of her features nor the emotion that might be assigned to them—and his inability made him remember, belatedly and with a stab of shock, that this was only the second time he and Farah had met.

A moment later, however, when Nasr's mother came forward and with much grave affection placed a garland of fresh roses around Farah's neck, he dismissed this shock. It was not, after all, so unusual that he'd seen Farah only twice. Their previous encounter might have been brief, but it had told Nasr all he needed to know: that the being behind the rupatta was composed and private in the very best sense. She knew the value of holding herself back, and her moderation was practiced not simply in the service of rituals but because she was receptive to forming a life with another person.

But just as he was thinking this, Nasr became aware that even though Jameela was hidden by the crush of bodies, he could picture, without effort and quite clearly, the expression that would be on her face—down to the tartness about the eyes and the missing warmth from what would have been her natural smile.

2

Everybody knew that arranged marriages were for desperate people: old-maidy, overeducated, semi-Westernized
girls who weren't pretty enough or meek enough to attract men
on their own and straight-from-India, computer-degreed guys
who had adolescent expectations and weren't patient enough, or
suave enough, or were altogether forbidden by their mothers, to
date. Nasr wasn't desperate, and this, he thought, when he finally agreed to let his mother find him a bride, would be his
chief tactical advantage.

Before consenting, he'd performed the usual evasions. He
pretended, during his entire first year in New York, not to hear
the long, martyred sighs his mother sent through the phone lines
from Montreal, nor to follow her logic that while it was good to

put efforts into one's career, one must remember that it was merely a stage in life—a time when one's focus, rightly so, was on oneself. But, like any stage, it must end, and other stages must be allowed to take their natural courses. Also, Nasr's mother didn't like that he'd changed countries, that she knew no one in Manhattan, that he wouldn't even go to meet their distant relations in New Jersey so that she could be assured he was eating well. During these conversations—the same conversation, really, reprised for weeks and then months—Nasr never mentioned how her own parents had let their children fling themselves across oceans without calling every other day. But his silence on the matter was, apparently, only encouraging. His mother became convinced that he was lonely and unhappy.

"Lonely for what?" he asked in a frustrated moment, one weekend evening when she'd called and seemed both satisfied and concerned to find him home alone, with no plans to go out.

"This is New York, Ammi. Just what kind of companionship is it that you think I don't have?" he asked, then mumbled, "Or couldn't get?"

"Someone of your own," she replied, "who will know you better than anyone—at least better than I do."

This remark, more than all her other words, made an impression, though Nasr didn't know whether to credit his mother for being astute or just getting lucky. He had begun to feel, after years of living on his own, in danger of becoming a cliché: the determinedly striving immigrant professional who'd been at his accounting job long enough that it was no longer something he set out to do every morning so much as something he *was*—a person who often attended meetings in cities across the Atlantic but for whom going out with his colleagues in London was beginning to feel a lot like going out with another set in Paris, a different map but the same bars and clubs.

At first, the charm of New York and of being away from home had been potent, and Nasr was happy doing what everybody else did: working ten hours a day, decompressing with a drink or two, finding dinner in a newly trendy neighborhood, smoking whatever was passed around. There'd been a routine to this freedom, but also an easy goodwill. He liked to think of it as sowing oats Western style, and he had prided himself on being, despite his upbringing, open-minded enough to try anything (within reason) once—including sex, although he considered these encounters casual in the sense that they could never, to his mind, have led to marriage.

In truth, Nasr had dated only a handful of women in his life (if going out with a bunch of people and finding yourself alone with one of them at the end of the night could be called dating), and each of his "relationships" had, to the last, fallen into the same pattern. The early parts of the evenings would be loose and undemandingly jocular. Through cocktails and dinner, Nasr would feel utterly in possession of the right opinions to be had on all subjects and would express them with a glibness that came so easily it was as if he'd read a script in advance. He'd hit his prompts and cues, elicit surprised smiles and laughter. His jokes, he knew, were often improved by his listener's initial expectation of what he would be: a polite, foreign-looking guy with a timid manner. He was, instead, insulting and challenging. "You Americans," he would begin, "are always thinking 'worldview' refers to what you can see out your back window. On a cloudy day, with the blinds drawn," and then he would give all the reasons why the national character of "we Canadians" was more considered, and therefore vastly superior and adult. These sorts of corollaries, perhaps because they highlighted the less serious cultural divide, were somehow softening, but they also enabled Nasr to feel as though he was blending in without giving up more than an inch or two of honesty.

But at some point in the evening—you never knew when: his passing on the "divine" prosciutto-wrapped appetizer; his admitting too offhandedly that he had no plans for Christmas; his accidentally venturing into a clever anecdote built upon the absurdity of his parents' generation's belief that leaving grand old Lucknow for a life in Montreal, with reliable plumbing, secure employment, and steady electricity, had been a comedown—there would be a crack, an opening across which a translation was required. His listener's beautifully made-up face would gain a puzzled look. She would pose an apologetic question ("Oh, what do you mean?" or "Really, is that unusual?"), then attach it to an understanding smile—and at this the gap would tear right open. It was not as though Nasr had anything to hide, but something about the questioning that followed felt disappointing and exhausting. Where, indeed, did he "really come from"? What was his family like? And why, come to think of it, would someone draw the line at prosciutto but happily drink beer after beer? The more inquisitive and hopeful his date became, the less willing he was to embark on explanations, and by the time they were in the cab or back at the woman's apartment, a tight silence would overcome him. He would become polite in that too-formal Indian way, which, consequentially, would require the woman to take the lead in the seduction. Some of these women were clearly dismayed by the change in his manner, but others were charmed, interpreting his hesitations and attentiveness as signs of unexpectedly deepening interest—which made the business of extracting himself more difficult.

One morning Nasr tried to explain himself sooner rather than later, to prevent misunderstandings before they multiplied—this was to the last woman he'd been with, at the end of their only week together. He got dressed early, made a pot of coffee while she showered, and delivered a mug to her bedside table, looking away when she parted her towel to flash him on route to her cavernous walk-in closet. Speaking to her from the door to the bedroom, he described how Indian marriage worked—how it was a merger of families, not just of a man and a woman, requiring considerations beyond love, such as compatibilities of religion, family structure, even regional rituals and codes, and so on. He went so far as to say that, given all the duties and obligations involved and how they were doubly complicated by the absence of his father, he didn't think married life was something he'd consider for years—possibly ever. Kate—that was her name—had paused while getting dressed, her blond hair emerging slowly from the top of her blouse, and laughed. "Well yeah, Naz," she said with a quizzical smile. "Kind of early in the morning for marriage, isn't it?"

Later that day, they met up with friends of hers for brunch, former Princetonians doing their parent-funded tours of duty in the city, and more than once she patted Nasr's arm affectionately or winked as if the two of them now shared a private joke. But on the subway home, when he was alone again, Nasr had the distinct impression of having become an amusing episode in someone else's life: the anxious Indian fellow who'd felt obliged to speak of marriage and his mother's worries a few hours after sex. No more than a pet, really.

*S*uch a sweet face the Kureishi girl is having now," his mother said with a sigh the next time they spoke. She'd recently attended a dinner party for a girl from their community who'd gotten married several months earlier and moved to Toronto; the new bride and her husband were back in Montreal for the weekend and enjoying, from the sounds of it, a hero's welcome. Nasr had learned of Rehana Kureishi's engagement with considerable relief—she was just the sort of unimpeachably suitable girl his mother approved of and he dreaded: wholesome, dutiful, college-bound but incurious, bursting with unquestioning agreeableness. Whenever Rehana's name used to come up, even his mother would concede that her looks were "nothing special."

"Arré, but now," she continued, "the quality of the skin, the eyes. Talat swears the nose even has straightened . . ."

Nasr stood by the only decent-sized window in his apartment, listening and eating leftover General Tso's chicken straight from the carton. It was over-microwaved, sticky but hardening fast. Outside the window, three stories down, was the building's narrow, littered courtyard. For the past week, a group of teenagers had found their way in and would spend a couple of hours each evening playing music, boasting loudly, probably drinking. It was summer, and Nasr couldn't imagine it was at all pleasant down there. Bits of trash occasionally swirled up, and a thick stream of noisy, hot wind poured in through the open window. And yet the kids kept coming back, each evening as the light was fading. So far tonight there were only two: a girl with swinging hair and a boy whose fluorescent yellow jersey glowed as he danced about and gesticulated.

It had been a few weeks since the brunch with Kate's friends, and despite their mutual decision to "wait and see" (her phrase), Nasr had called her this morning—then immediately regretted it. "You're a great guy, Naz," Kate had said, her voice lowered and thoughtful. She added that he was sweet and spoke of their time together as being special and to be cherished. Nasr supposed he should feel grateful that she was making it so easy. There was probably a kind word for how she viewed their relationship—a tryst? No, that would suggest an encounter that had been illicit, and thus had the potential to be of consequence. For her, their relationship had clearly been quite the opposite—not unpleasant but the sort of thing that happened all the time, involved bodies, and meant next to nothing. A friendly six-night stand.

Nasr heard laughter, a girl's, rising up from the courtyard.

The sun had dipped away by now. On the surface of the glass was his own black silhouette, cut out of a white square of reflected light. He moved closer and peered down, but all he could see was darkness.

"To be a young wife," his mother was saying—had she always been this pushy?—"there is really no other time like it in one's life."

Just then, while he was staring at the dark empty pane, an unexpected image, maybe something from one of those old Hindi movies his parents used to watch, rose up in Nasr's mind: a walk in moonlight away from the warm glow of a verandah, a hand slipping secretively but confidently into one's own, the soft clinks of a stack of glass bangles sliding against one's wrist.

"Are you sure?" said the girl in the courtyard, her voice high and scandalized but also pleased. A smudge of white stirred in the dark, someone's bare arm or leg? When Nasr felt himself actually craning his neck, he slid the window closed and stepped back. Without the whir of city air, his apartment felt large and silent. On the other side of the building, there were a number of lit windows, but certainly he was the only grown man spying on the furtive necking of teenagers. It was pathetic. He was pathetic.

"All right, let's do it," he heard himself say.

His mother, who'd moved on to detailing the problems of rinse cycles, paused, but just briefly. Then she continued with a description of her ancient dishwasher as though he hadn't said anything.

When they spoke again a few days later, Nasr waited for his mother to bring the marriage matter up. She didn't, for once. When she didn't in their next conversation, either, he knew she was aware that she'd succeeded. And when he finally managed to say that he wouldn't mind if she started looking for a girl, all his mother said was "Very good, beta," in a solemn, businesslike manner, before she went on to relate the virtues of the newly delivered dishwasher that he'd surprised her with. More than a half hour later, at the end of the call, she added, almost as part of her goodbye: "This is a very good thing you've done, masha'allah. For all of us." Who was this "all of us"? Nasr wondered, and he wished just then that he could take his consent back.

He'd expected glee, relief, tears even, but after a while his mother's restraint felt oddly fitting. More significantly, the image that had swayed him to her cause lingered and evolved: the moonlit path was now in Central Park, the hand was so soft and pliable it hardly seemed to contain any bones, its tentativeness made sweeter because there was no need, in this new setting, to worry about detection. His mother's years of talk had intimated a sacred enormity to the task of caring for someone, which had only made the prospect of marriage terrifying, like handcuffing yourself to a stranger and leaping off a cliff. But now Nasr could imagine how this leap might be exhilarating, even freeing. Just because the arranged-marriage system placed emphasis on social and familial compatibilities didn't mean that it couldn't produce someone he could love. And why should love necessarily entail meeting someone independently and unexpectedly, as if getting caught off guard were the key to its authenticity? The more he thought about it, the more Nasr recognized that he already had the life he wanted; all he needed was someone to share it with. He also came to see that the dangers of the leap would be mitigated by the precautions built into the system: the stranger could not, in the end, be all that strange. What was wrong with wanting his future wife to be someone for whom he didn't have to translate himself? Wasn't this just being honest?

Finally, Nasr discovered that all he truly objected to about arranged marriage was the path taken by most of its practitioners in his family: men who spent years delaying, squirming, making impossible demands, even charming their way out of engagements, only to turn forty (which was little more than a decade away for Nasr) and marry neutrally willing nineteen-year-olds who'd never struggled with the question of whether such a marriage would be like losing the game or giving up. Only Nasr's father had been different: married at twenty-four, three children by thirty-two. He had even died ahead of schedule.

A few days before the party in August, when Nasr and his mother called India with news of the engagement, the joke had already started circulating among some of those former bachelor uncles: "Arré, the prince is tired of the princely life already?"; "Why, the boy's not even middle-aged yet, Sultana," their voices bursting with laughter. "How can he be ready to give up heaven on earth?"

T he search for a bride began in earnest on Nasr's next trip back to Montreal. He, his mother, and his younger sister, Yasmine, who was essential to the process because she could communicate with their mother more efficiently, swept the local counties. They went to awkward teas hosted by nervous parents, sat in spacious, empty living rooms as well as cramped and steamy ones, pretending that the questions being asked were merely sociable: *Your family is from which region? Ah, yes, and before that, they were? And how long have you been away? All the children were born where, exactly?*

Every so often Hamid Uncle and his wife, Talat Auntie, would come along on these visits—lending the occasion some Old World formality. Even when the two of them didn't attend the meetings, they were almost always present for the lengthy discussions that followed, in which the merits of the latest prospect were debated. Sometimes these discussions spilled into the informal dinner parties Nasr's mother or Talat Auntie hosted when he was home visiting, or at fancier functions for the Eid holidays, and they also, Nasr suspected, went on when he wasn't around, for if his mother was on the lookout, all her friends—

an entire network of aunties—would also feel charged with the task.

When he was part of the debates, Nasr found that he didn't mind having other people in the room. It allowed him to say what he couldn't say to his mother when they were alone: Too young, too religious, too dependent, too quiet, too dowdy, too brainy, too ditzy, too Desi, too Pakistani, too modern, too American. To be fair, he often invited others to air their impressions: Yes, yes, to wear a skirt on such an occasion does show bad judgment, after all (his mother); Well, it's the quality of the family that is not what it could be (Hamid Uncle); I didn't like her brother—a total fobio (Yasmine).

Nasr was well aware that his mother wanted a certain kind of daughter-in-law, and that, although it had taken him a while to realize it, some of her requirements actually matched what he had in mind for a wife. Since Sunni Muslim girls from good families who spoke enough Urdu to teach it to their children didn't exactly hang out in bars, he was agreeing to an arranged marriage, yes, but his consent was not without certain conditions. Marriage to him would not mean what it meant to those bozos who came from abroad expecting fresh chapatis for dinner every night and who got nervous when the conversation turned to anything other than their work, their nostalgia, or the latest episode of *ER*. He didn't want an unassertive woman. Just the opposite, in fact. If one wasn't honest about such preferences, even brutally and publicly honest, wouldn't this whole thing be a waste of everyone's time?

"*Too* modern?" Talat Auntie said once, with a raised brow.

"I want a balanced individual, Auntie," Nasr replied, trying to be diplomatic.

She rolled her eyes at Nasr's mother sympathetically. "These children and their wanting."

But his mother waved away the sympathy, didn't need it. "No, but you will not be believing what goes on these days, Talat," she replied, "with some of these girls in this boyfriend business. No telling how many there have been in the past—or even in the present." When Nasr made this suggestion to his mother, it had been pure speculation, a convenient way to slip out of a prospect that was in danger of looking promising to everyone but him. The real problem was that he hadn't felt a spark, something that made him forget why he was there, but that was hardly an objection he could expect his mother to understand. "We think our people are so honorable," she continued, "but it happens all the time. One fine day, the father finally loses patience, wraps the girl up in a rupatta, and places her before unsuspecting people like us, as if she has been a namaazi all her life. One has to be careful. That is why I still like that girl Saman. Nice face, no fuss-wuss, very seedhee sahdhee."

Saman was a girl from Windsor whom they'd all met on Nasr's previous trip. He'd had numerous objections to her as well, but his mother was apparently not convinced that "too smiley" and "talks too much about the joys of knitting" were negatives.

"And then," his mother went on, "there are those others who tell you only so much about themselves, mention where their family most recently lived, as if that is where their people have always been from. Very chalaak—and, of course, it is working. How can these children be expected to know the difference between a Qidwai from Bare Goan and one from—" She paused, then began again as if from inspiration. "Now with Saman, we are knowing the full story. My maamojaan married into that family. Fine people. Straight from Chowk."

"The point is," Nasr said, "that for this to work she and I have to be as compatible as possible," without adding what would have seemed not only obvious but also irrelevant to his listeners: "since we're not going to start off in love."

Nasr's mother sighed mournfully. "If only the system was as reliable as it had been back home," she said, "where one could be confident about the histories of all the families worth knowing."

"Or where the children weren't so picky," Talat Auntie added with a sardonically curled mouth.

Nasr's mother's lips clamped into a frown.

"She's from *Windsor*," Nasr said, but failed again to make his point.

Shaking his head of carefully groomed silver hair, Hamid Uncle observed that in many ways an arranged marriage, at least these days and in this place, might be deemed as big a gamble as any other kind of union.

The mothers immediately agreed; and after breaking the impasse Hamid Uncle added, in a gentle but teacherly tone: "Well, then shouldn't the differences between living in a cultivated city such as Montreal (where one could expect to find a decent samosa) and, say, Windsor (whose municipal palate is as un-Indian as that of an American city) be given as much consideration as those between living in U.P. and Gujarat?"

Hamid Uncle wasn't a real uncle but a family friend who, after Nasr's father died, had adopted Nasr's mother as a sister. He was one of the leading figures in their community, which was now extensive but had grown from a small founding constituency, a handful of Indians who'd all come to Canada as young couples at about the same time—a window in the seventies when primarily engineers and doctors were welcome. A number of these early settlers, including Nasr's parents, had even come from the same place: Lucknow, a small, substantially Muslim city in north India. Hamid Uncle was not one of those much coveted engineers or doctors, though. Before taking an early retirement, he'd taught history for a number of years at a community college in Longueuil. But his native Lucknawi's aesthetic sense was finely cultivated, and he had long and widely been regarded as an authority in matters of taste and cultural fidelity. More to the point, he had overseen the major events in

21

Nasr's life: funeral arrangements, graduations, career choices, and now this search.

It was not that Hamid Uncle's presence felt exactly like that of Nasr's father, but he had known Anwar Siddiqui longer than anyone, including Nasr's mother, so there was a sense that his opinions were built on the same foundations: ten years at La Martinière, the architecturally ornate prep school in the south end of Lucknow, eating bun-tacs and attending vespers, during which the boys tried, in honor of their mothers, who would have been mortified, to keep from singing along with the hymns and chants that they somehow knew by heart; followed by university a few hundred miles away in Aligarh, where Hamid failed nearly every subject except English and British history, and Anwar set himself apart with a dedication to mechanical engineering. Threaded through this friendship, seeming in fact integral to it, was a childhood in neighboring compounds, sprawling homes that housed the extended family and whose daily mysteries the boys explored together and took for granted—and then spent the rest of their lives speaking about with growing reverence.

In all their descriptions and reminiscences, the life in Lucknow seemed so leisurely, so rich with adventure and supple in its demands, that Nasr couldn't help wondering why anyone would ever leave it. But leave it they did. In fact, it was Hamid Uncle who was responsible for Nasr's father's coming to Canada. To hear Hamid Uncle tell it, Anwar, who was back in Lucknow at the time, after spending a year in London on scholarship, must have received dozens upon dozens of blue aerograms imploring him to visit, to try it once, for a year. Montreal was a beautiful city, its people much friendlier than London's; the winters can be gotten accustomed to, construction projects abound (the Olympics are coming!), sponsorship would be easy to offer; we can be roommates again! Just try it, try it, try it. " 'After all,' I said to him, 'it is you they are wanting, bhai sahib, not me!' "

Hamid Uncle often told stories about Nasr's father that Nasr found surprising—the man whom Nasr remembered as unfailingly cautious and hesitant on the highway and shy with cashiers used to be an accomplished equestrian (such a daredevil that he'd been thrown once, attempting a bold jump, and had fallen into a coma for days). He also fell from a scooter (hence the scar on the side of his face), and on hunting parties he shot pheasant square-on, without wasting a bullet. "Best of all," Hamid Uncle would begin, sputtering already from the off-color nature of what he was about to say, "was his habit of carrying a rose into the bathroom to protect himself from . . . himself. Ingenious. Marvelous." Hamid Uncle made the quiet habits of a quiet man seem tantalizing and remarkable, as though they were choices, mysterious suppressions of a more worldly character, acts of will and therefore undeniable marks of the man having been a member of a distinguished tribe.

Nasr felt proud of the connection, although he wasn't always sure if this pride was for his father or the place his father occupied in Hamid Uncle's heart. And there were even times when he secretly envied Hamid Uncle, when he wished his own heart were as accommodating of Anwar Siddiqui. The only memory Nasr had of his father behaving as Hamid Uncle described was at a dinner party, when Nasr was around ten. His father interrupted a lecture Hamid Uncle was delivering on the delights of Lucknow's toonde kebabs to wonder why it was that Hamid had become such an expert in all matters Lucknawi only after he'd left the place. Hamid Uncle paused—Nasr had seen few people contradict or question him—and then, to everyone's surprise, burst out laughing. "You see how he keeps me honest."

What would his father have thought of this one? Nasr occasionally wondered upon meeting a new girl; but failing to imagine the answer, he often found himself waiting for it to emerge from Hamid Uncle's mouth.

"On to the next," Hamid Uncle said now, almost cheerfully.

23

With a few words, he sent glorious Saman packing. Sometimes he would say, "No matter. No matter. There's plenty of time," and Nasr would know he was safe from his mother's pushing. Every now and then, when Nasr made a firm rejection, it was Hamid Uncle who seemed to need consolation. He would pull on his hookah and sigh, declaring that the times were strange indeed when one found oneself glad to no longer be a young man.

A fter a few more rounds of searching in Montreal came a couple of trips to Toronto. Soon, Nasr ruled out the girls who'd arrived from India or Pakistan too recently. The half generation before his own—his older sister Saira's group—had suffered the growing pains of engagements made between first cousins (because that was the only acceptable option left) and marriages in which one or the other spouse was imported straight from India, as new to the West as an infant.

"We're not the same species," he told his mother, cutting off her protests. "It would be like marrying someone from your generation."

"So you and I are not of the same species?" she asked with alarm.

"Not in this way."

Once in a while, his objection of "too young" incited a full-blown quarrel. "The prescribed difference is six years," his mother would say, "and this girl is only five years younger."

"I mean emotionally," Nasr explained, then adjusted the objection to "not educated enough" or "not educated well enough" or too young in her career, or in what she wants, how she thinks. Having spent only a few supervised moments with each girl, he couldn't be entirely sure of the accuracy of such judgments—and to her credit, his mother wasn't always fooled. "What sort of virtue is age to look for in a girl?" she asked help-

24

lessly when the search reached its one-year anniversary. "Do you want me to marry just anybody?" Nasr countered. She didn't, of course, and her own natural prejudices often spared him from making the really crass objections. His uncles, those practiced bachelors, could and often did say, "Not pretty enough" or "Too fat already." But Nasr stuck to "Just not right," and let his mother mutter in agreement: "Yes, a big nose" or "The color is not clean."

It was during such exchanges that Nasr became most conscious of Jameela's presence. She happened to be there for many of these discussions (though perhaps this was because the only discussion being had these days when their families got together was about his search), and although Jameela hardly ever contributed much, and she often seemed sleepy, bored, or distracted, her eyes hooded and narrow, there were regular indications that she was listening. One time, when the rest of them were in the kitchen arguing vigorously and Jameela was in the den reading, Talat Auntie said, "Nasr Mia is a regular— Arré, what is the girl with the three—" "Goldilocks" came the reply in a dry tone from the other room.

In its second year, the search expanded into the States, then England—a radius so wide that it became impossible for anyone to come with Nasr on visits, many of which he scheduled around business trips, adding a day here and there. Whenever he could, he told his mother where he'd be going in advance so she could inquire about the prospects in that city. Despite how distasteful she found the business of relying on sightings from third or fourth parties who offered themselves as matchmaking experts, Sultana Siddiqui eventually accepted that the current times and circumstances required such measures, and she became more and more adept in her dealings. She would strive to locate these informants at dinner parties, mushairas, even weddings (it was the most socializing she'd done in years) without seeming desperate for their assistance. And she was always careful to say that she'd just started looking, or that her son was still so young and still having to work too hard (but reaping the rewards of it, masha'allah) and that she was simply hoping to get a head start for when he was ready to settle. Soon, Nasr followed up on recommendations made to his mother by friends of friends and contacts of contacts, people who knew people who knew people who had a daughter, a sister, a niece of marriageable age in this province or that country. Yasmine began, with the efficiency of the engineering major that she was, keeping a packet of his statistics ready for distribution, so photos were exchanged and résumés faxed before his arrival.

But Nasr always returned with bad news. Too Californian, too British, too loud, too shy, can't speak Urdu and doesn't care to learn, not willing to live outside Sacramento, Trenton, London, Dallas, too money-minded, too tall, has dirty fingernails, her mother's too conservative, her dad too imam-y.

Nasr's older sister, Saira, who lived in Texas with her husband and their three children, began lightly complaining: "I hope he's not expecting to meet Miss America."

"What is that supposed to mean?" Nasr asked when Yasmine relayed the comment to him during one of their phone calls.

Yasmine said that whenever Saira called home now she accused their mother of indulging her son's every preference when Saira herself hadn't had a say at all in her marriage—not that she wasn't perfectly happy. "The two situations can't be compared," Nasr said, sighing. Saira had married a distant cousin about a year after their father died. The wedding had taken place in India to make it easy on most of the family and the guests. She'd been nineteen, Yasmine ten, and Nasr and Jameela (whose family had come along, too) fifteen. In Nasr's memory, the tone of the whole occasion—the first wedding in their family—was set by their mother, who alternately burst into tears of grief (this being their first trip back to Lucknow since her husband's death) and tears of gratitude for the good fortune of marrying off a daughter under such trying circumstances.

"Apa thinks you've got a girlfriend somewhere," Yasmine said.

Nasr said that was ridiculous.

"Either way," Yasmine replied, "it's a good thing you live in New York—away from this phone."

Perhaps the time and effort required for the search wasn't fair to his sisters, but Nasr still felt that he had a right to be choosy. He had, after all, worked hard to become the youngest manager his department had ever promoted, and he still had his looks.

But Nasr hadn't expected the search to become a condition of his life. For almost three years, instead of going out with friends he'd spend a few hours with strangers in a strange city. And even when he did go out with people he knew, he wound up trying to appreciate the evening as if it were his last—his last time drinking, his last time returning to his apartment without giving a thought to waking someone else or keeping anyone waiting. If they went to a bar, he would drink steadily but not outrageously. If they were at a club, he would dance, but only until someone grew tired and suggested that they sit the next one out. He was never inspired to actually enjoy himself anymore, though sometimes, late in the evening, he would look up and it would seem as if the gazes of all the women in the bar were directed at him. This also happened in airports, stores, restaurants, offices, and on the subway—interested, almost rude stares, looks one fantasizes about receiving; shrewd but willing glances, coming over chins raised with cigarettes. At first he thought it was his imagination, but then other people began noticing. "You're not engaged yet," a friend said. "No need to live the life of a monk." But Nasr would ignore them, the friend and the women. Next week—he would think—or next month, he would meet the woman he would marry and this life would all be over.

He would drive a rental car an hour or two out of his way to her parents' home in the suburbs. He would be welcomed at the door as if he were a long-lost relative instead of a stranger who'd gained entry on the good word of a distant mutual acquaintance. Her father, gray-haired and froggy-eyed, with a professional but slightly apologetic handshake, would lead him into their living room. Nasr would be served tea by her mother. He would be fed a biscuit, a stale sweet dish, or pretzels. He would accept seconds of whatever he was offered, though it would taste like nothing in his mouth. Her mother, before retreating into the kitchen, would smile at him shyly but kindly, almost as if she felt sorry for him. An older brother, or younger (if he wasn't too young), would emerge and also shake Nasr's hand and sit down to chat with him and the father. The men would discuss the clarity of the directions, the father remarking, as though he were a native, on how rapidly this city—Atlanta, St. Louis, Cincinnati, Boston—was developing. They would talk about Nasr's job in New York, his career plans, how long ago his family had come from India, the brother's nervous hopes for med school or law school, a fondly remembered trip the father had taken as a boy from his own hometown to Lucknow (the "Paris of the East," he would call it with a sigh of approval or pride, as though his opinion were original). No one would say anything that alluded to the reason Nasr was there, but he would sense that everything he said was being noted appreciatively, especially the references to his family. In fact names and histories were sometimes so successfully recognized that it was as though Nasr had arrived with a ghostly entourage of long-dead grandfathers and great-aunts, all with enduring reputations for uncommon philanthropy, impeccably good taste, imperial piety, or simply an artful style of bringing a bite to their lips. In such a room, under all that warmth and expectation, Nasr would feel his manners expand and grow fine, his command of Urdu become crisp. He would answer the questions put to him as generously as was appropriate, with all the formal aaps and jihaans, and he would genuinely become what his interviewers supposed him to be: a lone but representative member of a formidable clan. With every smile her father sent his way, Nasr would feel himself being imagined into future gatherings of the man's family, introduced with glowing satisfaction. No one had ever worked this hard, Nasr would think, or acquainted himself with this many people in order to meet just one. Certainly not his own father, who had only been shown a pleasing photograph and told a name.

At some point, the mother would reappear, probably silently, in the doorway. She would be a stout, harshly aged figure in a shapeless shalwar kameez. Upon her arrival, the conversation would break; a hush would descend, after which another figure would appear. Slimmer, sometimes taller, almost always a shade fairer, she would stand beside her mother in a plain or ornate shalwar suit. She might have a rupatta draped over her head. Her hair might be black, thick, and glossy, or sleek and brown, with tawny highlights. The mother might have allowed some makeup, or she might have insisted on a strictly modest presentation. Nasr always felt that he could instantly ascertain the situation, guess, thanks to his sisters, the whole history of the preparation for this visit and the kind of battles that had been fought—all from one look, from how she stood there, from how she came into the room, smiling, and sat down quietly between brother and father. Sometimes people spoke for her: Sadia is getting her master's degree. Tazeen is studying to be a nurse. Sabiha enjoys cooking. Maryam will be nineteen in April. Sometimes she spoke for herself: "Is it cold all the time in Canada?"; "I've always wanted to see New York"; "How old are you?"

. . .

*T*he woman you want—the female equivalent of yourself—would never let this be done to her." When it was in the middle of a speech, Jameela's voice could seem sincerely speculative, as though she'd been open to your views and now you ought to extend the same courtesy as she delivered her own thoughts on the matter. But Nasr knew her well enough to recognize that this was a trap—a false reasonableness designed to disguise the fact that her mind was completely made up.

Jameela maintained her early habit of staying quiet during the group discussion about his search, but at some point she began letting Nasr know exactly what she thought whenever the two of them were alone. Lately, her approaches to the subject had become almost tactical, as if she were his rival in a debating society, and her voice was not the only feature that warmed to the task. Jameela had a long, narrow face and matching nose, and sharp cheekbones made more prominent by the amusement that constantly played across her thin lips. For an Indian, she had light eyes—almost hazel in color—that were often narrowed, darting from one spot to another with the formulation of an opinion. But during the debates related to the search her face seemed to transform. Everything opened up: her dark eyebrows grew wide and pensive, the amused gleam in her eyes dimmed, and there was even a sincere shape to her mouth. Her whole manner became matter-of-fact, almost patient, as if she were confident that he'd eventually come around. Once, she proclaimed with scholarly certainty: "The fact is it's an utterly corrupted process, run by well-meaning but utterly ill-prepared innocents. Why does anyone believe it will work when children, dreamy little children grown up in nineteen-fifties India, which might as well be Victorian England, are in charge? Sure, they're parents now, but the kind who have no common experiences with the children whose lives—whose *love* lives—they're attempting to arrange. I mean, okay, so none of the parents have ever gone on a date or to a prom. But I'm saying they've never *not* gone to a prom in the same way as us." Another time, she speculated that things might have been different if they'd come over in the sixties. "Then they might even have known there was a sexual revolution, might even have become the kinds of people capable of saying the words 'sexual' and 'revolution.' Though I doubt it."

It was only when Nasr talked to Jameela that he realized how relatively easy it was to handle his friends. Most of them were colleagues, and even if they weren't actually white and American, they asked questions like white Americans. They had confusions, but always confusions Nasr could resolve. He discovered that if he pitched it the right way, he could pull off any weird straddle of cultures he wanted. He didn't *have* to get an arranged marriage, he assured people, he was just keeping all his options open, indulging a mother who wasn't nearly as overbearing as some. "Look," he would add in a semi-offhand, semi-confessional tone, "it's the one thing she's asked of me"—not exactly true, but so what?—"and it means a lot to her, especially without my father around, that this one thing be on the up and up, culturally speaking." To the especially naïve friends who still wondered how he could submit to it, Nasr said, "It's only settling if I don't state my preferences, and I do" or "Well, of course, if I meet the woman crossing the street or lunching at the Oyster Bar, that'll work, too." And then finally, for those who asked about the principle of the thing—didn't his mother account for the possibility of his falling for someone who wasn't Indian or Muslim?—"There's this whole pool of promising candidates. Definitely promising to my mother and possibly to me. Wouldn't it be just as closed-minded to simply turn my back on *that* whole group because of a principle?"

But Nasr couldn't say any of these things to Jameela. With her, the more he talked about the search, the more ridiculous he felt. His explanations sounded overprepared, defensive, even self-delusional. For a long time, this didn't bother him. He appreciated Jameela's honesty. In a way, her challenges kept him sharp, reminded him to keep his standards high. Recently, however, she seemed to have gotten better at anticipating his next line than he had at hers, and after one of their marathon debates he felt like such a fool that he put the search on hold for three months.

*T*hat woman," Jameela continued now, "would have, like you on your better, smarter, more self-aware days, assessed the odds but come to a very different conclusion."

"And what's that?" Nasr asked, not caring if his irritation showed. This was back in June, when he was in Montreal for the sixteenth anniversary of his father's death. Yasmine was sitting quietly on the other side of Jameela, and behind both of them the café staff scrambled around, turning up the techno music and opening the door-size windows to let in the cool summer breeze as the place filled up with the typical Saturday-evening crowd: women in tight jeans and stilettos, men with gelled hair and bulging arms. For all Manhattan's variety, it couldn't beat Montreal's selection of women. Here they were all so polished and decorous. You hardly ever saw a quirky misfit with green hair, or unsexy piercings—at least not in the places Nasr frequented. He had said as much a few minutes ago. It was the sort of thing you could say in front of Jameela—in this way, she was like a male companion, distanced and assessing, though perhaps a bit more philosophical than necessary. But the comment had been a mistake, having somehow launched her onto this of all topics.

"She would have concluded that the odds are demographically stacked against her," Jameela said. "Look, theoretically a guy, a New World man such as yourself, still has enough candidates to make the whole arranged-marriage process work. He's got both New World girl, who grew up here, and Old World girl, born and raised in India or in some might-as-well-be-India situation. He can marry either without giving up any degree of freedom, because his habits, as we all know, are expected to rule the household. But the *female* version of yourself can only, realistically—if you think about it—consider New World boy, the one raised to expect his wife to have an opinion. So the pool for New World girl is already fifty percent shallower than yours. Never mind that she, unlike you, can't choose anyone younger than herself, either. So there she is. Stuck in a muck. And she can't hope to—wouldn't *want* to—attract the New World boy's interest by being passive, by being looked at and assessed literally at face value during chaperoned meetings that take place in rooms with parents and aunties looking on and thinking of her in terms of livestock.

"It's very simple really," she continued with a grim expression that Nasr knew actually signaled triumph. "Depth, which is what our girl will want and what she will want a future husband to want, can't be assessed visually."

"Nothing is being done *to* anyone," Nasr said, but before Jameela could finish squinting her eyes and ask him how he could be so sure, he remembered one visit in which the girl he'd gone to see had inadvertently made a dramatic appearance in the doorway to the living room. At the time, he had thought she'd tripped on a rug in the hallway, but in retrospect it seemed obvious that someone behind had, not very gently, helped her into the room. "And anyway," he said, "if it was, that person is not the one for me. Obviously."

Jameela's eyes lit up. "My point precisely."

Nasr shrugged. In the past, their approach to the subject of arranged marriage had always involved speaking hypothetically—he had thought this was an unwritten rule. But tonight she was aiming her criticisms right in his direction.

The waitress, black-clad with a long, slithery ponytail, came by with a fresh round of drinks. Reaching for their empty glasses, she smiled at Nasr. "You're all related, eh?"

Nasr nodded, then shook his head.

The waitress nodded, too, as if she understood. "I thought it was family night," she said with a friendly wink.

Jameela caught the wink and smirked when the girl turned to leave. "So 'decorous' means fawning all over you?" she asked, raking a hand through her hair, which these days was down to her chin and featured two thick dark-red streaks on either side of a middle part. The streaks disappeared momentarily, then swung back into place, curling about her face like the horns of a ram.

Nasr took a sip of his drink and shrugged again.

Yasmine slid up to the edge of the sofa. "So your point is that the choice for her, the New World chickie, is not so much between this or that boy but between one way of—"

"Exactly, exactly!" Jameela said, turning excitedly toward Yasmine.

"—life versus another?"

Jameela beamed. "Which is, of course, a much bigger decision," she said, pausing between each word. "For a certain kind of woman, it's the choice between submitting to a process that humiliates her intelligence while promising the narrowest margins of success—or not. Given those odds, it's pretty obvious what any thinking person would do."

Nasr watched his sister nod in complete agreement while sucking down her rum and Coke through a straw. Earlier that day, he had accompanied his mother and Yasmine to his father's gravesite, then to the masjid for a prayer. To have started the day there and ended it here felt like traveling centuries forward in time.

"It wouldn't be so bad," Jameela mused, "if Indians weren't so susceptible to commodification, which is all this is—the valuation of people as property. Daughters as childbearers, sons as future incomes."

Yasmine had apparently developed the patience required for Jameela's habit of discarding one topic and taking up another. She shook her head now as if she saw this sort of sad business every day.

Nasr had been surprised that his sister had wanted to come out in the first place. She was a notoriously dedicated sleeper. Usually her eyes would get droopy around nine-thirty, when other people her age began discussing their plans for the evening. Even more surprising was that Yasmine seemed not to mind Jameela treating her like a prized pupil. The two of them had hardly been close growing up, which was not unexpected, given the difference in their ages and temperaments. Unlike Jameela, Yasmine took no interest in pulling apart anything that she couldn't put back together. When she started college, she wanted to study engineering (her original preference had been chemical, but their mother thought this profession unfeminine and worked her down to civil), and now she was an engineer at a firm downtown and would probably be promoted next year. Although five years older, Jameela was still in school, where she had been a pre-law major, then switched to architecture, then social work, and now English. Ever since they were kids, almost everyone they knew had been a commuter student, living at home and going in to a city college, but as a teenager Jameela had her eye on schools in the States—an idea that didn't sit well with her parents. "Why did they get to come over oceans," she would ask, "to prevent me from going a few hundred miles away?" She'd collected several impressive acceptances, but at the last minute her mother made noises about her being the only child, and Jameela agreed to attend McGill. In exchange, she insisted on living in her own apartment downtown. Even this had created a stir in the community, with all the other parents fearing that she'd start a trend, which, of course, she did. But after a couple of years Jameela herself moved back home, back into her old room even, and started working in a bookstore and going to school only part-time. These days, Nasr had learned from Yasmine, she was for vegetarianism and against globalization.

"We've already gotten accused of being more English than the English," Jameela was saying. "This willingness to treat one's own children as investments is going to turn us into better dreamers of the American dream than the Americans."

Yasmine smiled grimly and rolled her eyes, as though she were an old hand when it came to postcolonial disgruntlement.

"Hold on," Nasr said. "Twenty minutes ago, you were saying the West is making mincemeat of the developing world."

Jameela paused, frowning. "That's because it is."

"But now what? Globalization begins at home? The poor materialistic bastards have been grinding themselves into mincemeat all this time?"

Jameela looked from him back to Yasmine, who also appeared puzzled, but not as concerned. Jameela's frown deepened. "Well, it's a continuum—the consumerism of the West on one end, the commodification of people in agrarian societies on the other. You of all people should know—"

"Arré, bibi," Nasr said in the thickest Indian accent he could manage, "but the question is being what kind of kebabs will all this keema make?"

Jameela's frown now began to struggle against a smile, and Nasr waggled a finger. He could always get her with this routine. "Best that little girls should keep eyes on the mirch masala, na?"

"You're impossible," Jameela said, sighing at his bobbling

head. She reached over and swiped the cigarette he'd just lit. "At least I have the capacity to think critically—instead of being ruled by assimilative instincts."

"What do you think you are, if not part of the big, bad West?"

"My sympathies are divided," she said, putting on a smug face.

"How convenient," he mumbled through the lighting of another cigarette.

"It happens to those of us who can see around ourselves," she said.

"Quite a little Mrs. Rushdie, are we?"

Jameela smiled, grudgingly impressed—she was always quick to get a reference.

Nasr was sure he'd successfully diffused that peculiar, challenging energy of hers, but now it was Yasmine who had to be dealt with. "So," she said from over Jameela's shoulder, "it's not a choice at all for New World chickie?"

"Of course it's a choice," Nasr said with a sigh of his own. "This isn't the Middle Ages. There are lots of choices. All you're doing is meeting people who've already made one choice: to get married. It's just not to you—me," he corrected himself. "Yet."

3

Two days before that night at the café, on Thursday, when Nasr first arrived in Montreal for this eventful weekend— the weekend he would, quite unexpectedly and after three years of searching, meet his future fiancée—he found his mother in the middle of telling a lie. "He's not coming until tomorrow," he heard her say, and then add that he was leaving early on Sunday morning. This last part, at least, was true.

Yes, she continued, a thoughtful tone checking the flow of Urdu, it would be a very short trip indeed, very hectic, but weren't all his visits so? It seemed to her, in fact, that she hardly ever got to spend any time with her son since he moved himself to New York. Which was why they would not, regrettably, be able to fit in a dinner invitation, and—her voice slowed here—

although he was not ever saying such a thing, she sensed the last time she spoke with him that he really just wanted to spend the time at home quietly, which, of course, made perfect sense as Saturday was such an important anniversary.

Nasr entered the kitchen and found his mother stirring a pot at the stove, the cordless tucked between her ear and her shoulder. She was a small woman, with short curly hair and a roundness of face and limbs that somehow didn't seem fat. She'd always taken meticulous care of her appearance. Although it hardly looked worn, her pale-pink shalwar kameez was so old Nasr could have sworn he recognized it from his childhood. For a number of years, she had been running a small babysitting business at the house in the mornings, so it was not unusual to find her on the phone in the afternoons after the kids had been picked up—making the rounds, as she put it, with her ladies' circle. Now she glanced over her shoulder, and though she must have been expecting him, her eyes widened. But she signed off calmly. "There you are. How was the driving?" she said, then made her usual fuss about how thin he was, and began plying him with tea and steaming channa and puris.

She turned from frying puris to rinsing potatoes without a break in her speech, and by the time she landed on her most recent deepening concern—she'd been getting fewer notices of eligible girls lately—Nasr forgot about the lie. She told him she was worried that they'd exhausted an entire generation, and that she might be able to take some comfort in anticipating a new set of graduates (her word) if he weren't so unreasonable about the age issue. "They will only get younger," she said, as if this were an academic point he had failed to consider.

When Nasr didn't engage his mother on this subject, she switched to gossip. She had an almost lurid fascination with a particular kind of scandal, and when she started down such roads the easiest thing to do was let her talk and offer a few words of surprise, preferably laced with disbelief. She took an interest in the usual catastrophes, of course: whose son had dropped out of medical school; whose daughter had shown up at last week's dinner party wearing a sleeveless blouse. But she had a particular fondness for near-escapes: whose daughter's potential marriage would have been tragic had a question about the mental stability of an uncle on the boy's side not been raised in the nick of time; which family learned that their future in-laws had hidden a son who'd been divorced. She related these stories, which she collected from the various continents where her relations lived, as though they were adventure tales full of scheming villains who were trying to invade the sanctities of certain families.

Fortunately, Yasmine came home and put an end to this talk about inferior bloodlines: "How do you know they are like that? You've never met those people." A few years ago, Nasr might have challenged his mother in the same way, but these days he was more inclined to think that while one should not rely solely on Old World presumptions, it was foolish to deny that there was some truth behind them. He was no longer so naïve as to suppose that a person's background was inconsequential, and by now even he could detect the difference between Qidwais from Bare Goan and those from Masauli: one group pretended to be family-loving, and the other actually was. This sort of thinking might seem unenlightened, but it was built upon an irrefutable fact: the influence of one's family showed. How your father or uncle or brother spoke, or how he presented himself to a stranger over a cup of tea, even how he lifted that teacup to his lips, was, to some extent, a product of upbringing. But this knowledge had begun to make Nasr's search even more trying. The visits seemed to be less and less about the girl, and in fact there were several times when she came into the room well after Nasr had already made up his mind. The last one he'd gone to see, in a suburb of Atlanta, chewed gum during the visit. Early on, Nasr might not have noticed such a thing, or if he did, he might have found it vaguely intriguing, but the first thought that had come into his head was "Gum—on such an occasion?" in exactly his mother's outraged tone.

I just don't understand why so much time needs to be spent together," Nasr's mother said the next morning. She had decided, she informed Nasr when he came down to a kitchen already fragrant with masala, to make aloo parathas for him, and had dispatched Yasmine to the grocery store for missing ingredients. "Never apart," she said, shaking her head as she adjusted the pressure cooker.

The kitchen was sunlit and spacious, with a deep porcelain sink and tall white cabinets, and Nasr's mother, barely over five feet, had always looked tiny in it. The two of them had had many conversations like this, with her busy at the counter and Nasr at the breakfast table, occupied with homework and then, in later years, the newspaper. Mostly, she kept her back to him, as though she were simply speaking to herself.

"Jameela is also working downtown now," she mumbled, standing on her toes to peep under the lid of a pot before turning to the sink. "They are meeting for lunch, and sometimes Yasmine calls to say they are deciding to eat dinner together, two girls by themselves in the city." Nasr noticed the shift in his mother's voice: yesterday's high-volume chatter replaced by a confiding and serious tone. "Or this concert is happening, then that event, and it must be seen because it will never happen again." The sleeves of her shalwar kameez were pulled up away from the dough she was kneading, and the two ends of her soft yellow rupatta hung down her back to the floor. She lifted a corner of it to dab her forehead. "Then there is this business of leaving the house well after one has come home—"

"Everyone goes out, Ammi," Nasr said.

His mother ignored him. "Jameela has grown up before my eyes like my own daughter, but sometimes one wonders how a person can have no sense of the worry she is causing her parents. Does not want anyone to look for a boy, and absolutely forbids Talat to raise the issue. And this is what it is called—an issue." She paused and gazed for a long moment out the window above the sink. "To have such strong opinions at this age—well, I suppose it is the parents' fault, too. Hamid Bhai was very broadminded. But is this a way for a girl to be?"

Nasr said there was nothing wrong with having opinions, when his mother turned to face him with a genuinely puzzled expression, one hand held up curled, like a claw, with bits of dough on the fingers. "Yes, but what does she say, beta?" she asked. "Are you knowing?"

"There's also nothing wrong with saying things," he said, shrugging. "At least Jameela's honest."

"Honest?" she replied, as if he'd said something obscene. "Arré, beta, there is a time and place for honesty, isn't that right?"

He shrugged again, and his mother turned away with a sigh of her own. She transferred the dough to the counter and began making little balls.

"It is they themselves who are suffering most now from all this toleration. Talat was saying just yesterday that Jameela told her that some friends were renting a hall and planning a big party to celebrate her thirtieth birthday, and she said to her, 'Arré, what is there to celebrate?' You know Talat Auntie. She can be so blunt and say the thing. But I was thinking the same myself—how could one not? Is this business actually something to be proud of?

"Okay," she added in a quiet voice, as if to herself, though of course Nasr knew better, "if one is not interested in marrying this way, fine, then do something, make some effort to meet a nice boy. As long as he is a Mussulman there shouldn't be too much problem—even Talat is saying this. She has begged Hamid Bhai time after time to say something to Jameela, make some insistence, but he refuses. In every other matter, one can be sure to get an opinion from him, but in this there is silence." She shook her head now and, glancing out the window again, sighed. "Given what happened with him, one would think he'd begin and end each day making sure his daughter doesn't repeat. Or"—another deep sigh—"perhaps he thinks he's the last person who can say any such thing."

"What do you mean?" Nasr asked. After a moment's hesitation, his mother began to tell him such a scandalous bit of gossip that he wondered how she'd managed not to reveal it before.

It had always been clear that Hamid Uncle and Talat Auntie's was not a marriage of compatibles. He almost always spoke slowly and thoughtfully, as though after much reflection, and with an extreme degree of consideration and politeness. Also, he was an avid fan of classical Indian music (ever loyal to the Sabri brothers over the "upstart" Nusrat) and a connoisseur of Urdu poetry. Talat Auntie was not coarse by any means, but, unlike Hamid Uncle, she was direct and almost defiantly practical. She was dismissive of the books her husband prized and had never been shy about proclaiming matters of poetry fussy and confusing; her preferred activities were clothes-shopping, party-giving, and keeping up with Bollywood movies. Jameela had long seemed accustomed to protecting one parent from the judgments of the other, and Nasr had always assumed the Farooqis' union was one of those arranged mismatches that were, if not inevitable, hardly uncommon. But now, according to his mother, this marriage had come together through "an unusual path."

"A love marriage?" Nasr asked, genuinely surprised.

"Nothing so crude as that," she replied contemptuously. "But Talat caught his eye. And he was insistent."

It happened at a time when Hamid Uncle was already living

in Canada, in the same apartment building as Nasr's parents. He'd gone home one summer to perform the usual duty: to wed and return with a bride his parents had chosen. A week into the trip, which his mother had spent taking him around the best drawing rooms of Lucknow, his father decided that a quick visit to the family's ancestral village in Kakori was in order. It was there that Hamid Uncle spotted Talat Auntie sitting on a cot, fanning one of his aunts. "You would not be knowing it now," Nasr's mother said, "with all this weight she has put on, but she was quite a beauty then." Hamid Uncle soon learned that she was not a village girl but a cousin from a distant and minor branch of the family who had recently been orphaned and shipped out from Lucknow while various parties figured out what to do with her next.

"Hamid Bhai had been living in this place and all these ideas had gotten to him." Nasr's mother shook her head. "No more looking—on this first sighting, he had found his bride. What could the parents do?" They had, as it turned out, disowned him, cut off all contact and support for the first several years of the marriage, so that Hamid Uncle, upon returning to Canada with his young wife, had been forced to get a job of consequence. "God only knows what he'd been doing before," Nasr's mother said. "Your father helped, signed for loans and whatnot. It was not an easy time for us. We were new, too—Saira was just a baby." After Jameela was born, Hamid Uncle's parents wanted him back—"He was the youngest child, after all"—and although he refused the restoration of income, he accepted their overtures, and the couple's standing in the family was reinstated. "But even so," Nasr's mother continued, "one couldn't help wondering if there were times when Hamid Bhai regretted how he used to boast about being able to describe the gharara Talat had been wearing when he first saw her. Which, with her being an orphan, had to have been of the very plainest of embroidery, no doubt."

44

Yasmine returned from the grocery store and regarded the silence in the kitchen suspiciously. Nasr's mother became involved in describing her plans for their weekend together. But Nasr found himself wondering if what she'd said about Hamid Uncle and Talat Auntie was a true secret. If so, why had she told him now? And did Jameela know?

When Nasr thought about his mother's complaints later that Friday, during the tedium of the shopping errands she'd scheduled for them, he knew he should have said something the minute she started in on Jameela. Or maybe he should have said something many years ago, in all those other, similar conversations he and his mother had had. The problem, really, was that key events had established Jameela's reputation among the parents of their community, and nothing would change their views.

The first happened in India, on the trip for Saira's wedding. The only response Nasr and Yasmine could come up with to the teasing they endured for being so American was to remind their cousins over and over again that Montreal was in Quebec, which was in Canada, which was its own country, entirely separate from the United States, like the difference between India and Pakistan, and that they were North Americans, not Americans. But this last bit only made the teasing worse. Someone howled, "Arré, maybe we should start calling the Pakistanis West Indians?" Jameela ignored the taunts until one evening when one of Nasr's cousins made a comment about how the *North* Americans probably didn't know the difference between bharatanatyam and bhel puri. "You mean this?" she asked, then popped up and began performing a classical Indian dance routine—complete with sliding neck, slanty eyes, and stiffly pointed fingers—that silenced everyone in the drawing room.

The second event took place a few years later, in Montreal, on Eid at the masjid, when he and Jameela were seventeen or so. The holiday had fallen on a cold and windy spring day, and Nasr was outside, huddled by a corner of the building, smoking. He heard a voice behind him say, "The namaaz isn't over already, is it?" He turned to see Jameela standing with her hands dug into her armpits. She wore a shalwar kameez for the occasion, but she had her black leather coat and heavy winter boots over it, and her red rupatta was tied diagonally across her chest like the bright sash of a military uniform. She was rubbing her arms and hopping from one foot to the other.

He shook his head.

"What are you doing out here?" she demanded, in her unflatteringly curious way.

He shrugged and said he could ask her the same thing.

She seemed to be taken off guard for a moment, but then she pointed to Hamid Uncle's car, which was still fogged up from the heater, and said in a rush: "Oh, you're not allowed to do namaaz when you're having your . . . I've been reduced to chauffeuring."

She looked away. The plastic bag she was carrying crinkled around her knees as she hopped. "The heels I'm supposed to wear," she said, catching Nasr's eye, the side of her face scrunching up. "Yet another reason why one should have been born a male child."

Nasr lit another cigarette and felt her watching him. "Why don't you just go inside and wait?"

She pushed aside her hair, which featured a stiff, Elvis-style peak. "You shouldn't smoke."

"I shouldn't do a lot of things."

"Like what?" she asked, her eyes narrowing.

Nasr ignored the question. He felt his head sag. Hangovers were still new to him, and it was when he'd imagined throwing up on his neighbor's socks during the prayer that he'd come outside.

Just then people began pouring out of the masjid. "Oh, let's go," Jameela said, and when they found their families she merrily rotated through the exchanging of Eid mubaraks—a dip to the left, a dip to the right, one more to the left—and looked genuinely interested in discussing what new Eid clothes would be worn to the evening dinner parties. At the time, Hamid Uncle was actively engaged in organizing poetry readings for the community, and Jameela, as his self-assigned assistant, was soon standing with a group of uncles debating which Urdu poets should be invited to the mushairas. Nasr gritted his teeth through all the jolting embraces and good cheer. His eyes burned; he couldn't manage the smiles they wanted, and he longed to be back in bed. If his mother had noticed that he left the namaaz early, she didn't ask why.

Yet by the end of the day the talk was all about how Jameela Farooqi had shown up to Eid namaaz in army boots and a battle-style rupatta. What a strange girl. And did anyone notice how freely she mingled among the men?

But all this chatter was unfair, in Nasr's opinion. Yes, Jameela probably *did* dance better than any good Muslim girl should. She *was* opinionated and didn't keep her opinions to herself, as any good Lucknawi would. But that was simply because there was a lack of exclusivity in everything she did. She'd refused to go inside and wait discreetly like the other indisposed ladies, but she had still come to Eid namaaz, still wanted to be a part of it. For everyone else Nasr knew, stepping inside a masjid, or going to a family function, or visiting your family in India, meant that your other life was put on hold, suspended without a second thought—a total submission. But not for Jameela. She acted confidently and spoke plainly, as if she had nothing to hide and therefore merited no reproach.

A few years after the Eid incident, however, Nasr learned that Jameela did, indeed, have a secret life—one that was so deeply and effectively obscured that her rebellious attitude was just part of an elaborate cover.

One evening, when Jameela was still at university full-time and Nasr hadn't yet moved to New York, he saw her crossing the street outside his office. Her big blue coat with its white trim and her white knee-high leather boots were unmistakable. He was about to call out, but when he realized that she was walking in the wrong direction, away from the metro station, he popped his collar and started trailing her.

They turned left on Avenue Docteur-Penfield and right on Rue Peel. They went past the big-windowed downtown stores and restaurants, and a row of competing ethnic bakeries. She had a long stride, and even though Nasr kept half a block behind, he could see that Jameela turned away from any looks she got from both men and women.

He thought he knew the city quite well, but soon he found himself in a neighborhood that he'd never visited. It bordered the back edge of McGill, a flat spot between the campus and Mont Royal. They passed used record stores and tattoo parlors. Nasr wondered if this was where the apartment she'd recently moved into was (he'd not been invited to come see it yet), but Jameela continued on at a determined pace.

Wouldn't it be strange, he began to think, if she was going to meet some guy? Had she been another girl from their community, this thought would have been ludicrous, but with Jameela, one never knew. With every step, Nasr could better imagine the sort of person likely to appear, some earnest poet-crusader with floppy hair and thrift-store clothes who campaigned for the environment or for orphans in China. Perhaps the kid would dare to sneak a kiss as part of his greeting—and what? Be shocked to find his interest forcibly batted away?

She paused in front of a brick building and then climbed the steps. It was an ordinary pharmacy—disappointing as a destination. Nasr crossed the street to wait for her to emerge.

That morning, his mother had mentioned that her sister back in Lucknow had recommended a girl whose family lived in Ottawa: she was nineteen, part of the pedigreed Rizvi clan, studying to be a doctor. Last week, there'd been a twenty-year-old from Edmonton. Nasr had pretended not to comprehend either of these hints, because for him there were already complications. He had just slept with Connie, his first, a rosy-cheeked Greek Orthodox girl with light-brown corkscrew curls who was a friend of a friend. She had surprised him by being so shy, after the notes and phone calls and the reaching over determinedly to kiss him in public. She had said, when it seemed too late to stop, that it was her first time, too, and for a moment Nasr thought she meant it was her first time at her house, in her bedroom. "Ever?" he asked, feeling his face turn into a cartoon.

Now the streetlamps came on, and their lights, though dim, glistened on the dark, wet pavement. The few people out walking seemed to glance at Nasr as though his presence struck them as out of place, which, given the formal overcoat and tie he was wearing, wasn't unreasonable. He considered turning back. What was to be gotten in an out-of-the-way pharmacy? Or, if Jameela lived nearby, why choose such an area, where there was litter along the curbs and the streetlights were barely doing their job? Just then she reappeared. She arranged her bag over her shoulder and, instead of turning back toward the metro, continued in the same direction as before. Nasr fell into step again, heading deeper down derelict blocks dotted by empty lots.

A few minutes later, the street grew quieter and darker, and eventually it was lined with brownstones. Jameela stopped under a lamp and took a piece of paper out of her pocket. She glanced up at the face of the brownstone to her left. The place had blacked-out windows and there were no numbers. Jameela looked down the street and then back over her shoulder and was climbing the stoop when someone called her name. He was more like a young professor than a boy, with long hair, glasses, and a satchel across his chest. He seemed to have emerged from a spot where he'd been waiting. They didn't kiss, but he did slip an arm around her waist after she turned to greet him with a bright smile. The two of them chatted for a while, standing shoulder to shoulder and glancing up at the building. Several times, his hand slid up and down her back. Eventually, they went up to the door, which opened without sending out much light.

Nasr waited, moving in a little closer. He assumed that the place was a club of some sort, so he listened for music. But there was nothing, not a peep of sound or a glint of light, and the buildings beside it were just as dark. He lingered for ten minutes, then fifteen.

During the cold walk back to the bus station, Nasr decided that one day he and Jameela would have an honest conversation, not just debate theories and speak in hypotheticals. He would tell her about Connie, confess the absurd thought he'd had after his first night with her: that he had already cheated on his future bride, even though he hadn't met her yet and probably wouldn't for years. Was the thought actually absurd, though? he wondered. Then: Who was that guy? Did he mean something to Jameela?

It occurred to Nasr that it was strange that they hadn't already had such a conversation, as the two of them had a long habit of candid talk, which began when they were young and he would walk Jameela home after family gatherings. These gatherings became more frequent when his father got sick and the local families assembled at the house for prayer vigils. By that time, Nasr's family had moved from Jameela's subdivision to an adjacent one of new homes, so their route was longer and more complex. Still, the two of them would wait and head out well after everyone else had left or fallen asleep. They would wind down Nasr's street, cutting across his development's freshly paved driveways and half-constructed lots, and make their way through a band of woods, toward a soccer field. At one end of the field, there was a tiny park with a swing set and a rusty slide, and extending from it a sandy footpath that led to the thick-treed blocks of the old neighborhood. Sometimes they would choose a different, more roundabout course. Nasr often didn't remember exactly what topics had carried them across streets and to the border of the woods, but afterward he always felt clearheaded, as if he'd spoken his entire mind.

"All right?" Jameela sometimes asked when they stopped in front of her house, a sort of polite "Are we done then?" She would wait a second, though they both knew that lingering wouldn't make a difference, that when he saw her again, in the midst of parents or parties, the nightly progress of their talk would have been erased and they would have to start all over, speaking clumsily at first, as though they hardly knew each other. After another moment, she would give a small nod, as if she'd gotten an answer, and head inside.

Now, walking alone in an unfamiliar neighborhood, Nasr took more than one wrong turn, but he eventually found his way to a mostly lit street and spotted a bus stop. In their community, there were a number of guys who claimed to have girlfriends, but Nasr had never known of a girl to talk about a boy, let alone be seen embracing a man—a white man—in public. Which proba-bly explained why Jameela hadn't told him about her, well, boy-friend. But wasn't it understood between him and Jameela that he didn't live by their parents' Old World rules any more than she did? Sure, he hadn't told her about Connie yet, but that was because it had happened just a few weeks ago; and anyway, he was hardly at the stage of making plans to meet up with Connie in strange, out-of-the-way places. Had Jameela moved out of her parents' house for this very reason—to facilitate such meet-ings? The more Nasr thought about it, the more obvious it be-came why Jameela had made no mention of this life to him. It was a pity. She'd clearly outdone him and she knew it. Here he was congratulating himself for his careful sneaking around, and all he had to show for it was a big mess: Connie had called him to say she wanted him to act like an actual boyfriend, to take her out to places and stop being so weird whenever they were in public, as though he didn't want to be seen with her.

Nasr gave up on the bus and hailed a cab.

Was he really supposed to introduce Connie as a girlfriend now? Just because they'd been together a couple of times? Having pioneered out beyond his community's frontiers, Nasr had thought he was alone in this narrowly defined quandary and would have to keep such questions to himself. But now he wondered if he could, even should, talk to Jameela. Clearly, his transgression was nothing compared with hers—she obviously had more experience, and a far superior sense of discretion. Not only would she understand the delicacy of such matters, she might even prove useful in sorting them out.

But when Nasr saw Jameela at a family dinner the following week he didn't manage to find the words that would initiate this honest conversation. A few weeks later, an opportunity to transfer to New York came up at the office. Nasr decided to take it.

4

His father's gravesite was a small plot on a bare hill about a half hour from their part of the city, and the masjid was a few streets away, in the same distant neighborhood. It was a beautiful Saturday morning. The mid-June sun was warm on Nasr's back, and the sky was bright and clear in every direction. The tombstone was pink and gray marble, and aside from the foreign name—Syed Anwar Siddiqui—it looked exactly like all the others beside it: worn and almost soft at the edges, with dark stains bleeding out from the letters. There was a time when Nasr would come to the cemetery on every visit back home, stopping either on his way to or from the airport. But on one visit he'd been distracted and missed the highway exit, another time he'd been running late to catch his flight and had to let it pass, and after a few more such slips, the habit had lapsed.

Yasmine was busy tidying up the grave. She'd even brought a few paper towels along to clear the dirt out of the lettering. Nasr's mother stood watching, directing Yasmine to a missed corner. She was surprisingly relaxed—reminiscent but not overcome with emotion, as she usually was on such visits.

After a half hour, the three of them decided to walk to the masjid, and Nasr and Yasmine moved slowly to accommodate their mother's short stride. "When we first came," she said, "this country was much too quiet for me—no honking horns, no shouting conversations, no call of street vendors. I wrote to my sisters that the loudest thing to be heard was one's own thoughts. Everybody said how can you be missing the noises—this is a luxury!" She shook her head, but with affection for her old silly ways. She had also filled those letters with descriptions of the parties she was newly attending, smoky and with mixed company; and how she'd worn her stiff and heavy wedding saris to months and months of such events, wondering why the other women, also young brides like herself, were so casually dressed in shalwar kameezes or even pants, until the first party she and Nasr's father had hosted themselves. Only then did she finally realize that the sari was a garment meant for a certain kind of woman: one with a cook who could stir the pots and fry the samosas, an ayah who could feed the children, and a maidservant who brought in the tea tray while you sat in the drawing room and obliged your guests by doing the pouring. "But we had left that behind," she said, sighing.

Nasr caught Yasmine's eye, and they waited, from long experience, for their mother to lose her composure, but she simply gazed around the neighborhood.

He felt his relief expand into an almost absurdly cheerful feeling. How could anybody not be cheerful on such a remarkably beautiful day, under the stir of thick leaves, with the smell of cut grass mingling with river breezes? He didn't know why they hadn't talked about the past like this before—without the customary silences and respectfully serious moods. His parents had, after all, been happy together. Nasr didn't remember them ever making declarations or even holding hands, but the evidence of their rapport was unmistakable. There was a harmony to the way the house was assembled and operated, and the couple spent patient hours together shopping and consulting to make sure their choices were mutually agreeable. It wasn't that there were no disagreements, but they were always friendly ones, between clear equals. Nasr's father was a daring eater, and particularly adventurous when it came to fruits, while his mother was suspicious of anything that wasn't pressure-cooked or deep-fried. He never succeeded in getting a blackberry past her lips, but she was always grateful that he pressed the raspberry issue: after one taste, she became a lifelong fan.

Yasmine's cell phone rang. "Jameela," she said. "I left a message about Bhaiya being in town. She's probably calling to see if we're free this evening."

Their mother let out a sigh but didn't say anything. This new carelessness in Yasmine's dealings with their mother was so annoying. It was as though his sister were regressing into adolescence—except that in her case adolescence had involved hours of quiet, serious study and remarkably little disaffection.

"It's okay, right?" Yasmine asked Nasr lightly. "I said after dinner." Then she answered the phone and walked ahead.

"There is one thing I just don't understand," Nasr's mother said in an urgent whisper, though Yasmine was ahead of them and well out of earshot. "If one is not interested in marrying, then complete some studies. Fine, if that's the path one has chosen for oneself. But those around one must be married." Nasr remembered then the lie—or half-lies, or liberties with the truth, whatever it could be called—that he'd overheard when he arrived. Had his mother been talking to Talat Auntie or Hamid

Uncle? Last night, when Yasmine asked if they should invite the Farooqis over, their mother had wondered what the need was and complained that Hamid Uncle was always monopolizing Nasr.

Now his mother said, "Already so many people have been asking about Yasmine. Have I started looking? Why am I taking so long? Let her finish the schooling, I have been saying. One thing at a time. I am just one person doing this, after all."

Her face transformed, the lips quivering and distressed, but she quickly brought it under control. Nasr realized then that it was not Hamid Uncle or Talat Auntie that his mother had been maneuvering to avoid yesterday but Jameela.

"But how long can one keep saying these things?" his mother continued. "I have told all this to Yasmine, only now she is refusing to talk about this 'issue' until your situation is finished. But a girl can't take the same time in such matters. She gets opportunities at a certain age that she may never get again. Soon it is said that she has her nose in the air."

"It's all settled," Yasmine announced, turning back, in her typically decisive but newly oblivious way.

As a building, the masjid was unremarkable: brown brick and slightly circular, with a small domelike rise in the center. It had been built in the mid-eighties, triumphantly but hastily by a forward-looking portion of the community who had grown tired of renting school gymnasiums for Eid namaaz. In the parking lot, Nasr's mother and Yasmine left him, busily adjusting their rupattas over their heads. He climbed the steps to the main doors.

The first time he noticed the way his mother and his sisters turned off to head to the ladies' entrance was also the first time he climbed the masjid steps alone, about a month after his father's death. At forty-three, Nasr's father had been one of the youngest men in the hospital ward, and his last stay had been his second, the first coming after a mild heart attack and the discovery of a murmur. That time, he was discharged with orders to follow a careful diet and cut back on the cigarettes. Six months later, he suffered a sinus infection, which, though minor, had traveled to a valve. He felt a numbness again, and the doctor asked him to come into the hospital for a few days of observation. There he was tired but cheery, until another heart attack struck, this time in the middle of the night. After that, the adults who visited huddled around his bedside. Yet even then he had been fully expected to return home. The prayer vigils that the community organized were simply a precaution, extra insurance for a speedy recovery.

A week later, Nasr and his mother and sisters were at a funeral, and then plunged into forty days of iddat, when the widow is supposed to spend each night in the house in which she had lived with her husband. In Nasr's mother's case, the house barely qualified—they'd moved in just a month before his father's first attack. There were still boxes stacked in the gleaming hallways, large rooms still empty in anticipation of new furniture. But this didn't matter to his mother, who had chosen a confinement that was far more stringent than the one prescribed: she didn't leave the house at all, hardly took a step out of her bedroom. Saira, who was eighteen and just out of high school, Nasr, four years younger, and Yasmine, just nine, followed suit, spending much of that summer indoors.

Now, in the masjid bathroom, after doing his wazu, Nasr caught sight of his reflection in the mirror above the sinks. He wasn't exceptionally tall, just over six feet, but his head came to the top edge of the mirror. His hair and sideburns were dark and wet, which made his face look thin, yet somehow oversized as well. Actually, he looked thin all over. But what surprised him most was how vacant his face appeared—uncluttered, even placid—which was all the more strange since his head felt full of thoughts.

As it was under the dome, the main room of the masjid was about a story and a half high, with white walls, small recessed lights, and high, narrow windows. Its silence was occasionally broken by murmurs, and more regularly by the popping sound of knees bending down into a prostrating ruku. Near the front were several rows of men in various stages of prayer, standing, kneeling, facing straight ahead, or bowing at the waist. At the back, the women prayed in clusters rather than rows, with small children moving in orbits around them. Nasr's mother and sister stood close to each other but slightly apart from the other ladies. Only the front of their faces showed from their tightly wound rupattas, and their movements were nearly synchronized: their eyes downcast, their hands together at their chests, the left under the right, their lips moving almost imperceptibly. When they straightened and were shoulder to shoulder again, Nasr noticed they were almost the same height. All those platform shoes of Yasmine's had finally fooled him.

As was his habit, Nasr took a spot at the end of the row of men closest to the exit. He lifted his cupped hands to his ears and began his namaaz. Even as a kid, he had always liked the look of this place. Its gleaming white walls made the space appear bare but clean and expansive, with a spareness that felt more suburban than severe, like walking into a new house before anybody has moved in. Even copies of the Qur'an were stacked out of sight in small recessed arches positioned at knee level (as if to encourage readers to settle themselves on the carpet nearby and pull the gold-edged volumes into their laps). At the front of the room, there was nothing to distract you or break your concentration—unless, of course, you were distracted by blankness.

Nasr sank to his knees, then pitched his chest forward until his nose brushed against the carpet's bright, clean plushness and he could almost smell how new the fiber was. New to him, he realized, but that could have meant it had been put in four or five years ago. He raised himself, sat back on his heels, and rested his palms on his knees. After the next verse, he dipped forward again, sliding his fingers through the ruts they'd already made.

Staying home for the iddat after his father passed had been surprisingly easy for him and his sisters; many of their friends had either drifted away during the move to the new house or actually were away on vacations. Various aunties would bring food over—groceries, but also tubs of shorba and daal. While their father was in the hospital, the three siblings, perhaps also because the house was brand-new, had been careful and restrained. And they continued to be so for the first week of mourning, mindful not to disturb their mother, who was on the phone with someone in India nearly every morning, having to shout private details across the crackling international connection: the state of the family's mortgage payments and savings, what insurance her husband had purchased, her health, the children's health, government assistance, her job skills if she had any. So even though it was tempting to slide across the shiny wood floors, they would tiptoe, finding by accident the creaks that could be heard on the second floor. But after a week or so of watching soap operas in the den, unpacking old board games on the carpet, and taking turns bringing tea up to their mother, they finally claimed the house as theirs. They spread out and filled its corners with discarded toys and clothes. When they ate, they left their plates in whichever room they happened to be in, and when they finished with Dune or cards, they set Monopoly up right beside it, or sometimes played both at once.

Occasionally, Saira tried to get some housework done—the

laundry or cleaning—but after an hour of stomping around, looking for the right detergents or sponges, she'd return to the game at hand or join Nasr and Yasmine in front of the TV. The hamper would get left in the hallway and closets would gape open, their contents spilling out. Sometimes Nasr and his sisters became conscious of their voices echoing in the largely empty house. But mostly they weren't aware of how their triumphant shouts and disagreements carried. Increasingly few people visited, but when an auntie did—usually Talat Auntie—she would take a tray up to the second floor and spend her time trying to persuade their mother to eat something.

On the fortieth night, Saira decided to prepare a full meal in case their mother came down. But an hour into her efforts the tadka for the daal had spattered on the ceiling, the potatoes in the aloo gosh from Talat Auntie had disintegrated because it had been wrongly stored in the freezer, and the rice had burned to a sticky brown crisp. In the midst of all this, they heard a door open upstairs, the soft pad of feet. Saira, in tears, said, "How should I know how to do this," and by the time she'd gotten the rice to stop smoking, their mother was standing in the doorway. She wore a plain white shalwar kameez. Her face was thin and blank, and her hair was drawn tightly back under a rupatta, as if she'd just risen from prayer. Nasr noticed the mail that had been piling up on the dining table and the jumble of the kitchen, the sink stacked with pots and pans, the garbage bin overflowing. Yasmine ventured toward their mother first. "I wanted pizza," she said in her usual solemn manner. Their mother gazed down at her, and after a moment, during which it seemed as though she was trying to remember something, she said, "Yes, beta." She touched Yasmine's cheek and actually smiled. "Your brother will order it for you." When the pizza arrived, his mother asked him—not Saira—to pay the delivery guy, and when Nasr returned to the dining room, he found that his father's place at the table was set for him. After they finally sat down, the others waited for Nasr to serve himself, and his glass of Coke was already full of ice, the way he liked it.

The next day, he was allowed to sleep in while the house was swept, straightened, swiped, and shined to its old polish. The day after that, his favorite meal was prepared. It was as though mid-voyage, while the ocean still roiled, the crew suddenly began treating a lowly seaman like a captain, in the hope that he would eventually become one. The sensation was satisfying but somehow unsustaining. And a few days later, when the four of them went to the masjid for Friday prayers, the way Nasr's mother and sisters broke off, wordlessly and without a backward glance, had struck him as irreconcilable with the weeks of mourning they had all just shared. Standing on the steps of the masjid, as men streamed by, he did not feel at all like a captain, not even like a grown man, just a kid who'd been knocked overboard while none of the crew were looking.

Now, nearing the end of his namaaz, Nasr sat up, then rose to his feet. He wondered in passing where Jameela had been that summer when his father died, and then he found himself thinking about the odd vehemence with which his mother had spoken of Jameela's influence on Yasmine. He was about to drop his arms when suddenly his lips stopped moving; the next line of the prayer hadn't arrived. He began reciting it again, from the top. He didn't know Arabic, so there was no chance of his piecing the sentiments together meaningfully, but he knew that if you didn't think about it, just let the memorized syllables trigger themselves, they came easily and swiftly. But his muscles reached the same spot and slackened. "It's selfish to be careless with one's own chances," his mother had said just before Yasmine rejoined them on the walk from the cemetery, her voice quavering. "But to be this way with another's—this is poison in the ears." Nasr skipped forward to the next prayer in the sequence, but again, after a few lines, he ran into dark, missing pockets of verse. Soon he was just emptily going through the motions,

praying the way he used to when he was a kid copying his father's timing: up, down, up, down, wait three beats, move your
lips. Around Nasr, the other men stood up from the last phase
of their namaaz; their chests widening and their backs straightening out of the humble posture, they dropped out of formation
one by one, like the disciplined members of a squadron.

5

*B*ack at the café on that Saturday night, before the conversation veered disastrously off course, Nasr and his sister
arrived to find that Jameela wasn't there. While they waited,
Yasmine updated him with gossip that was much better than
their mother's: which parent-favorite with a cherubic face was
secretly dating a French guy, a *black* French guy from Mar-
tinique, and which other one had been seen downtown last
weekend with his friends disturbing the peace, clearly high on
something. But as her stories grew juicier Nasr found himself remembering what a small, self-sustaining universe their community was.

Through the windows of the café, he saw a dark-haired
woman across the street, striding briskly. She was wearing a

T-shirt and black pants, with a jacket tied around her narrow hips, and she moved past the others on the sidewalk as though she was late but not prepared to hurry. She ran an impatient hand through her hair, a red streak glinting, and Nasr belatedly recognized her as Jameela.

It occurred to him then that, despite all their discussions in recent years, the two of them still hadn't had that real conversation, the one that would involve honesty and actual disclosures. Nasr's contribution to such a conversation would, of course, be much different now. Life in Manhattan had changed him. There was so little anxiety about running into anyone he knew that he could wake up and be the same person for most of the day. And that person, he'd discovered, was someone who found it easier than ever before to move between different worlds. He genuinely felt guilty the one or two times he'd shown too much interest in a prospective bride, only to realize that she wasn't the right one; on the other hand, he was no longer consumed with remorse for sleeping with someone he knew he couldn't love. The expectations of the two sides couldn't be more disparate, but the boundary between them had begun to feel porous.

Would he really confide all these things to Jameela? Probably not. But he might share a detail or two in exchange for learning where she'd gone that night years ago (even if that meant he'd have to confess to following her). Had she had more romances since then? For all the community's talk about Jameela, no name had ever been connected to hers, not one rumored association. Her discretion was remarkable. And, despite his own adventures since, Nasr found, to his disappointment, that he still couldn't imagine what was in that brownstone. He'd even gone back to that part of town in the daytime once, but hadn't been able to find the right street.

Nasr saw Jameela approach the café's entrance. Well, there'd be no revelations tonight, he thought—not with Yasmine around.

He was still sure, however, that when he finally heard about Jameela's hidden life—looked behind that door that had always been closed but from which came the sounds of endless activity—it would be like getting a peek backstage at a play. The room behind that door would be washed in red light seeping through thickly brocaded curtains; milling about would be a circus of people stretching, practicing lines, singing, leaping—representing all the eccentric interests that pulled Jameela this way and that. This morning, yesterday, last month, years ago, Nasr should have told his mother that if guarding such a life made a person prickly and opinionated, indelicate and unsuitable, then so be it. None of this—he thought, as Jameela made her way toward their corner and greeted Yasmine with a smirking "Hey, girl"—constituted poison. How could it?

*B*ut as the evening wore on Nasr found himself changing his mind. "Don't you think you've had enough?" he asked his sister while Jameela was in the bathroom. "This is just my second," Yasmine replied. She looked more disappointed than annoyed. *Gum—on such an occasion?* he might as well have said. Nasr supposed he ought to feel relieved that Yasmine trusted him enough to drink in front of him, but that she drank at all was news, and this discovery distracted him enough that he forgot his resolution not to be drawn into arguments with Jameela, especially when Yasmine returned them to the topic of marriage—*her* marriage. Their mother had apparently, despite all the whispering and secrecy of the past few days, broached the subject with Yasmine in her usual way: with direct orders for her daughter to submit her information to a matchmaking agency known as Mrs. Saleem's Family Connections.

"At first I thought it was for Bhaiya," Yasmine said, "but no, I was supposed to be checking it out for myself. Ammi said, 'Oh, it'll be different with you, much more efficient.'" Yasmine had always done an almost ruthlessly good impression of their mother's singsongy accent. "As if efficiency was supposed to make me feel better. I was, like, whoa, Sultana. I'm not ready for this."

The more Yasmine complained, the more Jameela sympathized ("Well, of course—who can be ready for marriage to a stranger?"), and the more Nasr found himself wondering why Yasmine shouldn't start thinking about her prospects. Not everyone could be like Jameela, and twenty-five was a good age, maybe even late by some standards. Truth be told, Nasr had never given his sister's prospects much thought before. But as far as he could see Yasmine was a friendly, hardworking, and practical girl. She was also pretty, with a ready smile and their mother's fair skin, and Nasr imagined she would be considered a good catch by any family. By any family that didn't know she went out drinking, that is.

Jameela, of course, had different ideas.

"It's incredible that people believe this sort of nonsense will work," she said. She grimaced and shook her head. "That, upon meeting someone for the first time ever, you're supposed to imagine how they would conduct themselves in a marriage. And you're supposed to do all this when you can hardly know such a thing about yourself!"

"But you're always extrapolating with fewer variables than you wish you had," Nasr said. "People date for a reason."

"Yes, but this is not dating," Jameela said. "It's dating's ugly cousin—profiling. It's coming up with the most complex extrapolation based on one undoubtedly artificial impression gained in the presence of parents and now professional God-knows-who-elses."

"You get more than one impression," Nasr said. He tried to keep his tone reasonable, hoping that the contrast with Jameela's would appeal to Yasmine's good sense.

"You mean somebody lets you take your girls out alone," Jameela said, "to dinner and a movie?"

Nasr ignored the "girls" part. "We live in the age of the phone and e-mail."

"And have you ever contacted a girl after going to see her?"

Why did she keep doing this, Nasr wondered—turning everything on him? What about her life—was it fair to have all these opinions without risking anything about herself? But being a person who'd long believed that the code of discretion should be mutually respected, he wasn't about to out her. Worse, he found himself answering truthfully: "No."

"And why not?" Jameela asked with a trapping smile, and she continued before he could reply. "It's because you trust your first impression, right? What I'm saying is that the *circumstances* of the assessing, which these parents of ours all dismiss as irrelevant, are not. Instead of being drawn *to* someone—as *opposed* to someone else—and *then* thinking about your future together, your mission here is to find the girl who best fits into the future you've already planned."

"It's not a *mission*," Nasr said. His imitation of Jameela's hissing emphasis drew smiles from both of them. "You're making it sound like the guy is on a hunting trip and the girl is some unsuspecting target. But both sides get equal opportunity—"

"Don't you mean lack of opportunity?" Jameela said. She and Yasmine were sitting on a love seat across from Nasr, and Jameela posed the question to Yasmine as if she were a judge hearing a case. "Don't you see each other for only an hour tops?"

"Fine," Nasr said, "but it's still equal."

"But equal doesn't mean it's fair," Jameela informed Yasmine. "Feminism one-oh-one."

Nasr sighed. "Well, I've met plenty of smart and liberated women through this process."

"And?" she said, turning back to him now with lawyerly posturing.

"And I've married them all in secret ceremonies in the mountains of Utah." Jameela rolled her eyes. "And nothing," he said, also addressing Yasmine, who now wore an appropriately impartial expression as she listened. "I wait for the right one. There's no gun to my head."

Jameela clapped her hands together and smiled. "My point exactly!"

"I don't even know why anyone would want to marry his 'female equivalent,'" Nasr said, trying to disrupt the self-celebration. "What does that even mean?"

He was pleased when Yasmine asked, "Yeah, what is that?"

"The normal stuff," Jameela replied. "Same level of education, same general sort of parents—"

"I'm hardly giving that up, going the arranged-marriage route," Nasr said.

"Same way of thinking," Jameela added. "Someone who has lived as you have, worked as you have." She looked pointedly at Nasr's glass. "And made decisions as you have. Look," she said, "it's one thing to be ready and willing when you've barely seen the world and have lived behind the iron burqa all your life. But there is no gun to your head, and yet here you are. Here so many people are, feeding yourselves to this thing that's still in existence—even though it's the twenty-first century and we live halfway across the world." Jameela's voice was attracting interested looks from the nearby tables, but she didn't seem to notice.

"Yes, but whether you like to admit it or not," Nasr said, "we all know there are practical matters to consider. In our culture"—Jameela winced at this word, but he continued—"one's family does matter, and it's best for all if one's spouse fits into it well. And, strange as it may seem to you, the culture is actually a fascinating one. I mean, India itself is a fascinating place. Just because certain customs don't always mix well—"

"*Fascinating place?*" Jameela said with an energetic cackle, eyes aglow. "Do you say that to people?"

Nasr took a sip of his drink.

"So you've spent three years looking for someone who can get along with Yasmine?" Jameela asked. "Hear that, lucky girl?" She elbowed Yasmine and shook her head with disbelief, and for a moment Nasr had the oddest sensation that something about Jameela's expression was overdone, a bit acted.

"Well, what do you suggest?" he asked. "What's the alternative?"

"Take the parents out of it," Jameela said. "If not out of the whole thing, then at least out of the room. Stop pretending that we're all innocent know-nothings who can be happy with any other innocent, warm-blooded know-nothing." She took a long, skeptical drag from her cigarette and blew a stream of smoke from the corner of her mouth.

"I mean, has there ever in the history of arranged marriage been a pool like this?"

"Like what?" Yasmine asked.

"Like who in fucking North America hasn't watched a *music* video?"

The waitress came by again, and Jameela slumped back in her seat. "One simple whiskey soda," the waitress announced to Nasr. He saw Yasmine catch Jameela's eye, and when the waitress left the two of them burst out, "Simply simplify!" This, for some reason, was extremely funny to Yasmine, so much so that she tipped into Jameela with uncontrollable laughter, and she couldn't stop grinning as Jameela explained to Nasr that the slogan was part of a classified matrimonial ad that they'd come up with for submission to *India Abroad*. "Simply S.I.M.P.L.I.F.Y. your life with me," it said, with the acronym standing for "Single Indian Muslim Professional, Lucknawi, Intelligent, Female—Young."

"Young-ish," Jameela added. "Thirty must still qualify, in some societies."

Yasmine confirmed this by raising her drink for a toast, a glassy smile on her face.

Nasr cast a vigilant glance about the café. One witnessed sip was all it took to be thought of as a person who drank. There was, after all, a reason that you ordered a rum and Coke. If Jameela had taken it upon herself to initiate Yasmine into a certain kind of life, then she should at least do it with the care that she applied to her own interests. Her glass, he noted during the toast, was still mostly full. Nasr also realized then what it was about the two women's appearances that had been surprising him all night. It was not just how similarly they were done up— it was that Jameela looked like Yasmine, rather than the other way around. Gone were the big, loopy earrings and the shabby, thick fabrics (which had looked like actual slabs of upholstery) that Jameela had worn the last time he visited. Her pants were as tasteful as Yasmine's, and there was no political slogan plastered across the front of her T-shirt. The two of them, though perhaps less scantily dressed, looked like many of the other women in the bar. Even Jameela's hair, aside from the red streak, seemed different—tidier, adventurous in a merely fashionable way. And for some reason, Nasr found her new aesthetic to be annoying, as though it was yet another one of her tactics.

"Enjoy yourself while you can, my dear," Jameela told Yasmine. "But just don't age. Turning thirty is like sending a nuclear weapon through their poor little hearts. It's when you have to start consoling them—and there's nothing funny about that."

Yasmine let out another vigorous laugh. What was the need, Nasr wondered, of turning his sister into a cynic?

"So what," he asked, "you're saying a person like you is too good to marry me?"

Jameela replied first with a lazy, dismissive smile, then said, "We're not talking about me."

"But that is what you're saying, right?" To Nasr's satisfaction, his tone of voice had stripped that unsober smile from Yasmine's face.

"Is this your way of popping the question?" Jameela asked, eyes still arch and unconcerned.

"What do you think?"

This time Jameela answered with a long look of skepticism that, after she mashed her cigarette into an ashtray, evolved into a dismayed frown. Yasmine's expression had also shifted, from surprise to nervousness.

A few months later, Nasr would recall the next moment with lingering self-consciousness, though what happened was so slight that it hardly seemed worth considering—just a quick sweep of Jameela's eye, a look lasting no more than a few seconds. Perhaps the very instantaneousness of this glance was what fooled him, made him think he'd finally gained the advantage in the conversation instead of noticing that he was being taken in, measured and brought like an object of curiosity to the center of another person's full and frank attention.

"Well," Jameela said finally, in an absurdly kind and patronizing tone, as if *she* felt sorry for him, "what is it that you want from this whole search business, then?"

"I want what everybody wants."

"Which is?"

"To feel something. A spark."

"Spark?" Jameela said. "What kind of spark?"

"I don't know—something surprising."

"How do you detect this spark?" she asked.

"You pick up stuff going about your own life." He felt as if she was feeding off his words. The more he gave, the more she would consume, yet he couldn't keep himself from blathering on. "You keep your eyes open, have an open mind. Meet people, get to know them. Figure out what's attractive to you, what's not."

"I see," Jameela said sternly. "So she has to be a clean slate, and as long as it seems to you, based on all your vast experiences, that the two of you would be good in bed, she's fair game."

"I didn't say that."

"Do you at least make any of this known to the people you see? That you're not looking for conversation or companionship? Just a good time with a pretty virgin?"

"Oh, come on. You know as well as I do there's more to it than that."

"More to what?" she asked, and then before he could respond: "Well?" Her lips were clamped together, and there was a scowling, closed fist of a look on her face.

Nasr had wondered for years when Jameela had lost her virginity and to whom—not *whether* she had at all. But he felt that he could see the truth now, plain as day. Hers wasn't the outrage of experience but of innocence.

"Not everyone has hopes as high as yours," he said.

"Hopes?" she asked. "What do you mean?"

The evening at that brownstone had thrown him off. But now, all of a sudden, Nasr wondered if he'd been deliberately misled, for it struck him as the height of hypocrisy. A betrayal, even. To have dispensed so much advice over the years, injected so many opinions here and there, counseled Yasmine as though she were some kind of expert—all from such a limited position, without an iota of actual experience. What a fool he'd been to have missed it.

"We don't all live in a Harlequin romance," he said, "saving ourselves for some perfect match."

Jameela's face drew in, her eyebrows descended into a flat line under her forehead. "You have no idea what I hope for," she said.

"Well, what is it that you want to know from me? The names of each girlfriend, optimal positions?"

Jameela's face now was drained of all expression. "I'm just saying, if I were on the other end, I wouldn't want—"

"Well, lucky for us, nobody's asking."

*T*hat was June. But before Nasr had time to consider that Jameela might be right, that she'd merely given voice to all the doubts that were mounting in his own mind—that he'd outgrown the process, that perhaps it was time to give up, that he'd wasted three years looking for someone who didn't exist—his mother, the next day, the Sunday of that weekend, said she'd received a call while he was out. It was about a family in Cornwall, a small town an hour west of Montreal. The parents had three daughters and were looking for a match for the eldest. If he'd stay one more day, his mother said, they could all drive out together for a visit. Nasr reminded her that Cornwall was on the way back for him—if these people were free, he could easily stop by on his own. And get it over with, he thought to himself.

The drive to the Ansari home took longer than expected, and until Nasr was actually put in front of Farah, all he kept seeing during the whole trip was the image of a slowly opening door. The room behind the door had a small high window in one corner, and in another, a bare desk and a chair. Apart from that, it was empty—a lonely, left-behind place. And the light in it was gray, as if the very air itself had accumulated a fine layer of dust.

6

The house, when Nasr finally found it, was tiny—a simple box of white vinyl siding with two small windows in front, one overlooking a narrow patch of yard, the other a black, shiny asphalt driveway. On both sides, it was attached to other houses that looked much like it, and the sad-faced trio was embedded deep in a treeless subdivision, around which Nasr had spent the better part of an hour driving, lost.

On a Sunday, Cornwall could be reached in forty-five minutes from Montreal, but Nasr was a full two hours late. He was greeted at the front door by a short man in his fifties, wearing a light dress shirt, untucked, over blue pants. The man, who introduced himself as Parvez Ansari, had graying eyebrows, but the trim beard (no mustache) contouring his jaw was very white. He smiled briefly and stood inside the house, holding aside the screen door but not exactly inviting Nasr in. Mr. Ansari asked how the traffic had been, and kept glancing back over his shoulder while Nasr made his apologies. Nasr couldn't tell whether the man was nervous or annoyed, and he was even more puzzled when Mr. Ansari suddenly stepped back from the door and began warmly gesturing him in.

The entryway was a cramped area with linoleum flooring; a half-step turn delivered him to a small carpeted living room. There, a middle-aged woman with a wide face, her hair completely covered in a white headscarf that looked as thick as a dinner napkin, stood beside a couch on which three girls were seated. Each girl had a rupatta lightly draped over her head, and they were all dressed in nearly identical shalwar suits of a plain, pinkish beige. Nasr saw their downcast eyes, their carefully crossed hands and scrubbed-clean, colorless faces, and thought, I'm getting too old for this. He nearly announced that he had a flight to catch and couldn't actually stay.

Mrs. Ansari gestured anxious fingers toward an armchair. "Come, sit here." Glancing back toward the girls, none of whom had stirred, she offered him a cup of tea. Nasr accepted, and stood waiting for Mr. Ansari to seat himself in the other armchair. But the older man stayed at the far end of the room by a saloon-style set of swinging doors as though he'd been planted there, and Mrs. Ansari now moved to join him. Nasr eventually sat in the seat opposite the three figures.

The room was dim and furnished with the barest of essentials: a sofa, two armchairs, a coffee table. Except for an unframed brownish-gold hologram of the Kaaba that hung above the sofa and a grocery-store calendar tacked beside the saloon doors, the walls were empty.

Mr. Ansari apologized for the complicated directions so hesitantly, as if he wasn't sure it was his place to speak, that Nasr wondered if the man's gruff manner at the front door had been accidental. Nasr assured him that the directions were absolutely right, and he made up a little story about how he'd misread his own handwriting and thus kept missing a particular turn on the way. None of the girls said a word, or even looked up. After years of meetings like this, Nasr thought he had perfected the art of disguising his glances at whichever girl he had come to investigate—he would usually do it while explaining something about his job to the parents, as though the daughter of the house were the last thing he was interested in. But with the three Ansari girls just sitting there and neither Mr. nor Mrs. Ansari asking him any substantial questions, he could hardly keep himself from openly staring. Up close, the major themes of the girls' features were apparent: smooth pale cheeks and thick dark eyelashes. But the lineup of profiles also accentuated slight variations: one girl had solemn, delicate brows, another soft but well-shaped and vaguely smiling lips. The middle one had more difficulty keeping her eyes down than the other two. Had the three of them been sitting like this for the past two hours?

Mrs. Ansari asked again after tea, and Nasr again said yes. She mentioned bringing out a small snack and lingered for another moment. Then, prompted by someone—Nasr couldn't tell who—she and her husband slipped out through the swinging doors.

The girl on the left (and therefore farthest from Nasr) spoke first: "One of us is Farah, and the other two are her sisters Suraiya and Rafia. You should speak freely, and direct all questions to Farah, as if you two were alone. Anything you ask about her, us, our family will be answered truthfully, to the fullest extent of our knowledge—"

"But not necessarily by the person you ask," said the middle one, who seemed relieved at not having to look down anymore.

"Our parents have agreed not to disturb or eavesdrop," the

girl on the right added. "Mummi may come back with tea, but that will be the only interference."

Nasr felt his mouth hanging open and immediately shut it. He'd been expecting something, of course, but the sudden animation was disorienting, as if statues in a museum had just come to life, and for a moment it seemed as though one voice were coming from three faces—or was it three voices from one face?

"This way," the girl on the right continued, "nobody has to feel self-conscious or in the spotlight."

"And we may ask you questions," said the girl on the left, with the delicate brows, "which must be answered truthfully unless they are too personal in nature. You may at that time say that only Farah will be told the answer to that question."

The right-hand girl, who was closest, said, "At the end, the other two will leave the room, and you can tell her the answers to those questions in private."

"If you choose correctly," the middle girl said.

"Oh, yes," the left one added. "You must decide, based on our answers, which one of us is Farah. If you guess correctly, you'll be allowed to speak to her alone. If you don't, or don't want to, or say you don't know, the whole thing is over and you can be on your way."

"And nobody's feelings will be hurt," the middle one said, looking proud.

"Since both sides will have a choice," the girl on the right finished explaining.

Nasr could feel the heat under his arms wetting his shirt and turning it cold. He was having trouble anticipating who would speak next and kept getting caught staring at the wrong girl.

"You go first," said the middle one, leaning forward in her seat.

"First?" he said, clearing his throat.

"A question."

"Are you all"—he cleared his throat again—"are you all the same age? How old are you?"

"You think we're triplets?" asked the middle one, a little gleefully. She had the roundest face of the three, and the roundest features. "Do we look it?"

The one on the right said, "There's about a year and a half between each of us." She seemed friendly but reserved, more inclined than the others to look down when she wasn't speaking.

"Which means Farah is in grade—?"

"Farah is twenty-three," the girl on the left said. She was not frowning, exactly, but she seemed concerned somehow. "Rafia is twenty-two, and Suraiya twenty." She had a slightly longer, narrower face. "We are all in university."

They had very dark eyes, Nasr noticed, especially for such fair skin, but he was beginning to distinguish shades now. "What is Farah—" he began generally, then turned directly to the one on the left, whose eyes were the biggest and lightest of the three pairs. Were they the large, serious eyes of an oldest child? Under an oldest child's long, serious forehead? "What are you majoring in?" he asked her.

But the middle girl jumped in to answer. "Farah is majoring in Mass Communications and Policy. She will complete her degree next spring and hopes to ultimately get a master's degree in health. Public health," she said—and that was it. Nasr eliminated her as a possibility.

"Where did you grow up—in Cornwall?" he asked. He watched the other two while the middle one continued in her scripted tones to explain that Farah and Rafia were born in Bombay, and Suraiya in Dubai, where the family had lived for a year before coming to Canada.

"Didn't they already tell you these things?" the one on the left asked, interrupting her sister.

Nasr felt all three pairs of opaque eyes on him. "I suppose," he replied, though he couldn't remember one word his mother had said yesterday.

"You might want to ask about something that only Farah can tell you," the serious one said.

"Like what?" he asked.

"Like what her favorite color is," said the middle one.

"Or something you really want to know," added the one on the right. She might have smiled at him—his glance back at her was a fraction of a second too late—or she might have smiled at her sister's suggestion. Or her perfect lips were always half smiling.

"What's your favorite color?" he asked.

"Red," answered the middle girl, then she looked at the sister to the right. There it was! Nasr thought—but then she looked, just as hesitantly, to the sister on the left, who said, "Actually, it depends."

Maybe they had more tactics than he guessed—orchestrated interruptions, preplanned vacillations. Maybe it was too easy that the responsive, clearly young one wasn't the bride or that the shy, serious one was. Or that the one smiling at him—flirting with him?—was the troublesome middle child. And what was his role? What was he supposed to do? Appeal to one, or to all three? He had never tried to charm three women at once.

"Depends on what?" he asked belatedly.

"Is it finished here?" Mrs. Ansari came in carrying a large serving tray. "Farro, come on, beta."

The middle girl made a squeaking noise, and the other two jumped up to relieve their mother, telling her that she should have called out when the tea was ready. Mrs. Ansari relinquished her platter unwillingly. "Now, Nasr will be wanting to talk to everyone." She seemed ready to assert herself, but then the girl on the left took command of the teapot, and the one on the right said, "He'll get plenty of chance for that," in her quiet but final tones. Which one of them had signaled to their mother that she should leave Nasr again wasn't sure, but that there had been a signal was apparent, for the poor woman turned on her heel and left without another word.

While her sisters busied themselves with serving the tea, the middle girl asked Nasr about his job, and if he could be anything else, what would he be, and if he could live anywhere in the world, would it still be New York? Also, when was his birthday, and what kind of music did he listen to? What was a typical day in his life like? Did he enjoy travel? Was he close to his sisters? What were his nieces' names and ages? What were his hobbies, and the last movie he'd seen? And would he say he did any cooking? They were not the questions a parent would ask, but still easy enough, and Nasr took his time with each answer. By now he felt comfortable looking away while the middle one was speaking, a definite advantage.

"Not enough sugar?" the girl on the right asked.

"Perfect," he said, taking a sip from his cup.

She nodded and smiled, or the smile that permanently hovered over her lips deepened into her cheek for a moment. She handed him a plate and a samosa, then passed him a fork. "Was all this Farah's idea?" he asked, finally catching her eye in the midst of these transactions.

"Yes," she said, then turned to serve her sisters.

The samosa was delicious—just the right crispiness and well-seasoned softness; he took another sip of tea.

"But Farah designed the whole thing?" he asked. The middle girl nodded emphatically, a cheek swollen from chewing. "Where did she get the idea for it?"

The girl on the left said, "That you'll have to speak with her about."

"How many times has it been done?"

The girl on the left hesitated for a second.

"More than five?" he asked, and, when she kept nodding, "More than ten? And the setup," he continued, "is always the same?" More nodding, but from all directions. "What if my mother or sister had come here with me?"

"They would have been asked to wait with our parents," replied the girl on the left.

He wished the other two—the one on the right, actually, whose black eyes seemed to grow in size every time he caught a glimpse of them—would answer more of his questions. Was it his imagination or were she and the sister in the middle hanging back now? "How did you get your parents to agree on all these rules?" he asked, quizzing those black eyes.

But the girl on the left answered again. "They don't know them all," she said in that low-voiced manner of hers.

Nasr was impressed with all these mechanics, but he couldn't help thinking that there was a problem with the way the whole thing worked. What would happen if he wound up selecting the wrong girl on purpose—or, rather, if he chose the one he liked best and it wasn't Farah? Would he be allowed to talk to that girl, then? Or was it Farah or nothing? Most families maintained strict codes about the eldest daughter marrying first.

"Have you asked enough questions?" the girl on the right wanted to know.

He turned to her and shook his head. "So if I guess correctly, I speak to Farah alone?"

"Yes," she said.

"For how long?"

Again, the girl on the left interrupted—ah, yes, taking over as a prospective bride might. There was clearly a plan to let her emerge from her shell. "As long as you and she like," she said.

"Just once?" he asked, though he was reluctant to turn back to her.

"It depends."

"And that's all—that could be it?"

"Yes," she said, a frown developing on her face. But the girl on the right asked, "What do you mean?"

"I mean"—he paused, noticing that his and the middle girl's heads were turning from side to side in sync; he stared straight ahead, looking into her saucer-round eyes—"I mean that this talking would be just the next round, right?"

"Right," the girl on the left said, again in a tight, dry voice, her lips pursed. She knew exactly what he was getting at. "You don't marry her just for picking her out."

It was the tense expression of an older sister holding up the line, knowing the other two, one with her sweetness and the other with her beauty, would have an easier time of it. Or it was the hurt expression of an inventor who's been made to notice a flaw in her design, for it couldn't be denied that a serious flaw was there, especially if the whole purpose of this scheme was that the interested parties would have a choice and no one's feelings would be hurt. Where was Farah's choice? If she didn't like him, which, now that her identity had been revealed, was plainly evident, and he chose correctly, she'd still have to reject him (or he her). Wasn't it a bit risky to give the visitor the choice and make everything depend on that? The expression on Farah's face was still watchful. What about the sister with the smile—and her choices? Nasr wondered. He reached for his cup and noticed that it had been refilled, that in fact it had been full every time he'd taken a sip, and that there was a new samosa on his plate. How many of those had he eaten?

"Of the other guys," he said, leaning forward and not taking his eyes off the girl on the right, "exactly how many got to speak to your sister alone?"

There was a silence, and then the perfect lips finally (maybe because everybody was staring at her now) answered a question from him without immediately looking away. "None," she said.

"That many men have guessed incorrectly?" Nasr asked, not bothering to hide his skepticism.

At which point he was rewarded with not one but three sly smiles—not identical, but each smug in its own way.

The middle girl leaned forward with her hands clasped together. "Do you know who she is?"

"Yes," Nasr said, taking a deep breath. He couldn't help staring at the girl on the right. What a pity, he thought, that he couldn't get out of the attachment with Farah and simply choose the girl he liked best. But really the bigger pity to his mind was that this girl wasn't the designer of the test, for it would have been perfect: he would have solved the puzzle, impressing her where all those others had failed, and she would have been the one he was truly most inclined to pick. A genuinely natural match, a sign of fate even. But instead it was just going to be an empty victory, delivering him, three years—plus yet another afternoon—later straight back to where he'd started, with nothing to show for his efforts. On the drive over, Nasr had felt the waste of these years of silly prattle, swift judgments, and mutual rejections. What did he *want*? What *did* he want? That empty room he'd seen and thought was a representation of Jameela's life—wasn't it his life as well? Lonely, neglected, narrow. If he'd ever once really, actually, ventured out of that cell, might he have met someone and fallen in love—who cared where she was from or whom she was related to?

The girl on the right held his gaze; then her smile deepened into her flushed cheeks. "You're right," she said. "I'm Farah."

7

The engagement party gave the Siddiquis and the Ansaris an excellent opportunity to consider how deeply two Indian, Muslim families on Canadian soil who had mutually and voluntarily pledged to unite (or, at least, to interpenetrate and proliferate) could misunderstand one another. It began when the Ansari family arrived in a block: men of modest height behind trim beards and white skullcaps and women in pastel headscarves tumbled out of three minivans and settled in the Siddiquis' foyer. "Thush-reef lai-yay . . ." both Hamid Uncle and Nasr's mother said again and again, while shawls and shoes were shed. They gestured into the waiting house: "Please!" But far from budging, none of the Ansaris had quite acknowledged their hosts' presence yet. They clung to the tiled border of the foyer so steadfastly that the Siddiquis could not have been faulted for wondering if their guests had superstitions concerning hardwood floors. Finally Mr. Ansari, probably concluding the test had been failed, said to Nasr's mother, "You have no doubt completed the Maghrib prayer," then apologized for his family's poor planning. "Perhaps we should hurry down to the basement before the namaaz time expires?" he suggested, evidently under the impression that the lower level of the Siddiqui home had been relinquished, as in his own house, and served as a permanent prayer space.

After sheets were hastily laid and prayer rugs were secretly liberated from suitcases in the guest bedroom; after the Ping-Pong table had been tucked away and the eastern wall stripped of Nasr's vintage posters of U2 (so long there that they'd become invisible to Yasmine, who almost left Bono interposed between the basement and Mecca); after Hamid Uncle had ushered the Ansaris down and most of the other guests had guiltily felt obliged to pray as well, engendering the need for shifts and some delicate traffic control (men first, women to follow, of course); after everyone had trooped, relieved, into the living room and was briefly warmed by a universal agreement concerning tea, only to trip into the freshly awkward exchange of ring and watch between the shy betrothed, there was a short period of smooth accord in which they all began to feel that perhaps the essence and true value of marriage lay, after all, in the clumsy chemistry it inspired.

The most unlikely product of this chemistry, to Nasr's mind, was Jameela's animated presence in the midst of the Ansari sisters—smiling with them, whispering, even smirking. Jameela wore a slinky black shalwar suit with silver mirror-work, and rather than draping the rupatta modestly across her chest she had flung it around her neck like a winter scarf—the prime minister, stepping into the room, could have instantly picked her out as the thing not like the others—yet she seemed to pass. How chummy, Nasr thought, though it made him a little queasy. He wondered whether to credit the younger Ansaris with more tolerance than he had or Jameela with more guile and charm.

In any case, he was soon distracted by the innovative misunderstandings that dinner inspired. For a long time after the dishes had been laid buffet style and a first wave of plates had been filled, the seekh kebabs rendered from an heirloom recipe belonging to Hamid Uncle's mother were left to toughen from neglect, the hilly platter of pullao remained unexcavated, and the nihari was so unharassed that a crinkly skin formed on the curry's surface. It seemed that the Ansari guests had all limited their attention to the appetizer of dahi vadas, the side dish of aloo gobi, and the salad of sliced cucumbers and baby carrots, which was an afterthought—half decorative, really. Nasr's mother's matchmaking between guests and meat dishes slipped from cordial to coercive—she circled the living room with a tray of kebabs, encumbering plates uninvited—until one of the old Ansari aunts held hers away and said, "I'm sorry, daughter, but I can't start eating non-halal at this age."

"Arré, but who has said these are not halal?"

"Who do they think we are?" she whispered to Yasmine, or perhaps to herself, in the kitchen a short while later. It was only after all the guests had left that she discovered the little nest of plastic toys and smelly, half-eaten sandwiches in the corner of the den, and learned that midway through the evening her granddaughters had persuaded their father to drive out for McDonald's Happy Meals.

After dinner, when it seemed that there was nothing left to go wrong, Mrs. Ansari approached Nasr's mother (who smiled broadly, perhaps in expectation, finally, of a compliment) and gave her a small piece of paper. "If you don't mind, Sultana Baji," she said, pausing apologetically. "We have some elders on our side who feel it would be best to keep future sleeves to this length at least."

This was just after dessert and more tea had been set out, and Nasr was standing with his mother and Yasmine in the foyer, bidding an early farewell to guests who weren't able to stay for the last course. Mr. Ansari joined his wife, and for the second time that evening, the spacious foyer, designed to impress, with its high cornice window above double front doors, felt cramped.

Nasr's mother accepted Mrs. Ansari's note with a surprisingly mild "Oh. Was there a problem?"

Over her shoulder, Nasr could see two neat columns on the paper: neck, shoulders, arms, sleeve length, wrist, chest, waist, hips; 11, 19, 21, 15, 5½, 34, 24, 38. The 15 was circled in red, but the other numbers were more intriguing. The length of Farah's arm was twenty-one inches? Almost two feet? And those tiny wrists were actually five and a half inches around? There was a movement then in the corner of Nasr's vision, and he quickly lifted his eyes.

Mrs. Ansari was shaking her head. "Not a problem, really," she said to his mother with a kind smile. "Perhaps a bit more supervision in the future—"

"But she liked that one—" Yasmine said, stopping when their mother raised her chin.

A matrimonial tradition that Nasr's mother took particularly seriously was that of the groom's side being responsible for providing the bride with various outfits, including the wedding suit. She had, in fact, begun planning a long shopping trip to India for February, in which she would consult with her four sisters about the design and tailoring of these garments. But since the giving of that gift was far off, she had also asked the Ansaris if she might purchase an outfit for her future daughter-in-law to wear to the engagement party. The suit would, regrettably, be of the ready-made variety, but what could you do in a country like this? Mrs. Ansari had agreed, and Nasr's mother had put Yasmine in charge of shopping. Yasmine enlisted Jameela's help, and Jameela suggested that the bride herself come along since she was going to be wearing the thing. After some resistance, Nasr's mother relented on this point, but she insisted that no such input would be solicited when the wedding suit was made. Yasmine, Jameela, and Farah, along with her two sisters, scoured all the Indian shops they knew, but to no avail. They were considering a trip to Toronto when Yasmine learned that a number of enterprising aunties who went back to India regularly had set up showroom-like boutiques in their houses. After two full weekends of shopping in converted dens, basements, and garages, fattening on pakoras that could not be declined and delicately negotiating empty-handed exits, the girls had discovered a pale-green Hyderabadi-style suit with gold-mesh embroidery and sheer, short sleeves.

"Not to worry, beta," Mrs. Ansari said to Yasmine, as though to assure her that she wasn't being blamed. "Farah told me that you and Jameela Begum were very patient. And you all have chosen a nice color indeed. Very unusual." Mrs. Ansari was wrapped in a thick rupatta, and every time she closed her eyes and nodded, the fabric pulled the wrinkles around her eyes smooth and gave her a placid look. "Really, all this business was Farah's mistake," she added. "I told her, 'Why didn't you simply ask for one in the same color but with decent sleeves?' " Then her voice dropped. "And no see-through, please."

Nasr saw his mother wince, but Mrs. Ansari continued on, shaking her head with proud disapproval: "Sometimes our daughters are so modest they cannot even bring themselves to insist upon things."

As this was the very sort of reticence that Nasr's mother would herself find most appealing, she merely smiled.

Mr. Ansari stepped forward and complimented Nasr's mother on the management of the party, noting in particular the capability of the house to accommodate such an event. She had been right, he said, sending a confirming but unmet glance back at his wife. Certainly their own home would have been too small for a party of this size. Then Mr. Ansari wondered if Nasr's mother might by chance know how many guests their side would be expecting for the Nikaah?

Nasr's mother hesitated, said it was difficult to know.

Was it possible to give an estimate? Mr. Ansari asked. "Ballpark total?"

"Well," Nasr's mother said, "there is first the family to consider—both the ones here and back home, of course. And then old friends who may as well be family—"

Mr. Ansari nodded. "Perhaps double this quantity here?" he asked, gesturing.

"Yes—at least." She began describing the bounty of their community. "There are the Alvis, Husains, Ahmad-Khans . . ." At one time, she explained, there had been so many children that the adults decided to group them together and throw one big birthday each month—one for all the January-borns, then February, and so on.

Mr. Ansari owned a convenience mart in Cornwall, and while Nasr's mother was speaking he took out a small pad on which he began listing names as though he were tallying inventory.

"Then, of course, there are people who've moved away," Nasr's mother continued, eyeing the pad as entries were made. "To America and whatnot—Rizvis, Naqvis."

Mr. Ansari nodded, and continued making notes. But as soon as there was a pause in Nasr's mother's speech, he said, "So one-fifty you are thinking?"

"Arré, is it settled?" asked the auntie who'd put the watch on Nasr's wrist. She came marching into the foyer, pulling Farah behind her. She turned out to be Mr. Ansari's eldest sister, Farah's Noreen Phuphi.

Nasr tried to make room for Farah beside him, but she slipped in between her parents, taking careful steps as if not to disturb a single fold of her shalwar suit.

"I brought this one along to see what progress we are making with her marriage," Noreen Phuphi announced.

Farah's face was angled down and to the side. Standing as still as a vase, she displayed the perfect degree of embarrassment at her aunt's words, and there were smiles of approval in all directions.

"Let's not forget that tea and mithai are in order, and there should be paan as well." Nasr's mother gestured for them to head toward the living room. Nasr noticed that her admiring eyes lingered on Farah. And why not? She was beautifully assembled. The sleeves of the suit might not be "decent," but the pale color perfectly set off her creamy skin.

"I've sampled the paan," Noreen Phuphi declared, but it would have been hard to say whether the thin lines of red on the inside of her lips were from a recent tasting or permanent habit. "Well, what did you decide?" she asked her brother. "Is it to be the first week in October or the third? You know how these people are—they will not hold it."

For the next few minutes, Nasr's mother listened in polite bafflement, even bemusement, as though she were expecting the punch line to a joke, as Mr. Ansari explained that, because the town of Cornwall didn't have the facilities of Montreal, he had already begun searching for halls. With the help of Noreen Phuphi, the Ansaris had found a place—a former elementary school that had been converted into a party center—but they'd been told that the availability was extremely limited. Only two weekends in October remained free, and to secure one of these they would need to put down a deposit as soon as possible.

After a moment of silence, Nasr's mother shook her head,

the deep furrows clearing from her brow. "I was thinking you meant October of this year," she said, waving a hand apologetically for the silly misunderstanding.

Mr. Ansari glanced at his wife and cleared his throat. "The deposit has been put, actually," he said. "For the first week. But this date can still be shifted to the third."

"But two months?"

"Best to get these things done quickly," Noreen Phuphi said with a toothy smile.

The corner of Farah's rupatta had slipped off her shoulder and was grazing the floor. Mrs. Ansari seemed to have noticed this at the same time as Nasr—he had the sensation that she might have been following his eyes. She adjusted the fabric as though she were working at a mannequin.

"Well, we, of course, are very eager to settle matters as well," Nasr's mother said with sudden readiness. "I was just saying to Hamid Bhai whatever is the fashion of these long engagements everyone is having these days?" She was all smiles now. "But he reminded me that our weddings are such a trial of patience—oof, so much to be done." On the surface this was a mild statement, but Nasr understood that the note of apology here was a stylistic courtesy that had nothing to do with the content of what was being said, which, in fact, was *No, there is absolutely no way this wedding is taking place in the month of October.* Recognizing the mood shift that his mother's expansiveness signaled, Nasr suddenly found himself both curious and filled with mortal dread about where the conversation was headed. And it only made matters worse when his mother said, "Oh, here is Hamid Bhai now," with such sunny energy that Nasr's uncle could not fail to immediately read the desperation at hand.

· · ·

The people of Lucknow, at least those fortunate enough to be able to cultivate a life of sufficient leisure, are known for their conversation—not just because of the language they use, the artful Urdu, in which it is purportedly impossible to even construct an impolite phrase, but also because of their attitude toward communication: it must involve no unpleasantries whatsoever. One's listener must be kept amused and engaged, whether the topic of conversation be the dinner at hand or the riot in the street. To be Lucknawi was to be agreeable, especially when one disagreed. There were, of course, drawbacks to this position. After a while (or, more likely, after the fact), a listener who'd been plied with sweet formulations found it difficult to decide where his companion's opinion fell. It was through such evasions that Lucknawis earned the additional reputation of being a people of spongy sincerity—noncommittal, unrevealing, and either ambiguous or ambivalent, depending on how much patience you had.

Hamid Uncle, who was from one of the best-spoken families in Lucknow, would always illustrate his native people's character with an anecdote he'd heard as a boy and embellished: Two gentlemen, each a principal of an old landed family, arrive separately at a train station with much fanfare. For each man, a team of coolies is dispatched to handle the luggage. Trunks and valises of all sizes are loaded onto the heads, shoulders, and backs of underfed men, who then walk a pace behind as each principal makes his way to the train car. The platform is crowded. In addition to the business travelers and the permanent inhabitants of the station (beggars, fruit-cart vendors, stiff-capped railway personnel), there are large families parked in camps, their possessions spread about them, eating from tiffins, the children scurrying and disobedient. The whole of Lucknow seems to be setting out.

As the train approaches, there is chaos, a press of bodies, shouts, and flaring tempers. Fortunately, the gentlemen are headed for the less congested sleeper cars at the front of the train. They arrive at the entrance of their berth at the very same moment, and each immediately begins insisting that the other board first—Pehle aap; you first; no, you please; kindly do me the honor—until the passengers behind them lose patience and push past. Oh, no, please, you must—through the first whistle, and the second. Soon the train has chugged away. The next day, the coolies are rounded up again, bags are again hoisted and navigated through crowds to the front car, where the same thing happens. "For weeks, this process continues," Hamid Uncle would say. "It would seem that the men, once they become tangled in their politeness, can never manage to get on their train. They are helpless do-nothings, totally ineffectual, one might say. But"—Hamid Uncle would pause—"where was it going, the train?" He would wait a beat, then deliver the punch line: It is a train destined for Pakistan, and the year is 1947, of course. The journey is to a brand-new country, forming just as its future citizens are making their way to it. This land is to serve as a haven for every Muslim in the north of India, and they ought to be flocking to it, to self-rule, to finally stand in the majority, to live where one is wanted, among one's kind, under a government that is built on the foundations Allah holds dear. But there have been rumors that this new nation is also a place where trains are arriving charred, their boxcars full of smoking bodies. Were the men on the platform inept weaklings, missing out on the most desirable passage of the day, or did they recognize the moment for what it was—a time when it was wiser to show that you wished to leave than to actually depart? "This is the question," Hamid Uncle would say in conclusion, though of course to him it never was.

• • •

*P*erhaps the Ansaris already knew all about the Lucknawi character—or perhaps they merely intuited what they would have to face when Hamid Uncle drew the group out of the foyer and entered the discussion. He and Nasr's mother, as though responding to some long-dormant but native capacity, slipped into an elaborately coordinated debate in which one of them wholly adopted the Ansaris' position and the other played devil's advocate, with heavy doses of regret. Without seeming to consult each other at all, they would sometimes switch positions, argue the other side just as tenaciously, but neither of them ever addressed the Ansaris directly.

Hamid Uncle opened by saying that he didn't see any reason to delay, and if they were all back in Lucknow he would have been able to pull the whole production, no matter its size, together within a month. The Nikaah would have taken place at Baradari, of course, where Nasr's parents themselves had married, and the other events would have been hosted at the Siddiqui and Haq family homes, with one more small reception, if they would all permit him, at Jamshed Manzil, the Farooqi residence.

But as this was impossible, Nasr's mother said, a dream of a dream, the next best thing—a trip home to collect what could be transported across the ocean from such an idyll—ought to be pursued. For this very reason, she'd already begun planning a visit to India to assemble Farah's trousseau, and by her estimate a wedding date in the spring would provide sufficient time for a certain darzi who made the clothes for all the future brides of all the sons in the family to be put to work. She spoke at great length about Rozi Mia's long allegiance to the family, but mentioned that a specialist would have to be hired for the embroidery on the shaadi gharara. For this she would need to rely on the recommendations of her sisters back home; but no matter how skilled this specialist was, he would still have to be given instructions and patterns, and—Nasr's mother added, her voice dipping—monitored, of course.

Was there not any way, Hamid Uncle asked, with an expression of dismay, that these important tasks could be done so that the third week (or even the fourth) of October was possible?

Nasr's mother shook her head wistfully. The other problem with an October plan, she explained, was that it would mean that she would have to schedule her trip for no later than September. That is, buy a ticket within the next week—at what prices on such short notice? October was simply too soon. One might say impossible, yes.

What of November? Hamid Uncle asked.

November, the Ansaris reminded Nasr's mother and Hamid Uncle, as well as the handful of remaining guests who had been drawn to the living room and were gathered around the edges, was complicated by Ramzaan.

Nasr's mother agreed with the Ansaris that November was out of the question, most certainly. She and Hamid Uncle then speedily did away with December and January as months available for Nasr's mother's trip, as these fell in the high season of travel; and February would be much too cold. The two of them nearly agreed on a March trip, which would mean a wedding in April; but then Nasr's mother's confessed to always having wished for an old-style outdoor event, and Hamid Uncle concluded, with a show of reluctance, that May would then be more suitable.

The Ansaris listened to this exchange with polite interest, and after a moment Mr. Ansari wondered if any materials might be ordered and then shipped with a cousin-sister who was returning from Bombay in a month.

Nasr's mother acknowledged that this was indeed very kind, but she shook her head. Oh dear, even if they managed somehow to get the tailors started, one shouldn't forget that there was also the jewelry to think of.

Mr. Ansari made a joke about Cornwall being a small place and, unfortunately, limited in its resources—hence the need to act quickly on the reservation of the hall.

Hamid Uncle nodded in absolute agreement. "For all the conveniences of this country," he observed, sighing heavily, "living here becomes most problematic during the important events of one's life."

But it soon became clear that the Ansaris would not settle for sympathetic philosophizing and agreeable evasions. They wanted a wedding date, caught and speared, before they left.

The eagerness of Nasr's future in-laws ought to have been flattering. But nobody asked him when he was free, and nobody seemed to think it was odd that both he and Farah were mere spectators at this discussion, as irrelevant as the nieces playing about in the den. The negotiations simply went on and on, the two parties waging a battle by spraying each other with small, ineffectual darts.

Nasr began to feel like a piece of driftwood floating on a river of talk. The worst part of the situation was that he had no contact with Farah. He tried to follow her out of the foyer, but he got the distinct feeling that she was being ushered away by her mother. Now she sat tucked between her sisters on the love seat across the room. When she wasn't turned toward the conversing parents, her rupatta obscured half her face, making it impossible to catch her eye. Somewhere in all the folds of her rupatta, Nasr thought, was the ring he had given her. Was she aware of it? Did it feel strange or, dare he hope, pleasantly weighty? At this rate, he'd never find out—in fact, the whole evening could go by without his exchanging a word with her beyond hello and how are you.

None of this would have been nearly so awkward for Nasr if for most of the discussion Jameela hadn't resumed her edge-of-the-conversation presence. Unlike during the search, when she would occupy her post with boredom, usually on a distant couch, tonight she was positioned a few feet from Nasr, at the other end of the living room's archway, watching the parents avidly. More than once, Nasr thought he'd glimpsed a peculiar smile playing about her lips. Was she *enjoying* this?

"People with three daughters don't have the luxury of waiting," Noreen Phuphi suddenly declared, adding that while their own family didn't have these old contacts in Lucknow, she was sure they would be able to find tailors and jewelers who could do the work in half the time and at half the cost. This comment drew several of the other Ansari members into the discussion, which then prompted a long, group reminiscence of the Ansari family's arrival in Canada: how various branches had for a number of years shared one home in order to build their savings, and how each brother who arrived from abroad worked in a sibling's convenience store until he could set up his own place, and now there was a real family chain, with four locations in the greater Cornwall area.

During the recitation of this history, Yasmine's lips were pursed with uninterest. Jameela, on the other hand, was leaning forward as though she didn't want to miss a word. Earlier in the evening, as everyone was heading downstairs for the namaaz, Nasr ran into the two of them standing in the doorway of the kitchen, watching people stream by. He stopped in the hallway. "Ladies first." "I don't think that's really the way it works," Jameela replied with a cursory smile. "Do you?" Ever since then, Nasr often found himself in a silent dialogue with her, defending by turns his mother, the Ansaris, and Farah herself. If Jameela would just come right out and say whatever was clearly on her mind, he thought now, then at least a person could defend himself. But it was just like her to sit back in judgment, making jokes, risking nothing. If she were at all a reasonable person, he might even be willing to admit that he himself had, over the past few weeks, tried to imagine Farah in his life—at family functions in their community, or in New York with his friends—and failed. But this was only natural. You couldn't just insert someone into a scene as if she were a cartoon.

Mrs. Ansari capped the family history—or interrupted it—with a non sequitur. "We understand that the children are wanting to spend time together," she said, glancing kindly in Yasmine's direction. "Some party is being planned?"

A few days earlier, Yasmine had proposed to arrange an event to introduce Farah and her sisters to the younger generation of their community. She told Nasr's mother that the party would take place at a restaurant, so there would be none of the usual parental anxiety about what to prepare and which dishes to serve it in. Nasr had been all for the idea—it would provide the perfect chance to get away from the parents' watchful eyes.

But Yasmine refused to be drawn out by Mrs. Ansari's question. Everybody else was managing to hold smiles on their faces, but her expression was distant and mutinous, and her arms were crossed at her chest—she would neither confirm nor deny the plans, as though she sensed a trap.

To cover Yasmine's silence, Nasr's mother answered: "Yes, to allow them all to get to know one another. You know how the children are these days. But these things are easily cancelled," she offered as way of sacrifice, but it was too late. The trap had sprung.

"If there is such eagerness," Mrs. Ansari said, "why delay?"

"People don't become engaged just to start a romance, after all," added Noreen Phuphi.

A silence fell over the group. Nasr looked up and saw Farah's chin dip down, impossibly lower into her chest. Even from this angle, it looked as if she was trying to conceal a smile. Had she just been looking his way? When they'd spoken back in July, less than a month ago, when it had been just the two of them, when a week of phone calls had ended with Nasr finding it surprisingly easy to ask Farah if she would consider marrying him, she had said, "Yes, of course." Just like that—without a moment's hesitation, as though her interest were a foregone conclusion, and shame on him for bothering to put words to the question. He'd been standing at his usual spot in his apartment, staring out the window, remembering how this smile of hers had played on her lips at their first meeting. As in their previous phone calls, they had begun by talking about small matters, rambling through their backgrounds—which schools they'd attended, how much French each spoke, all the places she'd lived. Somewhere along the way, they discovered that they both liked movies, real movies—the bigger the release, the better. She confessed to finding the Bollywood films from their parents' time a little tedious, and asked if America had cinemas that showed the latest releases. Nasr hadn't seen a Bollywood film in years, so he didn't know; she assured him that the stories and sets were much more lively now, and he promised to find out where in New York they might be seen. "Perhaps we'll go every weekend," she said. Her voice was inviting and amused, and the allure of this confidence was undeniable. Now, across from him, at the other end of the living room, Farah's chin dipped again, unmistakably hiding a smile. Nasr then saw something he'd never seen before on an Indian person: a front of color, splotches of the palest red, rose up from Farah's jawline and into her cheeks. Could it be that *she* was the one who wanted to set the wedding date this soon? That she had put her parents up to all this?

"There's no sense in waiting," he said. "Not if everybody's willing to do it sooner."

The room's attention fell on him. His mother's face flared with surprise.

"Why don't you do a shorter trip?" Nasr said to her. The ticket would be expensive whether they bought it now or later; and perhaps a short trip would make November possible. His mother frowned; Hamid Uncle smiled and benignly ignored him. "Maybe you could get things with those tailors started with a phone call," Nasr said.

"But an elementary school, beta?" his mother replied, with suddenly open exasperation.

Nasr thought he should have guessed that the source of her objection would be something trivial and snobby. The blush on Farah's face was still there. What else could make her blush? "This way," Nasr continued, feeling inspired now, "Farah can transfer to a college in the city for the spring session." Probably in any culture it would be untoward of a bride to insist upon an earlier date, but a groom could do it, couldn't he? Play the eager, besotted fool? He wondered what Farah would think of this extremely practical reason he'd offered. "Also, she'll get a chance to be there before her studies begin. We'll have to get another apartment—mine is too small. She'll need time to get settled, get used to—" Here Nasr might have paused, maybe even smiled accidentally, because he was thinking "married life" even though he ended up saying "city life."

The silence that followed wasn't as extreme as the one that had preceded it—it involved murmurs and nods, shuffling and half-smiles. When the discussion resumed—tentative at first but soon returning to the familiar impasses—Nasr couldn't tell if the Ansaris were pleased with his support.

In the end, it was Talat Auntie who nudged the Ansaris to see past October—suggesting that Ramzaan, being such a time of sacrifice and contemplation (plus, of course, all its bodily prohibitions), might not be ideal as a first month of marriage for the young couple, and that if the families waited through November, the Ansaris would be able, perhaps for the last time, to have their daughter all to themselves for the holy month. This was a trade-off the Ansaris hadn't foreseen but could appreciate. Soon the wedding was set for late December. It was also agreed that the two events to be hosted by the bride's side would take place in Cornwall, while the groom's events would be in Montreal.

Nasr was momentarily compelled to speak up again when

both parties looked as if they were headed toward Christmas Day, with all its "convenience" in terms of vacations. He reminded everyone that a number of the guests—namely, his friends and colleagues from New York—might not find this option at all convenient. He vetoed New Year's Day for the same reason (without adding that he didn't want either date as his anniversary).

He looked over to Farah in hopes that he'd get more signals about her preferences, which he felt willing to voice and defend on her behalf. But she had turned her attention back toward the parents. Jameela was still planted a few feet away, but her demeanor had changed considerably. In place of the avid smile, there was a stern but distracted profile, which Nasr occasionally heard emit a sigh of sorts. He couldn't help being pleased. Despite all the difficulties, the families had reached an agreement, and the system had worked: smiles were once again exchanged, and Hamid Uncle joked that surely another round of tea was in order to celebrate the coming together of two such caring families. Afterward, as they were leaving, Mrs. Ansari patted Nasr's cheek.

8

Just after eleven, Nasr was in the basement. The rest of the family was scattered throughout the house; his mother didn't like the detritus of parties to linger, and having recently discovered the Happy Meals, she had started cleaning with new ferocity. Nasr was assigned the task of returning order to the basement, which actually meant positioning the mismatched furniture and games back into their comfortable jumble. Every once in a while, as he worked, there would be a faint rush of footsteps and the ceiling above would creak.

In July, on the phone, Farah had been curious about Nasr's travels, and of all the European capitals he could rattle off, she was particularly impressed that he'd been to Milan. She had, as it turned out, an interest in fashion design, and the shows of

Milan, Nasr learned, were where "the season" began. She readily admitted that she would never wear anything that appeared on the runways, but she found it so interesting to follow the trends: which designer had actually done something new and different from the others; who was being copied; who had brought out his old favorites, without giving a second thought to recent tastes. The depth of her enthusiasm was charming, even more so as it seemed both tinged with embarrassment and marked with expert knowledge of cuts and biases and how the designers chose only the models who made their clothes *move* as they should.

Another girl her age, with such an abiding interest, might already have done a summer in Europe, Nasr thought. It didn't seem fair to him that Farah spoke as though she would never see such things, that she was content to watch the shows on TV or read about that world in magazines. Her life apparently involved only attending classes, dropping off or picking up one sister or the other, working in her father's store in the evenings, spending Fridays at the masjid with her parents, going to Ansari family events on the weekends. She described this routine and then shifted to the wonders of Milan without a sigh of complaint.

Though the Ansari girls had moved around quite a bit in their childhoods, their lives, Nasr gathered, had been genuinely sheltered. Farah had been abroad, of course. In Dubai, her family had lived in a lower-story flat of a tower designated for foreign workers, and thus packed with Indian and Pakistani families. In Canada, the Ansaris had initially lived with Noreen Phuphi, and then in a series of apartment complexes, until they were finally able to buy their current house, which Farah spoke of as though it were the most accommodating of residences. Having seen it, Nasr could just imagine the earlier places.

The night after he proposed, Nasr called up a few friends in the city. He'd intended to make an announcement, let people buy him rounds. But somehow he didn't get around to it. Instead, while nursing his drink and trying halfheartedly to follow the thread of bar talk, he found himself making plans. He and Farah would take a trip every year—not a cheap, watch-every-penny, stay-with-relatives Indian-style trip but one that involved B and Bs and fine hotels. They would thoroughly explore the cities of Europe, go to museums, tour the old palaces, coliseums, cathedrals. Having already been to many of these places, he should know the sites to be seen, but of course he hadn't been on holiday when he'd gone and his work commitments kept him from sightseeing. In any case, he knew enough to make sure the two of them wouldn't miss anything important. Perhaps Farah would prefer to visit markets and fashion houses instead of ruins. He would let her decide, projecting her excitement at the prospect of setting their travel agenda—how this excitement would beautifully occupy her face, produce that smile that appeared to emanate from some internal point.

Nasr hoisted up an armchair that belonged in the den and began climbing up the basement stairs.

"The boy ought to know his own mind by now." The voice seemed to be attempting to whisper, but the tone was harsh— one Nasr had never heard Hamid Uncle use.

Nasr waited a moment, letting a corner of the armchair rest on a low step.

There was a reply, but so hushed that it was impossible to make out, and then Hamid Uncle said, "Now that he's made a decision, who are you to second-guess?"

Now came the sound of footsteps, retreating. Nasr set the chair down and took the basement stairs two at a time. He felt his heartbeat in his head. At the landing, there was no sign of Hamid Uncle or the person he'd been talking to.

Nasr searched the guest room (empty), the first-floor den (Saira's younger daughters sitting too close to the TV), and the kitchen (also empty, but hot with steam), and finally found

Hamid Uncle in the living room, sitting with the rest of the group: Saira, Saira's husband, Rizwan, blinking sleepily; Yasmine, in the corner playing checkers with Saira's daughter Aisha; Talat Auntie and Nasr's mother, exhausted but cheerfully discussing how many times the dishwasher had been loaded. When Nasr stepped into the archway, they all turned to him and smiled.

Hamid Uncle said, "Ah, there is the groom-to-be." He pushed his hookah stand aside and patted the empty seat beside him on the sofa. But Nasr didn't move. The blood was still loud in his ears. He scanned each face again, wondering which one of these people who'd known him nearly all his life was smiling falsely.

"You are setting a very good example, Nasr Beta," Talat Auntie said. "You have found yourself some stubborn and very practiced bargainers, masha'allah. Good straight-talkers—none of this yes, yes, perhaps business. And fortunately for us, they are afraid to let you get away."

The front door opened, and Jameela came into the living room from the foyer. She had changed into a black kurta and jeans, and her face was washed of makeup. She walked across the room to hand her father a pair of glasses without saying a word to anyone, and then retreated to sit beside the checkers game.

"It was so important to your father that you children be married well," Talat Auntie said, but she'd turned away from Nasr to speak more generally to the room. She was a large woman, and her tight, glittery pink shalwar suit was quite wrinkled, but there was a sharp precision to her face and it was not hard to imagine her having been a beauty. " 'As soon as possible,' he used to say. 'A family like our own is the number-one thing we can provide for them. When that is established, then we will know that coming here was not the wrong decision.' Arré, Bhabi"—she turned toward Nasr's mother, whose eyes had begun watering at the first mention of his father—"do you remember how he used to worry about this business? Yes, they will go to the better schools, and buy big houses, but what will they have given up because of our decision? We will not know until they are grown."

"I would say," Talat Auntie continued, " 'Arré, Anwar Bhai, every week I am writing to my mother-in-law about the fancy diapers they are having here and how one can buy this baby food in the stores that makes one's life easy, and in every reply she is asking, Well, how easy can it be when you are doing it all yourself—no ayah, no maidservant, nothing? And now you are saying I must wait until the children are not just grown but married before we can know if all this was the right thing to do?' Then he would put Nasr in my arms and take Jameela, and say, 'Here, behen, your suspense is over.' " She dabbed the side of her face with her rupatta, then clicked her tongue. "Oof-foh, look what I've done to us." Shaking her head, she put her arm around Nasr's mother. "No, no, you have nothing to worry about," she continued. "Nasr is a very good boy. Usually, it is the other way around—the girls setting the example for the boys, but no matter. What is important"—a coy pause—"is that some of the people in this room will follow it."

"Don't get your hopes up, Mother," Jameela said without looking up from the checkerboard. "Not everyone marries for the sake of setting an example."

Talat Auntie either didn't hear Jameela's reply or she did a good job of ignoring it. Nasr's mother seemed to have missed the comment as well. But Hamid Uncle had heard. He stiffened and clamped his lips closed, and it now became perfectly clear to Nasr who the older man had been talking to on the landing near the basement.

In describing their shopping excursions, Yasmine had mentioned that Jameela and Farah had spent a lot of time chatting together. What was there to talk about? Nasr wondered all of a sudden. The two women couldn't be more different, and they hardly knew each other in the first place. If all that talk was merely about the engagement suit, how did it turn out to be such a mistake? Come to think of it, the business about the sleeves was so strange—surely Farah would have known her own parents' preferences and avoided getting something that was unacceptable. Nasr felt his face grow hot. Might Jameela have actually *steered* Farah into choosing sleeves that would get her into trouble with her parents? But why do something to create tension between the families? Was this just her knee-jerk instinct for testing limits, or—Nasr's mind began leaping ahead now; this evening's missteps and awkward moments, its unflattering presumptions and peculiar insinuations, were like stones jutting up from the surface of a pond—did Jameela hope the confrontation would expose something about Farah's parents? That they were set in their ways, that they could be hardheaded about petty matters? There was another leap here—to a conversation Nasr had with his mother in July after the Ansaris had phoned her to ask which masjid he attended in New York, how close it was to his home, and whether his employer allowed him to take time off for the Friday prayer. "I reminded them," his mother said, "that it was not so easy for everyone to pray five times a day, especially with these kinds of jobs you all have, but that you manage to do what you can." Nasr offered to find out about local masjids, and in return his mother sighed. "But of course they are not having sons," she said. It was through such exchanges that Nasr and his mother had, over the years, worked out a carefully but tacitly negotiated understanding regarding his loose observance of religious duties. She didn't, like other mothers Nasr knew, pretend she didn't know that such neglect happened in the world. Instead, she subscribed to a theory that men in general, and young ones in particular, were constitutionally incapable of maintaining wholesome living on their own, and as long as the major holidays were observed and the minor prohibitions unchallenged in public, she asked Nasr no questions about what he did and did not do. Her attitude had evolved incrementally, but even she was aware of its radical nature. During the years of the search, she had deemed matters of observance to be private and best resolved between a husband and wife. She hadn't asked whether Nasr had told Farah about the choices he'd made. She seemed to believe this wasn't her business. So it certainly couldn't be Jameela's, Nasr thought now with a fresh wave of anger.

For the next hour or so, as the evening's success was reviewed and another round of tea was served, he could hardly contain himself. If Jameela, with her inane fixation on equivalents, was hoping to prove something to him, to imply that because Farah couldn't assert herself on a matter as small as sleeve length, she wasn't his match, or, worse, that she was a dim bulb who couldn't speak up for herself, then she had failed. If she was hoping to change somebody's mind—the Ansaris', or Farah's, or his own—with this pathetic scheme of hers, then she'd failed miserably. The families had not only cooperated, but considering the circumstances, they had come to a remarkably quick and amiable agreement on the wedding date. The three and a half months until December now began to seem to Nasr like too much time, rife with opportunities for Jameela to interfere further. He resolved to fix whatever damage she had already done and to make sure that anything she might say or do in the future wouldn't take seed. He would do this by telling Farah everything—about his drinking, the kinds of friends he had, the life he had cultivated in New York, maybe even his experience with other women, if she asked. Perhaps he would even tell her about this summer's visit to the masjid, and his not being able to do namaaz on the anniversary of his father's death, about how he had felt the division happening within him again—that exclusivity of the two halves of his life, one half asserting itself, the other being expected to fall away—and how he'd resisted the total submission that was demanded in such moments to the point of breaking his prayer.

Nasr had always supposed that these sorts of intimacies would be shared in the natural course of matrimonial life—either that or they would never come up, become irrelevant. But he saw now that he would have to hasten their disclosure. He would do this by driving up here for as many long weekends as he could, by taking Farah to dinner, movies, shopping, whatever she wanted to do, by drawing her out, by being open and honest himself.

The irony was that in trying to prove a stupid point Jameela had cleared a path: with the wedding date set, the Ansaris had no reason to object to him and Farah spending time together, and any hesitations Nasr might have had about speaking frankly with her were moot. In fact, he and Farah were freer to be themselves. Recalling the blush that had spread across her face, Nasr was sure she would accept him. Farah may have had a sheltered life, but she was not what you expected. She had an intelligence that didn't require experience. It was built on an adroit and practical instinct for determining what was important and what wasn't. Above all, she was the designer of that perfect plan that Jameela herself would probably admire. The longer Nasr's thoughts lingered on their first meeting, the more confident he became that he and Farah would, like so many earlier generations of couples, find a balance between what they knew of each other separately and what they discovered as they forged their own way of being together. The only thing he would ask of her was that she not make them live as though the parts of their lives that didn't fit into prayer times had no value at all.

A t about one in the morning, after Hamid Uncle and Talat Auntie had driven home, the sounds of Nasr's mother and

Saira putting the kids to bed had quieted, and Yasmine and then Rizwan had gotten up sleepily to say good night, Jameela caught Nasr's eye. "Walk me home?" she said in a mild voice, and headed out of the living room before he could respond. He found her in the foyer, standing in a thin slice of light, still and patient, a hand on the doorknob, the nearer half of her profile in shadow.

"I can't," he said, and watched the words land on her face. "We're all going to Farah's tomorrow for breakfast."

A light outside made the embroidery on her shoulder glow in bright white lines; her eyelids were bare and serious. Nasr knew which two of the streetlamps on the way to her house hadn't worked in years, and which intersections the other four lit up. He also knew just how silent the neighborhood would be at this time of night, and that, despite this, their conversation wouldn't carry. He could hear himself recant, hear the very words he would use: *All right, let's go*. In fact, he was sorely tempted. This was how she'd always made him second-guess himself, even about what he most wanted—and it wasn't exclusively her fault. This was his essential weakness, wasn't it? Like so many times before in his life, a firm resolve he had just arrived at would instantly begin to crumble at a mere suggestion. Not this time. He wouldn't look at her.

In June his mother had spoken of a kind of careless talk that can unravel one's intentions and sabotage one's chances. She'd been worried about Yasmine, but what if she'd also been warning him? What if Jameela's talk of the past three years hadn't been careless? What if it had been deliberate and methodical—a poison? Nasr bravely turned to see what Jameela would look like through the prism of this revelation, but she had slipped away, leaving the front door ajar.

9

*T*he terrible event happened, once, twice, then over and over again on the television. So many times that people no longer wanted to say what had actually happened but chose to speak in metaphors. "Like a giant felled to its knees," one friend said to Nasr. "But then the knees disintegrated."

Back in August, Nasr's cell phone had been overflowing with congratulatory messages about the upcoming wedding. "Oh, no," wailed Pete, calling on the day of the engagement party. He was a burly blond Missourian who was Nasr's colleague and oldest friend in New York. Many of Nasr's friends had known he was going the arranged-marriage route—not details, of course, but enough to recognize that the results were long awaited. He had told them the good news a few days before leaving for Montreal, and he'd been grateful that it was received like any other engagement announcement—especially by Pete. "Man down, man down," the message continued, with Pete barking out military-style rescue orders, until a female voice interrupted abruptly to offer proper congratulations. "You'll have to let us take you out for a drink, Nasr"—this was Pete's long-time girlfriend, Laura—"after Pete grows up." The messages from family on various continents were brief, declaring communal happiness and wishing Nasr and Farah blessings (in the form of children) for a joyous future.

In September, Nasr's voice mail was overflowing again, with different daily messages from many of the same far-flung international numbers. Had he been hurt? Was he all right? How was his mother? But then people he'd only ever known as names called back, wanting details. What was it like? How did it sound? Had he felt anything? Did the whole island tremble? And what was going on now? Were the Americans having a curfew? It didn't seem to matter to these uncles and aunts and cousins that Nasr hadn't actually been in town that week, that he had in fact been in London on a business trip. Nor did it matter that he didn't work in that part of Manhattan, hadn't gone to "visit" the site, and didn't plan to. Although he was up-front about his absence at the beginning of every such conversation, the callers insisted that he tell them what had happened. "You already know," Nasr would reply in the very early days—Wednesday, Thursday, Friday—while walking down into a tube station or along the Thames. "You're an eyewitness, like everyone else who has a TV." Several times Nasr tried to suggest that what had happened was unspeakable, shouldn't be referred to in such curious, gossipy tones. Then, for a while, he avoided answering his phone altogether.

But when Nasr got back home to Manhattan, something about being in the very city made him feel like a reporter filing a story—patient, detached, obliged to explain—and he gave in.

What he began to describe, however, was what he saw on his own TV: looping video of the buildings driving themselves into the ground, which one station had accidentally played at double speed, so it looked as though the building were being erased off the bright white board of a sky; various angles of the sickeningly stately ride of the planes, their determination through the sunshine of that day; live street coverage of the hospitals on alert, their staffs waiting expectantly in scrubs near the sliding doors of the emergency entrance. He talked about how impressive it was that after the initial shock, after the smoke and the dust stopped pouring in from around street corners and sirens stopped coming from all directions, there had been no riots, no angry, loose-eyed mobs. Perhaps, Nasr speculated, this calm was a testament to the character of the city's citizens. They would not be undone so easily. But none of these descriptions seemed to satisfy his family, and Nasr slowly began to realize that what everybody was really after were those shocking details that the cameras couldn't or wouldn't zoom in on.

Nasr's friend with the metaphor, Javaid, was actually a distant cousin who'd left Montreal for the States a year or so after him. He was a banker, and had been in a business meeting in a nearby building when he felt the shudder and turned his head to see the first plane hitting. As one of those deep-voiced, grim-faced guys who looked much older than they were, Javaid already had the manners and formality and five o'clock shadow of an uncle. But every time Nasr saw him now, his eyes looked tender and glittery. Once he said to Nasr: "The way they were climbing over each other at the windows, I didn't think they were people. But what else could they have been?" Another time, Javaid described how the smoke had taken on different shapes. At first it was thick, black as ink, dribbling from the gash in the building; then, as the first tower sank, it gushed out the bottom, a gray and swift effluent, and after this came the most imposing transformation: the smoke swelling up and up, like a

113

genie from a bottle. A moment later, what he saw wasn't so much a genie but a thundercloud—tall, vast, teetering. The cloud rose to an immense height and then began advancing toward Javaid's building. It tumbled down the canyon of the avenue, rolling over cars on the street and eating up intersections. The smoke had remained so white and full against the blue sky, dignified even, as it approached, that Javaid fooled himself into thinking that passing through it would be like moving through a mist. But then the sound caught up, and soon the cloud slammed against the windows of the conference room, heavy and solid, and whatever was in it began to thrash against the glass. Tiny sounds like pebbles hitting—but thousands upon thousands of pebbles, coming in waves. The room darkened and stayed that way for long minutes. "You'd think we'd been caught in a storm," Javaid said. At first, he thought the building had lost power, but this must not have been true. "We could see everything on each other's faces—it was almost too visible. Everybody had stepped back from the windows, and we were lined up against the back wall. But nobody made a move to leave. There we all were—seven men, one lady, gathered together in a corner where normally nobody ever stood. I'd never noticed how huge that room was, so much wasted space. It all looked so different. So did the people. You couldn't tell who was who—the client, my colleagues, all their faces had the same expression." Here Javaid shook his head and looked away. Sometimes he would begin a thought—"But to have woken up that morning as usual, gone to work, and then spent your final moments hanging out of a window, in some stranger's office, in a part of the floor you'd never paid attention to, that . . ."—then trail off, as though he'd forgotten he was speaking. Other times, he spoke in urgent whispers: "It's just that there are too many layers you can think about at each moment—the people on the lower floors or in the other tower who couldn't help feeling lucky, saved, grateful, the people on the nearby floors who'd

114

lived to see the planes come in, the people on the planes who couldn't see the building in front but could see that the ones on the sides were getting too close." Once, he wondered if any passengers had seen him, through the windows of the conference room, in that meeting, sweating stupidly about losing an account.

Nasr borrowed what he could from Javaid for his reports to his relatives. After a few weeks, he forgot to mention that he'd initially witnessed the whole thing as a foreigner in a silenced pub. In fact, much of Nasr's time in London rapidly retreated from his mind. For most everyone he knew, the shock of Tuesday began in the morning, but for him the morning had been routine (a short meeting, followed by a successfully delivered presentation), and the grimness arrived in the afternoon and lingered into a night that was spent watching the events of another continent's tragedy unfold. Perhaps this was why the trip began to feel like someone else's experience, as if another person had sat in that pub in the midst of co-workers who, he suddenly sensed through the glaze of a long lunch, were avoiding looking in his direction. Someone new to the group, who'd been briefly introduced to Nasr, said across the table, "Hey, Nick, we're very sorry for you blokes." And tried to add, "Not even you people deserve that." A joke, perhaps because it was a pub. The people sitting closest to the new guy grimaced. "Americans," he said, looking around puzzled. "What?"

But Nasr had been so relieved to be spoken to, he'd said thanks, not bothering to correct the guy about his name or to say what was usually on his lips when his nationality was mistaken: "I'm Canadian, thankfully." Moments later, Nasr's phone began ringing—this was not unusual, most people were taking calls—but he saw the number and quickly turned it off.

• • •

115

*F*or the rest of that week in London, he continued going in to the office, but there was nothing for him to do. He would have left on Wednesday morning had the flight schedules not been postponed indefinitely. Because he was visiting, there was no desk available for him to occupy. Each day, he wound up storing his briefcase in a coat closet and searching for a free computer. He spent mornings sending e-mails but received few replies from New York, as though, aside from a few friends, his office had forgotten he was still here. After that, he would wander over to where other people were milling around and listening to broadcasts, waiting with the rest of the world to see what would happen next. Nasr's cell phone continued ringing during this time, and because most of the calls he took were from relatives, they required him to speak Urdu, or shout over distant, scratchy connections, or both. He tried to keep these conversations short, but when he couldn't, he would excuse himself and go outside.

On Thursday, sitting on a bench talking to an uncle in Delhi who was telling him that tragedies such as this were always happening and the important thing for the Americans to do was not to start believing that they were being singled out, Nasr overheard a guide leading a group of solemn tourists. He watched the visitors listen with intent faces to a speech about the Great Fire that left much of London destroyed and then let themselves be herded across the street. As soon as Nasr hung up with his uncle, the phone rang again. He decided to ignore it, and instead slipped in behind the trail of tourists as they made their way to a large white building with a high dome—St. Paul's Cathedral, the guide said, had been resurrected from ashes.

On Friday, when the airline said he wouldn't be able to get a flight out until the weekend, if not later, Nasr decided to skip the office altogether and head into the city. For him, London was a strange place—essentially unknown but with recognizable street names and sights. And as was the case with many cities, he was more familiar with its suburbs, which he'd seen on visits to prospective brides. He signed up for an overpriced walking tour. As his fellow tourists were led past Parliament and Westminster Abbey, toward Buckingham Palace, then up to Trafalgar Square, the young guide recited a script about the last great empire's imposing history almost apologetically. Despite this, Nasr found himself, at least at first, charmed by London: the grand form of its buildings seemed to him tastefully undercut by their modest scale and the harrowing spectacle of the narrow, sharply angled streets.

Once the tour ended, Nasr returned to Buckingham Palace. There were flowers at the gates, as there had been at the time of Princess Diana's death. Yesterday the American national anthem had been played there, and other memorial services were planned in the days ahead. It was a venerable show of sympathy for the former colony. In the park nearby, Nasr bought a sandwich to eat while watching people go by. It was easy to spot the honeymooners, with their Fodor's guides and camera-ready clothes. They would stop to pose for pictures in front of the palace. One couple, tall blond Australians, asked for Nasr's help. Staring into the viewfinder, he centered their smiling faces in front of the ornate façade—how strangely possible it was now to imagine a building not being there anymore, wiped clean from the sky as though it had never existed.

His feet ached as he left the park, but he felt pleasantly tired. Absently, he reached into his pocket and turned on his cell phone, and the moment he did, it began ringing, as though it had been ringing continuously this whole time, during all these hours he had spent trying to escape it.

· · ·

Nasr considered deleting the messages Jameela left, but at the end of each day, back in the stale hotel room, he wound up listening to them—and with every one, his fury grew. Most of the messages were frantic apologies, and many were hard to follow, but it was clear what Jameela had to tell Nasr, and the confession—of her meddling and interference—was even worse than he had imagined. She had indeed pressed Farah into getting the suit with the short sleeves, knowing full well how the Ansaris would react; also, when the Ansaris had once asked her about namaaz arrangements, she had assured them that they would be able to pray at the Siddiquis' house, even though she knew the basement wouldn't be set up for it. Worst of all, she'd told Farah about the search—when it began, how long it had gone on, how many girls Nasr had rejected. But she'd done all this, she said, only because she wanted him to know whom he was marrying—and the other way around. Or maybe not only because. But she had no idea that the Ansaris would force the issue like that—press, instead, for an earlier wedding. Hearing this, Nasr couldn't help feeling both as though he'd narrowly missed the worst of the outcomes and that he'd been tricked, that they'd all been manipulated and deceived by someone Nasr hardly recognized, someone who would try to ruin others' chances just because she couldn't be happy herself. He'd been right about Jameela—or he'd underestimated her.

In his mind's eye, he saw again that room that he'd imagined in June on the way to Farah's house. This time, he was standing inside it, seeing the desk and the high window so clearly that they might have been features of an actual place he'd been to. For a moment, the stillness in the room seemed just as lonely to him as it had before, but then the door swung open and sent the dust whirling into thick gray clouds, as though the tiny chamber had been invaded by invisible forces. It seemed clear now that if Jameela was removed from his life—if not only the spiteful and jealous things she had to say and do but all that she intimated in silence, and stood for, were gone—nothing would be easier for Nasr than to be happy with Farah. Perhaps the last truth about all this compromise he'd embarked upon three years ago—this reconciling of sometimes seemingly incompatible elements of one's self—was that one had to know when to finally draw the line. He and Farah did not need Jameela in their life together. It was up to him to make the eviction absolute.

10

*O*n Nasr's flight back to New York, the woman next to him, white-haired and grandmotherly but with a moneyed air—a native New Yorker, he soon learned—had asked, "Are you British?" There was a hopeful edge to her question, as though she was seeking assurance. Nasr said he wasn't and then answered all the other questions she had for him—why had he been in London, where did he work, for how long, where was he born, was he married (she was pleased to learn that he was soon to be), where in Manhattan did he live, whether he'd ever heard the story of how the island had been traded away from the Indians (not his kind) for twenty-four dollars, had he been to the museums, would he like to know how the boroughs had come to be formed? She had a significant number of facts at her fingertips, and though he knew some of them, it was easy to be suitably impressed.

Midway through the flight, after they'd chatted comfortably through the serving of dinner and dessert, Nasr found himself describing Lucknow—what kind of place it was, how its people were famous or infamous for their cordiality. He discovered that he could recall with almost startling accuracy a tour he'd taken with his father, when he was ten, of the grounds of their ancestral home, which was set a few miles out of town in what was known as the village country. They'd begun at the house, which didn't have the twenty-foot ceilings, multiple rooftops, and colonnades of the home in town but was nevertheless immense and rambling. It seemed to Nasr that he and his father walked for hours, past the rooms where the family still lived, down dark, neglected corridors that led to more courtyards and dusty drawing rooms. His father would periodically point to empty corners and describe what sort of treasure each had contained—hooks where fine swords had hung, a spot that had featured a waist-high porcelain vase instead of the dull brass spittoon, massive squares on the walls, faintly paler than the surrounding stucco, that were formerly occupied by the tapestries an ancestor had collected and later generations sold off.

The woman, Mrs. van der Luyden (Lillian, she insisted), had listened avidly, her exclamations of pleasure and approval rising over the quiet of the cabin, and Nasr's own voice kept up as he told her what his father had told him: about the stables that the estate had maintained and the horses the family would get to ride; how the animals were retired from the police force, where they had served in government parades. Among the lot there'd been a handsome silvery-gray stallion with finely defined quarters and a black mane—his father's favorite when he was a boy. Nasr found that he could relate all this so fluently, describe

121

events and circumstances as if they were part of his own memories, with details he hadn't even realized he knew: the ride of this particular horse, its eagerness to speed across an open field at hardly a prompt, even how there had been much speculation about its parentage, rumors of the races around the world that its forebears had won, and how those rumors, when connected to the ones about the stable's having originally been donated to the police by a sultan, had led some to believe that the barn might, in fact, be filled with creatures of such quality that they could be . . . "*All* Arabians?" Lillian gasped—too loudly. Her voice carried throughout the dark cabin, which seemed to be hanging perfectly still and silent above the black Atlantic, though surely not everyone on board was asleep.

Back in New York, when Nasr was among friends comparing stories—Where were you when you first saw "it": the plane(s) striking, the building(s) fall, the fire, the snowing ash, the people running?—he didn't, as he normally would have, turn this or any other incident from his London trip into an amusing anecdote. He imagined that everybody had other things on their minds. Perhaps some of them had begun, like him, spending their free minutes concentrating on how far away an airplane should sound. Whenever Nasr heard one now, he stopped typing or walking, even swallowing; he risked the burn of holding coffee in his mouth too long—not to look, but to train himself to *sense* the appropriate quality of the rumble: distant and dispassionate, lapping like a forceful ocean in a seashell. Although he did a lot of talking to his family these days, he didn't share any of this with them, either. Once, he tried telling his mother about how the memory of that time with his father had come to him so easily and vividly. His mother replied that her own family had had horses as well, out on the farm; they might not have been as fancy as his father's, but a horse was a horse, after all, wasn't it?

. . .

As the days passed, there seemed to be more and more details that were no use sharing with anyone. Better to let them slip from his mind. Who would it help to know that there were times during those airport inspections at Heathrow when Nasr was nearly impressed with the officer for not taking one look at his face and spitting in it? Or how he suspected that the bottle of scotch he'd been bringing back for his boss's anniversary might have helped get him through the security checks? The sight of it rolling out of his carry-on had made an impression on more than one official—at least those smart enough to recognize that, if anything, the bottle was evidence that it was Nasr's people who should be suspicious of him. In any case, there was no point dwelling on whether or not he had consciously put that bottle on top.

Another thing best left unexamined was that during those days of wandering around London there were times when the woman Nasr was engaged to would fall out of his mind completely, and when he did finally think of Farah fully and properly—back home from the airport, in the unfamiliar daytime shade of his apartment, when he'd unthinkingly turned on his phone and Farah's voice had sounded so hesitant in her message, stumbling over the use of his name as she hoped he was okay— it had, for some reason, surprised him that she even knew what had happened in New York. "Everyone here is saying how nice it will be, insha'allah, to see you," Farah had said. It was a voice of concern, but not panic—clearly being overheard—in a call made on behalf of other people. From the moment he'd met her, Farah seemed to exist in a world that was adjacent to and neighboring Nasr's, but also sequestered and protected. Her world may have had its mysteries, but in general he had thought he would always be able to see into it, that it was a life whose customs and codes would always be decipherable. But hearing the message, it occurred to Nasr that when she married him he'd be taking her into this new wound on the map, and that although the distance between Cornwall and the border was not even country-sized (just a few hours on the highway), America was, nevertheless, a country Farah had never been to nor perhaps had ever wanted to see. He wasn't sure which, as he'd never thought to ask.

At the end of that flight back to New York but before the descent, while they were still high above the clouds and the airplane was still dim, with many of its shades drawn, a need had gotten hold of Nasr, an instinctive reaction, and his lips had begun moving out of an old habit. He had tried to keep his tongue still, but the words then began vibrating along his teeth, through his nose, and in his cheeks—strings and strings of them, the prayer coming back in full.

Something like this had happened to him once before, a long time ago. It had been on the third day after his father's burial, during the bakshana, when the dead are required to be released, sent off to heaven with as many complete recitations of the Qur'an as can be read before the high sun of the noon prayer. Hamid Uncle had organized a group reading to commence at dawn, and the adults had sat in the living room, quietly reciting the chapters Hamid Uncle had assigned to them. Nasr's mother had hoped they would be able to finish two readings, transfer the sawaab of a full sixty chapters. In another room, the children who were awake had also been given assignments, but small ones—repeating a kalma a few times, helping the very little ones recite the ayat al-kursi. Nasr had joined the adults. He was known at the masjid school for being a fast reader—a star pupil, with his quick but unmarred articulation.

Instead of a few thin chapters, he'd taken a full copy of the Qur'an to a corner beside the sofa, and when he'd begun reading the words had glided out of him, over his tongue and under his breath, as loose and rapid as water. He kept them intelligible with a feverish grip but just barely, for he found it impossible to slow down, didn't even want to, as if this reading were imperative, as if his father might not have done enough to secure his own passage into heaven. Nasr's throat had burned for hours, expanding and constricting as the hot breath poured out.

He'd felt this burn again on the plane, but then sensed himself come awake. There was a dull hissing silence in the cabin, and though it must have been only minutes later, the drawn shades were now edged in the bright tinsel of sunshine. In sleep, his neighbor Lillian looked like someone's grandmother, her cheeks slack with wrinkles, a faint crosswork of red lines where the rouge had collected, the skin around her jaw quivering slightly. Nasr remembered finishing the last chapter minutes short of the noon deadline, his eyes tired and sticking, heavy from the blurry daze that had never quite eclipsed the questions no one was willing to ask aloud, let alone answer: What was going to happen now? What would their lives be like? Would there ever be any return of the known and familiar? The overhead lights flickered on, progressing down the length of the aisle. There was the ring of a bell, a few electronic taps on a microphone, as though someone were preparing to speak, but then only crackle and silence. Drifting again, Nasr let his eyes close. There was a tipping sensation, the grind and strain of gears turning, a slow, dreamy tumble to the left. Would you always have to wonder now who was steering? he thought. And into what?

PART two

11

*I*n the weeks following the attacks, the wedding preparations resumed with breathtaking speed. For Nasr, many of the major decisions concerning his future were made on the phone: his mother on one extension in the den, his sister on the echoey upstairs line. Of the three of them, Nasr's mother had been the quickest to recover her focus, and she declared that critical time had been lost without dwelling on whether it was politic to make such a claim. She made Yasmine call florists, renters of fine linens, and decorators. But finding these vendors, or, rather, keeping them committed, wasn't easy. It seemed many couples were deciding to get married these days: middle-aged ones who'd been living together for years; others who'd met recently (perhaps even on *that* day); previously engaged pairs who'd decided to move their wedding date up. The trend had been observed in the news. Who knew what was around the corner?—the interviewed lovers said, valiant and solemn as they spoke of the joys of matrimony and of not wasting another day. With so many hastily pulled-together ceremonies in progress, one needed to be ready to search widely, act fast, and, if necessary, offer competing bids—all of which meant that Nasr's mother's instincts had been right.

One relentlessly contentious issue was the guest list. Nasr's mother's feeling was that the sending of an invitation was not so much a request for attendance as a courtesy—a gesture made to assure the recipient that he or she had been remembered during the planning of this momentous occasion—and this courtesy should be extended with broad generosity: to the legions of actual and extended (by marriage or tenure) relations that circled the globe; to the multitude of Siddiqui and Haq acquaintances from Lucknow and neighboring villages; and even to visitors who'd passed through town (five years ago, seven, ten, fifteen) and had been kind enough to inquire after the family. Nasr's mother insisted that all of these people must be invited simply because most wouldn't, couldn't possibly, attend. The guest list (even before it was combined with that of the bride's side) swelled from 175 to 250 in the course of a week, and reached 300 by the end of the next. The Ansaris, who had kept themselves to a modest 120, were not the only ones dismayed. "What if half of them show up? We'll still be in trouble," Yasmine said to their mother with a civil engineer's outrage about building codes. The capacity of the school the Ansaris were renting for the Nikaah was 250, and while the hall they themselves hoped to get for the Valima was larger, it, too, would be nowhere near adequate.

"These capacities are just estimates, beta," Nasr's mother replied. "And this is just a matter of a few hours. Why, back home we hosted weddings of much greater size in our houses."

"Well, if you don't want to follow any rules, why don't you go to Lucknow and do the shaadi there?"

Nasr's mother sighed. "I would do that without one minute of hesitation, beta, but your brother's preferences must be considered, after all."

This was the first time Nasr had heard this line of reasoning, so he hardly noticed its implications, but it soon became a common refrain. Whenever Yasmine identified a difficulty, Nasr's mother would become adamant in settling the matter for "your brother's sake" or because "it is what your brother is wanting." The intimation evolved and snowballed. First he was portrayed as having been merely eager, then not only eager but desperately so, and in no time he became the one who'd been set on marrying as soon as possible. Finally, by some perverse turn, the alleged urgency on his part was presumed to be connected to this thing that had happened in the world. "At times like these," his mother had taken to explaining to Yasmine, "it's only understandable for a boy to wish to settle down." Not only was the determination of the Ansaris forgotten, but so were the timing of his first meeting with Farah, the years of searching, and his mother's long and pressing investment in the matter. Once uttered, this presumption was surprisingly difficult to refute. Nasr couldn't very well say he wasn't eager. Nor could he mention Jameela's interference. For one thing, he wasn't even supposed to know about that; and for another, he could hardly give a reason that suggested that he (and the Ansaris) had been tricked. So he went along and accepted this miscast blame. In a way, it was a trump card for both of them: because there was no objection Yasmine could make, the card, once played, ended the argument in his mother's favor and immediately got Nasr off the phone.

As tedious as the wedding preparations could be, they were a welcome diversion. A growing invitation list, however controversial its progress, was more pleasant than the growing death list printed in the newspaper on a daily basis. His family had experienced moments like this before, when the chatter of practical matters was welcomed after a long, uncertain silence, so they were perhaps better at recovering than one ought to be. Still, it was sometimes impossible to hear about the intricate web of connections and relations that his mother could provide to justify a new invitation without wondering how each dead body might be connected to, depend upon, support so many others still living, or how wide the circle of acquaintances who would have to be informed of the death might extend. Two hundred and fifty people might legitimately be invited for one person's wedding? What about for one person's funeral? And for some three thousand funerals?

For Nasr, his family's swift recovery served another practical purpose. It was key to his campaign to get close to Farah. Upon returning from London, he offered himself up as a liaison between the families, the members of which didn't seem naturally inclined to coordinate their efforts. He made sure that when his mother chose linens or flowers, the information was transmitted to the Ansaris. He did this by calling Farah, not every day but several times a week—relaying decisions, gathering opinions, speaking to her mother and father if necessary. No detail was too minor or inconsequential, and Nasr applied himself to the task.

He hoped for more success in these conversations (even if they began with the topic of dinner napkins) than he had in late August, when he'd gone to Montreal for a weekend to see Farah and failed miserably to make a good impression. This was a couple of weeks after the engagement party, and the Ansaris had somehow been persuaded to allow the "children" to go out on their own for an evening, but not before the two families had met for a requisite, formal dinner, this time at the Ansaris' house. The men had segregated into the living room, balancing heaping plates of food on their knees, and the women had stayed in the dining room, behind those saloon doors. The following evening, Nasr and Yasmine took Farah and her sisters to a nearby bowling alley. Yasmine had asked Jameela to come along (Nasr could hardly object), but fortunately she had declined.

The Ansari girls had never been to a bowling alley, although this one was just down the street from their house, and they were good sports about the very specific lessons they received from Yasmine. Suraiya, the youngest, bowled three strikes in a row, and the Siddiqui siblings were soon informed that she was the athletic one. "She doesn't actually play any sports, though," Rafia said. Yasmine, who seemed to get on well with all three sisters, asked Rafia which "one" she was, and Rafia replied, in the same flat, possibly sarcastic tone: "They think I'm the sober one." "And you?" Yasmine said, turning to Farah. "Oh, just the old one, I guess," Farah said with a self-mocking sigh. If that was the case, Yasmine replied, she wondered what that made her, at the ancient age of twenty-five.

As the evening progressed, Nasr got the sense that contrivances were being made to leave him and Farah alone—as alone as two people could be in a crowded bowling alley on a summer weekend. Their sisters congregated at the opposite end of the bowling booth, and several times they went off together to fetch Cokes, then snacks, then to explore the cavernous outer banks of the arcade room. But Nasr felt tongue-tied all night. Farah's hair wasn't, like her sisters', covered in a headscarf. It framed her face in deep brown sheets. This was the first time Nasr had seen her in Western clothes, and he was relieved that she, for whatever reason, didn't do hijaab, had a trendy haircut, and was, if not initiating conversations, then at least listening with a friendly smile. Sitting beside him, she looked like any other girl. But this wasn't any other girl. This was his future wife, and tonight was their first date—presumably, her first date ever.

He inquired about school, but was careful not to ask when exactly Farah was finishing up, as he didn't want her to think he was being pushy about her transfer. He tried to avoid topics directly related to wedding preparations—they seemed presumptuous on a first date. He didn't feel he could talk about her family—he knew enough about them, as much as was appropriate, and if he asked more, it might indicate that he hadn't been paying attention or had paid too much to the wrong details. And there was no way to tell her any more about his own family without feeling that he was bragging or repeating himself, like a salesman pitching a product. He tried not to stare when it was her turn to bowl, but when he was up, he couldn't help noticing that it was like standing on a stage, with every angle of yourself visible to spectators. Out of desperation, he mentioned that he couldn't come up for the next couple of weekends as he was heading out to London for a business trip. "But I'll visit again as soon as I get back."

Farah nodded politely. Did he like London? she asked.

"Very much," he said, adding that it would be fun to introduce her to the city sometime. He hoped to tell her something about the place, but nothing came to mind—not one single detail—which was frustrating, as he now thought of London as the city abroad that he was most familiar with. "It could be our first stop," he added helplessly.

Farah looked puzzled, but she listened patiently as he began a clumsy (perhaps even pompous and not altogether appealing) description of the grand world tours he had planned for the two of them: "England would be the easiest place to start, language-wise, then France. But I really want to take you to Milan. You don't speak Italian, do you?" Fortunately, Farah was saved from responding—and he from continuing—by the return of their sisters.

Despite all this, Nasr hadn't thought that the silence between him and Farah was all that uncomfortable until Yasmine made a comment about how Jameela had told her that bowling shoes would soon be the height of fashion. Farah laughed and clapped her hands together. "Too true," she said, and confessed to having spent the past half hour trying to figure out how to walk off with her pair. For the rest of the evening Nasr glumly wondered what he might say that would produce such a genuine and spontaneous response.

12

*F*arah's parents were polite when Nasr called, but they didn't do anything to encourage him. There was always an awkward moment, as if they didn't know—couldn't even imagine—why he was asking for their daughter. "Farah?" Mrs. Ansari would say. "Yes, she is here. Would you like to talk to her?" Likewise, each of his conversations with Farah began with polite exchanges, first consisting of reports on the well-being of one another's families, then of news and related trouble, brewing locally and globally. When no progress was made beyond this, Nasr would be forced to make the inquiry that had ostensibly prompted the phone call. This turn toward wedding matters somehow felt even more impersonal, and thus a step in the wrong direction.

In all of these calls, the practical and sensible tone of Farah's speech made their conversations in July seem distant and irreconcilable, even inexplicably candid, as if there had been an opening in the summer through which a whole person had nearly gushed out, but now that person had retreated into a cloak of correctness and manners. Nasr considered buying Farah a cell phone, but he didn't think her receiving an expensive gift from him would help his cause. He would have preferred to visit, of course, but the unsuccessful bowling weekend made him hesitate. Plus, he reasoned, with a name like his, it probably wasn't the best time to make frequent excursions across the border. (Fortunately, Nasr had, with his firm's help, filed the paperwork for Farah's immigration back in August, and since then, his supervising partner had had papers drawn up that authenticated his employment—"Just to be on the safe side.")

He still wanted to be open and confiding, to tell Farah about himself. But all that certainty he'd felt back in August at the engagement party was based on an assumption—that she had secretly been behind her parents' insistence on an early wedding date. Now, with Jameela's voice-mail confessions factored in, this assumption seemed rather bold. If Jameela's interference had actually motivated the Ansaris, it was likely also to have influenced Farah. But the question was—in what way? What did she think of all that Jameela had told her about the search, with its many years of rejections? What a mess Jameela had made, Nasr thought every once in a while, and a crust of rage would form before he remembered that she was no longer allowed into his thoughts.

After several more phone conversations with Farah, in which it felt as if he were assailing a fortress whose defenses were impregnable, Nasr tried e-mail. He composed long, detailed messages, endeavoring to be as natural as possible, as if he were writing to an old friend. Without implicating himself

135

too much, he tried to give Farah a sense of who he was and wasn't.

He began by writing that everybody in New York was very eager to meet her, and he warned Farah that there would be a number of parties for her to attend when they got back from their honeymoon. He let the word "honeymoon" sit there, unelaborated upon at the end of the sentence, and wondered what she would think.

In a reply, Farah, also perhaps ignoring the reference to "honeymoon," asked about his work, and Nasr quickly produced several paragraphs and sent them off. But upon a rereading, they struck him as no more interesting than dry job descriptions, so he wrote another e-mail—about the office, the building, the company, and also the people: which of the partners were Canadian and friendly, which were assholes (he kept the word) but influential. He narrowed "everybody" down to friends—Pete, Laura, Ramesh, Martin, Cynthia—and explained all the connections and histories, not bothering to hide the fact that there were several couples among them who weren't married. He described the projects for which he'd done so much traveling over the past few years, but also assured her that he'd requested a cutback—and then September had come and imposed one, of course. Soon Nasr found himself writing about those early days: how it had been impossible to concentrate; how even if you wanted to get something done, your mind floated away; then your body would get drawn from your desk by the TV in the coffee room. Or you would linger after fire-safety drills to chat in whispers—why whispers?—with your co-workers. When these chats ended and people returned to their cubicles, they sat so quietly that you would have thought large pockets of the building were empty. Now, only three weeks later, you could—were in fact encouraged to —talk about something else, something that wasn't happening down the street. Down the street had become the West

Bank, Bosnia, Oklahoma City, Northern Ireland, the Congo—
frenzied, sincere, patriotic, ribboned in red, white, and blue, be-
leaguered, defeated, overexposed. It was not New York. And you
couldn't look at it. Or rather, you couldn't both think of it and
set about explaining to your secretary how you wanted a certain
memo formatted.

One person who didn't stop talking about it was Javaid. For
Javaid, the "it" was still the ever-changing smoke—now billow-
ing across town, this way then that. After his company's building had been cleared for reoccupancy, he spent a whole week at
his desk staring out at the smoldering ruins. One day he called
Nasr to tell him that he'd decided to take a few days off, and the
next time they met for dinner, he said of the smoke: "Sometimes
there was an orange light at the back of the gray, winking like
someone was searching with a flashlight, and then it was green."
Javaid looked up at the ceiling, exhaling deeply. As usual, he had
arrived first at the restaurant, a Turkish place in the East Village,
and chosen to sit in the quietest corner at the back. Although he
wasn't going to work these days, he had still shown up in a tie,
with not a hair out of place, his dark goatee precisely rounded
and trim.

Javaid had moved to New York six months ago from
Boston, where he'd been getting his MBA at Harvard. Growing
up, he and Nasr hadn't been particularly close. The relation—
Javaid's mother was Nasr's father's uncle's daughter—was not
that distant in Indian terms, but Javaid's family had moved to
Canada from Pakistan when he was in his early teens. By that
time, Nasr's father had been dead for a number of years, and
that experience had so sealed the family's relationships that it
was impossible to get close to new people, even if they were
blood relations. It didn't help that Javaid was a few years
younger than Nasr, observant about drinking and eating halal
only, and that, even as a kid, he had a very direct and serious
manner. But as Nasr got older, he came to appreciate, even en-

joy, this seriousness. Javaid would earnestly consider an issue even if you'd brought it up casually, and you could get into a satisfyingly long conversation on why it was that Canadians still had Britishers on their money, or how, nuclear weapons or not, India and Pakistan still needed to be saved from themselves more often than from each other. The two cousins had been on increasingly friendly terms since college, and Nasr wondered if he'd half inspired Javaid to come to the States, though of course the numerous scholarships he'd been offered had no doubt done most of the persuading.

Last year, when Javaid was finishing his degree in Boston and considering job offers, Nasr hadn't pushed him toward the ones from Manhattan, but he had made a case for the city and its various resources (among which he included himself)—and he'd been pleased when Javaid had come down in April. Early on, Nasr invited him out with friends, offered it as a way of seeing different neighborhoods and building contacts in a new place. But Javaid always declined, usually calling back from his office, even though it was after nine or ten, to say he still had some work to finish. The two of them eventually settled into a pattern of meeting every other week on their own for a meal, during which Javaid was sometimes almost manically loquacious, jumping from one topic to another. Nasr often got the impression that his cousin's usual stoicism was the result of a powerful self-restraint that reined in the workings of a mind that was anything but quiet. After a couple of months of these dinners, Nasr realized that he was still Javaid's only friend in town, and also that Javaid might have passed much of his time in Boston in silence.

This night, the two cousins talked, as they had at their last few meals together, for a long while about the evolving nature of the rescue and recovery efforts. According to Javaid, factions had developed among the volunteer crews—some people felt as though they were not being allowed to do enough or as much as other groups. "They want it so badly, they're actually fighting over it," Javaid said, incredulous. "They're like us now."

"How's that?" Nasr asked.

When Javaid spoke, it was always clear who the "they" was. And whenever he expounded on a new theory, Nasr couldn't help noticing the ways in which coming over as a teenager (as opposed to being born here) had made Javaid's sensibilities fall between his parents' generation and his own. Now, as he described how the Americans were finally getting a taste of what it was like to be an immigrant—to feel paranoid in familiar neighborhoods, to suspect that everyone around them had mysterious motives, to find it was impossible to communicate with anyone who didn't feel exactly as they did, to believe they were a certain kind of people without realizing how much they had already changed—Nasr wished his cousin wouldn't lean in as though the two of them were sharing a secret.

"They've lost their confidence," he concluded, and promptly sat back. The waiter had returned with dinner.

During the meal, Javaid asked how the wedding plans were proceeding. He apologized again for not being able to attend the engagement party, but mentioned that he'd met Farah when he went home for a visit last weekend (his mother had hosted a little party). The Ansaris seemed to him like very fine people.

Nasr gave a barely exaggerated description of Sultana Siddiqui's commitment to sending an invitation to any and all living organisms that might expect one. "She'd invite the dead if she could."

This drew a smile from Javaid, but in the brief lull that followed their ordering coffee, he suddenly said, "I walked in it."

Nasr nodded. He had developed a habit these days, and not just in conversations with Javaid, of anticipating when a discussion would turn back. With others, he'd occasionally been mistaken and the solemn tone had come back into his voice too soon, but he never made that mistake with Javaid.

"I still keep finding ash in my clothes," Javaid said, then stopped just as abruptly. Perhaps he had detected the note of pride in his voice that Nasr always found so strange. But a moment later Javaid added, as though he couldn't help himself, "I've never been that close to such a thing."

"Of course not," Nasr replied.

"But I mean all of it," he said. "I've never been to a funeral or to a birth or to anything. Whenever something happens to people we know, it always seems so far away."

The next morning on his way to the office, Nasr considered composing an e-mail to Farah that rehashed last night's conversation. Perhaps she, having also been born outside of Canada, felt as Javaid did. But he was soon distracted by a strange thing that was developing at work.

"I didn't even know you were seeing anybody," a receptionist said to Nasr as he passed by, with the first smile she'd ever bestowed on him. "Was it love at first sight?" she asked. Nasr smiled and shrugged, then he headed quickly to the elevators, letting her think what she liked.

It seemed as if interest in the wedding had grown and spread across floors and management levels, and now there were at least a couple of office parties being planned—one for before and another after, when Nasr got back with Farah. All of which would have been fine, except for the fact that people in the office, from secretaries to senior partners, had also apparently decided that this was the only thing to talk about with him. If he wandered by during a conversation on the latest topic in the news—whether or not to bomb Afghanistan—people would welcome him into the circle, not to ask for his thoughts but to inquire about when his fiancée would be visiting and what, exactly, an Indian bride wore. They demanded photos of the engagement party. How did Nasr propose? Did he get down on one knee, or was that not part of the religion? Some of his colleagues wondered—politely or ironically, depending on how well they thought they knew him—if he was going to make Farah cover her head, and whether she would be allowed to have a job. And how come he didn't wear a turban? The Americans were so cheerful and friendly and respectful through these inquisitions that Nasr half wondered if the prospect of military action—someone doing something about it—was making them feel generous again, even curious.

From the questions asked, Nasr guessed that many of the people he worked with seemed to have known that he was Indian but had hardly noticed that he was Muslim. And, in truth, why would they? He'd always been rather proud of not being one of those people who pushed their differences on others. (Recently, the lyrics of that "Come, Mr. Taliban" song had found their way into Nasr's in-box. He took this as a sign that the person forwarding the e-mail either recognized that there was no connection or hadn't stopped to consider that there might be one—flattering either way.) But Nasr now found himself standing in copy rooms explaining that no, Islam was not like this. Like all religions, it had its extremists, but violence was not a central tenet. In fact, at the heart of Islam was moderation—moderation of thought and deed. Did the Crusades mean that violence was essential to Christianity? And: Oh, well, yes, sure it was possible to be a moderate and a believer. These extremists were no more like Muslims he knew—*real* Muslims, he suddenly took to calling them—than those right-wing people were like the majority of Christians. The views of a renegade minority couldn't—shouldn't—be extrapolated to an entire group. In such conversations people didn't interrupt, and Nasr would accidentally drift into lectures, and sometimes he would say things he wasn't sure about, with more conviction than he actually felt.

Questions were just questions—no more, no less. But sometimes the attention made Nasr feel as though his life in New York over the past few years had been taking place in a drawer that had now been pulled open and its contents rummaged for clues to a mystery. Occasionally, this feeling extended outside the office. A stranger sitting across from him on the subway or, more often, in a crowd heading toward him, would suddenly make eye contact and hold it—a gripping, silent stare. In such moments, it was hard not to become conscious of the dimensions of one's own face. What would it be like, Nasr wondered, if this person followed the impulse showing in his eyes and came over and punched him? When the person merely passed by or eventually looked away, Nasr felt unexpectedly reprieved. Sometimes he couldn't help admiring the stranger's restraint and goodwill.

W*as* it love at first sight? The answer to this question idled somewhere back in that afternoon of his first meeting with Farah. Nasr had yet to tell anyone about the scheme Farah had devised with her two sisters. He was so desperate to impress someone with it—to have it sifted for clues and confirmations— that he nearly confided in Javaid. But his cousin was often so preoccupied that Nasr felt guilty dragging his attention to a new topic. How could he suggest, in the midst of soldiers on the street, barricades and armed checkpoints, wild reports and hasty evacuations, that there was another world, of petty delights and even pettier anxieties? Nasr considered telling Yasmine about the scheme, but that would have its own awkwardnesses. Plus, there seemed to be only one way he and his sister could talk about the wedding: through the event's most tiresome logistics. The ideal person to talk about it with would have been Farah herself—that afternoon in her parents' living room was part of their past, something to reminisce about. But how could he compliment her on the scheme's design without also seeming to congratulate her for its effectiveness in, well, getting him?

That left Nasr's friends, mainly Pete. But recently even Nasr's interactions with him had become complicated. A few days earlier, Mrs. Ansari had requested that there be no wearing of sleeveless blouses at the wedding, a restriction that was most likely to affect one group of guests—Nasr's invitees, specifically his female co-workers from New York. Nasr asked Pete for his advice about whether it was better to talk to each woman or to send out an e-mail and thus avoid having anyone feel singled out.

"So you'll give 'em a chance to buy something new," Pete said. "Not like anybody's going to complain about that. Anyway, do I whine when the Christmas party is black tie only? Well, yes, I actually do. But hey, as long as I don't have to wear a turban to your shindig, I'm fine."

Nasr nodded absently. Pete was probably right, he thought to himself. People accepted all kinds of restrictions for formal occasions.

But Pete suddenly got a strange look on his face. "Sorry, man," he said. "I didn't mean that." Nasr had never seen his friend apologize before, not sincerely. "Look, don't worry about it," Pete added. "Aren't all eyes supposed to be on the bride, anyway? Everybody gets that."

To tell Pete about that first afternoon with Farah, Nasr would have to explain what the other, more typical visits to prospective brides were like, and to do that would put a certain, very foreign scene into his friend's head—all that before the guy even met Farah.

143

One day in early October, Nasr finally encountered the Farah of his first meeting. The occasion was prompted by his mother calling to say she was ordering an eight-place table setting for him and to ask which color he preferred. She thought a classical ivory white would be best, but Yasmine and Saira claimed that people these days liked more colorful patterns.

"Oh, that's nice of her," Farah said when Nasr called to ask her preference. "I hadn't thought of the dining table, or even of the dining room." There was a pause, then Farah remarked that his mother was always so considerate, and then another pause. "Wouldn't the color depend on other choices?" she asked, then broke off yet again. "This is so very nice, but—but can we wait and see? Maybe choose later? When it's just us?"

A beat later, she was telling him about her family's plans for the Canadian Thanksgiving this weekend, but Nasr's ears were still prickling. Her voice had changed with that last question—the words had come out low and whispered, the intimation in the tones designed to remind him that there were people listening, but also: *Let's hold them off, shall we?* Just before hanging up, she asked if his company gave him Thanksgiving off. Not this one, he said, and pledged to make arrangements to come later in the month. "Oh, that's nice," she replied, her voice reverting back to its neutral tones. But Nasr followed her meaning perfectly. We may not be the classic sort of lovers, Farah might as well have said, but we could still enjoy the romance of getting to know each other.

13

A few days later, when Nasr called Montreal, Jameela answered the phone. His mother, she told him, had gone with Hamid Uncle and Talat Auntie to dinner at another auntie's house. She was waiting for Yasmine to get ready so the two of them could go out. Nasr asked after her parents; Jameela assured him they were fine. They made their way through a little more small talk, and all the while, Nasr's voice felt creaky, which he attributed to his having succeeded in putting Jameela out of his mind.

"But are you okay?" she asked, the question rushing out like a horse breaking free of its reins.

Nasr replied that he was. There was a silence, and he

thought maybe they were done. Well, that wasn't too bad. But then the horse galloped back through.

"There was a while when nobody heard from you," Jameela said. "They didn't know where you were, which country, airline. People tried calling—did someone confiscate your phone?"

With a quickness that surprised him in this moment as much as it would later haunt him, Nasr said, "I lost it." A lie.

"Oh."

"I had to get a new one," he added. He heard the sound of a long breath being expelled.

"Guess nobody thought of that," she said eventually. "Hold on." She broke off for a moment, then came back to report that Yasmine said she would talk to him tomorrow. Jameela fell quiet again, but she seemed in no hurry to hang up. Nor would she say something to keep the conversation going.

"She's getting ready, eh?" Nasr said.

"I'm only on the fourth 'Just ten more minutes.' "

"I hope you brought a book," Nasr said—he found he couldn't help himself.

Now Jameela laughed. "Getting that kid dressed for her wedding will be a nightmare," she said. "My nightmare," she added, finally sounding more like herself. After a moment, she began asking Nasr some of the same questions about life in New York that other people had asked him. By now, he knew the answers to such questions by rote, and even though Jameela's versions were peppered with her typical demand for strange specifics—"What train do you take downtown?" and "How close is the river to the site?"—Nasr could, despite her interruptions, deliver the story like a speech. He was in the middle of describing the daily reports that came in about the volunteer efforts, people who'd dropped everything—jobs, college classes—to come and help, when Jameela said, "Oh, I know. Suddenly everybody doesn't mind being part of the great American family. Yesterday I found myself explaining to the whitest boy on the planet that, no, actually, at a time like this, we didn't all just become Americans—we became white Americans. The guy was actually lecturing me about wearing veils, how repressive they are, how backward—all TV sound bites. The whole class had to stop and we all had to talk about it. Burqa this and burqa that, life as a hidden person, as if it's all just fucking occurring to them. 'Oh, my God, there are people in the world who aren't allowed to wear what they want? *Buy* what they want? How can that be? That's not freedom.' " Nasr heard a long, and what seemed to him showy, sigh. "Just give them three seasons, I say," she continued. "Three fashion seasons, and all the stores will be selling little 'berka' caps, with a piece of gauzy mesh floating down from the top. Part of some designer's Muzzl'em collection. It'll be all that comes out of this rage—or outrage—or whatever it is."

It seemed to Nasr that an age had passed since he had heard anyone—in the office, on the street, TV, or anywhere—speak in a complaining voice, and the sound of it was grating.

"It's amazing nothing happened to you," Jameela said.

"What's amazing about it?" he asked.

"Weren't you trying to fly back?"

"I did fly back."

"And you—there was no trouble at all?"

Yes, he'd been stranded, Nasr said, like everyone else. And yes, he'd been misidentified once and asked to step aside at the airport, but he was sure other people had been, too—and anyway, he was correctly identified soon enough. To the Interpol officer who asked his name, the nature of his trip, he'd said, "All business," and described his job as many times as he was required to, and reconstructed each day of the business trip without losing his patience, because these were all fair questions.

Jameela made some sort of squeaking sound. "But you shouldn't have had to—"

"It was fine," Nasr said. He was glad he hadn't told her that the Interpol officer had been paged specifically to question him. Or said anything about how he'd spent much of the interview relieved that he'd paid for those walking tours with a credit card, so there was a record of his activities. He'd also felt a pang of relief that he hadn't visited the home of a prospective bride on this trip, only to remember belatedly that he didn't need to make such visits any longer.

"Still, they can't single you out like a criminal," she said, but Nasr ignored this. The hands of the boy who'd searched his overcoat had trembled, he told her—leaving out how the boy's supervisor had plundered through his briefcase and broken an inside latch.

In another kind of country, Nasr said, wouldn't there have been immediate riots, hysteria, revenge killings—instead of apologies and embarrassment? And hadn't this caution been for his own good as well, as a passenger? He tried to speak clearly and evenly. He wanted to make sure Jameela understood all this before she said something else stupid and rash—not so much to him as to someone else. What could not be forgotten, he continued into the silence building on the other end of the line, was that all the laws and protections had been in place and working, and that in the end, just days afterward, he, a Muslim man, had been allowed to board a flight. And yes, of course, he'd received looks when he stepped on the plane, but they were looks that he himself would have shot, in any reversal of the situation. But here, too, Nasr had to pick his way through the details. After going on board, he had taken his seat quickly, ordering the first of several drinks, and when the passenger beside him needed something from the overhead compartment, he had stopped himself from reaching to help her with her carry-on. Standing in the aisle, he'd put his hands in his pockets at first; then crossed his arms so his hands were visible; then let the arms drop to his sides in case that made him look angry.

Before takeoff, when the pilot asked all the passengers to introduce themselves to one another, Nasr promptly shook hands with all six of his neighbors, two forward and back, one to the side, and another across the aisle, realizing for the first time how surrounded a person is, even in business class. The pilot suggested that the passengers think of themselves as an army of a hundred and seventy-six, that it was their responsibility to speak up if they saw anything suspicious.

"He said 'army'?" Jameela asked.

Nasr said yes and nothing else. He hadn't meant to tell her that.

"That's it?" Jameela said.

He said yes again, and now there was real silence. The embarrassing truth of that flight was that he'd chatted with his fellow passengers the whole way, and hoped these strangers noticed his suit and the company's logo on his briefcase if these things made them feel better. Hours later, at the other shore, when the plane had cleared the clouds and the wreckage had come into view, still smoldering at the far end of the still distant skyline although the smoke was no longer as voluminous as it had been on TV, there had been gasps and cries all through the cabin. The pilot had asked everyone to observe a moment of silence, but his deep voice had wavered and he could hardly get the sentence out. Nasr caught a few glimpses through the windows, but he didn't strain or overreach like the other passengers. Lillian van der Luyden caught his eye and patted his hand kindly, as though she knew what was on his mind. "Look, love," she whispered with perfect sympathy, "there are always those bad apples ready to give the others a bad name." And then, as if to cheer him up, she asked when he was going back home to Lucknow next. When Nasr replied that he didn't know, that the last time he'd been was when he was fifteen, her eyes narrowed, as if she thought he was playing a trick on her. But she thought he half lived there, she said. No, he said, he'd grown up in Canada.

Lillian turned away then, and stared out the window with pursed lips. He thought maybe they were done. But a few minutes later she nudged him with her elbow. "Have you been to see her?" she asked, pointing at the Statue of Liberty. He hadn't. "You must do that," she said, reproaching Nasr almost affectionately. "Introduce yourself." Nasr assured her that he would, first thing, and as if that weren't enough, he added, "I've heard it's something to see," and then "All countries should have such a grand welcome"—acted like a buffoon really, as if he were coming to America for the very first time.

The silence on the phone line continued. Bad apples. If he told Jameela this, she would give him the benefit of the doubt. She would ask why that woman Lillian had *presumed* he was trying to distinguish himself.

"I called you," she said suddenly.

She didn't specify when, and there was an almost challenging note in her voice, as though she meant to surprise him. What actually surprised Nasr was that she would bring up those calls at all. In total, there had been a dozen. Along with the messages in which she confessed to meddling with the Ansaris, there were others that were nearly incomprehensible. Sometimes the messages cut off abruptly; at other times, they ran on and on until the voice mail cut Jameela off. Many were long, rambling pronouncements about there being no rules any longer, nothing to prove, how nature didn't take its course. He'd won, she said in another message; he'd won. There was no reason to prove anything. Whatever the game was, she gave up. Just would he please call her—or anyone—and tell them that he was all right, safe. At one point, it became horribly clear that she thought she was talking to herself, a dead line. "Oh, God. Oh, God. Hello?" Impenetrable whispers followed, then static. A short while later, she seemed to have finally learned that he was in London, not New York, but the phone calls kept coming.

Now there was a wet intake of breath. It was a sound Nasr thought he had successfully blotted out. Since returning from London, he had decided that when he spoke to Jameela again— *if* he did—he would say something. He meant to, the first chance he got. Someone should. So why had he let her off the hook by lying about his phone? So why did he now find himself saying, as lightly as possible, "Did you?"

There was that sound again, followed by a recovering gasp. "Guess it doesn't matter now," Jameela said eventually, a dull waver in her tone.

Probably not, Nasr meant to reply. But for some reason, he felt his own voice catch in his throat, sit like a stone.

14

What is inevitable—the accumulation of small, tacitly agreed-upon concessions, decisions, willing and unwilling cooperations? What qualifies as surprising, legitimately catches you off guard and leaves your intentions asunder? And how far do you have to go down a trail of linked circumstances and subtle couplings to find the true source of a change of mind?

In mid-September, a car was driven into a masjid in Cleveland, and not long afterward Mrs. Ansari decided that there would be no wearing of sleeveless blouses at her daughter's wedding. Now, almost a month later, a threatening call is made to the Ansaris' masjid, and she decides that bare knees would also be unacceptable, and skirts should be avoided. Is this a reaction to feeling besieged? Or is the timing between these events and decisions coincidental? Or should one have anticipated from the very beginning that the Ansaris would expect others to conform to their ideas?

"What am I supposed to do—specify a length on the invitation?" Nasr asked his mother, who had called to both break this news and proclaim that she'd helped get the restriction relaxed. Skirts (or dresses) with hemlines that came to the ankle were now permitted.

"Many of these women are my superiors," he said. "I can't tell them what to wear." In fact, he already had. After much procrastination, he'd finally sent that e-mail out to his female friends and co-workers asking if they wouldn't mind wearing long sleeves to the wedding. They had all been good sports—Pete's girlfriend, Laura, promised to leave her bustier at home. But it was hard for Nasr to imagine how a follow-up request wouldn't be seen as peculiar and demanding, if not insulting.

"Beta, now this is their wish," Nasr's mother said. When Ansari demands didn't affect her, she received them calmly, and even came to their defense. "It will be too cold for this skirtswurts business anyway," she offered, then immediately interrupted herself: "One thing you must do, beta, is speak to Javaid." According to her, Javaid, who had left town a few weeks earlier on a leave of absence, was returning to New York to quit his job. "And he has done nothing to find a position here. Masha'allah, they are people who can afford for him to do such a thing, but your Shazia Phuphi is very worried. You have to explain to him that this isn't the time to make these kinds of decisions."

"Are you sure he's actually quit?" Nasr asked. "A lot of people are taking time off."

"But how does one take time off from one's life? One cannot avoid things. Things happen in all places. Arré, did your grandfather decide every time there was Sunni-Shia trouble that

153

the family should just close the factory and leave Chowk?" This was exactly how she'd been a few weeks ago when Nasr and Yasmine had such a difficult time arguing her out of her shopping trip to Lucknow. She didn't see why she shouldn't travel by herself. A quick flight, two, three weeks. What was the harm? The whole of the world hadn't been knocked out of alignment, after all. They reached a compromise when they learned that the wife of Nasr's uncle Masood had a fine sewing hand and could, if all the fabric was cut, dyed, and embroidered, bring the materials and finish assembling the bridal suit (as well as the other garments Nasr's mother had ordered) by herself. After much wrangling, Nasr's mother was convinced—bullied, she felt—that sending tickets to bring Masood Chacha and his wife to Canada would be wiser than going on the twenty-hour journey herself.

"You children have not seen such things," Nasr's mother continued, "but the best thing Javaid can do now is settle down. There is just no sense in running away."

"How do you know he's running away?" he asked.

"The sooner he is settling down, the more he will feel at home—just like you, beta. This is what I was saying to Shazia. Let Nasr talk to him. You can explain the value of having such an important matter in one's life decided. Yasmine also is not thinking practically. She refuses to listen to one word. 'Oh, he's my cousin. That is gross.' What nonsense. Some of the best marriages I've ever known come from marrying within. And these two are not even first cousins!" She went on excitedly about a new plan of hers to get two ghararas made—one for Farah, another for Yasmine—and also to have two sets of jewelry ready in case something developed.

It was the most ridiculous thing Nasr had ever heard, and he wondered if his mother, in her wedding fervor, had lost her grasp on reality. Even as children, Yasmine and Javaid never got along. It was almost a joke how adept Javaid was at irritating her. Since then he'd grown up into the kind of person who spoke to women in exactly the same way he spoke to men—never rude, but also never accommodating. Yasmine had always complained that talking to Javaid was like being around a disapproving uncle.

But the more Nasr's mother listed the many benefits of settling down, the clearer it became that she didn't believe Javaid was leaving New York any more than Nasr did—and also that she truly imagined a match was possible. Soon, Nasr found his own wheels spinning. There was no doubt that Javaid, with his job and his sense of responsibility, was desirable son-in-law material. And, at least on paper, the match between Yasmine and Javaid was attractive. They were the right ages (twenty-five and twenty-eight, respectively), and both were intelligent and articulate, good-looking though not intimidatingly so. Most significantly, they both had jobs that were careers to which they were dedicated. Truth be told, Nasr had always felt that Yasmine had never given Javaid a chance. He was a good person, if a little stiff.

When Nasr mentioned Javaid the next time he and Yasmine spoke, she clicked her tongue. "Oh, him."

For a moment, Nasr thought his original instinct was proved right, but then she went on: "The story is that he's trying to quit, but they won't let him. The firm keeps offering him more money and time off—they'll do anything to keep him. At least that's what his mother's saying. Anyway, he's spending his free time getting the parents riled up into all these arguments. Jameela says he's not that bad, but I think that's just because she needs someone to go with her to all her protests."

There wasn't a positive word in any of this, and yet, Nasr noted with interest, his sister didn't sound quite like her old, irritated self. Remembering his visit home back in June, when

Yasmine's manner had struck him as increasingly sour and inconsiderate, Nasr couldn't help thinking that a solid person like Javaid might be the very sort of grounding his sister needed.

*L*ater that week, Javaid called him to ask if he was free for dinner.

"You're in New York?" Nasr asked.

Javaid admitted that he'd been in Manhattan for a couple of days but was heading back to Montreal the following morning. He apologized for not phoning sooner but he'd been in meetings at his firm.

"To tell them you're quitting?"

"News travels fast, eh?" Javaid replied in a dry voice.

"Is it true?"

"Well," he said, "not exactly." His supervisor had somehow gotten the company to grant him an indefinite leave of absence. In exchange, he would have to take some work home, and, of course, he couldn't accept a new job.

"That's awfully generous."

"But I do want a change of some sort," Javaid said immediately. "I was so worried about telling Edward that I wanted time off, but the moment the words came out of my mouth, they felt right. You know the story, you get on these 'career paths,' and you do what you're supposed to do just so you can make it possible to continue doing what you're supposed to do, but it doesn't seem to have an end. I mean, as Jameela says, this isn't a time to sit back and build your résumé."

"Well, Jameela would know," Nasr said sarcastically. Was he misremembering or did Javaid used to call her Jameela *Baji*—big sister?

As it turned out, Nasr wasn't free that evening—his friends

were taking him out for a very belated happy-engagement dinner. He invited Javaid to come along and, quite unexpectedly, his cousin accepted.

Javaid was already at the restaurant when Nasr's party trooped in. There was Pete, of course, and Laura, a tall, willowy redhead with dark-brown eyes. Also Cynthia, who was in Laura's department. She'd been part of the group from the very beginning, though no one could ever quite remember inviting her along. Martin, a junior vice president, and the only native New Yorker, sort of—he actually grew up on Long Island. Martin's pretty but harried-looking wife, Claire, who was a doctor, caught up with them on the walk from the subway. And, finally, Ramesh, whose family was from Delhi, by way of Nashville. He was the only Indian person Nasr had ever met who proudly admitted to liking country music.

Javaid was sitting in a booth near the maître d' station instead of waiting at the bar as someone else might. He was dressed as properly as ever (tie and collared shirt), though his face looked a bit scruffy. The trim little goatee wasn't gone but was clearly being grown out, along with his hair. The new, youthful appearance immediately sent Nasr speculating about his mother's hopes for Yasmine. People change—Yasmine certainly had.

But as soon as the introductions began, Nasr could tell that the old Javaid wasn't totally replaced.

Pete, who could always be relied upon to break the ice with an off-color joke or a well-timed but affectionate insult, extended a surprisingly polite hand. "Nice to meet you, Jay."

"Javaid. Likewise." Javaid shook Pete's hand, but said nothing more, and he greeted the women en masse, with a tip of his head. While drinks were ordered, he quietly asked the waiter for an iced tea, looking away from the table as though he didn't want to be implicated in what was happening there.

For much of the next hour, Nasr's friends toasted him repeatedly, made him cut a not-so-unexpectedly-produced cake, and took the customary pleasure in exchanging exaggerated stories of the "escapades" of his bachelor days, but Javaid didn't catch any of the party's spirit. When somebody asked him a direct question he answered truthfully, in monosyllables, and otherwise sat back in silence, listening with a watchful or bored expression.

The waiter came by for another round, and Pete pointed a thick, possibly drunk finger across to Javaid. "Another Long Island iced tea, young man?"

Javaid sat up and put his hand on his glass, his fingers covering the top of it. "Just iced tea, please," he said. "No alcohol."

"Fair enough. Fair enough," Pete said with a cheerful nod. He turned to solicit others, but Nasr could see that he was embarrassed—and who wouldn't be, with the way Javaid kept his hand in place, as if whiskey were raining down from the ceiling.

By the time the conversation turned to the wedding, Nasr was weary and ready to go home. But among this group were some of his closest friends, people who had booked their tickets and hotel rooms and would be cutting their Christmas vacations short to attend, so he felt obliged to answer their questions. *Are all Muslim marriages arranged? Why doesn't the bride wear white?* Some of these pertained to Hindu weddings, and Nasr could, thankfully, deflect them to Ramesh. Others involved matters Nasr hadn't given any thought to. The significance of henna? Well, what was the significance of lipstick? he wanted to ask, but he didn't. Instead, he did his best to describe what his guests should expect. There would be four nights of events, and the people around the table would be attending three of these.

First was Farah's Mehendi ("a henna party," he called it; "a sort of shower, where they decorate the bride's hands and feet"), primarily for the bride's family and guests. Then came a corresponding event for Nasr (minus the decorating) hosted by his side, followed by the Nikaah (the actual wedding ceremony, hosted by Farah's parents), and then the Valima (a post-wedding reception, thrown by his side).

As Nasr spoke, he felt his voice regulate itself as though he were narrating a documentary. The table became quiet. He wished Javaid weren't around while he was doing this. It was not just that his friends had been asking so many questions lately; it was the way they listened, like children in a schoolroom, so that you felt you were speaking on behalf of Indians or Muslims but not quite as one: *This is the unit on how the creature known to us as the Muslim organizes his cultural activities. Lesson one, mating rituals . . .* But wasn't it irresponsible, Nasr thought, not to explain, to just let others speculate and get things wrong on their own? Still, as he continued he couldn't help despising the stuffy and ambassadorial tone of his own voice, the glided-over mistakes and exaggerations. It was also hard not to despise his listeners a little, too, for being so easily duped.

He was describing how the bride and groom are kept separate until the Nikaah when Laura said, "Oh, I've been to one of those. Are you going to lead her around the fire?"

Relieved to be interrupted, Nasr said no, that that was another Hindu custom. "The only sparks you see flying at a Muslim wedding are between the in-laws." A cheap joke, but judging from the smiles, it was the right thing to say.

Even Javaid felt compelled to join in the conversation: "Aren't our weddings more like waterworks than fireworks?"

"Very true," Nasr said, adopting a large, jolly manner. "Don't forget to bring your Kleenex."

"I believe the technical term among our people is 'hankies,' " Javaid said. He seemed pleased to have inspired some actual laughter.

"I remember that, too," Laura said. "I've never seen so much openly expressed despair at the prospect of marriage."

Winking at Nasr, Pete said, "Well, if Farah knew what she's getting into with this one, the girl'd be bawling her eyes out every night till December."

No matter what Nasr did, Pete still pronounced "Farah" as if it rhymed with "Sara"—as in "Farrah Fawcett." Yet if Nasr had had to choose a best man, it would have been him.

When Laura said, "Javaid, you've met Nasr's fiancée, right?," Nasr decided, not for the first time, that she would probably become one of Farah's first friends in New York.

But Javaid simply nodded. It was, of course, his usual odd way with women, but how was Laura, who was expectantly leaning forward as though she hadn't heard the rest of his answer, to have known? Nasr sighed. He decided, once and for all, that his mother was on the wrong track. There was a time and a place for a certain kind of seriousness, and though Javaid wasn't totally humorless, he could be a bit of a dud. And even when Javaid did speak, he formed his words too carefully, which gave the impression that he was either struggling with or—even worse—trying to hide an accent. There was no way Yasmine would tolerate that. Nasr couldn't help smiling at the thought of his sister sitting beside Javaid in full bridal costume, rolling her eyes and checking her watch while her groom conferred seriously with some uncles.

"So what is she like?" Laura asked with friendly impatience. "We haven't been able to get one decent piece of information out of Nasr."

"She's a very nice person," Javaid said, but then he actually smiled again when half the table groaned: "Oh, really?" and "We thought she might be a sociopath." "Well," he added after a moment, "I guess her bowling abilities could use a little work."

This drew a flurry of questions, and to Nasr's surprise Javaid began answering them. It turned out that bowling excursions had become a habit back home, and Javaid had gone along several times. At first, he provided Nasr's friends with details that Nasr knew (Farah was studying mass communications, but her real interest was public health; she had two younger sisters, with whom she got along very well; she spoke nearly perfect Urdu), but then he declared that Farah was one of the most approachable people he'd ever met—always interested in the well-being of those around her. He added that although she was quiet, it didn't mean she wasn't listening or following the discussion, and you knew that because every once in a while, late in a conversation, she'd make an observation or a connection that nobody had thought of.

Nasr had the extremely unpleasant feeling of being tempted to ask a few questions of his own: approachable—really? After that promising moment on the phone last week, the fortress's defenses were not only back in place but had been reinforced with moats of politeness and walls of correctness—the cannons of subject change pointed straight at any topic Nasr brought up that might be too intimate.

"Oh, and one more thing," Javaid continued, and if Nasr didn't know him better, he could have sworn his cousin was showing off. "I don't believe there are enough shoe stores in the world for Farah. But she has very high hopes for New York."

Laura made a joke about she and Farah being soul mates. "Look out, brother," said Pete, nudging Nasr with an elbow. Nasr decided he might prefer the dud Javaid over this new, cheery one.

"But why aren't your weddings happy occasions?" The interruption came from Cynthia. She glanced about the table, making eye contact with every person, like a teacher reminding her students to focus. Then she fixed her attention back on Javaid. "I mean, all weddings should be joyous. Isn't that the point?" Nasr saw Pete roll his eyes. Cynthia had a way of seeming victimized by the unfamiliar.

Javaid was serious again, and, like an infection, his seriousness soon spread. Wonderful—we're back to square one, Nasr thought. He began, clumsily, to explain to Cynthia that it was just a difference. Why is it, he asked her, that in this culture a funeral reception is the kind of event where people are supposed to mingle and eat and smile and tell funny stories?

"That *is* different, though," Cynthia said, looking at Nasr with that intense, slightly glazed expression of hers. "At least people are making an effort to feel better." She looked around the table again, as if she were speaking on behalf of the group. "Isn't it disturbing that everybody in your family is crying their eyes out while you're getting married?"

"Actually, it's the bride's side that does the majority of the weeping," Javaid clarified.

But this nuance was lost on Cynthia, who demanded, "But doesn't anybody wonder what's making them cry like that? Why participate in something that's making people so unhappy?"

"Well, it's not so much unhappiness," Javaid replied, "as it is sadness." He cleared his throat. He'd been in the middle of rolling up his sleeves but now pushed them down, and sat up, striking a straight-backed, businesslike pose. "It's less true now, I suppose, but, historically speaking, the sadness has its sources in village life, where you don't have much, but what you do have, what you *can* have, is a daughter. She is something you can value and protect. A son you send off to learn the trials of life, but a daughter you shield. She's your dearest possession. But unlike a possession, of course, she has feelings. Devote yourself to her, and she devotes herself back. The apple of your eye has eyes, and they're only for you.

"The crying," he continued, "is just a measure of how much we value what we're losing. I mean, suppose you are a parent in this system and your eyes are dry on the wedding day? Can you imagine how that looks? By not weeping you might make the groom's side wonder about the fairness of the whole arrangement." He shook his head. "Your dry eyes could practically ruin your daughter's welcome into her new family, jeopardize her happiness."

Javaid finally appeared to notice the long faces in his audience. He looked as if he didn't quite know where his little speech had come from, but was pleased that it had been available.

A lot of what Javaid had said, however persuasive, wasn't exactly true. Sons were far more prized than daughters in Indian families. But Nasr wasn't about to make such a correction here. "Just hold on to those faces," he said, though it was clearly too late.

He didn't know why he'd spent so much time attempting to convince his friends that the wedding would be like any other they'd attended, its differences merely decorative.

Nasr left this dinner and ran straight into a puzzling wreckage of thoughts. He wondered if he should be pleased for his mother that Javaid had clearly started thinking about marriage himself, in particular the intricacies of marrying off a daughter. Perhaps this was the vibe she had so astutely picked up? Or maybe those bowling weekends had helped Javaid and Yasmine get to know each other. Something about Javaid's speech had a naggingly familiar ring to it, not so much its content as its tone. But the most perilous feeling Nasr had as he returned to his apartment that night was that everyone seemed to know Farah better than he did. In what sense was she approachable? he wondered again. To what sort of person?

15

"What it is, is filthy," declared Hamid Uncle. He brought one end of a long blue- and gold-threaded cord to his mouth and took a puff from his hookah. "It's filth, and we are letting them do it," he added with theatrical offhandedness. The living room was crowded, but he directed his comments to no one in particular or, you could say, to everyone at once, as though he were addressing a committee.

"Arré, bhai, you are speaking as a gentleman believer," Masood Chacha said in mock dismay. An extremely thin man, with a dark, pockmarked face and a bushy black mustache, he was Nasr's father's only brother, but the family resemblance was nonexistent in both looks and manner. Where others, especially Hamid Uncle, pirouetted around conversations, Masood

Chacha barreled through, finding contentious topics and sensitive family matters that other people, mindful of speaking in front of prospective in-laws or relations they hadn't seen in years, would have avoided.

This was a Saturday in mid-October. Nasr's mother had talked him into coming home for a visit to honor his uncle's arrival earlier that week from India, even though Nasr already had a flight to Montreal (the trip he had promised to Farah) booked for the very next weekend. "Masood is waiting to meet your in-laws," Nasr's mother had said, as if this explained why Nasr's presence was absolutely essential. The visit had, naturally, prompted a dinner party, to which Nasr's mother had invited a number of Ansari relatives as well as Javaid and his parents.

Upon the Ansaris' arrival, the sexes had separated into different areas of the house and stayed apart. The women had taken their plates and their conversation downstairs to the den, while the men occupied the living room. Hamid Uncle was in his usual spot, stretched out in one corner of the love seat. Mr. Ansari's brother, Adil, sat beside him, more primly, in the narrow space that was left. Javaid and his father were on the large low sofa, and next to them was Masood Chacha. Nasr and Mr. Ansari closed the circle, in the remaining, symmetrically arranged armchairs.

Already the group had been treated to several lectures by Javaid on the not-so-economic decision-making of the World Bank; a discourse from Mr. Ansari and his brother about the new government rules being developed for the collection of charitable giving; and a recitation by Hamid Uncle of a couplet mourning the loss of civility. According to Yasmine, such discussions were now a regular feature of life in Montreal. With all this practice, it was no wonder, Nasr thought, that the uncles sounded so much like those Mideast experts all over the radio and TV these days who offered, in similarly timbred voices and semi-British pronunciations, the same sort of living-room opinions that nobody had been interested in before.

"Where there once was thameez, thehzeeb," Hamid Uncle continued, "manners and consideration, mildness, tolerance"—with each word, he gestured toward the middle of the room as if a pile of these qualities were resting on the coffee table—"now it's something one doesn't recognize. Can hardly belong to at all. It's just an excuse now, nothing more. A thing in shreds, caught in the teeth of these jackals."

"But this is your Islam of the nawabs, Hamid Bhai. Noblesse oblige." Masood Chacha held his cigarette low in the scissor of two extended fingers, and when he took a drag, his open hand covered up the bottom half of his face so you couldn't tell what kind of smile was there. He shook his head and caught Nasr's eye. "What we are needing now is the people's Islam. Isn't that right, beta?" he asked, smiling, possibly.

Nasr had been warned that there was no way to agree with Masood Chacha and be done with an issue. He tried a noncommittal shrug, and Masood Chacha promptly called out across the room: "What do you say, Ansari Sahib?"

When Mr. Ansari nodded and smiled but could not be drawn away from the discussion he was having with Javaid and Javaid's father, Qamar Phupha, Masood Chacha held Nasr's eye and raised his eyebrows meaningfully. Earlier today he had asked Nasr if "his Ansaris" were connected to the illustrious Ansaris from Ajmer, and when Nasr said he had no idea, Masood Chacha said, "What do such things matter in this country, anyway?" He waved his hand blithely but still managed to imply that there was a sinister laziness to such democratic inclinations. His expression now suggested (and thereby attached mysterious significance to the fact) that Mr. Ansari wouldn't, of course, have any understanding of the pity that the wealthy classes might take on the poor. Nasr felt a curl of annoyance that he'd already, after just ten hours, been schooled in interpreting his uncle's insinuations.

When Nasr arrived at the house that morning, it was in disarray. Barely saying hello, his mother asked him to take out the heavy silver and unpack the bone china, so that she and Yasmine could begin rinsing. A few hours later, when she finally had a free moment, she drew him aside and confessed to being at a loss as to how to deal with Masood Chacha. He apparently expected to be fêted most days of the week, seemed to think that groceries appeared in the fridge by magic, and refused to drink tea from a bag, as though servants were available to brew a fresh pot at any hour. And then there was the ten-month-old child he'd brought along, whose sleeping habits had yet to adjust to the time difference. Masood and his wife slept through the crying, or perhaps expected an ayah to materialize out of the ether.

Nasr soon saw that she wasn't exaggerating. Early that evening, Masood Chacha welcomed Hamid Uncle into the house as though Hamid Uncle were the visitor from abroad, and when the guests began arriving, he greeted them as if he were the head of the Siddiqui clan. Then at dinner, when the men and women finally crossed paths, Masood Chacha cornered Javaid's mother, Shazia, who was his second cousin and whom he hadn't seen in forty years. He marveled at the change in her: from a mere slip of a girl hiding beside her mother to, well, there was such a healthy glow of proportions now. She had become a "ditto-copy" of her father, who, as everyone knew, had always enjoyed his fair share of good cooking. The more Masood Chacha reminisced, the more his observations drifted beyond the limits of flattery, but Shazia Phuphi dipped her covered head and smiled as though she were accepting compliments. Everybody within earshot could only watch helplessly and hope that she was embarrassed more by the scrutiny itself than by its nature. The poor woman was finally rescued by Nasr's mother, who came charging over to let her know that the ladies would be eating downstairs.

At first, Nasr thought that his mother was simply helping Shazia Phuphi escape. But a few moments later, when she came back to supervise the self-serving and Nasr asked her if dessert could be put out in the living room along with extra chairs, she deflected his suggestion: "Oh, I think we should keep it as is." Nasr realized then that his mother would be making no effort at all this evening to promote mingling across gender lines.

He found himself both surprised and disappointed that she'd caved so easily to the Ansaris' preferences. Fine, it was only good manners to have had the basement set up in advance this time for namaaz and to have been prompt to break for the prayer, but what was the point of reinstating old ways that their own community had chucked years ago—ways that hadn't even been enforced during the engagement party, when she was surely more desperate to impress the Ansaris? Shouldn't a person be free, in his own home, to go where he likes—to sit beside his fiancée and tell her how beautiful she looks? When Nasr gave in to his mother's pressure to come for the weekend, he'd hoped for a reward: Farah in close quarters, a little attention thrown off by the visiting relations. But he'd seen Farah a total of three times tonight: first a hasty and impersonal exchange of salaams when the Ansaris arrived, followed by a glimpse across the buffet offerings at the dining table, and then another sighting from the end of the hallway. She was, as usual, prettily assembled, in a plum-colored shalwar suit. But even when the two of them managed to make eye contact, some relative always lurked around, ready to run interference.

The worst part was that Masood Chacha had overheard Nasr speaking to his mother, and afterward came over to sympathize. "Arré, you all have become very formal here," he said, laughing. "But what is the need for these medieval practices? Who are we having to keep up appearances in front of now?" Who, indeed? Nasr wondered, doubly fuming over the extremely unpleasant circumstance of being in agreement with his uncle.

*T*here was a pad of footsteps along the far edge of the living room, and Jameela appeared in the archway, followed closely by Yasmine. They were on tea duty—one held a tray of cups, and the other a smaller tray of milk and sugar. They knelt down at the coffee table and began soliciting orders.

"Still talking filth, Dad?" Nasr heard Jameela murmur as she handed Hamid Uncle his teacup. Father and daughter exchanged matching smiles, then Hamid Uncle took a hurried sip and returned his attention to the conversation, as though he feared losing his place.

"All right, listen to one thing," Masood Chacha said, brazenly speaking over the other men in the room. "On my flight to this place, one fine fellow—Amreekan, going from Delhi to Amsterdam—began asking me this why-do-you-hate-us business. 'Tell me something, Mr. See-dee-kee, why is there so much venom? Where does it all come from? What have we done?' "

In his imitation, Masood Chacha made the man whine, and now, as he looked about the room and clapped his cigaretted palm against his forehead, he was the picture of incredulity. "I had half a mind to say, Arré, baba, that you can ask me this with your unlined face and your open borders, not living next to any neighbor who dares invade you." He playacted this exchange as if the man were sitting before him, a dunce in the center of the room. "When your concern is not for us, but what we *think* of you? That you have the luxury, the innocence, the stupidity to be posing such an absurd question—*Why?* you ask, and I say, Why not, my fine fellow? When you are the steadiest supplier of reasons." Masood Chacha's scowl deepened, and he cast a roving frown about the room.

Just then Nasr caught Jameela's eye. She gave him a quick look of complicit amusement, the kind that might pass between preschool teachers having to manage a rabble of students. For better or worse, her manner toward Nasr had become sisterly since they last spoke. She made friendly and uncomplicated small talk. *How are you? How's work? Yes, the weather has been remarkably warm.* Mostly, Nasr was relieved. He supposed he'd always known that an eviction of Jameela from his life would be too ambitious. She would always be around. But this new attitude of hers, though a bit cool, made the prospect of dealing with her (this is how he'd begun to think of their interactions) manageable. He smiled back, but Jameela was already looking away.

Masood Chacha intercepted the smile, however, and returned a knowing smirk. "Well, Nasr Mia, what do you say?" he asked. "Or are you too busy thinking about your bride-to-be."

A silence descended upon the room, and Nasr felt all eyes turn to him. Masood Chacha wore a deeply inappropriate, semi-lascivious grin; Nasr kept his profile to Farah's father. Who knows what the man might have thought of this. The expectant silence was momentarily interrupted by a high and nervous laugh from Qamar Phupha. He was a shy and soft-spoken man, but his laugh could be so helpless-sounding it was hard to imagine that he was the chief of staff in an oncology department.

Still, nobody said anything, as though they actually expected Nasr to provide an answer to a question he'd forgotten. Even Jameela looked curious.

"The whole thing seems pretty rhetorical to me," Nasr said,

clearing his throat. "I think there can be misunderstandings on both sides."

Nasr knew instantly that he had disappointed. He drew none of the nods of agreement or encouragement that had been so generously distributed all evening—and, perhaps more tellingly, no one disagreed. Jameela was back to filling and sugaring teacups, as though his answer had been not merely unimpressive but distinctly uninteresting.

Despite all this, Masood Chacha's face cleared, the brows unfurrowed and the frown evaporated. "Spoken like a diplomat," he said, practically beaming with some mysterious satisfaction. "Lucknawi to the core, just like his father—"

"But did you actually say all that, Uncle?" Jameela interrupted him, without looking up from her pouring. "To that man?"

Masood Chacha gave a dismissive shrug. "One can't say such things to a person's face, beta." He leaned forward to crush his cigarette. "Especially when the poor fellow is so depressed about this business that he is practically in mourning."

"Maybe he lost someone in the attacks," Nasr suggested, trying to make up for his dismal performance.

Masood Chacha shook his head in mild reproach. "No, not a single acquaintance. But this is the point. They are taking this thing so personally." He sighed now. "It has changed them—no one is doubting that."

But Mr. Ansari's brother, Adil, looked quite doubtful. "Your fellow passenger was an exception, Masood Bhai. In our store, I see the typical Canadian, man off the street. He is wanting to buy his sharaab at ten o'clock in the morning, and screaming with his wife and whatnot in front of the cashier, no matter how many people are looking. For better or worse, this is the person my business depends on, and he will never change. This is just the way they are. Confused, childish. They don't know what they want. We try to say something to them, involve ourselves in their communities, but our opinions are unacceptable. We keep to ourselves, then we are secretive. One very long-time customer said to me last week, 'Oh, you did not tell me you are Muslim. I thought your family was from India.' I haven't seen him since that day. I have been special-ordering his cigarette brand for ten years, and now I have a whole box that nobody is buying."

"Yes, yes," Hamid Uncle said impatiently, as if the conversation had completely gotten off track. "But what we must not forget is that it is not their problem only. There are jackals in our midst, committing filthy, abhorrent, inexcusable actions. And they must be booted out, plain and simple."

"And yet these people's grievance surely isn't filthy?" Masood Chacha replied. "Nor is the desire to spread the faith—"

"But to put one's desire above goodwill?" Hamid Uncle asked. "Above simple kindness, charity? Above culture—since when are we doing this?" It was his turn to shake his head with extravagant incredulousness. "If we are, as they wish, to go back to the illustrious Muslim past, let us go, then. Let us go back all the way to the benevolence of the Prophet and the freedom— yes, freedom—of thought he himself embodied. It was based on a very simple idea in which only Allah is above all, and the rest—all the rest—is below. This is what a life of moderation means."

"Well, it's a little more complicated than that, isn't it, Uncle?" Javaid asked.

"Yeah, Abba," Jameela said. "There's got to be something else going on there." She was perched beside Hamid Uncle on the side arm of the sofa, her legs dangling. She looked tall and thin in her dark-blue shalwar kameez, and for a change her rupatta was actually tied about her head. As Yasmine slipped out of the room, Nasr noticed that her rupatta was also arranged traditionally.

Hamid Uncle had politely noted Javaid's suggestion, but now looked taken aback by his daughter's contribution. "There is nothing, beta," he said to her. "Not one thing. Nothing that is not in Christianity."

"I mean," Jameela said, "something in it that might lend itself to such abuse." Yasmine had escaped at the first chance, but Jameela seemed in no hurry to leave. She, of course, wouldn't care a whit about his mother's imposed segregation, Nasr thought with grudging admiration. In fact, he was surprised it had taken her this long to join the men's discussion.

"Islam does not ask its followers to identify an enemy," Hamid Uncle said, sending a puzzled frown in Jameela's direction. "There is no call for the death of innocents. You know that."

Jameela said, "I mean in its history—"

"What do these jackals know of history?" Now Hamid Uncle sat up, straight-backed and with both feet planted on the floor. "They are fixated on one period. And then in one place only. Fifty years in the middle of the desert is to have been our golden age. Forget the Taj—forget Nur Jahan, Ghalib, Faiz Ahmed Faiz, Begum Akhtar." He shook his stately silver head. "Our people have triumphs, but we didn't achieve them by living in isolation. If you are to have a true history, you must accept the fact that history includes progress."

"But there's always a bias, Uncle," Javaid said gently. "I mean, look who you've named."

"All Hindustanis!" Masood Chacha exclaimed.

"Actually, I meant there were no politicians," Javaid said.

"Oh, yes, quite right," Masood Chacha agreed as if this was just what he'd meant as well. "And you're forgetting the intervening British, Hamid Bhai—who unified the place by hook and by crook."

"And then divided it up into future war zones," Javaid added in a dry voice. He leaned forward in his armchair. Recognizing the posture, Nasr braced himself for a lecture. "But, actually," Javaid said, "I agree with you, Hamid Uncle. There is nothing but wisdom in Islam's basic framework. I also agree that this situation is both our problem and theirs. The Americans are as bad as ever, and we, I'm sorry to say, are as blind as ever. And what we are most blind about is the extent to which our very judgment is corrupted by the West."

Not being the sort of person who was often contradicted or (perhaps consequently) easy to placate, Hamid Uncle received all this agreement with the tip of his hookah held between pursed lips.

Javaid, however, pressed on, undiscouraged. "Every time these people say something accusing about Islam, we simply point back to the Qur'an-shareef and the teachings of the Prophet, sallallaahu 'alayhi wa sallam, believing that the obvious purity of their message ought to be enough of a defense, but it's not." Javaid's speech had always been peppered with the proper insha'allahs and masha'allahs when he spoke to the parents, but now he seemed to use them all the time. Upon arriving this evening, he'd greeted Nasr with a cheery "Looking forward to the big day, alhamdu lillah?" In fact, Nasr had never seen his cousin so forthcoming and genial. The new, trim beard Javaid had grown since that dinner a few weeks ago with Nasr's friends might have aged another man's face, but it made Javaid's, for some reason, seem spry and boyish. "What one can't forget," he continued, "is that religion and political life are entangled. And that a religion, for better or worse, comes to contain the experience of the people who follow it and spread it. Take Pakistan, for example. It has a very rich past, culturally and politically—"

"Otherwise known as the history of India," Jameela said.

Nasr burst out laughing, and then the rest of the men followed with unruly laughter and jokes. It was a cheap shot, especially in a room where the Indians outnumbered the Pakistanis seven to two, but it was just the right cheap shot. Jameela earned an affectionate pat on the arm from her father. Even Javaid had to smile and offer a concession—"All right, yes, there is some overlap." But this only inspired more laughter. There was no one who enjoyed Pakistan-bashing more than an Indian Muslim, and they ganged up quite shamelessly, led by Masood Chacha, who repeated "Overlap?" gleefully, like a child testing out an unfamiliar word. "Yes, yes, perhaps the way one's skull overlaps one's brain."

For Nasr, it felt so good to laugh that he suddenly wondered when it was that he'd done it last.

Javaid could do nothing but wait until the jokes subsided, but when they did he continued on just as seriously as before: "My point is that we Pakistanis are constantly apologizing to the world for the 'factions' developing in our country. There are skirmishes in a couple of tiny villages, and immediately we are on the phone: most sorry, Mr. Bush, a thousand apologies, Mr. Blair—yes, sir, the matter will be resolved pronto. But why are we sorry? Often, the issue is a simple disagreement or misunderstanding that hardly deserves global review. Citizens of a country ought to be allowed to disagree with each other, shouldn't they? And even if it's more than that, what are five, ten, even fifteen years of civil disagreement in the life of a young nation? Aren't these simply the growing pains of history and progress?"

Hamid Uncle's sociable smile was back in place, but he showed no eagerness to take issue with the reference to his words, which allowed Adil Ansari to say he didn't know about all this global review business, but he thought it was progress that friendly customers had recently recommended to him that the Ansaris' store should display a Canadian flag out front. He himself considered this to be a good idea, but Farah's father wasn't so sure.

Masood Chacha, who'd now been in the country for all of seven days, said the Ansaris should put up not only the flag but also a notice that the establishment was Indian-owned.

"It's not the Canadians, Masood Bhai," Mr. Ansari said grimly. "It's the Americans. They are not knowing the difference."

"Even so, you must show it—educate," Masood Chacha said. "A simple sign with nice lettering: 'Sirs and madams, kindly take note . . .' "

Out of the corner of his eye, Nasr saw Jameela's hand suddenly fly up to adjust her rupatta, a river of blue fabric that nevertheless poured off her shoulder to the floor. She snapped it up and began repositioning the material over her head. Then she did something even more surprising—she sent a quick checking glance in the direction of Javaid and his father. Was all this observance to impress Javaid? Was this why Yasmine was also properly attired? All at once, the use of the good china and silver (neither of which were put in service at earlier dinners with the Ansaris) finally made sense: they'd been brought out to make an impression on *another* set of prospective in-laws. Nasr hadn't even thought to look out for any difference in Yasmine or Javaid's behavior tonight, though of course he'd had no chance to observe them together. He remembered now that Javaid's parents' parties were always segregated. Of course. But none of this explained Jameela's cooperation. Unless—he thought with a pinch of dread—unless she knew that Yasmine was actually interested in Javaid.

"It won't work," Javaid said, interrupting the uncles, who were still working out the phrasing of the note that should be written to the Ansaris' customers. It wasn't clear if his disgust was directed at ignorant Americans or the men who'd missed his point entirely. "We know everything about them—how to take their exams, how their holidays work, what one should and should not say at business lunches. But we ourselves don't show up in their minds at all until something happens."

"Well, what do you suggest we do, beta?" Adil Ansari asked. He was a practical man, open to solutions, and he might have been referring only to his store and what other signs of conciliation should be installed.

But in response Javaid's face became sly. "I think we should go," he said matter-of-factly.

"Go where, beta?" Hamid Uncle now inquired with a grand tone, an olive branch to erase any earlier rudeness on his part.

"Back."

"Back?" Adil Ansari echoed.

"Back home, to Pakistan. To India for you all. It's the only way."

Nasr saw his own surprise reflected on the middle-aged faces around him. The uncles subjected Javaid to a friendly barrage of questions, but their relaxed nature dimmed as they began receiving answers: Was he actually suggesting that one give up one's livelihood and shift countries? (He was, yes.) Fine for a young man, but how could one do it at this age? (At the current rate of exchange between the rupee and the Canadian dollar, and with some proper investments in these emerging economies, they could go home and live like millionaires.) But how, when one's children's education was bound to this place? (Wasn't it commonly known that India had excellent schools, graduating tens of thousands of Ph.D.s every year?)

Only Masood Chacha continued smiling, with a new admiring light of interest in his eyes. "Oh, yes, listen to this," he said. "The children are knowing these things."

"I think everybody knows that we are no longer wanted."

The uncles conceded that yes, well, Javaid did have a point there. Mr. Ansari brought up the murders of those poor Sikhs in Texas. How was it possible that a Sardarji could be mistaken for an Arab? "Do these Amreekans not have eyes?" Masood Chacha exclaimed. "One is averaging six feet, and the other is a weasel of the desert!" Most troubling were the local incidents, of course. Last week the windows of three different Muslim student associations in Toronto were broken overnight, and in the news earlier today there was a story about an attack here in Montreal on a girl coming back from school. She was hounded at an intersection, pushed to the ground, and told to go back to Afghanistan. The girl's parents were actually Greek Orthodox, and the mother had said to the TV reporter: "Look at us. Do we look anything like those people?"

"If your neighbors have changed at all," Javaid concluded, frowning triumphantly, "it's for the worse."

"But these are the acts of crazy people," Nasr said, "indulging themselves during a crazy time. If you did a survey of any type of hate crimes at any given moment, the numbers would be just as shocking."

Javaid said, "So now that we contribute to hate-crimes statistics we belong?"

"But is the solution to this really to leave the country?" Nasr said. "Isn't that a bit drastic, not to mention impossible for a lot of people—maybe even most of the people in this room?"

Javaid shrugged. "It's not something they haven't done before."

Nasr wanted to say the obvious: that it was one thing to go when you're twenty, young, and adaptable, and another to go in your fifties or sixties, when the thought of, say, taking a different route between your house and the grocery store was—as in Hamid Uncle's case—disorienting. He could no more imagine his mother, fastidious and organized, riding around in an auto-rickshaw in Lucknow now than, say, on a desert camel. But there were so many toes to be stepped on here that he wound up replying, quite lamely, "But they've spent more than half their lives here now."

Javaid, who apparently had no qualms about discussing the people who sat before him, pounced on this. "Yes, but they always talk about returning. My parents regret it every year they don't."

Qamar Phupha confirmed his son's words with a helpless giggle, and Nasr knew, of course, that this had been true of his own parents. But the people who had left India weren't the same as the ones who lived in Canada now, Nasr wanted to say. Instead, he chose a different tack: "If threats to safety and well-being are what you want to avoid, you're not exactly proposing places free from danger. There's pollution, disease, bribery, crime—"

"Arré, arré," Masood Chacha exclaimed. "We are not the lowest of the low."

Nasr ignored the interruption. "Not to mention sectarian violence right next door in Ayodhya, and then, of course, there's the Sunni-Shia conflicts—"

"We came here to get away from all that nonsense," Hamid Uncle muttered in agreement.

"Arré, but what Javaid is saying is that the nonsense is at your doorstep now, Hamid Bhai," Masood Chacha said. By now, he seemed profoundly impressed with Javaid, besotted, won over, but Javaid didn't need his support.

"What's left for them here?" he asked Nasr. "Retirement with a dwindling income, children living far away or so caught up in their busy lives that they're unable to help, even if they wanted to. All the daily tasks will only become harder and harder for them to do as the years go by. The whole support network of extended family, not to mention servants, that would have been available back home is nowhere in sight. And now they will have to do all this with suspicious neighbors and hostile new laws. I'm saying the life there would, if anything, be easier."

Hamid Uncle appeared out of sorts. One might even say a look of terror contorted his features. The other men were somber and pensive. Nasr would never have guessed that Javaid could be such a bully.

"What about your job?" Nasr asked. He found that, under

179

the right conditions, it wasn't all that difficult to raise your voice in outrage. The more you did it, the more satisfying it became. "Haven't you tried to quit? Hasn't the company, the Americans, done all they can to keep you?"

"I'm an investment for which they haven't got their return yet. And besides, I'm still quitting."

"My son is a great believer in problem-solving and long-term planning," said Javaid's father, smiling weakly. "He sees much farther into the future than the rest of us."

"Look," Javaid said, "maybe it is filthy—at least, not fair—what's being done in the name of Islam, but it's also possible that this perspective on the events is an essentially and deeply Western one. All I'm saying, Abba, is if they aren't going to leave us alone, maybe we should get away from them."

Qamar Phupha said, "Perhaps we've had enough discussion for today, beta," after another lingering moment of silence.

It was then that Nasr noticed that Jameela had hardly said a word on the issue of moving them all "back home." He had half expected her to speak up as an ally, since she wasn't the sort of person who would ever hesitate to challenge a bully. But Nasr didn't get a chance to speculate further on her silence, for the next words uttered in the room made his spine tingle.

"I am agreeing with you, Javaid beta," Mr. Ansari said gravely. "Questions must be asked. These are unenlightened people. They can study as much as possible, but they will always be ignorant. Look how quick they have been to assume that this thing was done by Muslims." The media and the politicians, Mr. Ansari went on to explain, often colluded to obscure the truth; for example, not one reporter had ever asked whether an outside investigation or even a simple review of the government's evidence would be conducted. "Like everyone else, I condemn such actions, and I would do so if they were committed by Muslims, Jews, or Christians. But are we not needing the proof first? As Muslims, shouldn't we at least question this?"

Hamid Uncle cleared his throat; Qamar Phupha's hand fluttered about adjusting his collar, but there was no helpless laugh this time; Jameela began collecting teacups, and Javaid rose to set his on her tray. Masood Chacha lit a cigarette and held Nasr's eye as if to say: What do you think of your Ansaris now?

Hamid Uncle spoke first, but he directed his words straight at Nasr, as if he were replying to a question Nasr had posed. "Every system, beta, can be used properly or misused. Every religion. Every point of power. The problem with my point was that I had listed no politicians—look at Akbar. He governed with such generosity toward the Hindus—"

"Aha," Masood Chacha said. "But for every Akbar, there's an Aurangzeb."

"The point, beta," Hamid Uncle said, his voice booming over the interruption, "is simple because the idea, the religion itself, is simple. Submission to God and moderation—that is all it requires." It was strange to be spoken to with such intensity—surely Hamid Uncle knew that Nasr was in complete agreement with him. But as the older man continued, Nasr realized that his uncle wasn't actually speaking to him at all. He was broadcasting a message for other ears: "Moderation, of will, of practice, of consumption, and, yes, one must even moderate one's—"

Masood Chacha let out a shriek. "Arré, you are suggesting the believer ought to moderate his very beliefs?" he asked. He swept up the Ansaris in his outrage as though he were speaking on their behalf, but his indignation hardly seemed genuine, considering how pleased he looked.

"I was referring to one's emotions," Hamid Uncle said, his lips tight about the tip of the hookah. "Moderation of anger and self-pity."

16

The assault on Nasr's focus—his determination to concentrate on Farah and Farah alone, to corner her if necessary, to relax and be himself in her presence, to initiate, beg for, demand some progress in their relationship—began the moment he arrived in Montreal the following weekend. Masood Chacha seemed to think his nephew had come to visit him again, and complained of neglect when he learned of the evening plans. Nasr's baby cousin, Raza, happened to be crying as Nasr and Yasmine headed out after lunch, and Masood Chacha joked that his son knew when he was being left behind.

The plan was to take the Ansari sisters bowling (of course), but first Nasr had to go downtown to pick up Jameela and Javaid, who had spent the day at a protest. The weather had recently become very cold, the clouds sinking close. When he and Yasmine pulled up to the designated meeting place, Javaid and Jameela were nowhere in sight, but a girl waiting near the bus stop began heading toward them so determinedly that Nasr assumed she was a friend of Yasmine's who'd recognized the car. The girl wore a white headscarf and a pale trench coat that came down to her knees, and it was not until she had climbed into the seat behind Yasmine and closed the door that her placid face was recognizable as Jameela's.

"Heat, heat, heat," she said, making various shivering sounds. Following Nasr's eye to the headscarf, she said, "Battle gear."

"Against whom?"

"Never know," Jameela replied with a shrug, but she had already begun sliding the scarf back off her head.

Nasr had been about to say that he didn't think there was such a thing as a born-again Muslim when the other back door opened.

"Assalaam'alaikum," Javaid said, his deep voice almost jolly. He greeted Nasr in the rearview mirror with a mockingly formal salute, touching the fingertips of his right hand to the bridge of his nose. "Nasr Sahib." He apologized for being late, but the cold had finally broken him down, and he'd raced in for a coffee—not so much to drink as to hold. "Looks like I've lost my tolerance for these temperatures," he added, quite pleased.

At first, the conversation on the drive to Farah's house was light enough. The topic of shoes came up—Yasmine and Jameela wanted to get matching ones for the dance they were planning to do for the wedding.

"Forget shoes," Javaid said. "Where can I get some dancing feet?" He was evidently playing the male lead in this dance, which had been adapted from a Bollywood movie they all seemed to know well.

"But why do you need dancing feet?" Yasmine said. "You

183

know all the steps." She sat twisted in her seat, facing the back. Nasr found himself looking for secret signals, smiles, nervousness, any clue to his sister's true feelings for this new Javaid.

"I meant warm feet—they're essential for my moves." Javaid was sitting deep in the seat, and had thrown an arm over the back headrest behind Jameela's shoulders.

"Moves?" Jameela asked, her voice low with amusement.

"Signature ones. You'll see."

Jameela burst out laughing. "I guess we all will."

Yasmine then made the mistake—to Nasr's mind, a grievous miscalculation—of asking how the protest had gone. At first, Jameela and Javaid merely described the ridiculousness of the improvised songs they had been made to sing—"No more innocent bombing" to fit with the melody of "Imagine."

"There were so many Indians there—" Jameela said.

"South Asians," Javaid corrected, but Jameela didn't seem to mind. "The South Asians," she continued, "came up with some lyrics that drifted rather, um, off topic."

"Hell no, we won't chalo," Javaid chanted, to which Jameela added, "Arré, make some tea, why don't you—not this war business."

For the next endless hour to Cornwall, Javaid went on and on about how we as immigrants, especially children of immigrants, have allowed ourselves to be shortchanged. It was not that coming to Canada had been a terrible mistake—it was probably the right thing for our parents to do at the time, and each of us had certainly benefited from the endeavor in many ways. But we should remember that the migration didn't have to be a permanent one—not in this day and age. Plus, there were real benefits to returning to one's own homeland. Don't we all go around wondering what we would have been like as natives of a place?

Despite Nasr's success at remaining out of this conversation, he could feel his attention dividing: so Yasmine did know of his plans (such as they were). Yet she didn't seem at all fazed. What did this mean? By the time they got to the Ansaris', Nasr found himself thoroughly distracted by his speculations. He forgot to tell Farah (discreetly, of course) how nice she looked—her figure in the pants and mannish collared shirt was a tidy arrangement of curves and delicately formed limbs. But maybe that was because she had surprised him by appearing at the door in a headscarf much like her sisters'. In fact, the three of them looked so much alike at first glance that Nasr accidentally called Razia by Suraiya's name, and caught the frown in the serious sister's eyes a second too late. Then his plans to steal Farah away were immediately foiled—she had an economics exam on Monday and, as Mrs. Ansari twice reminded her when they were leaving, she would have very little study time tomorrow because she was scheduled to teach the Sunday recitation class at the masjid.

The bowling alley was busy with the electronic beeps of arcade games and the woodenly dull spills of pins. As soon as they walked in, Javaid broke off from their party without a word, then returned a few moments later to report that their "favorite" lanes (two adjacent ones tucked in the corner far from the arcade) were free. When they paid and got to the cozy enclave, Razia immediately sat down at the scoreboard and began entering their names; Jameela and Javaid went in search of bowling balls; Yasmine and Farah fetched trays of popcorn and drinks. There was little consultation among the group, as though each person had long been assigned a particular task. Nasr was left with Suraiya, who, while chatting about her last performance (when she'd nearly hit five strikes in a row), warmed up her arm with swimming-stroke stretches. It was so strange to see a girl in a headscarf move her limbs so forcefully—not caring about the attention it might attract. When Farah returned, Nasr wondered whether her headscarf was a temporary measure (and if so, for whose sake?) or a permanent addition. And then he wondered if he was entitled to ask such questions. At first, he supposed he wasn't, but then he reconsidered. Wouldn't it be an addition to his own life as well as hers?

At some point on the drive over, Jameela had replaced the headscarf she'd been wearing with a colorful piece of fabric she wore like a do-rag and had removed the trench coat to reveal a gray denim kurta over jeans—a common uniform of her school years. Her face, now that Nasr was seeing it more directly, seemed, strangely, to be missing something. When she dipped forward into a patch of overhead lighting, it suddenly became clear that she, like the Ansari girls, was wearing either no or very little makeup. In her case, the absence of color made her look older.

For much of the evening, Yasmine and Jameela held forth. They sat in the center of the bench, exchanging familiar stories from childhood—how Yasmine had tried to be a Girl Scout once but had given it up when the troupe learned to make s'mores and she'd been revolted by the look of melted marshmallows, and how the babysitting business Jameela had started in her early teens had not survived its second summer.

Javaid joined some of these trips down memory lane. The person he seemed to remember best was Yasmine. "She hated me," he told the Ansari girls.

"I did not." Yasmine looked dismayed, even embarrassed.

"No, you really did," Jameela said, patting her hand.

"See, see!" Javaid said. He was sitting backward in the chair at the scoreboard, facing Jameela and Yasmine.

Eventually, the reminiscing landed on Nasr's childhood. His career in elementary school, according to Yasmine, had been so illustrious that she'd suffered in its wake. His youthful obsession had been starting a business: a lemonade stand, tea stand (at Eid namaaz), lawn-mowing service, newspaper delivery, pet sitting (very short-lived), snow shoveling. "But he wouldn't do the work himself, remember?" Javaid said. "He'd hire us hanger-ons, at cut rates." Yasmine and Jameela said that while they remembered being recruited into employment, neither could recall ever being paid.

The Ansari girls shook their fingers at him, naughty boy. They were clearly enjoying themselves. Nasr couldn't help feeling that the person emerging from these fond memories was not quite who he remembered being. But if Farah was pleased to hear about this Nasr, he was happy to play the part.

"Oh, and if our people had any such thing as an altar boy," Jameela said, "he would've been it."

"Okay, but it wasn't that bad," Nasr said, as though he were being forced into an unwilling confession. "I can't help it if the imam took a liking to me for some reason."

"For some reason?" Jameela replied, rolling her eyes. "He was such a goody-goody," she told Farah. "Even when he wasn't up to any good."

"What do you mean, Jameela Baji?" Farah asked, leaning forward. She was sitting beside Nasr but turned away, and the back of her shirt had lifted out from the waistband of her pants to reveal a thin stretch of pale skin.

"He never did anything wrong," Yasmine said flatly.

"Nothing that could be detected at least," Jameela muttered. The Ansari girls found this, as they seemed to find nearly everything that came out of Jameela's mouth, scandalously funny. "Don't you remember," she asked Yasmine, "whenever we went to Nirj Auntie's house how he used to make us constantly ask our parents when we were going home or he'd even pretend to be sick, all because he didn't like playing with little Irfan? He was a true sneak."

"I wouldn't have thought that," Farah said. She glanced back at Nasr, shaking her head but smiling. What would you have thought? Nasr wanted to ask.

"Well, don't ever expect him to play the bad cop with the kids," Jameela advised her.

Farah's sisters burst out laughing again, though they immediately caught themselves at the sight of their older sibling's embarrassed face.

In the next round of play, the groupings shuffled, but Farah stayed beside Nasr. Their talk remained small and local: her exam was on microeconomics; the professor was notoriously crafty. When they weren't talking, Farah seemed lost in her thoughts. After a while, Nasr felt his own thoughts branch and thin, and every time it was his turn to bowl, he did so mechanically, hardly noticing where the ball rolled.

Most distracting were the snippets of overheard conversations. He heard Jameela explain to Javaid the reason that she refused to use the phrase "nine eleven." According to her, September 11 was already a significant date in history—the day in 1973 when the CIA backed a coup in Chile that ripped out the country's democratically elected government and replaced it with the tyrant Pinochet. One country shouldn't get to take over and reserve a date on the calendar, she said—but if the world was going to allow that, then the Chileans had first dibs. This led her and Javaid into a discussion about the plight of the Afghanis and the U.S.'s not-so-covert arming of the mujahideen, and how a country that meddled in such ways shouldn't be surprised when the chickens came home to roost. The two of them said these things offhandedly, as if they were or should be common knowledge, but also proudly, in loud and assured voices.

Nasr found the whole conversation both hard to take and hard to ignore. They just went on and on, alternately lecturing and debating (speaking freely, Nasr would have liked to point out, without any restrictions on their persons), cooking up a pseudointellectual, recklessly naïve version of events—events that hadn't and wouldn't, if you really thought about them, actually affect one single aspect of either of their lives, though both pretended that they already had. But what was most irritating was the manner in which Jameela listened to Javaid. She wore an amused expression when he spoke, and Nasr kept expecting her to set him straight—tell him that throwing one's career out the window wasn't the way to reform Islam; and that one person's return wasn't going to change the state of any affairs of any country. But she didn't.

Yasmine stayed on the rim of Javaid and Jameela's talk. She didn't seem annoyed with its chumminess, but she did seem to be following the conversation carefully. Nasr could only hope she was seeing the shallow and self-serving manner in which Javaid tossed out his opinions, but the evidence continued to be mixed and puzzling. And then there was Farah. Occasionally, Nasr would turn to find her looking at him with a penetrating, mysteriously thoughtful gaze, but whenever he tried to bring up a topic, all he got was one-word answers. He wondered what other stories she'd heard about him from Jameela and Yasmine. He wondered when she'd ask him a question about himself. He wondered if he'd always feel like this in her presence, simultaneously assessed and ignored.

*L*ater, in the car, when he was finally alone with her (his other passengers had piled in with Farah's sisters for the short drive), Nasr remembered what he wanted to ask her. He turned into her subdivision, and decided it was an encouraging sign that she didn't say anything when he slowed through the residential streets.

"You all seem to know each other so well," Farah said, then turned away from him. Her headscarf had slipped back, exposing the front crown of smooth dark hair, but she didn't seem concerned.

Nasr cleared his throat. "Thirty years of growing up together will do that."

"It must be nice." She faced forward now, but there was a glum curl to her mouth.

"It is. Sometimes," he said. Glancing over, Nasr wondered for a moment if she was crying. But no, it was a trick of the light. Her eyelashes were so dark and thick they could look damp, like the tips of wet paintbrushes.

"Your mom told mine that Javaid Bhai has been spending a lot of time at the house, and she has hopes for Yasmine Baji. She is not wanting to push them, but if it happened naturally . . ." Her voice trailed off.

Nasr couldn't believe his mother had made her wishes so public—it suggested a confidence that still, to him, seemed unfounded, if not brazen. But after a moment Farah said, "I suppose the timing would be convenient," and Nasr finally noticed the tired, even peevish, tone of her voice. What bride likes to share the stage with another?

"You know," he said, "there's no chance of a double wedding or anything—"

"But it's not impossible," Farah said, turning frank and anxious eyes toward him. "Sometimes people reach a certain age, and they change their minds."

"Not this much," Nasr replied firmly, feeling absurdly accomplished at having accurately anticipated her concerns. Perhaps this was what had been bothering her all night. "Even if anything were to happen," he continued, "it wouldn't happen within a month. Those two have known each other for years and nothing's come of it." Then, in case this might seem like a judgment on their own speedily assembled situation, he added, "I mean, Yasmine doesn't do anything that fast."

"But it has to fit in Javaid Bhai's schedule. He wants to go back to Pakistan in the spring."

"Well, that settles it then," Nasr said. "I don't see my sister leaving Canada, let alone the First World, in a matter of months. Do you?"

Farah smiled now, finally. "Your mom seems keen," she said in a small voice.

Amid family, and especially in those fancy shalwar suits, she could look so molded and inaccessible, but tonight he'd seen another side to her charm: the cute concentration when, for a stretch, she actually tried to compete with Suraiya; brightly giggling when she and her sisters shared old jokes.

"Hey," he said, continuing to steer gently at the turns through the darkened neighborhood. He couldn't help feeling impatient; these moments of being alone were too valuable to be spent on others. He didn't reach across and take her hand, but the phrasing of the question finally came to him in full.

"Yes?" she said, eyes on her lap.

But Nasr hadn't driven slowly enough. There was her lawn with people gathered on it, siblings and parents on the lookout for their return.

He pulled up to Farah's house. Already her fingers were on the handle of the door, but she paused. "Were you saying something?" she asked, looking him square in the eye, the curve of her cheek so purely formed—all of a sudden childlike.

Nasr cleared his throat. "Good luck with your exam," he said.

She thanked him for the evening and slipped out, toward her mother's approaching figure.

It didn't feel like timidity or modesty, or even unwillingness, exactly—so what was it that always stole in between them? Nasr's mind wheeled back then to the words, lost now, that he'd concluded would be best: *When am I going to get to kiss you?*

I don't believe this," Nasr said a week later into the phone. The cubicles around his were festooned in Halloween orange. He was finding it difficult to keep his voice down as he learned from Yasmine that Mrs. Ansari was not keen on having music at the wedding. "But there's always music," he said. This latest directive from Mrs. Ansari felt like a surprise attack. Nasr imagined his friends sitting around at their assigned tables, already not being served any alcohol, already mortified by the seriousness of the occasion, already wondering which of the events they were attending would show recognizable signs of celebration, and now, on top of all that, being subjected to moments of actual silence, with nothing to buffer the foreign happenings.

Yasmine explained that his future mother-in-law would be fine with the typical family-sung wedding songs, but she didn't want professional musicians or a dj.

Considering that Yasmine had spent the better part of the month of October searching for a hall with a sound system (in addition to an extra room for namaaz and a separate entrance for ladies), she delivered this news rather calmly. To further complicate matters, the manager of the place Yasmine had found had called today to say that he needed the balance of the deposit by the end of the week. His company treated short engagements (he'd somehow discovered that the engagement party had been back in August) as a higher risk for postponement or cancellations. If they needed more time to decide, he would find it necessary "in the interest of seeking a firm commitment" to raise the deposit amount by a third. Also, he asked that the Siddiquis provide a list of all guests and accept that people would have to check in at the door.

"Why check in?" Nasr asked.

"They claim that they're afraid of damage to the facility."

"Isn't that what the deposit would cover?"

"Not that kind of damage," Yasmine replied. She said there'd also been some talk about whether scheduling a Muslim wedding at a time like this was more about making a statement than anything else.

"Nobody's making a statement," Nasr said. "My getting married has nothing to do with that."

"Right," she said, as though she were placating him. "But the thinking is that things have changed, and plans can change." Apparently, someone had gone so far as to wonder if, especially under the circumstances, one or the other party might decide to wait a month or two in order to avoid having a "cloud" hanging over a happy occasion. And some people were talking about how it might be best to hold the wedding plans off, perhaps even indefinitely, until things calmed down.

"Are these guys trying to lose business?" Nasr asked, and then had to check his voice again.

"I told him we'd hire security if we had to," Yasmine said in a grim tone.

"Security?" Nasr had a vision of his friends arriving for the Valima and having to line up, as one did in so many buildings in New York these days, to show IDs and endure a plundering of their bags or persons. Yes, yes, just another quaint ritual from the old country. "Is this even legal?"

"Probably not, but under the circumstances—"

"What circumstances?" Nasr asked, though as soon as he did, he heard his mother's unreasonable tones.

"Anyway, if we can't have music, should we let this place go?" Yasmine asked. "It's pretty expensive, but I don't think we can start looking again, either. Can you get Farah's mom to change her mind?"

"How am I supposed to sell a dj to her?" Nasr replied. Although initially bold, the hiring of a dj had become a common wedding practice in their community over the past few years, especially since more and more Indian djs who could play both techno and bhangra music (along with older Bollywood songs for the parents) were available. "This is so stupid," he muttered. "Why do we have to do everything they say?"

"Well, you don't," Yasmine said.

"Don't what?"

Yasmine let out a long sigh.

"What?" Nasr asked.

"I mean, people change their minds all the time."

"But I haven't changed my mind." What Nasr meant was that he himself still wanted music—no change of mind there, but his sister said, "Yes, but everything did come together quickly, especially with all that's happened—"

"Not because of that," he said.

There was silence.

Nasr felt a weary annoyance. He wished he had not let his sister think he was part of the marriage-eager horde. "And how long are we supposed to wait, anyway? Something like this doesn't just blow over," he added, but he was further annoyed by the distant presence in his mind of a desire to agree—at least admit that well, yes, perhaps it was true, things had progressed a bit hastily.

He was about to offer to speak to the manager himself when Yasmine said, "Oh, just forget it. You know how people around here are."

"What people?"

"I just wanted to warn you."

"About what?"

Another pause.

"What are we talking about?" Nasr asked. In this next pause, it occurred to him that his sister might finally be telling him about her feelings for Javaid. He tried to remember all that he ought to say. It couldn't be anything too negative, but she had to be made to see Javaid clearly.

"We'll just go with this place," Yasmine said. "It's the right size—that's the important thing." And before Nasr knew it, she had hung up.

17

Farah was right, after all. There was another engagement. In fact, Javaid and Jameela's party was scheduled for the very next weekend, the first Saturday in November—too soon for Nasr to make arrangements to attend.

There was, as one might expect, much surprise and speculation back home. When had all this developed? Had the parents been consulted? Was Jameela merely two years older than Javaid? Hadn't she always seemed more somehow? Nasr was subjected to earfuls of his mother's conjecture, but only after she had recovered from her initial disappointment and was allowed to express annoyance at having to share the nuptial spotlight. Eventually, she came to the magnanimous conclusion that the burden lifted from poor Hamid and Talat's shoulders was much greater than any she faced with Yasmine.

Nasr supposed he ought to have been relieved. Now there was little chance of Jameela continuing to interfere with his plans.

The night of Jameela's engagement party, Nasr worked late and went out with friends to a very different kind of celebration in Williamsburg—a belated Halloween party at the loft of a friend of Pete's where there would be separate prizes for the skimpiest and the scariest costume. Among the usual ghouls and fanged Draculas were a guy roaming with a noose around his neck calling himself Hanging Chad, women who looked as if they'd simply stripped down to their underwear ("I'm Miss Ohio," a busty brunette in a red bra said to Pete by way of introduction), and a number of men in street clothes wearing fake mustaches and beards with checkered handkerchiefs over their heads. One member of the group had a red-and-white bull's eye taped to his back with a note: "Kill me now."

Nasr hesitated over his first drink. The beer bottle felt like a prop, part of a bizarre costume of the Muslim guy who wanted to pass, especially when he joined in the drinking jokes with a few comments himself about longing for the days when he could drink himself silly. He said this enough times, though, that a kind of nostalgia took hold, and by his third beer he was anticipating the buzz, if not quite savoring it yet. Wouldn't this be one of his last nights of freedom, of doing what he wanted? Well, no—maybe not. But didn't he deserve this? Why should he care what the Ansaris would think? They would never know. And why should he care that Jameela and Javaid's engagement was being treated as a love marriage—with all the investigating gossip focused on how those two rascals managed to hide their blooming feelings? Jameela and Javaid, Nasr decided, deserved each other. They were both impetuous, disagreeable, prone to arguing for argument's sake—and, as far as he was concerned, they could spend their love marriage talking each other to death.

He left the party early, just before two. There was no moon on the walk back to the subway, no clouds—just a deeply empty sky at the base of which the city lights shone and winked out from the black lines of buildings like the final embers under a pile of logs. He hardly remembered the subway ride that followed, or the short walk to his building, or even the elevator up to his carpeted hallway—only the pillow that seemed to materialize finally under his ear, the cool stealing softness on which the dreams began.

Nasr's family—minus, for the first time, his father—was in Lucknow for six weeks, the first three spent in mourning, the final three in preparation for Saira's wedding. That trip, Nasr's last, remains in his memory as a blur, a shuffle of ceremony and distraction, punctuated by vivid images. India could pull time out of solution, leave you with effects that had no apparent connection to each other. Airports at which horse-drawn carts wait outside the baggage claim. Squatters hanging laundry in some former emperor's abandoned palace.

The wedding finery had escalated with each evening event, so that by the night of Saira's Nikaah it seemed as though the full fortune of the family was on display. The women wore ancient, multi-jeweled necklaces, earrings that pulled slits into their lobes, and antique saris with so much silver embroidery the borders had tarnished. The men were no less eye-catching in black, crisply ironed silk sherwanis over starched white pajamas. Tonight's event was the culmination of a chaotic but successful effort to ensure there would be no mistaking that these people—

Nasr's people—lived a certain kind of life. Standing in their midst, in the vast hall (made intimate by the attention of an undetectable army of servants), it should have been easy to believe in grand and consequential unions; that this one, to which Nasr's sister was being contributed, was no simple marriage but the coming together of tea barons and gentlemen farmers, a solemn merger for which one sets aside one's personal feelings. Even happiness was beneath the dignity of the occasion.

But happy was the last thing that Nasr was feeling, although this trip had started off unobjectionably enough. For many weeks since their arrival, he had rather willingly taken his mother on customary visits to the old families. At fifteen, walking first across thresholds, being led into the living room with the other men, and congratulated for the most meager performances of graciousness had its charms. Nasr didn't ever wonder if he deserved this royal treatment, or what might be demanded in exchange for it. He simply went about collecting compliments and fond remembrances of his father.

But a few days ago a curtain had lifted and Nasr glimpsed the inner workings of this place and its people. He had learned of a plan hatched among his cousins to play pranks on the bridal couple on their wedding night, which would be spent, like that of all new Siddiqui couples in recent memory, in a small rooftop room that had been prepared as a bridal suite. The pranks were also part of a tradition, apparently, and when Nasr heard the conversations and discovered their nature, he immediately went upstairs to inspect the room. It was on the third floor, a bare little cell with low light and shiny bedding waiting to be unfolded. Following up on the details he'd overheard, he saw that there were indeed peeping holes drilled in the massive wardrobe that dominated the room's back wall. And the basket where a snake—not an actual one, but still—would lie in wait was already in place. Nasr found his mother and ordered that a room at a hotel be booked instead—no matter how many traditions it would break. She was in an understandably difficult position, being here among her in-laws, but Nasr insisted that she do something and she eventually agreed to ask for a change of plans. Since then, not one of Nasr's cousins, boys he'd spent other summers playing with, had spoken to him straight. No one had said an accusing word, either, but it was clear that they all knew who had sabotaged their fun.

Now, standing in the immense, twinkling hall, Nasr began to wonder how his father, a modest engineer and a good citizen, who had been upstanding and pious, had ever fit in here, amid this grandiose costuming and lurid theatricality. Then he wondered if his father would have done what he did—break those customs to save Saira? Would he even think of it as saving Saira? And finally there was another thought, one that Nasr had resisted for weeks here in Lucknow, and for months back at home while he was acquainting himself with bills and insurance papers, but here it was in full: wasn't it true, when you were really honest about it, that Anwar Siddiqui was a bit of a forgettable figure—not unaccomplished, but unremarkable, unvivid, and disappointing? Easily replaced. Hadn't Nasr himself, a mere teenager, already taken the man's place?

At the end of the Nikaah, during the Rukhsati, Saira was a small but heavy bundle against Nasr's arm. The two of them were at the head of a procession, beside the groom, whose parents, along with Nasr's mother and Yasmine, followed half a step behind. Their progress was slow: somebody had needed to lift the stiff hemline of Saira's gharara out of her way and Nasr was required to keep the Qur'an he was carrying centered above her bent head. No one said anything, and the only sound heard above the shuffling and sobbing was the thin wail of the shehnai, the instrument's single tone reaching its long, wavering climax when they arrived at the curb, where a creamy white Ambassador stood waiting to take the newlyweds to the hotel. The car was draped from hood to trunk with a thick net of jasmine, marigold, and roses.

Someone came forward to open a door. The maroon leather seat was polished to such a shine it looked wet. Nasr felt his sister slump into his shoulder. Her weight was flush against him, and he wondered, momentarily, if she'd tripped, and then if she'd fainted and he'd have to lift her and place her in the car—and whether, if he had to, he would. She was twenty, but seemed childlike in the bridal costuming. Up to this point, she had known Rizwan just as Nasr and Yasmine knew him—as an older second cousin who was studying electrical engineering in the States. At twenty-six, Rizwan was already stooping and paunchy; he spoke English with a singsongy accent, and made self-conscious jokes about his thinning hair. He was probably a perfectly nice person, but until this moment he'd simply been one name, among many, to keep track of. Nasr felt his arm grow sore. He turned to look over his shoulder for help, and that's when he saw all the faces: tears were pulling black streaks down the women's cheeks and bloating the men's features, so that, with their glassy eyes and red noses, they looked drunk.

It was a cast of mourners, not wedding guests. And yet they had all wanted this—each one of them had played a part in arranging the marriage: badgered his mother about the need to get her daughter married as soon as possible; recommended the nearest groom available in the family so insistently that she could hardly object without giving offense; demanded that the wedding take place in Lucknow so they could attend.

There was a squeeze now of Nasr's hand, his sister seeming to revive. All evening, her rupatta had hung over her head and halfway down her chest, and now a curtain of fat roses was tied over it. He was standing not six inches away from her, but he couldn't guess her feelings. He couldn't even be sure that she knew it was his arm and not a stranger's she was grasping. Nasr wished just then for something to happen—something short of an aunt keeling over or a child being struck down, though he would have taken those. A proper distraction. Any excuse for the chance to grab his sister's hand and get away into the dark street.

This feeling Nasr had wasn't only about Saira. How many times in the past few weeks had he found his mother caught in whispered and urgent discussions two, three relatives thick— who knew how broadly the conspiracy extended—conferences in which she was being urged to consider how much better off she would be if she came back. A woman alone, a widow, ought to be with her family. *We don't belong here*, Nasr wanted to remind his mother, and to the heads huddled together in consultation, he wanted to say: *Leave us alone.* He was speaking now for all of them—his sisters, his mother, and even his father, who was made more and more foreign by each of his relatives' reminiscences. And by "here" he meant everything—the place, the people, the demanding entanglements, and the arcane rituals. He had no use for any of it. He wanted nothing to do with them. He didn't know it yet, but the residue of this feeling would linger with him for many years, fueling a rebellion, first showy, then secret, that would take him through his adolescence and early twenties, perhaps even until the time he moved to New York, when the anger suddenly exhausted itself and he felt he had finally outgrown it. But during his sister's wedding, it was still fresh and piercing, and he was willing to aim it at everything in his way. Lucknow, he had told Jameela the previous night, during a rare moment alone with her, was the most backward place on earth. "We don't belong here." He'd finally said the words. She replied, surprising him: "But if we don't belong here, then where do we belong?" Nasr immediately resented her tolerance: why did she always have to twist everything and complicate it?

But what really stung was that even she didn't understand that he was beyond this point already—had no desire to belong to anything, least of all Lucknow.

The weeping around Nasr intensified. His father had died just nine months ago, but this wedding, Nasr thought, as he lowered his head to ask Saira if she was okay, would always be the saddest moment of his life—he remembered hoping never to see anything like it again. But here, on this night of dreams, there is a transformation, as if the brain feeding at the bottom of an ocean of memory has floated up to the surface with something new. "I'm sorry, sir," a voice says over Nasr's shoulder, "but I will need to see madam's complete visage to identify her." The frazzled end of a dirty red rug and the stretch of broken pavement between the curb and the waiting car have now become the blue-gray carpet of an airport terminal—Heathrow, where a security official in an adjacent line is speaking to a man with a thick beard in a gray suit. "The rules have changed, sir," the official continues. "She cannot board the plane unidentified. Please remove the headscarf, madam." The bearded man is pale-skinned but big-chested and stocky. He is holding one child high in his arms, and another is clinging to the side of a woman in a black burqa. "Please," the man says, raising a hand to keep the official from speaking directly to his wife. "This is not acceptable for us." He speaks in a deep, grave voice. "She has gone through the machines. These are her papers, with the photo and fingerprint." The official is joined by another, and by this time every passenger at the gate has turned to see what will happen. The second official also says the headscarf must be removed, and when the Arab asks if a lady official can be called and if there is a screening room, he is told that the airport cannot grant special requests because it would then have to make exceptions for every passenger, and that would be impossible, wouldn't it? "But this is unacceptable for us," the man says again. Looking up and down the boarding line, he catches Nasr's eye. "Perhaps someone can explain," he says. "My English is not working." The screener who happens to be inspecting Nasr's bag is mild-mannered, with a boyish overbite. He pauses to look past Nasr's shoulder. Four men in green military uniforms are striding toward the gate. "But I am with my family," the Arab is saying loudly now. "My children. Look, ask him. He must be knowing. There." The screener turns Nasr's inspected bag over to him but holds on to his boarding pass. "Is that man referring to you, sir? Do you know that man?" Nasr pushes the bottle of scotch down and zips up the bag. "No," he says, holding the screener's eye. When the boarding pass is offered, he tries not to snatch it, and in the jetway he wills himself not to hurry.

The eyes in the burqa's face panel were familiarly shaped, deeply brown with dark lashes, lined in black kohl. They had snapped up for a second and met Nasr's across the sea of anxious and pale faces. How strange to be hated like that—so openly and without envy.

BOOK
two

PART *one*

18

*T*he sign in front of the masjid announced that a snack to open the roza would be served first, followed by namaaz, and then dinner. For Nasr, the timing was more important than the food at this point. He was early. Even doing his wazu slowly wouldn't kill forty-five minutes. He had half a mind to go home; his apartment was only a few blocks away. He should have known the roza today—his first in more than half a dozen Ramzaans—wouldn't go well. He should have planned better, drunk more water, filled up with more coffee, loaded his fridge with food he could imagine consuming before daybreak. He should have ignored the impulse to impress Farah. *Yes, of course, I'll be fasting*, he heard himself say during their conversation last night. *In fact, as a kid*, he'd added rather idiotically, *I* *was known to keep all thirty for several years in a row.* The achievement was true, but it was well before caffeine and cigarettes had entered his diet.

The headache had slinked into a corner of Nasr's brain in the afternoon, around two o'clock, just as people were returning from late lunches or finishing up their microwaved lasagnas, and the office was full of the odors of overheated oil and plastic. The pain had crouched in the right-hand quadrant of his head until the next hour struck. Then it was as if an alarm had gone off. All the nearby lights and sounds swirled and magnified, the hard *ding* from the hallway elevator reverberated against the tender walls of his skull, and Nasr ran out of the office. The city streets and the subway were no quieter, but the blur of sounds was a relief. Walking also helped, especially when his footfall happened to match the throbbing rhythm of his headache and there was a wonderful little cancellation of pressure.

The masjid was set back behind iron fencing, on a narrow lawn, its base a few feet above street level. It loomed like a fortress, with its thick windowless walls and blocky angles. There was a dark metallic dome at the top, and a skinny, squarish minaret to one side. Sunlight had settled in a thin bright band along the lowest floor of the building, but the time, when Nasr checked, was only 4:03.

He turned on his heel, strode around the corner, heading, for no reason, away from his apartment. Last night, Farah had called him for the first time ever. She'd discovered that a rather well-known masjid was in his—and her future—part of the city. "It's supposed to be something to see," she said. Did Nasr know of it? He didn't. (When she told him the address, Nasr didn't mention just how close he'd lived to the building without noticing its existence.) She'd wondered if he might stop in to take a look sometime—guessing (accurately) that the masjid would have made some sort of arrangements for Ramzaan to offer both the iftar and dinner meal. "That way, you won't have to open your fast alone," Farah said. This wasn't pressure, exactly, nor did it feel like a tactic. It simply hadn't occurred to her that someone could choose *not* to fast during the holy month.

But Nasr was actually more than happy to discuss Ramzaan with Farah. He preferred the topic to the latest focus of their phone calls: the progress of Jameela and Javaid's matrimonial plans. He had already endured a full report of the engagement party, which had been limited to close family and friends and had taken place at Jameela's parents' home. According to Farah, the newly engaged pair had done more mingling than sitting together, and there was very little posing for pictures. Jameela Baji, as Farah (being younger and always properly respectful) called her, had worn a simple shalwar suit. It was pale-gray silk, with an A-line cut and black embroidery. Everyone (meaning the Ansari sisters) had agreed afterward that the suit was not entirely as formal as one would have expected. "Too bad," Farah said rather wistfully. "I would have liked going shopping with her again. She helped me so much." Hearing this, Nasr suppressed his exasperation. But maybe it was best that the victim had no sense of being victimized. All in all, Farah concluded, Jameela and Javaid's party was a very nice affair. She was being kind. Nasr learned from Yasmine that the celebration had been modest by any standard—at Jameela's insistence and to Talat Auntie's chagrin. There'd been no decorating, no welcoming of the future in-laws with handmade garlands, no exchanging of gifts—only the food had been extravagant: Hamid Uncle's famous rogan josh and fall-apart pasande kebabs, along with shaadi pullao.

Last night, before the topic of Ramzaan came up, Farah updated Nasr with the latest news: Jameela Baji had announced that she and Javaid Bhai would marry no earlier than the fall of next year. Farah's mother believed that this was to give Talat Auntie more time to prepare, but Suraiya thought the pair simply wanted to spend time being engaged and in love. Nasr wondered why Farah cared so much, and whether her days were filled with anything other than gossip and wedding talk. Did she know anyone outside her family relations? And—most troubling—why couldn't she detect his lack of interest? But then the conversation turned suddenly. She said, "I wish you could come here for Ramzaan," and began expressing such care and concern over Nasr's meal plans that he had found the prospect of coordinating their eating schedules appealing.

Now a cloud passed overhead, momentarily darkening the street. Nasr imagined Hamid Uncle's kebabs—smokily fragrant and soft as can be. He felt his mouth fill, and turned his head to spit.

"Hey, over here." The man had a closely cropped salt-and-pepper Afro, and there was a faint, almost dusty sheen to his black skin, which made it appear gray, even metallic. Not only was he speaking to Nasr, but he was emerging from the alley and heading straight for him. "You're a brother, aren't you? Hey, where are you going?" The man had raised his voice. The sound echoed up into the alley, and the muscles of Nasr's neck, already tight, quaked in protest.

The man pointed up to the sky, knowingly. "It still isn't time yet."

Nasr mumbled an apology and tried to step past, but the man was standing before him now, his arms spread and his hands open. He wasn't very tall, but stocky, with an upright posture. His fingers showed through his torn red gloves, and he wriggled them, as if to suggest that he was carrying nothing, harmless. "Listen," he said, leaning in but also glancing back over his shoulder, "you just got to be careful, that's all I wanted to say."

Nasr also took a quick glance up and down the block—it was one of the shabbier ones on the Upper East Side, with an old warehouse on one end and a few graffitied stoops on the other. The black dome of the masjid peeked above buildings, a couple of blocks away. How had he gotten so far from it?

"You *are* a brother, right?"

"Sorry?" Nasr said. He concentrated on the man's hands, in case they plucked a knife or a gun from the thick brown coat, which was torn in spots but hung robelike down his front. The man stepped closer, and a tangy odor of sweat sprang up between them.

"Look," Nasr said, "I'm sorry. I've got a little something." Was one supposed to reach for one's pocket in these situations? To offer? Or did admitting that there was something to be offered imply that there was more hidden elsewhere?

"Look," the man replied, with almost the same intonation. Nasr couldn't tell if he was being mocked. "All I'm saying is, they're profiling big-time now. I mean, I would take different routes if I were you. You see those guys up there? On the roof. No, over there. All right, don't look just now. It is the oldest trick in the book." His hands dropped to his sides. "Been on the trail since '97," the man said in a low voice, "and I've never seen anything like it. Coming from both directions. You don't know whose is whose."

He rolled his eyes up, keeping his head still as he indicated that Nasr should really take a look at the top of the building behind him. Then he shook his head, seeming suddenly to give up. "Yeah, you're right," he mumbled. "Not yet." As though to pass the time while they waited for a better opportunity, he began describing how he used to get chased out of the upper Nineties on a daily basis—they'd come around with flashlights and sometimes sticks, truck people out but not always very far. This went on for years (his eating spots were down here, so he'd let things cool off and then come back), but now, as long as he stuck close to this area, the cops walked right past him. "Couldn't give a shit. I could be waving a loaded gun and they wouldn't stop."

Nasr felt his heartbeat in his throat, the blood surging in odd spots; his legs were stiff and useless. He had the impression that the man was somehow standing across the entire sidewalk, taking up the whole space between the car parked on the street and the trash cans to the right.

The man cocked his head toward the rooftops again. "The mayor put them up there—the old one—to protect you guys. You believe him, that's your business. But you know they're all around your mosque there." The "they" were sharpshooters, and the first day he'd noticed them, he explained, they'd scrambled out of sight so quickly he didn't know what he was seeing—probably kids messing around or something. But over the course of a week or two he'd staked them out, pretended he was sleeping in the alley, and eventually they'd emerged—thin shadows in the sun, but even so you could tell they were big men, walking along the roofline and then crouching down. Three, maybe four at a time. Probably they were stationed all the way up and down this whole block. Probably had rotations, shift changes—just like any job. But you could be sure as shit that someone was up there around the clock. Two four seven. That meant now. The man paused meaningfully. And speaking of numbers, he continued, did Nasr ever notice how the numbers all worked? Nine plus one plus one equals eleven. Eleven is what the towers looked like—a big, beautiful number, the first plane was eleven, too, Flight 11, and of course in America nine-one-one has always meant emergency—help for some, run like hell for others. "Different strokes for different folks," he conceded with a casual shrug. "But why are those guys up there? Not as if they don't have the patrols on the street, and every morning they got more barricades around the place. You all seem right protected to me—you know what I mean? Why do you need shooters?" He suddenly held Nasr's eye. "Got any idea?"

Nasr didn't know what to think. Pain held him in place as much as anything. It was as if the headache had scalped him, left parts of his brain exposed. Was it best to ignore such a direct question, or did ignoring make people angry?

"Think maybe your sheek knows? He got out of town in a hurry, didn't he?"

Nasr watched the progress of a woman walking down the street, a plump figure in a pink tracksuit. She wasn't walking very fast, but she'd crossed to the other side now and was no longer looking in their direction. The man might have moved closer, or maybe not, but the smell had grown, tightened around Nasr as though it had arms, and when the guy finally asked him, a bit disappointedly, "Well, all right, what do you got?," Nasr let his breath out with relief.

Where Nasr's wallet should have been was a pack of cigarettes, and when he drew it out, the man said, "Yeah, I'll take those." He struck the pack against his wrist a few times. "You guys gotta give a lot, don't you?" he said. "Especially this month, right?"

Nasr felt himself nodding—he turned his wallet to keep the credit cards out of view. He had a fifty, a ten, and some small bills.

"Yeah, I know all about Ramadan," the man said as he accepted the money. His dad, he said, had been a Muslim named Mustafa (he pronounced them "Ramadawn," "Muzlum," and "Moose-taw-fah"). "He didn't do all of it, but he knew what he was supposed to do. Mustafa," he repeated slowly. Counting the bills, he let out a low whistle, in no special hurry. "Oh, if those guys up there only knew. Got a light?"

Nasr's fingers shook as he held the lighter. The flame wavered, refusing to connect with the tip until he concentrated, aimed. It was fear, of course, but also withdrawal. As soon as the cigarette was lit, the smoke cut through the fog in his brain like a sharp refreshing cure, and he almost asked for one back.

"But you don't really give to everybody, right? You just send the money back to your countries?"

Nasr nodded again, less definitively.

The man had taken a few steps, head tipped back, blowing smoke almost thoughtfully, as if he were pacing a living room, but this had left an opening between the sidewalk and the car. "You can't be strolling around and around here."

"Yes," Nasr said. "I'm sorry."

"Not when you don't know who's protecting you and who's out to get you."

Nasr agreed again—yes, he was absolutely right—taking a small step with each word. Just as he edged around, the man glanced over, delivered a penetrating stare but then waved his hand, as though dismissing a secretary. "Hey!" Nasr heard a moment later, but he didn't turn, striding briskly now. "Just remember, brother—they're not gonna come when you call. You know that, don't you?"

Nasr didn't return to the masjid that day. He hurried to the closest convenience store, bought a pack of cigarettes, and smoked three on the walk home, plus a few more while waiting for the delivery guy from the Chinese place across the street. It was not the ideal way to a break a fast, but soon the combination of nicotine and food began chipping away at the headache. Just as he finished eating, Farah called—the second time in two days—to ask how his first roza had gone. She was disappointed that he hadn't seen the masjid, but when he began telling her what had happened, she drew a sharp, disapproving breath.

"You have to be careful," she admonished. "You can't take such chances these days."

"Walking around in broad daylight wasn't taking chances." By now the pain was tamed and dull, and Nasr felt the return of his perspective. He smiled when Farah suggested that he try, whenever possible, to travel in groups.

"He was harmless, truly," Nasr said, adding that if his head hadn't been pounding, he would've seen this from the beginning—or avoided walking straight toward the guy in the first place.

"What did the police say?" she asked.

Nasr replied that he hadn't called the police, nor was he planning to.

"Why not?" Farah asked, her voice high like her youngest sister's.

"You don't call the police for a simple mugging."

"But how do you know it was just that?"

Muggings, he said gently, as though he were reminding her of something she already knew, were a sad reality of living in the big city. Nearly everyone he knew had a story of an unfortunate incident. Most, in fact, involved desperate people, who hadn't eaten for days. This downplaying on Nasr's part was not simple bravado—he could just imagine how the episode might be received by her father as yet another attack on a Muslim carried out by someone who was probably being paid by the police as part of a large conspiracy of harassment. Or maybe that was too simple: maybe the man had been an undercover agent, either CIA or FBI, with a mission to try to spook Nasr out, or, even better, to befriend him in order to recruit him into some kind of infiltration effort that the government had wasted no time in launching. To Nasr, this sort of paranoia was not only unseemly, but exactly the kind that begat more incidents, and while he supposed he couldn't do anything to change Mr. Ansari's thinking, he had no interest in letting Farah scare herself to death before she got here. He'd been lucky, he told her, not to have been mugged before in all the time he'd been in New York—and today, he was lucky it hadn't been worse.

"But that doesn't mean you can simply ignore everything," Farah said with vehemence. "How would you feel if I encountered such a person on the street by myself?"

215

Before he could form a reply, she cut him off: "Hold on one second." There were sounds of footsteps now, muffled voices, a door closing. The Ansari house had a basement that half served as a prayer space and half as a thin-walled bedroom shared by the two older sisters.

There was silence now, not even the sound of breathing, and something about the absence caught Nasr's attention. He had never seen the interior of Farah's bedroom, but he imagined her taking the phone into a far corner, perhaps sitting on a bed, hunching away from the door. And just as the idea came into his mind, so appeared the image: the faint rise of color in her fair skin, expanding up her neckline—a blushing bride, he thought— holding her breath over a silence he knew she wouldn't break.

"Hey," he said, "why don't you come visit me?"

Now there was a small gasp on the other end, followed by a light chuckle. "Come there?"

"Why not?"

"All by myself, I suppose."

"The more alone, the better."

She laughed again, even more softly. She couldn't possibly, she said—there was too much to do.

Another silence formed and grew, and, desperate to keep her on the line, Nasr asked about the progress on her gharara.

"The bottom half of the suit came in twenty pieces," Farah said. "Each panel is so heavy, with all the embroidery." She sounded faintly relieved, and the rush of words continued on: "Masood Chacha told us that there were fifteen tailors working on it at one point. Saleha Khala made them sit together in a circle, work on a small section, then pass it on." Nasr couldn't help liking how she'd already taken to referring to his relatives as if they were her own. "Fifteen people—Masood Chacha said they filled the whole lawn."

"How does it look now?" he asked.

"It's very beautiful," she said with a sigh, then fell quiet.

"But what does it look like?"

"I can't tell you that." Her voice had risen in outrage.

"Why not?"

"It's bad luck."

"But isn't the gharara coming from our side?" he said, laughing. "Maybe *you're* the one who shouldn't see it."

"Well, it's too late," Farah replied, but she seemed distracted now, and her voice was fainter, as if she'd pulled the receiver away—untucked it, Nasr imagined, from between her chin and shoulder. He wondered if someone had come down to the basement to check on her.

"Will you be visiting home soon?" she asked in a low voice.

"I'm not sure," he said slowly. "I would like to, to see you—"

"Promise you won't look at my gharara when you're home?" She paused, as if catching her breath. "Not even in December."

"I promise."

"Or ask anyone about it?"

"Yes," he said. What was it, Nasr wondered again—a shift in accent, a new lilt or manner—that could make her sound so different suddenly?

"And promise you'll be careful."

"Yes."

They both fell silent now.

"Look," he said, "all you have to do is pack a bag, a small one, write a nice note, and call a cab to the airport—or *tell* them, even. The whole thing's on me." No answer. "I'll meet you right in the terminal, a seven-minute walk after you step off the plane." Still no answer. "If you don't want to fly, there are trains—even buses. Straight shots. You leave at night, sleep through most of it, get here in the morning. Then I'll see you at the door, the moment you step off."

"Oh, sure," she said—there it was! "I'll just get into a taxi and say Mummi and Daddy, don't worry, I'm just going to the States for a few hours. Be back in time for dinner."

"Well, I don't know about dinner," Nasr said, and there was another sweet silence. He couldn't believe he was missing all those blushes!

19

For the rest of the week, Nasr wasn't able to get away from work early and ended up breaking his fasts at his desk, with junk from the vending machine. After a few more days of headaches, it made sense to actually wake up early for the sehri, make some coffee, and have a few cigarettes. Gradually, the pain climbed in later and later in the afternoon, and throbbed less when it was there. By the end of the weekend, he had cut back to one cigarette in the morning, and replaced the others with a couple of aspirin.

Farah called every day wanting a full report of what Nasr had eaten for iftar and dinner. She was interested in whether he was the type to break his fast with the traditional dates and bananas or with more substantial things like samosas, dahi vadas, chana, and the like. He was definitely the latter, he told her, but he'd had to settle for chips, popcorn, a Coke. At the mention of each item, Farah groaned or admonished him, but she listened with sympathy to his story about how one of the worst things his mother had done to him when he was a kid was tell him that he shouldn't swallow his saliva—that even such a small amount of liquid would compromise his fast. Afterward, for years of Ramzaans, every time Nasr thought about how he shouldn't, his mouth would water, and he'd have to go running out of class— and now out of meetings. Farah laughed heartily at this, but the next day she complained that he'd passed the curse to her. She herself, she confessed, hated dates. To her, this, the holiest of fruits, had always looked like a cockroach, and nothing about its gritty insides contradicted the impression. "I don't know what I'll do when we go for hajj," Farah said, then added merrily, "but I guess we have plenty of time to figure that out." While none of this could qualify as lovers' talk, it did feel as though he and Farah were finally sharing genuine intimacies, details not intended to impress.

Although Farah didn't ask Nasr to return to the masjid, she did often wonder if he was going to be "alone again" for the iftar and then why he always "went everywhere by himself." Nasr decided to give the masjid another try. It seemed wiser to prove to her that it was possible to attend a prayer in Manhattan without incident. But the next day, as he made his way from his apartment to the glinting dome, he found himself taking the most public route and casting vigilant glances at the oncoming faces. Once he actually glanced up at the rooftops of the nearby buildings.

As before, the masjid rose in the distance like a grand and imposing mausoleum, guarded by police tape and water barrels—not the least bit welcoming in any way. By the time Nasr arrived at the entrance, a narrow corridor of sidewalk set back from the street and leading to dark glass doors, he was ready to turn back. And he would have, were it not for the stream of people pressing in behind him. Above the chatter of activity—Arab mothers prodding distracted children forward, and black men in colorful skullcaps reaching across to greet one another heartily with "Assalaam'alaikum, brother"—there was the noise of the massive construction project under way to one side of the masjid, large orange machinery blaring and hissing in a big dirt hole. But the moment he crossed the threshold into the small dark foyer, those sounds disappeared, as though he'd entered a sealed vault. Around him now was the busy last-minute activity Nasr remembered from his own youth: children being herded toward bathrooms or away from them with washed hands, held up and away like miniature surgeons'. Several men came through, carrying platters above their heads—the iftar snack. Well, maybe he'd have a sample and leave, Nasr thought. He followed the platters into a large side room, where they were settled on buffet tables, and he was disappointed to see their offerings: dates, cuts of melon, nuts. Nothing warm or particularly appealing. He waited beside a tray of cashews, hoping he didn't look as desperate as the other single men. At the prescribed moment, a hush fell over the room, and Nasr whispered the requisite words and broke his fast with a small handful. "Isn't it so nice," Farah had said the night before, "to imagine all of us, all over the world, bringing something to our lips at the exact same moment?" This wouldn't be true, of course, if you factored in time zones, but her question had made Nasr think of her lips—exceptional in every way; and he wondered now what Farah would have said if he'd told her this. Next time, he thought, he wouldn't let such an opportunity get away. He grabbed another handful of cashews and almost absently followed the crowd.

The stairwell to the second story was marble and airily designed, with fancy glass inserts, but at the corner turn there were brown water stains running down the walls. The impression of grand wealth was reestablished by the prayer room, however, an expansive cube, three stories high. The top third of each wall was composed of large blank cement squares with narrow windows at their edges that admitted precise grid lines of light. Without ceremony, a small dark man in simple white robes stepped up to a microphone to lead the prayer. Nasr took his place at the end of the back row of men and was relieved when the rhythms of the namaaz came easily and automatically.

Afterward, much of the praying public stayed seated on the carpet to hear the qutba. Speaking in perfect English but with a thick accent, the imam delivered a surprisingly standard lecture on the charitable message of Ramzaan, stressing sacrifice and self-discipline. There was not one mention of the attacks, despite all the building's security measures. Maybe Farah wouldn't find this place any more appealing than he did, Nasr thought. It was not as if saying your prayer in a masjid made it any more valid. In fact, weren't the duties of Islam designed to be portable?

People soon began to leave, and the imam, as if sensing light interest, finally made some remarks about how at a time like this the families of those who died in "recent incidents" should be remembered, the life of every person being God-given and precious. Nasr sighed. Rising to go, he recalled that the man who'd mugged him had said something about a "sheek." He must have been referring to this imam, who was now offering platitude after platitude about Muslim pride and the need to rededicate ourselves to our exemplary faith in a way that might have seemed totally inoffensive and mild back in August, when it wasn't so obvious what topic he was avoiding. "They're not going to come when you call," the mugger had said to Nasr. He'd had such a strange manner, not desperate or angry or particularly agitated—oddly sympathetic, in fact.

• • •

After namaaz, Nasr's plans to leave were once again waylaid. In the red-carpeted room downstairs, the platters of finger food were replaced with large metal trays, emanating warm tentacles of steam. A man beside Nasr said, "The boti kebabs are as tough as they look, but my wife's homemade achaar can make anything edible." He was wide-faced and broad-shouldered, and looked to be in his early thirties. Introducing himself as Malik Khan, he pointed back at a table of diners and made a joke about how, despite the admirable variety in the masjid's congregation (from black Muslims to our Latin American brothers and sisters), the South Asians in the room always managed to gravitate toward one another. "Gene-pool radar," he added, in a friendly but confident manner, so it wasn't surprising to learn that he was a doctor, a surgeon in fact. "There's plenty of mango pickle to go around," Malik said. "You're welcome to join us."

"Us" was a loud and crowded table of about a dozen people. Friendly faces turned to greet Nasr and room was hastily made for him to sit in the center of the action, as if he were an honored guest. Some of the women's heads were covered, some were not; a few of the men wore white skullcaps.

"So where are you in life?" a woman leaned over to ask. She was small, with a long face, and her pale skin was made even fairer by her black headscarf and the dark lining around her eyes.

"Sorry?" Nasr said.

"Already set up, being set up, or still in denial?" She turned out to be Malik's wife, Rashida, of the famous achaar.

Nasr told her, and by extension much of the table, that he was in the first slot. Rashida asked for details, and Nasr supplied them tentatively at first. No one blinked at the timeline: a first meeting in June, a marriage in December. No one asked if it was love at first sight, or how he'd proposed—or any questions that forced him into some weird evasion or lie. Instead, they made jokes about what Nasr and Farah could look forward to now: "If you're expecting to be left alone after you get married, forget it," Rashida said. "All this 'Arré, good, my final duty in the universe is done' is a sham. The next demand is for kiddies." Her warning drew supporting testimony from around the table, with each successive speaker having an even more impressive complaint about the unsubtle hints he or she had been subjected to. But this exasperation was mild—as though the parental demands were considered neither too odious nor alien, just a necessary and comedic fact of life. The Khans had already given in to such pressure—they had a four-year-old and a two-year-old at home with the nanny. "This is our night out on the town, if you can believe it," Rashida said, elbowing her husband. She and Malik seemed to serve as the seniors of the group, encouraging others to take seconds as though they were hosting a party. Rashida's mango achaar was very good. "Next year," Rashida added, "he'll probably take me to do umrah for our anniversary."

It was not the type of comment one expected to hear at a masjid dinner, especially during Ramzaan. Or, rather, its content was fitting but the ironic delivery was not. Nasr was impressed. His inclination to hang back evaporated, and he soon found himself offering all sorts of similar opinions.

As the evening progressed, Nasr discovered that the group was composed of people much like him: American- and Canadian-born Desis (with the occasional Pakistani) who'd grown up in a suburb of a major city and pursued the usual mix of professions—there were engineers, doctors, and lawyers, with one or two graduate students tossed in. While individual details were different, of course, each story seemed to Nasr like a minor variation on a common and familiar theme of hard work in expensive private (and often Ivy League) schools, "poor" years in cramped two-bedroom apartments with ill-chosen roommates, marriage tucked in somewhere before or after graduate school, then finally the first job—and with it a flush of income to wash away all the inherited penny-pinching of the parents' generation. One of the couples had just upgraded to a one-bedroom apartment in a swank new high-rise; another was buying a loft on the Upper West Side. The men were beginning to play golf, and the women starting to not feel guilty about buying expensive shoes and going to hair salons. ("Arré, why do you always tell your mother how much the coloring costs?" Nasr overheard one woman ask another impatiently.)

To Nasr's surprise, he was rather enjoying himself. The goodwill around him, the laughter and jokes, all felt like minor acts of rebellion, and he couldn't help admiring how nobody in the group seemed out of place in the masjid or disturbed by the fact that theirs was the loudest table in the hall. At the end of the evening, Rashida asked Nasr to join them at their home for dinner the following Friday. "You can't eat this food every night," she said.

Oh, you must go," Farah told Nasr in a tone both pleading and firm. Before he could reply, she began wondering which part of India the Khans were from and how long they'd been married. Did they live near Nasr? Were they from New York? How long after they got married did they have their son? And what did Nasr think was in Rashida's achaar that made it so exceptional? Nasr happily rode the river of her divergent and enthusiastic speculations to the next Friday, when, as he was heading out to the Khans, he had to promise twice to call her the minute he got back—no matter how late.

Malik and Rashida lived in a tasteful duplex with hardwood floors and pale leather furniture artfully arranged in stations rather than in a massive circle around a central coffee table. Even their children were picturesque—little Farid clinging to the nanny, who was a small dark woman from Sri Lanka, while Muneezeh toddled about imperiously, black hair curling around her gold hoop earrings. The kids were led in and out at various intervals during the evening, fed separately from the adults. Shortly after Nasr arrived, Rashida asked if he smoked and then led him to the balcony, where a couple of other men were gathered under a toasty outdoor heater. "Try to give it up before Farah gets here," she said with a smile, handing him a plate of dahi vada. "Nonsmokers can't stand the stuff in their hair. You'll see."

At dinner, Nasr found that once he started eating he could hardly stop. One of Malik's hobbies was fine cuisine, and that night he spent as much time in the kitchen as his wife. When he finally emerged, it was to call everyone to a feast of lamb curry, dal makhani, fried okra garnished with lemon, and tangy eggplant baratha—served with separate courses of freshly made naan and biryani.

In the course of the conversation, Nasr received advice about real-estate markets, halal grocery stores, how Crate & Barrel was the only decent place to shop for home décor (no matter how much the parents complained about its prices), and where in the city Farah might be able to pick up a tolerable off-the-rack shalwar suit—though nothing compared with going back and getting them tailored yourself, of course. He also discovered that the folks around the table had been attending the East Side masjid for several years. Two of the men, Jimmy and Rehan, coached basketball in a Muslim association's program for disadvantaged youth, and Rashida and her sister, Shahida, volunteered with other lady doctors from the masjid at a Muslim women's clinic. Even so, there were varying opinions about whether the Islamic Center's masjid was the best option in town. It was conveniently located, sure, but the overcrowding could get terrible, and during Ramzaan all its internal politics made the news. The latest episode involved the masjid's previous imam, who had quit and left the country suddenly in late September. The man's departure was eventually traced to remarks that he had made in an interview abroad and that a local news organization had recently picked up—something about how the Jew-controlled media in America was covering up the fact that its own people were responsible for the terrorist attacks and his fears about Jewish doctors harming Muslim children. "What was he thinking?" Malik wondered, shaking his head incredulously. "You don't say something like that." The people around the table agreed, but they didn't seem disenchanted in the way Nasr would have expected. They spoke of poor administration and mismanagement, of wishing for a system to elect new imams, and mostly of wanting a better alternative. Remarkably, no one seemed to consider the possibility of not attending a masjid.

For dessert, there was warm gulab jamun. The little balls of dough floated in a perfectly sweetened syrup and melted at first bite, topping off what Nasr considered to be one of the pleasantest evenings he'd ever had. The fine food helped, but a large part of the evening's appeal was the surrounding urbanity: uncomplicated manners, easy conversation, interesting art on the walls (a Mughal print from the Shahnama, and those abstract splashes of paint on large white canvases turned out to be Malik's original watercolors). At the Khans' that first night—but also in the homes of the other couples Nasr visited during the course of the following weeks—the men occasionally gathered around a toy (somebody's new flat-screen TV or Harman/Kardon speakers), but apart from that, there was no separation along gender lines. Some of the women were dowdy, others not exactly beautiful, but they were all assembled fashionably, with manners that were familiar to Nasr but modulated, less intense somehow. They alternated between motherly concerns (what had Nasr been feeding himself this week?) and lightly flirtatious teasing—knowing voices attributed each of Nasr's "lapses into silence" to him missing his fiancée.

It all felt like a scene from a certain kind of movie, but tilted slightly askew: the wineglasses contained no wine (all the toasting—for there was toasting—was done with water or Coke); none of the stylishly dressed diners had failed to pause and whisper a quick prayer before taking their first bites; the soft music in the background featured someone doing jazz improvisations, but on a tabla. It was this askewness, Nasr decided, that was most seductive.

*F*arah couldn't get enough of Nasr's new friends. "I wish we could invite the Khans to the wedding," she said the next day with a wistful sigh. "All of them really."

Nasr let out a laugh. "You haven't even met them yet."

"But soon I will. They'll probably be my closest friends."

"You're worse than my mother," he said. "How do you know you'll like them?" But even as he asked, he realized that what she'd said was very likely to be true. Pete and Laura were just as friendly and welcoming and eager to meet her, but they wouldn't stand a chance beside these people.

Over the next few weeks, Farah's appetite for details became so insatiable that Nasr found himself attending more dinners than he'd anticipated. She was particularly interested in Shahida Naqvi, who would be marrying Aamir at the end of May, after she finished her master's degree. At the beginning of every phone call now, Farah asked how the girl was managing her wedding plans. Today Nasr had learned that Shahida's mother had started insisting that the food served at the Mehendi ought to be home-cooked. "Home cooking for three hundred people!" Farah said with a pained croon. "Three hundred and fifty now," Nasr said. He and Farah had discovered that a weird pleasure could be had in reviewing the demands of other people's parents, and that this vicarious outrage made the logistics of their own ceremony easier to resolve.

One day, when Nasr broached the subject of having music at the Valima, Farah suggested that her parents might be comfortable with instrumental recordings—"Maybe some tabla or classical stuff in the background?"—but then listened while he explained why that wouldn't be enough. His friends and colleagues—in fact, most people these days—expected music at weddings. "It's part of the celebration for them," Nasr said. "It puts a good face on things." He stopped himself from saying that this good face was especially important now, and instead reminded her that they would be having music only at the Valima, his side's event—not at the Nikaah.

"They're just worried about dancing and things," Farah said.

Nasr understood fully, assuring her that his mother also wouldn't want dancing to be formally added to the program. In the silence that followed, he said, "The music's okay with you, isn't it?"

"I just don't want to make anybody uncomfortable."

Nasr offered to speak to her parents, take full responsibility for the decision. "But, you know," he added, "people would take the cue from us. If you and I were to dance, they would. If we didn't, they wouldn't. They'd be just as happy listening. It's just something additional to enjoy."

"Oh, I know."

"Unless," he said lightly, "what you're trying to tell me is that you're one of those people who can't help but start dancing at the sound of music."

"Me?" she said. "What dance would I do?"

"We could do the tango—nobody will even know you're enjoying it."

Farah laughed again, a bright and now familiar sound. "Okay, let's do it," she said. "I'll talk to them." A week later, she had gained permission for both the music and a dj.

*E*very once in a while, Nasr would see the homeless man on his way to the masjid, though he didn't tell Farah this. "Hey, didn't I tell you not to come this same way?" the man would call out in a joking manner, as though the mugging had never happened. The first few times, Nasr froze, immediately began assessing his escape route. But the man would greet him in full view of others, call out boldly as if they were friends. The third time he said, "Maybe you can buy me the lunch you didn't eat today?" No guilt, just a suggestion. The fellow even introduced himself— Leonard (his mother, he said, hadn't been into the Muslim thing). *Was* he being recruited? Nasr wondered, then immediately dismissed such thoughts. Leonard was old, older than his manner, and much of the bulk in his shoulders was due to the many coats he wore. The next time Leonard approached mentioning a missed meal, Nasr found himself handing over a few bucks.

During this stretch of weeks, Nasr rarely saw Pete and his other friends outside of work, but he figured that that was probably for the best, at least for now. The one evening he had gone out with them, he'd wound up having a drink or two (there was no way of getting out of it, he reasoned, without making a fuss). He'd come home early, and then found himself left with hardly anything to tell Farah about during their evening call. Also, the drinks hit his nearly empty stomach hard, and it felt strange talking to Farah in that state—especially in a month so devoted to self-restraint.

· · ·

*I*n mid-November, Farah told Nasr that Javaid and Jameela were coming to New York. "He's quitting," she said with such certainty that Nasr couldn't help believing her. So he actually did it, Nasr thought.

Javaid and Jameela would drive down the next week to move Javaid out of his apartment, so they were staying for a few days. Nasr supposed he would have to see them, and he braced himself for the ordeal—two smug people, showing off their supremely paired happiness. His mother, whom Nasr usually thought was too quick to judge, was probably right in her recent intimations that for Jameela this was a golden opportunity. However, Nasr didn't believe, as his mother did, that Jameela had angled for the proposal or intentionally competed with Yasmine. (All those mixed signals he thought he was reading from Yasmine were in fact not signals at all. If his sister was softening toward Javaid or being kinder, it was probably for Jameela's sake.) But Jameela probably had been susceptible and made herself available. At thirty, you weren't a girl by anyone's standards, and in their community if you weren't married, you weren't treated quite like a woman, either. Nasr's thoughts lingered near this insight, of being stranded in womanhood, but he soon let it go and returned to dreading Jameela and Javaid's arrival. There was no way to avoid them really. He sighed and heard an echo on the other end of the line.

"When is the Sultans' housewarming dinner?" Farah asked tentatively.

"Next month," he said. The two of them had consulted lengthily on an appropriate gift. Since it was the first they would give together, the item, Farah felt, needed to reflect their combined taste, and after combing the Crate & Barrel Web site, they had eventually settled on a tea set of stainless steel and bone china. Farah had been pleased, as though the project was a preview of the future synchronicity of their tastes.

"Oh, good," she said.

"Why good?"

"No reason," she replied hastily.

But he'd begun to know when she'd left something unsaid, and when he pressed her, she explained that Jameela and Javaid were coming on Thursday and would be in New York only through Sunday.

"And?" he asked.

"And"—she began in a small voice, clearly embarrassed—"and I was just hoping to be the first to meet everyone." Until then, it had never occurred to Nasr that a person's possessiveness could be endearing.

20

*B*y a perverse twist of logic, the various parental commit-
tees back home had decided it would be best if Jameela
stayed with Nasr while she was in New York. Or, rather, she'd
been forbidden to stay in the apartment of her fiancé, and once
the cost of Manhattan hotels was fully appreciated, staying with
Nasr, who was, after all, like a brother to her, was deemed the
most appropriate option.

"There's no reason to actually do it," she said, impatiently
cutting herself off in the middle of this explanation. "It's so stupid. I have my own sleeping bag; they never have to know."

"No, we should," Javaid said. "We don't want to have to lie
to them." He caught Nasr's eye. "I mean, paying for a hotel is
fine, too—"

Nasr quickly assured them—what else could he do?—that he had plenty of room. In fact, Javaid could stay, too, if his apartment became uninhabitable during the packing process.

Jameela glanced about the restaurant with an exasperated air. She was sitting between Nasr and Javaid. She and Javaid had already been there when Nasr arrived, at a small table in the rear: she with a gray hijaab over her head and a nearly naked face; he with a full beard and a small white topee at the back of his head. It was like coming upon a middle-aged couple, a timid uncle and auntie, who looked small and foreign huddled together in the booth. Nasr hadn't been sure what to do—he held out a hand to congratulate Javaid on the engagement, but his cousin rose to embrace him warmly. He would have hugged Jameela, but she remained seated and accepted his best wishes demurely. They'd had a long drive, they explained, made longer by a thorough inspection at the border. "I asked the guy if he'd be interested in checking under the hood," Jameela said. Javaid speculated that it would be longer in the other direction, when the car wasn't empty. Jameela rolled her eyes. Occasionally, her expressions were so incongruous to the tunnel of fabric in which they were framed that it was like seeing a bizarre spoof of a woman in hijaab. But they seemed happy enough to see Nasr, and all three of them took turns talking in bursts and lapsing into the silence of eating after an especially long day of abstinence.

Javaid patted Jameela's hand now, not exactly a bold gesture, but it did signal a certain degree of comfort. Did they hold hands? Nasr wondered. The engagement party was the only time he'd ever held, let alone touched, Farah's hand.

As if roused to attention, Jameela asked, "Where, exactly, are we?" Javaid named the cross streets. She shook her head.

"You'll figure it all out tomorrow," Javaid assured her. His manner toward her was attentive, but there were times—Nasr couldn't help noting this with a measure of satisfaction—when he seemed to revert to the old Javaid, solemn and nervous.

During the course of the evening, Javaid explained (also to Nasr's satisfaction) the true uncertainty of his job situation. Yes, he was definitely leaving the city, and they had indeed come to move him out, but it was not clear whether he would be leaving his firm altogether. Jameela thought it was too drastic to cut all ties, that Javaid should be open to the possibility of returning, or at least inquire about a transfer to Montreal. "You said you always liked the work," she reminded Javaid. Then she turned to Nasr. "What do you think?"

Nasr promptly agreed that the job, as everyone knew, was tremendous, but Javaid could find another one.

"But won't it be more difficult to return, given the climate?" Jameela asked.

"Considering how hard the firm is fighting to keep him," Nasr said, "one might say Javaid is in a position to create his own climate."

His words weren't exactly supportive of her position, but Jameela looked pleased, and Javaid listened to them both with a surprisingly willing ear for someone who only a month earlier had spoken as though he had a suitcase packed for Karachi.

"What does this mean for your Pakistan plans?" Nasr couldn't resist inquiring. Javaid and Jameela stared at him blankly.

"One major life change at a time," Javaid replied eventually. "Anyway, we'll see," he added with a shrug.

Nasr insisted that dinner was on him, a belated engagement present. And after another small fuss it was also settled that Jameela should be dropped off at Nasr's tonight, as it was too late for her to see Javaid's apartment.

• • •

*T*he next morning there was a faint knock on Nasr's bedroom door. It was still dark. The light from his alarm cast a green glow about the bare walls.

"Hey," came Jameela's whisper. She had not accepted his offer last night of taking his room while he slept on the pullout sofa. "You're not going to eat anything?"

Nasr got out of bed, remembering just now that he had run out of bagels and the fridge was probably as empty as ever. When he opened his door, Jameela wasn't there, but there was a warm smell of milk and something toasting. Did he have a toaster? Nasr's was a railroad apartment, with the bedroom at one end of a hallway that branched off twice, into a closet and a bathroom, then opened to a living room and dining area, and finally a galley kitchen. The kitchen's overhead light lit a shadowy path through the darkness of the apartment, and under it Jameela was moving about in a bright-blue hooded sweatshirt and jeans. Her hair was in a high ponytail, her running shoes squeaking on the linoleum. She met him with a cup of tea, the steam rising in the soft light.

"Sorry about that," he said, indicating the fridge. He couldn't remember the last time he'd made himself tea in the apartment, doubted that there had been milk on the premises in years.

"There was a place open around the corner," she said, shrugging cheerfully. Back in the kitchen, she pulled open the oven door.

"You're baking?" The tea was strong and sweetened just right, made—he saw the pot on the stove now—with heated milk and a brand of leaves he didn't recognize.

She pulled out a tray of bread slices. "I couldn't find any bagels. I thought I'd be tripping over them in this city."

"I didn't know you were a morning person," he said, watching her butter the toast.

She smiled, pushing a plate his way across the breakfast

counter. "Neither did I." She glanced at her watch. "You're going to have to hurry. It's almost time."

When Nasr saw Jameela again, twelve hours later, she and Javaid appeared flushed and tired in his doorway, back in the uncle and auntie garb. Javaid had picked her up from the apartment that morning on time, but his meetings downtown had run long—they took polite turns narrating the story—and they'd gotten off to a late start. "Start at what?" Nasr asked. Jameela, as it turned out, was no aimlessly wandering or even casually informed tourist. She had an agenda—a list of places to see and a schedule to follow. After Javaid was free, they'd gone to Ground Zero, which both of them agreed (to Nasr's surprise) was the saddest thing ever to be seen, then made their way uptown. They checked out the Metropolitan Opera House and the Museum of Natural History, followed by a look around the Columbia campus. They'd stopped in at Javaid's apartment, had dinner, then headed to the masjid for namaaz. Tomorrow's itinerary involved a couple of museums and Washington Square.

"And Bergdorf's," Javaid said in a dry voice.

"A site of great cultural significance," Jameela said, actually sheepish. "And we have to start packing, too." She headed to the kitchen to brew the tea.

Javaid said his former supervisor had asked him for some help in training a few people before he left, which meant that he would need to be in the office tomorrow for who knows how long and all the packing would have to be compressed into Saturday. He scratched his beard, and then looked back at Jameela, who was rooting through the fridge. "You wouldn't by chance be free tomorrow afternoon, would you?" he asked Nasr. "It would just be for a couple of hours." Nasr shook his head—sorry.

"I'll be fine," Jameela said, bringing over a plate of three steaming mugs. "I'll keep your cell phone and we can meet when you're done."

Javaid didn't seem to like the idea of her going about alone and began to mount a proper objection when she suddenly bounced up and went back to the kitchen. She returned a moment later with an envelope from Nasr's pile of mail.

"What is this?" she asked, handing it to Nasr.

"Just an invitation," he replied, opening it to show her the embossed card.

"Fancy. Who's inviting you to the National Academy of Design?"

It was from this woman he'd met on a trip back from London, he explained—and then had to tell the whole story, of course. Over the past few weeks, he'd received a number of invitations from Lillian van der Luyden. This card announced a birthday gala for her sixtieth.

"Are you going?" Jameela asked.

He didn't think so. He'd accepted one invitation, to a swanky party in a restaurant overlooking Central Park, and discovered upon arriving that he was one of the few guests who didn't have grandchildren.

"That's really her last name—van der Luyden?"

"I presume so."

"Hey, isn't this place on your list?" Javaid said, examining the invitation.

There was a curiously excited look on Jameela's face as she explained that the National Academy of Design was originally a residence, a grand house that had been designed by someone her favorite writer, Edith Wharton, had written a book with.

"Do you want to go?" Nasr asked. "I'm always expected to bring a guest." Jameela gave a dismissive but unconvincing shake of her head, and Nasr added, "I'm sure they wouldn't mind my sneaking in two guests," when he saw her glance in Javaid's direction.

"Think so?" Jameela said, her smile almost inappropriately sardonic. "In this day of heightened insecurity?"

"You two should go," Javaid said. "When is it—Saturday? Who knows how this training business is going to go—"

"We still have your packing to do."

"It'll be fine. I'll take care of it."

"But I can help—"

"It'll go much faster if I don't have to supply a history for how each object came into my possession."

"Very funny."

"Funny but true?" Javaid offered, almost impudent. He was like her little brother, Nasr thought, a bit cruelly.

All this would have been the very edges of civilization," Jameela said the next day, sweeping an arm past the glittery, Christmas-glazed storefronts on Fifth Avenue. In the end, Nasr had decided, to his own surprise, to take the day off and escort her around the city. Now the two of them were strolling through the upper Fifties, bundled too lightly against the sudden cool breezes that swept down from the park. The map Jameela used to make these proclamations of hers was evidently from a novel, or several novels, by Edith Wharton, who wrote—Nasr learned today—about a "wealthy but highly stratified and stagnant society" of nineteenth-century New York. The members of this society, Jameela explained, hardly ever ventured north of Gramercy Park, and the center of their universe was Washington Square. "These fancy streets before you," Jameela added with a mock shudder, "were where everyone thought the morally depraved nouveau-riche tribes lived."

For someone who'd never been to the city, who had in fact hardly traveled outside the place in which she grew up, Jameela seemed to know a lot about New York, or, rather, about the New York of the late 1800s. Her expertise put Nasr's—of the landscape's best restaurants and bars—to shame, made it feel functional and colorless. But he was rather enjoying listening to her theories and notions; he had trouble following along sometimes, but this was part of the excitement, to just be keeping up, to occasionally offer an interjection or question when he'd caught on. Jameela was most interested in the people of this time, though she admitted that they weren't an admirable or even particularly exceptional bunch—not the makers of fortunes, or the explorers of new lands, or strivers from a plucky immigrant class. "They were ones who inherited the wealth and lived off it for years, risking nothing. Which made the society totally clannish, insulated, fearful, terrible for women, the poor didn't seem to exist. Sound familiar?" she asked, and typically answered her own question before Nasr could: "It's amazing how much they were like us."

"Us?" Nasr said.

"Well, our parents, with all their proprieties and protocols and manners—what shouldn't be said, or done; how this or that might look. There was so much these people could hardly say to each other. You get the sense that they just went through life taking wide circles, never connecting with anyone."

"But isn't it too easy," Nasr asked, "to believe that just because they didn't talk it out, they were repressed? Is stirring things up always the best solution?"

"Maybe you're right," she mumbled.

Their conversation today was like a little car that, by some mutual but unspoken decision, they steered past certain topics; if the car took an unexpected exit, one or the other of them would calmly lead it up the next ramp and back onto the highway of neat and speedy talking. Now something caught Jameela's eye, and she stepped toward a department-store entrance with an investigating air.

That morning at the Met, where they'd started their touring, Nasr discovered that Jameela was not the sort of person who kept track of where her companion might be. He would often turn around and find that she'd drifted into a distant corner of the gallery or down the hallway into an adjacent room. As he made his way over toward her, he'd notice again what a strange figure she cut in her gray headscarf, tight about the forehead and settling on her shirt collar, and her silver boots that peeked out from under flared jeans. He also noticed that he wasn't the only one who stared, and found himself trying to intercept the glances Jameela attracted. He wondered why this press of attention felt so different from those times he'd spent with Farah's sisters, who always did hijaab, until he realized that his and Jameela's walking together signaled that they were a couple, and if they were a couple, that meant he was somehow responsible, that he wished for his woman to be modest and she was complying for his sake. But Jameela herself, who would surely be aware of this presumption, didn't seem to notice or mind the looks. She walked about as if she didn't even realize she had anything on her head. Perhaps all those years of wearing odd clothes were good practice. In fact, perhaps it was the oddness of her current appearance, rather than the headscarf, that was attracting all this attention. If strangers peered toward a covered head in expectation of a placid or meek creature, they were in for a surprise: there were bits of color on her lips and eyes (which hadn't been there yesterday), not to mention scowls, open declarations of excitement, wrinkled eyebrows. Jameela was a talking, walking mixed signal: Look at me. How dare you look at me.

Joining her now before a series of gold plaques at the department-store entrance, Nasr was ignored. At the museum, he would find her planted in front of paintings like this: her arms crossed and her feet slightly apart, not modest nor particularly feminine. And yet every time he came to stand beside her, he realized with surprise what a small person Jameela was—not only narrow-faced but also petite in the shoulder and hips. Maybe it was because she carried herself erect and took long strides, or because she often gestured so boldly, that one got the impression of a larger being.

"The Beaufort Mansion was up here somewhere . . ." she said, distracted, walking along the building to another entrance. Nasr followed a step behind. An hour earlier, in front of an image of a ballerina, she'd said, "This one is my favorite," in exactly the same way: as though she would have said it whether he was standing beside her or not.

But there wasn't any sort of mansion in sight, only fashionable storefronts and department-store windows, one of which depicted a slim and young Santa in red cashmere dipping a bikini-clad Mrs. Claus into a kiss.

Jameela frowned at it, then turned to glance up and down the street. "Maybe I've got the numbers wrong—"

"Isn't it possible," Nasr suggested, "that there's some made-up stuff in that novel?"

Jameela looked at him, as though he'd broken her reverie, and then laughed. She would always reward you well for saying the right thing.

They stopped at Bergdorf's but, no matter how much Nasr pressed, Jameela refused to buy the bright-orange-and-blue scarf that had caught her eye on the way in and again on the way out. As long as she wasn't interested in spending money, why not stop at Tiffany's? Nasr asked. "Yes, why the hell not?" she agreed, and they circled the sparkling glass cases, testing each other with the price of things. From there, they walked to Rockefeller Center, which was not on Jameela's list, but she seemed willing to depart from the agenda. Her enthusiasm was infectious, and when she mentioned an interest in old libraries, Nasr took her to the main building of the public library, just down the street. At the sight of the reading room, with its high, ornately gilded ceiling and balconied shelves, she let out an appreciative gasp that was too loud and a little dramatic but satisfying nonetheless. "This is exactly what I thought these places would be like, except this is a hundred times bigger. Beautiful."

At Washington Square he thought she'd want to see the park, but instead she drifted up and down its nearby streets, gazing again at buildings. To him, they were simply old buildings with NYU banners and students milling about, but Jameela stared at the walls and façades intently. They paused in front of a redbrick structure with white stone windows, and Nasr suddenly saw how it could have been a house. Yes, take away the labeling and the air-conditioning units and the modern glass doors and you had what could have been somebody's townhome. A grand one, but there it was. Were these the mansions she was looking for? Nasr was about to ask when Jameela said, "I applied here."

"To NYU? Did you get in?"

She nodded. "Also Columbia." She had wanted to study her favorite writers in the place that they'd written about.

"But they didn't let you come," Nasr said, thinking he knew the story.

"Yeah, sort of," Jameela said, looking disgusted for the first time that day. She fell silent and began walking ahead. Nasr caught up to her, thinking they were headed back onto the highway of lighter talk, but to his surprise Jameela began explaining that yes, her mother had made a fuss, but that fuss had involved blaming her father. Apparently, Talat Auntie had a habit of dredging up sore points, and in one argument she complained that Hamid Uncle, for all his big talk, had no ambition to improve the quality of their lives, even to buy a more suitably sized house, and now as they were getting older, he was encouraging their only child to leave them. Worst of all, he would do nothing to improve her marriage prospects, and in fact he was only making them worse by letting her pursue this senseless and expensive study in yet another country. Jameela said her father usually sat out such tirades, but this time he'd argued back, and before anyone knew it he'd told his wife that if she carried on with this sort of backward nonsense, she'd soon have a daughter who was as uneducated as she was. Talat Auntie demanded to be returned to India, she was finished with this; they didn't speak for days. Jameela thought she could solve the problem by accepting McGill's offer. But when she tried to follow a course of study there, it wasn't satisfying—not when she knew that she could have been walking around in the very streets she had read about. "It was a bit rash," she admitted now, but what was even more stupid, she added, was spending her time in college feeling as though she'd lost her one and only chance to do something.

It sounded terrible, Nasr said. He had no idea it was that bad.

Jameela shrugged. "That's what you get from the world's worst marriage ever to be arranged," she said, examining a store window. She loosened the fabric under her chin, then expertly tied an elaborate knot.

Nasr remembered now what his mother had told him about Talat Auntie and Hamid Uncle's past. So Jameela didn't know, he thought. He considered telling her, but she caught his eyes in the window and said something that sent his mind spinning in an entirely different direction.

"If we ever live here, I might get back into it. Who knows."

Nasr pondered this "we" for a long, senseless second. She meant Javaid, of course. And her unusually judicious insistence that he not burn any bridges at his company now made sense.

By afternoon, it was difficult to avoid the smell of food—warm and inviting fragrances poured out of restaurant entrances and emanated from food carts. Last night, on his way home from work, Nasr had bought eggs and bagels, and for sehri this morning the two of them had a full breakfast. The meal had still been provisional—at the kitchen bar, and with most of the lights in the apartment off—but at the time it felt enormously filling. After so much walking, though, Nasr felt his stomach protest. Jameela said hers was complaining, too, but then quickly changed the subject. It was bad form to tempt a fellow fast-keeper into thoughts and discussions about what they might be eating if they could. They ducked into a bookstore, but the air was thick with alluring smells from its café. The SoHo Guggenheim was sufficiently sterile but small. They did a few circuits around its narrow galleries until the iftar hour, at which point they shared a candy bar in the gift shop. For dinner Nasr mentioned a favorite Korean place not far from there. "But it's not halal," he warned, as Jameela dialed Javaid to see when he'd be free. She nodded and turned away to speak; a few moments later, she returned to report that Javaid's trainee was a slow learner and he would be taking dinner at his desk. "Let's try your place," she said with a decisive snap of the two halves of the phone.

*T*he restaurant's exterior was nothing special, Nasr warned, as they emerged from the subway, but every time he'd been there, there was a line winding out the foyer. Jameela groaned, and Nasr promised he'd take them somewhere else if there was a wait. But it was much too early for the dinner rush, especially on a Friday night. They were allowed in immediately, into a narrow and dark chamber with a dozen candlelit tables.

When the food came, they ate in solemn, grateful silence. As this Ramzaan had progressed, Nasr had begun to think that he couldn't remember any time in his life when food had tasted so good; with every bite another area of his tongue came awake with such a jolt it was as though his mouth had been dead. While delivering the appetizers the waiter glanced at Nasr and suggested, "Tsingtao?" in such a knowing and casual manner, he agreed without thinking.

When the beer came, it was too icy and refreshing to be regretted. But when, a few sips later, Jameela asked, "Won't you need to sanitize your apartment?," Nasr knew immediately that she was referring to the bottles in a kitchen cabinet of his: scotch, whiskey, a tawny port—all still full.

He had bought the bottles years ago, during his first month in New York and in a place of his own, but the funny thing is he still wasn't sure what he had expected—to host parties? Drink hard liquor alone? But, of course, the larger implication of Jameela's question was not lost on him: Did he feel guilty for drinking this beer, or the casual, almost instinctual way he'd ordered it? Was he aware that these habits would need to be changed soon? Had he thought about what other changes married life would entail? "I'll probably throw them out," he said, but it felt as though he'd declared: I'll bend as far I need to, of course.

Jameela nodded, accepting this, and it was as if the little car of their conversation, having veered toward an exit, was now heading back, yet again, into the express lane. Nasr felt an uncharacteristic interest in where the exit would take them. If he would have to make compromises, wouldn't she as well?

"So you're really doing that now?" he asked, gesturing toward her hair, which was free, but only because the headscarf had unraveled in the wind on the way to the restaurant. "Isn't it restricting?"

"Oh, it's not that bad." She combed her fingers through the flattened curls. "It took some getting used to, but if this is all it takes, it seems like a fairly small sacrifice."

"For Javaid?"

She laughed. "No, for getting the job done—for getting me in."

"Into what?"

"In with *them*," she said, with two pumps of her eyebrows. "Javaid's been going to the masjid back home lately, and now when I go I can actually talk to the women there. When you're dressed like this, they're not staring at you or trying not to stare at you from a distance, or wondering why you're there. All that stuff is gone, and we can really talk."

To say that it was odd to hear that Jameela Farooqi was trying to infiltrate the masjid would be an understatement. She had been one of the earliest dropouts of their Sunday school, and Nasr could still remember the fuss she made because she hadn't liked that they never learned the meaning of the words they were made to recite. She would spend much of class interrupting the poor volunteer teacher to ask for a translation of the Arabic.

"But isn't that a little deceptive?" Nasr asked.

"I don't know about that," she said, then pursed her lips. "You always manage to ask the most annoying questions."

"Me?" he said.

"Yes, it's a long habit of yours."

"I think it's a pretty obvious point that anybody could make."

"Maybe, but nobody would make it. At least not with me—they just let me go about being the freak I am. They might wish I would stop being a freak, but they would never think to ask what my reasons are."

"What *are* your reasons?" Nasr asked, but they were interrupted by the arrival of dessert.

Jameela ate a few spoonfuls of ice cream, then said, "Look, those women at the masjid aren't so very different from me. They have their doubts and questions and such. It's just a big stereotype that this garment, which is, after all, just a garment, is like some sort of cloak on thinking. I mean, a headscarf itself might be a signal of modesty, but the act of wearing it here requires some resolve. You put it on, and you can feel how imposing you become almost immediately. It's even more amazing with the burqa." She'd apparently tried one of those, too—attended a protest in the full gear. "That was a bit weird, hard to walk in," she said. "Plus, you could be sticking your tongue out and nobody has any idea." She fell quiet for a moment. "My mother hates it—the whole thing. 'Arré, how does it look that I go to a hairdresser but my engaged daughter won't even put on a bit of makeup?' As if they all didn't spend their first twenty years in burqas." She sighed. "Talat is just going to have to get used to it, because the only way to effect any sort of change is to be a person who gets inside and corrodes from within. To find them where they—"

"Are hiding? Smoke 'em out of their caves?"

"I should have known we'd hit a low point in your humor soon."

"Okay, okay—what do you have to say to these poor women? No really, I want to know."

"Oh"—she shrugged—"that Islam is open to interpretation."

Nasr chuckled. "I don't think we as a people do interpretation."

"That's not true," Jameela said. Did Nasr know, she asked, that in medieval Islam there were actually levels corresponding to different kinds of forbidden fruit? And that once upon a time Islam was so flexible and accommodating that it classified human actions into five (or four, depending on which school you followed) categories. Between the two well-known extremes—total prohibitions that were haraam and actions that were absolutely required—there were gradations to allow for the realities of life. "Those early followers were very clever about accounting for human nature. And they knew there was nothing so simple as this right and wrong business. One category was for things that were detestable, but doing them didn't count as sin. Another for extra-good deeds that you could do, but if you didn't, again this was not a sin. And a final one for actions that were neither good nor bad. The idea behind all this is that to judge human action you must also judge intent. And only a person can know his or her true intent, therefore you are your own best judge. Pretty reasonable, I would say."

The candlelight flickered. She was looking at him expectantly. The ins and outs of clerical jurisprudence had surely never produced such a deep sparkle in anyone's eyes.

"So what"—Nasr said, struggling a little to concentrate (had he become such a lightweight that one beer tipped him over?)—"you could drink as much as you wanted, but if you didn't intend to get drunk, it was okay?"

"Not exactly. Drinking alcohol was, of course, forbidden, but a little hashish might simply be strongly discouraged. If you were with friends, known comrades, adults—then it might be lightly discouraged."

"And now you want all the ladies at the masjid to revert to medieval Islamic law and start smoking pot?"

"All I'm saying," Jameela replied, "is that Islam used to figure things out—used to try at least."

Yes, Nasr thought, this was something he knew about her—when Jameela was on a roll, when her voice got raspy and avid, she lost her sense of humor.

"I know my father can sound like a broken record, but he's right. The Middle Ages were better for us. We flourished because we were flexible," she concluded.

"And you think of yourself as corrosive?"

The wry smile was back in place. "At least vinegary."

21

Although it seemed entirely the wrong thing to do, you entered a small octagonal-shaped bookstore first, with wood paneling and museum art books propped for display. From there, you stepped through a narrow passage with a gold-doored elevator to the left and a coat check to the right. Now you encountered the low, excited murmur and bustle of ladies being helped out of their sleek furs and silver-haired men sliding off their broad jackets and silk scarves—these were the first clues that you were in the right place.

You emerged from this into a rotunda with a head-tippingly high ceiling and a cream-colored marble staircase with a wrought-iron railing. The staircase rose in a spiral along the curved wall to the distant second floor. In the center of this room, there was a black statue of a girl balancing on one leg and pulling an arrow back from a bow. Above her, hanging from the gilded dome, was a lantern with candles that lit the room to a soft, burnished sparkle. A bar was set up in one corner, but a crisply uniformed waitstaff was also weaving through with trays of fluted glasses. And if you had Jameela by your side, you learned, as Nasr did, that the statue was of Diana, the Roman goddess of the hunt, and that this grand space was merely a humble foyer.

Before this building became the headquarters of the Academy of Design, Jameela continued in a low tour-guide voice, it was the Huntington House—townhome to Archer Huntington, a railroad heir, and his sculptor wife, Anna (it was her Diana they'd just passed). Ogden Codman, the architect friend of Edith Wharton who was hired by Huntington to redesign this house, believed, like Edith, so passionately in symmetry that he would put in false doors and blank walls purely for the sake of aesthetic balance. "That explains the coziness," Nasr said dryly, but the luxurious atmosphere was already pervading his senses, and as the two of them followed the crowd up wide steps and past tall black windows, he could hardly keep track of Jameela's talk of frock coats and dressmakers and visiting cards.

The second story opened into a large gallery with a parquet floor and paintings on broad walls. A long, narrow table in the center of the room featured an ice sculpture and decoratively arranged hors d'oeuvres: shrimp balanced, fins up, on stiff cream and toast; caviar sitting out for indiscriminate spooning; and a chocolate fountain with fruit and cake cubes at its base. Beyond the gallery was yet another vast room. At its threshold, Jameela drew an appreciative breath. Before them lay a ballroom with checkerboard flooring of silky marble. There were pillars along its walls, plants as tall as trees in distant corners, and larger-than-life-size statues residing in precisely fitted niches. The room's most striking feature, however, was a trio of arched windows that extended from floor to ceiling and offered long views across the darkening city.

A small orchestra was playing something faintly jazzy. Jameela drifted toward the windows, and Nasr followed.

*T*his morning, he had woken up a bit late and missed the sehri. When he came out of his bedroom, the apartment was bright with sunshine—and empty. The sofa was back in place and its bedding stacked neatly in a corner beside Jameela's small suitcase. There was a note on the kitchen counter: she'd gone to Javaid's place to help pack and would return in the afternoon. What a sharp, brief sensation of loneliness he'd felt, but then he'd remembered that they still had this event to attend and found himself looking forward to it for the first time.

Nasr spent the rest of the day trying to distract himself from the demands of his stomach, which had in the three days of Jameela's trip already grown accustomed to filling up before dawn. It began churning midmorning and grew more insistent as the day progressed. Nasr called Javaid to ask if they needed help. Javaid said that things were under control, though not in an entirely convincing way, then he asked if Nasr had an iron. Jameela apparently needed one for her evening clothes. Nasr said yes, then promptly went out to buy one, and also an ironing board. That took care of an hour or so. He was actually grateful when his mother called, though there was nothing for them to talk about—especially since her chief complaint, Masood Chacha and his family, was away visiting the wife's relations in Toronto. He tried to watch a little football, but it failed to hold his interest. He picked up his laundry from the cleaners across the street, then came home to find a short message from Farah asking how the visit was going. When he called her back, Farah wondered how the "gang" was, and for a moment Nasr had no idea whom she meant. Oh, the Khans and Shahida, of course. They were all fine, he supposed, busy with weekend plans. Did he have any plans for the weekend? she asked. Remembering her anxiety about Jameela and Javaid meeting the gang before she got a chance, Nasr felt free to tell her about Lillian's party. But for some reason this information came out as though he felt obliged to attend, had gotten stuck with performing an odious hosting task—and he didn't quite make it clear that Javaid would not be coming along.

In the afternoon, just before the iftar, Jameela appeared at the door with two massive shopping bags, looking harried. She'd gone to some stores in Javaid's neighborhood, managed to pick up a pair of serviceable shoes, a faux-pashmina shawl, and a decent evening purse. She still needed to iron, though. Did he have starch? What time should they leave? My God, she was starving. Nasr told her to get started with her shower, and he raced down for slices of pizza and a spray can of starch. There was a madcap element to the final sequence of their preparations, as they skirted about the tiny apartment, consuming pizza, showering, getting dressed, downing several rounds of tea—so when the cab came, Nasr had the feeling that they both sank into the seat with hearts thudding from equal parts relief and accomplishment.

A waiter came by, and Nasr declined, but he caught Jameela watching the tray of champagne glasses float away.

"Want some?"

"No, thanks," she said. But he'd seen the hesitation.

"Isn't it okay, according to your scholars, as long as you're not intending to get plastered?"

"I'm thinking that the intricacies of religious exegesis are not your forte."

For all Jameela's jokes about showing up at the gala in pajamas, she cut an eye-catching figure beside him. The fabric of her shalwar suit was a sandy raw silk, almost the color of her skin, and its stiff texture was enhanced by the fact that it was hardly interrupted by embroidery or embellishments. The kameez came down to her knees but was form-fitting across her chest and shoulders, and its neckline was a V composed of a simple series of faintly scooping arches. The rupatta was drawn loosely across her chest and caught up around one arm, leaving her hand to swing free, and a longer end hung artfully down the back of her other shoulder. He'd seen her at work lining her eyes, putting a dark, earthy red color on her lips, and sweeping up her hair, but the elegant result of these efforts surprised him somehow. And he had been grateful for the lurching cab ride, in which she'd tried and ultimately failed to affix her headscarf. It was not that he didn't want to stand with a woman whose hair was covered—or, not just that. He simply discovered that he liked the view of those escaped curls that sat on the soft mounds of her spine.

"Well, perhaps you shouldn't," Nasr said with a meaningful sigh. "You have others to think about now."

She turned to him, bemused. "What are you talking about?"

"Javaid."

"What about him?"

"He may notice it," Nasr said. He tapped his nose. "The smell."

"Why would he?"

"Well, you'll be a married woman soon," he said, leaning in as though with a secret. "I don't know if you know this, but there are practical matters to be considering now. Married women do this thing called kissing. The engaged have been known to as well."

"And you would know?" she asked.

He shrugged. "I've heard things."

She shook her head, laughing lightly. Another tray of glasses came into view, and Nasr caught her eye.

"Oh, all right," she said. "It looks nice to hold anyway."

They wound back to the gallery, where Lillian caught sight of Nasr and gestured with a warm smile. In her sleek black gown, silvery bob, and enormous sapphire necklace, she looked both smaller and more formidable than she had on previous occasions. To the balding man standing beside her (her lawyer son-in-law, George) Lillian said, "Nasr is the young man I flew home from London with." She offered no more details or elaboration.

She'd made this same kind of introduction at the charity dinner Nasr had attended. In a dimly lit restaurant perched high above Central Park, Lillian had taken him around, interrupting conversations to present him, then she'd step back, as if she were waiting for Nasr to do or say something—perhaps launch into an anecdote? It was hard to imagine what she thought he might be capable of among those people—men and women whose manners reflected a native possession of wealth that the suave and striving partners Nasr worked with couldn't fake. Becoming acquainted with members of this set might be considered an enterprising young person's dream, but Nasr was at a loss. He asked a few questions, hoping this would let the group return to its previous conversation, but once it did, Lillian would hook an arm through his and lead him to a new circle of strangers, to repeat the awkwardness.

Tonight, if George had no idea what his mother-in-law was talking about, he didn't show it—or, rather, Lillian didn't allow him to. She cast an admiring glance at Jameela and demanded introductions, and began chatting with her while the two men fell into the usual inquiries about work and workplaces. Nasr accepted George's invitation to fetch drinks from the bar and plucked Jameela's glass out of her hand (it was, he noticed with not a small measure of satisfaction, empty). When he returned to her side a few moments later, he found her asking Lillian if she was of Dutch ancestry. Lillian said she was from Buffalo, but her husband's people did indeed have Dutch connections. How had Jameela known? Jameela then explained the academy's connection to Edith Wharton—apparently, some characters in a novel were named van der Luyden.

"Imagine that," Lillian said, drawing the attention of a petite brunette in a soft gray dress. It was her daughter, Katharine, married to George and oddly resembling him somehow. Lillian's own husband, James, a less robustly aged figure with bushy white hair and red cheeks, was also called to join their group. He didn't seem entirely pleased about his family's possible literary connection, as if it suggested that his name was made up. By now, an audience had gathered around Jameela, and when asked, she could describe how the building they were standing in might have been differently furnished during the Gilded Age, what embellishments might have appeared here and there, and even how both Wharton and Ogden Codman were opposed to such flourishes. They preferred simplicity of arrangement and a measure of functionality.

Dinner was soon announced, to take place on yet another floor of the mansion. When seating assignments couldn't be found (Nasr's RSVP hadn't arrived—not surprising, as he hadn't sent it until yesterday; and, anyway, the plan tonight was to stop in at the birthday gala, and then meet Javaid for a late meal), the van der Luyden family made room at their table, which, like the others in the long dining chamber, was candlelit, with glistening silver cutlery and bright-white centerpieces of calla lilies.

Once they were settled, dinner—a spoonfully soft filet mignon with some sort of balsamic-vinegar reduction and crème fraîche—was too difficult to resist. Jameela, in a conspiratorial whisper, decided (for both of them) that they were hungry enough to eat here and again later with Javaid.

Nasr was seated beside her in such a way that he was forced

to spend much of the evening chatting with two of Lillian's other children, Jerome, the eldest son, and Henry, the youngest of the family—a Robert Redford look-alike whose long hair sat brightly about the collar of his black dinner jacket. Henry was in graduate school for film but had taken a leave to do some traveling—Spain, Tunisia, Cyprus. India was next on his list (of course), and he wondered if Nasr had any recommendations. Nasr suggested the big cities—Delhi, or Bombay if he was interested in the movie industry. Other people at the table had gone to India, and they protested. Oh, no, not the metropolises, they said. They recommended this or that "quaint village," perhaps without realizing they were referring to mid-sized cities, with populations in the millions, just as much pollution, and far fewer provisions for foreign tourists. Nasr was happy enough to let the focus drift away from him. He kept overhearing unsatisfyingly small snippets of Jameela's conversation with Lillian and Katharine. After a while, he saw Henry leaning in their direction, also trying to eavesdrop.

"I think what people—women who actually wear the veil— are saying is that feminism for them is always a question of priorities," Jameela said. "I mean, can you imagine someone coming to you and saying that the only way you'll feel liberated is if you conduct all your private and public activities wearing a bikini, which is what a shirt and pants feels like to some of these women, and that this exposure is the first step to feeling free?"

Lillian declared that she didn't believe any sort of freedom could be pursued until the whole thing was chucked off, and that until then, no one would see people so much as walking sheets of fabric. "Maybe I'm old-fashioned," she added with polite irony.

"No, I agree with you," Jameela said. "But these women have a point, too. All they're really asking is why start with our clothes? What about a little access to education? Voting rights? Why do we have to be revolutionaries with our bodies?"

"But, dear," Lillian said, a troubled note in her voice, "isn't it constricting on a basic level?"

"It might be to us, Mother," said Katharine, "but that's because we're not used to it. What Jameela is saying is that these women are—it's a standard of dress for them."

Where others might have left an old woman, especially one's hostess, to her opinions, Jameela pressed on. "Strange as it may seem," she said, "some women consider the veil absolutely essential to a happy"—here she did hesitate, but only briefly—"a happy home life."

"Oh?" Lillian said. "How is that?"

"Well, if you were a man, wouldn't you always be wondering what's under there?"

Henry burst out laughing. "That's certainly an interesting way of looking at it," he said to Jameela, eyeing her as though he wouldn't mind discovering her at the bottom of a burqa.

Lillian smiled, but indulgently now, as if the conversation had gone beyond her interest. "In any case, dear, you wear yours beautifully."

Here Jameela didn't, as Nasr expected, point out that the rupatta she was wearing was not really anything like a veil. And when another woman at the table asked for the name of the designer of her outfit, Jameela caught Nasr's eyes in mock alarm, as if to say our jig is up. "Yves St. Nobody, I'm afraid," she said with an embarrassed laugh.

A few moments later, when Katharine took Jameela to the ladies' room, Lillian leaned over to whisper, "Your fiancée is very charming, dear. A perfect complement."

After dinner, Nasr and Jameela followed the party into the ballroom, but waves of people came in after them, and they let themselves be pushed by the crowd into the far corner, under the fronds of a large palm. They obediently accepted champagne from a passing waiter, cheered with the other guests when the band struck up "Happy Birthday to You," and sang along as a massive white cake was wheeled out—its pencil-thin candles lit and their flames wavering on all four layers. They laughed along when Lillian made a joke about fire hazards, smiled like everyone else when she recruited her children and grandchildren to help with the blowing out of the candles, and happily contributed to the hearty bursts of applause that came at the end of each toast and speech.

During the last address, Jameela raised her glass and whispered, "To Naah-sur dear and guest," imitating, though not unkindly, Lillian's pronunciation of his name. "The vulgarians who got away with crashing the party."

Nasr clinked her glass. "For a vulgarian, you seem to have accumulated a number of admirers."

Jameela nodded. "I'm always a big hit with sixty-year-olds."

"Not just them." He pointed out Henry, who was near his mother at the front of the room, flinging his hair off a broad shoulder. "The son stopped me on the way to the washroom to ask about your status."

"Status?"

Nasr nodded. Actually, Henry had asked if Jameela had a sister—a twin sister.

"Did you tell him that I'm spoken for?"

Nasr nodded again. "He was deeply disappointed. Could have really used one of those loopholes à la medieval Islam."

"Mmm." To his surprise, there appeared on Jameela's face a look of plain embarrassment.

"I felt terrible for the poor chap," he said, wondering what would happen on her face now.

She grew serious and was quiet, but only for a moment. "Well, there is actually this thing, a sort of—a sort of temporary marriage that men and women who weren't related and therefore weren't allowed to see each other, let alone spend time together, would, could, set up."

"And how would one go about that?" Nasr asked. "I'm asking, of course, for young Henry."

Jameela smiled, her eyes immediately lively with good humor. "Well, let's suppose Henry and I were interested in, um, exchanging investment strategies—we would then declare our interest to our local imam. Once he sanctioned the merger, we'd be perfectly free to, well, mingle our portfolios."

"Very civilized."

"Don't you think?"

"How much mingling are we talking here, exactly?"

She shrugged. "As much as we'd like, I guess."

"But are we talking holding hands here, or—"

"No, no, a proper merging of assets, Naah-sur dear."

"And then what?"

"What do you mean?"

"Then you two would go your separate ways? Marry others. And the families are perfectly fine with this?"

"I don't know about families, but as far as jurisprudence goes, it was all permissible."

"Well, that's a relief."

She looked at him with an assessing eye. "You don't believe me?"

Nasr shook his head no, most definitely not.

Before she could reply, a waitress interrupted to serve them cake, and Jameela cut into hers with relish.

"Do you know what my mother said to me after your engagement was announced? One fine day, she suddenly says that if there was someone I wasn't telling her about, then I could consider marrying him. Even if he wasn't a Muslim, it was fine—as long as he was willing to convert, of course. You see that? For thirty years, there was only one possible path to a respectable life and a constant paranoia that I would screw it up, then suddenly all the rules get thrown out, one blink. Just don't embarrass us. And if there wasn't someone waiting around—if, contrary to all apparent expectations, I didn't have a disgraceful secret ready to spring on her—she was giving me *permission* to find him. Yes, yes, go ahead and have a life now. But of course all you can do in such a situation is be humiliated to disappoint her in this new way—sorry, Talat, no secret lovers."

"And you're sure about that?" Nasr asked.

"About what?"

"This not having any secret lovers business."

"I think I would know," she said with a faint smile.

"How about something in the tall, thin, European-looking variety—ring any bells?"

She turned to him and stared.

"Professor type, floppy hair, book bag, can't keep his hands to himself—"

Her confusion suddenly evaporated. "Oh, Sebastien?"

Nasr heard this confirmation with a curious dread—it was as though he'd played a joke on himself.

"Mmm, yes, Sebastien Savon," she continued, as though savoring a memory. She drew out each "s" as a hiss. "He was something. Very octopussy. But he was no professor—"

"A first love, then?" Nasr said.

"Very funny. No, more like a contact man. My in." And now something happened that Nasr recognized could only have happened with Jameela. You pressed open a door to her interests, and where you expected one thing—in his case, a secret romance with an older man—you encountered something entirely different and hardly to be believed. There had been a group on campus, she said, that was interested in reviving the tradition of the private library, and its members had been trying to persuade

261

the owners of those old city mansions to donate their properties to the university. The group had managed to get one, and they were petitioning for more. "No, really, it's true," she said, catching Nasr's expression. "The idea was to create a system of them, like here in New York. But really the best part was that hardly anybody would know about them. You could have them all to yourself, for hours—these perfect spaces, quiet and pretty, with books and armchairs and low tables, in these beautiful old town houses, where you can go and find yourself reading in what was once someone's fancy salon."

Nasr knew that it was true, of course.

"How do you know about Sebastien?"

"I spied on you," Nasr confessed, to his own surprise.

"Oh, of course." She nodded, thinking he was back to joking.

But her eyes narrowed as Nasr described the streets, the night (he added a fog to give it a moody feel), the long cold walk, her strange pit stop at a pharmacy, her blue coat with the furry white collar, the white boots. Finally, he could see that she believed him—the dark brownstone, with no lights, no sound, so you couldn't tell whether it was a bar, restaurant, strip club, who knows what—

"What were you going to do if it had been a strip club?" she asked.

"Bust the door down probably," Nasr said.

She barked a laugh and he joined in.

"What? You can't see that happening?" There was yet more helpless laughter, perhaps beyond what was flattering.

The ballroom was emptying, first imperceptibly but now more steadily. On the dance floor, a dozen tenacious couples lingered.

"The problem with champagne," Jameela said, after they turned over their plates and glasses to a nearby waiter, "is that it's like truth serum."

She turned to gaze out a window over traffic along Fifth Avenue.

"What's wrong with the truth?" Nasr asked.

She covered a yawn with the back of her hand. "There's a time and a place for it. Just as you said yesterday—something to be said for not disturbing surfaces."

"Maybe I was wrong."

Jameela shook her head no; there was a droop to one side of her mouth. She smiled, but the muscles provided insufficient scaffolding, and the corner drooped again. "Sometimes water should be left under bridges." There was a desultory tone in her voice, as though she, too, felt the clock ticking on the inevitable end of the evening. "Otherwise, it just gets too complicated."

"What if by complicating one thing, you can actually simplify something else, something more important?"

"Like what?" She was staring at him now, with not a bit of expectation.

A frond of the palm was grazing the top of her head, but she didn't seem to notice. They were a tiny island of two.

Nasr raised his hand and felt Jameela's eyes follow it as he pushed the frond aside. His hand then drifted to a lock of her hair. He pushed that aside, too, out of the path of those normally inquiring eyebrows. "Like what if I got out of it?"

Her face shifted, the eyes widened fractionally—whether from confusion or recognition, it hardly seemed worth knowing, for the lips he pulled toward him were warm and soft. The mouth was hesitant at first, then he felt it leaning toward his own, willing and pliant. Her rupatta grazed the backs of Nasr's fingers, and then he felt the cool panel of glass that he'd pressed her against. All those great big gestures and expressions, and she turned out to be this tiny and easy to squeeze. There was a ringing sound, a murmur of laughter, a long floating note of music, a burst of distant applause; something heavy but soft landed on Nasr's shoe. Her hands were on his chest, pulling away but also

263

clutching; foreheads resting against each other, a bitten lip, blinking eyes, her face too close for the features to come together, the breath in her chest pressing unsteadily into him. A phone is ringing: in the purse by his feet. The lips sway forward, and he catches them in his teeth, surprising the mouth into opening finally, then wider, the tentative flicker of a tongue, fleshy and slick. Still, the sound of a phone. Her gasping breath as she pulls away, the face turned aside. Nasr hears himself growl—feels the burst of her laugh against his chest. With one hand fixed on her hip, to keep her from breaking contact, he reaches down for the purse, but regrets this immediately, as the sound of the device, once she frees it, is lurid and brassy.

"Yes, this is she," she says, out of breath, heavy-lidded, not looking at him. But soon the sulky half-smile on her lips melts off in pure fright.

*T*here were two deep lacerations on the face—one across the cheek, another under the chin and down the front of the neck—that were now covered in bandages. His left hand and wrist were in a cast because of a broken thumb. His jaw wasn't broken, but the skin along it was swollen green and yellow, as if it had been trampled, and one eye barely opened, though you could see his pupil sliding from side to side in the narrow slit like a fish. There was a faint smell about him—urine mixed with something flowery or possibly soapy, and bright blood stains bloomed across the shoulders of his hospital gown as though he were still bleeding. "We did what we could when he was brought in," a nurse had told Jameela and Nasr on the way to his bedside. "But then he woke up."

Javaid's bed was in a dark corner of the ER, around which the curtains had been drawn. The overhead fluorescent panels were left off—as though someone had hoped he would drift back to sleep. But when the nurse let Nasr and Jameela in, Javaid immediately asked, "Can I go?"

At the sight of him, Jameela, a transformed figure in her headscarf, had taken an involuntary step back, and Nasr instinctively put an arm under her elbow to steady her. A moment later, she'd slipped out of his grasp and was by Javaid's bedside, concerned but composed. At Javaid's request, she turned on a light. Then she poured out a cup of water from a nearby pitcher and urged him to drink. The light restored a sort of solidity to his face. His flesh looked bruised now, badly, but no longer punctured and ghoulish.

Javaid couldn't be released without the authorization of a doctor, so Nasr, sensing a privacy growing around Jameela's ministrations and eager to be useful himself, left them to search for the attending physician.

"It's against hospital policy to release a person in your friend's condition," the doctor explained as he walked back with Nasr. He spoke in a careful voice, as though this was not his first time delivering the information. Javaid had made it clear that he did not want to be in the hospital any longer by refusing to sign any forms, including one that allowed for the administration of an IV. "He said it would ruin his fast tomorrow," the doctor said. He had a vaguely Eastern European accent and a soft, narrow face. "But, frankly speaking, a person with his injuries shouldn't be fasting in the first place. He's already verging on dehydration."

When they entered the curtained area, Javaid was sitting upright; he hardly leaned on his pillows. He didn't say a word while the doctor spoke of having admittance forms drawn up. It was very possible that Javaid would need to spend only one night in the hospital; he might even be released early the next morning, in less than twenty-four hours. When Javaid stared silently at the blank monitors beside his bed, the doctor looked over to Jameela but seemed unsure whether he should address her directly, and she certainly wasn't helping: her face under the headscarf was calm but unsmiling, and attentive only in Javaid's direction. Finally, he turned to Nasr and said, "I just can't in good conscience release him tonight," lamely, as though he knew he was speaking to the person whose opinion mattered least.

"We'll come back if we need to," Jameela said with sudden decisiveness. "Thank you."

"Without a release form," he told Jameela, "Mr. Husain would be leaving at his own risk, and I wouldn't be able to authorize any prescriptions. If there were complications tomorrow or another day, Mr. Husain would have to find a doctor and make an appointment to receive even the most basic treatment, and to do this he would, of course, need health insurance." He again glanced in Javaid's direction. Did Mr. Husain have health insurance in this country? he asked, somewhat rhetorically.

"I believe," Jameela said—she was adjusting the small blue light so that it wouldn't shine directly on Javaid's head—"it's well within a person's rights to accept or refuse treatment, isn't that correct?"

The doctor admitted that this was of course true.

Well, she continued, if the required tests had been done and it had been found that a patient didn't absolutely need an IV at the moment and the patient had expressed a wish to avoid unnecessarily invasive procedures, then the patient's wishes should be respected, should they not? Now, if the doctor's conscience was troubled, she added, perhaps he should find another way to provide his patient with the pain medication he might need. Surely there were over-the-counter options?

Looking more exasperated than annoyed, the doctor said he would give them all a little more time to decide.

As he left, the doctor drew Nasr outside the curtained area. "There is also the matter of the police report," he said quietly. "He really should file one tonight—these things have a way of getting forgotten." With a tip of his head, he indicated the uniformed officer at the far end of the ward who was leaning against a counter and chatting with a receptionist. "We've had a number of such incidents lately, and not one single filing, which to the police means nothing is happening that they can do anything about."

When Nasr returned to Jameela and Javaid, they were discussing who should be called: Javaid's parents, certainly, and perhaps Hamid Uncle, too, even though it was pretty late. Nasr volunteered to help. They gave him the phone numbers.

Then Jameela said to Nasr, "On second thought, I'll call my father tomorrow." Nasr nodded. Of course, whatever she thought was best. He was still obedient from the shock. But he noticed that Jameela was speaking now with an almost alarming composure. Her voice was formal, as though he were one of the outsiders against whom she must insulate herself. He sought her eyes out for recognition, but there was emptiness in them. And she hovered about Javaid with soothing sounds that it was impossible to begrudge. But the memory of their kiss still lingered, blotting out good sense, and despite himself Nasr wondered when he might speak to her again, really speak as they had in that radiant, twinkling ballroom. Now he saw that she was asking him something. Yes, of course, what did she need—oh, something for Javaid from the cafeteria. "There's probably nothing halal," she said, "but maybe a vegetarian meal?"

Grateful to be useful, Nasr rushed down the hallway and called Javaid's father, who, being a doctor himself, was immediately professional, with no trace of his usual nervousness. "Have they done an MRI, beta? Have any points of internal bleeding been established? Can the X-rays be sent to my hospital here?" Nasr didn't have the answers to many of his questions, and eventually Qamar Phupha asked for the attending physician's name. Nasr didn't know this, either, but he said he would call back with the information. In the meantime, the signs for the cafeteria had disappeared, he'd lost the trail, and now he was on a strangely dim floor with an empty, abandoned-looking hallway. Eventually, he found an elevator, then a nurse's station, and asked for directions. The hospital was the one near the masjid in Nasr's neighborhood, and with sudden inspiration he asked if Dr. Khan was on call tonight. No luck. In the elevator down to the cafeteria, he decided to call Malik at home. "Don't leave," Malik said. Like Javaid's father, he had come alert instantly.

At this hour, the cafeteria was reduced to an overly lit series of mostly empty glass counters. Nasr went to inspect the sandwich offerings, and felt his own head lurch sickly.

"Can I help you?" It was the policeman from upstairs. He was standing beside Nasr, bent at the waist, peering at the yogurts and fruit cups.

"No, thank you," Nasr said, and made to walk past him.

"Are you with the Husain party upstairs?" the officer asked, straightening. He was tall and thick-armed, with a block chin and shaved blond hair—up close he looked young, no more than twenty-five. Before Nasr could answer, he said, "Is Mr. Husain a resident of Manhattan?"

Nasr nodded, then shook his head, then stopped. He wondered if he'd been followed.

"What is your name, sir?"

Nasr hesitated again.

"Have you been in this country long?"

"Yes," Nasr said, finding his voice again. "I live here," he added more forcefully, then, not sure if this sort of questioning was legal, he chided himself for volunteering such information.

As though guessing the direction of his thoughts, the policeman said, "Well, then I'm sure you know that we have laws."

He was frowning, but this further exposed his age—he looked like a kid imitating an adult's disapproval. "We can't help you," he said, "or your friend if you don't work within our laws."

Nasr thanked him again and went to the cashier, but the officer lined up behind him. "You're not actually going to try to pay for that yogurt, are you, Stan?" the cashier said over Nasr's shoulder. She was a large woman in her sixties, with pink skin and almost pinkish hair. "I'm no freeloader, ma'am," the officer replied, familiar and affable. "You just keep getting the bad guys," she replied, in a motherly tone, "and let me worry about my drawer." The two of them continued chatting as she rang up Nasr's purchases.

After much coaxing, Jameela persuaded Javaid to take a few bites of the cheese sandwich and drink some juice. He seemed exhausted from the effort, and finally lay back on his pillows. Soon his eyes were closed, and Jameela began tidying up the remains of the meal.

"Can I talk to you?" Nasr whispered.

To his dismay, she was instantly suspicious. "What is it?"

He suggested they step outside, which was another mistake.

"You can tell me here," she said.

"There's a policeman waiting," Nasr said.

She showed no surprise at this information.

"The doctor said that if the officer leaves," Nasr continued, trying to keep his voice low, but she'd retreated to the other side of the bed and he was speaking over Javaid's sleeping form, "Javaid might lose his best chance to file a report and—"

"I don't want anything to do with them," Javaid said. His eyes were still closed, and he spoke through clenched lips.

Jameela patted his arm. "Why should you? Just rest," she said lightly, as if the matter wasn't worth discussing.

The curtain behind Nasr stirred. "Knock knock," Malik said. In his hospital coat, he looked stockier than usual, low to the ground and solid. "Assalaam'alaikum."

As Nasr made introductions, Malik checked the various monitors near Javaid's bed, striking up light conversation as he conducted a quick examination. While listening to Javaid's chest, he inquired where he was from. "Where in Pakistan?" he asked, and also could Javaid Sahib move these fingers here— very good, now like this? "My mother's side is from Lahore," Malik continued. Had Javaid Sahib ever been? Beautiful place. Truly the city of gardens.

Malik chatted on until the patient had finally slipped off to sleep. Then he drew Nasr and Jameela out into the hallway.

"Kiya hoowah?" he asked in Urdu, and out of some instinct the three of them kept their voices low as they explained that while nobody knew all the details, Javaid had obviously been attacked. It had happened near the masjid. He'd been left on the street, might have been unconscious for some time, but eventually someone had called the police.

Malik, too, seemed to know about the other incidents in the neighborhood and asked if Javaid had talked to the police. But when Jameela said, "He just wants to go home. Be away from all this attention," he didn't press the issue. His main concern, he said, was internal bruising, or bleeding. Javaid's condition was serious enough that one ought to be careful about moving him. Was there any way Jameela could persuade him to change his mind about staying at the hospital?

"You know, he can always make up those rozas," Malik said with semi-fatherly sternness. "I'm not even sure you're allowed to keep one in this state."

She had tried already, Jameela said, sighing. "We can take him out or he'll walk out. I think respecting his wishes is the least we can do for him."

Malik asked where Javaid lived, what floor, and whether his building had an elevator.

Harlem, the fifth, and no.

Malik smiled grimly. "I'll be right back," he said, directing them to the waiting area.

Nasr asked if he could get Jameela some coffee, a bit of food, but she declined. She dropped into a chair, and he took the seat beside her.

"You know he really should file that report," Nasr said.

"I tried," she said. She stared straight ahead. There were several other people in the room, variously interested in the late-night movie that was showing on the TV, black-and-white, with lots of overacting.

"If there's no report," Nasr continued, "there will be no investigation." He persisted, though he was conscious of having made an argument against this reasoning just a few weeks ago to Farah. Farah. Why was it that she would leave his mind so thoroughly sometimes? Whereas Jameela seemed to occupy a place so permanent and ingrained that, back in September when he had tried to dislodge her, he had had to work hard, fill his brain with so much other material—and that effort had succeeded only in pushing her deeper in. "I can call for another police officer," he said. "Let me help." His voice then changed. "Tell me what to do. We have to do something."

"Can we just not talk about this now, please," Jameela said.

Nasr felt his heart constrict. Of course, later. They would talk about it later, he assured her. He tried to take her hand, but she slipped it away to cup her hands together in her lap, and began whispering a prayer. The silk of her pajamas, at least the bit showing above the heel, was crushed and stained, a watery dark line running along the hem. Jameela remained so still and quiet that after a while Nasr wondered if she might have drifted off to sleep. Soon, he felt his own eyes drooping.

The kiss could be dismissed. Not easily, but the setting had been so suggestive—a ballroom, a band, a rich meal, not to mention the champagne. But his words—*Like what if I got out of it*—rang in his ears, as though he'd shouted them. He couldn't have, of course—shouted them, that is. Wasn't it possible, he wondered, that Jameela hadn't even heard? Or if she had, maybe she hadn't known what he'd meant? What *had* he meant? The silk suddenly stirred, and Jameela sprang up. Malik had returned with good news. He'd pulled some rank and found that he could arrange a release by accepting full responsibility for Javaid's care. But he'd do this, he said, only if Javaid agreed to come to their place for the night—and allow Malik to call for an ambulance to transport him.

Jameela didn't appear in the least bit grateful. She said she wasn't sure Javaid would agree, but she looked as if she herself wasn't convinced that this was a good idea.

"We'll tell the EMTs to keep the sound off," Malik offered, then turned from Jameela to Nasr with a puzzled expression.

"His wife's a doctor, too," Nasr said, hoping this would help.

"She won't mind," Malik said reassuringly.

But still Jameela hesitated, and Nasr suddenly knew what was troubling her. "Can she stay there, too?" he asked Malik.

"Of course!" Malik replied. "Rashida's already getting the guest rooms ready."

Jameela drew a breath and nodded, looking relieved to be consenting.

Javaid wanted to go home, first to his apartment, then to Montreal, as soon as possible. His lips hardly moved, and everything came out angry. Jameela asked Malik and Nasr if the two of them might have a moment alone and drew the curtains around Javaid's bed. The moment developed into an hour. Nasr got himself a coffee, and when he returned to the waiting room,

Malik came by to tell him that if they wanted an ambulance they really ought to get going. Nasr headed back to the ward.

There was a parting in the curtain. As Nasr approached, he saw Jameela dip forward and kiss Javaid's hand—so slowly and softly that he wondered if Javaid was asleep. But then there was a murmur, Javaid's deep voice, and Jameela's reply: "We'll do that, too—yes, all of it. Just get better first."

She loves him. Nasr knew he could have told himself that these actions were automatic—a show of loyalty, an instinctively feminine response. But no, there was love in the way she had urged Javaid to eat and drink and love in the way she was still holding his hand now.

Nasr coughed and stepped forward to announce that the ambulance was waiting.

They turned his way at the same instant. Jameela's hand slipped down into her lap, but neither looked caught out or disturbed. In the cab to the hospital, there had been an eerie, purposeful deliberation in the way Jameela had pulled a maroon scarf from her purse. Soon her hair and ears had disappeared, and after this she'd wiped her lips with tissue. For a brief moment, Nasr saw her mouth moving, the swift whisper of prayer, but for the rest of the ride the tightly wrapped profile had stayed turned away. He sensed now that what he'd seen was not just a transformation of demeanor or a change of costume—it was as if the tissue had cleaned away the past few hours.

"Good." She put on her coat and handed Javaid's to Nasr, speculating aloud that the EMTs would probably wrap him up in blankets. Unless he wanted it laid out on his chest? Did he? No, he didn't. And could Nasr let the nurse know that they were ready to go?

As the EMTs wheeled him out, Jameela continued talking. Could she come along in the ambulance? Dr. Khan had promised that the siren would be left off—was that still possible?

How long would the ride be? There was probably no traffic at this hour, right—though who knew with New York? Her voice wavered ever so slightly through this parade of chatter, but there was no real break in her composure, except that there were tears in her eyes, welling but not spilling, and her features were not so much calm as held steady, as though clenched in a sort of fury.

22

*T*here had, as it turned out, been other incidents. (Nasr learned this over the course of the next few days, but he had to piece the details together from different sources—some from Malik and Rashida, who admitted to prying, but mostly from Yasmine.) Jameela and Javaid had been spat at, back home and in New York—they were, in fact, pretty accustomed to this sort of reaction. Somebody'd thrown an egg once; another time, a couple of boys sprayed them with shaken-up beer cans. But mostly it had just been name-calling or simple threats, shouted out across street corners at rallies or from passing cars, muttered in grocery-store aisles, written with lipstick on their windshield in the mall parking lot: *dirty killers, paki fag, cowards, chauvinist, ugly mosquitoes, butchers, go home, fucking arabs, we'll get* *you back. How dare you, how dare you*—this from a fellow respectful tourist at Ground Zero who thought Javaid had dipped his head to say a prayer. At least she had apologized afterward.

This time the incident, according to Javaid, was a simple mugging. (Nasr heard the echo between these words and the ones he'd used to dismiss his own mugging, and he wondered if Leonard had anything to with what had happened to Javaid. But there was no way Leonard could have inflicted such wounds, he thought, reconsidering; at least not alone, he reconsidered again.) After breaking his fast at the masjid, Javaid had decided to stay until the Isha prayer. An hour later, as he was heading back to the subway, someone stopped him to ask for his money, and when he said he had only five dollars the guy struck him a few times and ran off. It was as simple as that, Javaid said. He'd been in the wrong place, perhaps with the wrong face, at the wrong time.

Nasr parted with Jameela and Javaid at the hospital that night—he tried to go along, but Jameela climbed deep into the ambulance beside Javaid, and Malik blocked him off at the door, urging him to rest and come over in the morning. "You're already so close to home," he pointed out. In bed, Nasr fell into a well of sleep. He felt himself plummeting down an airless shaft, deeper and deeper, and just when he thought he might touch the bottom and get some actual rest, something hauled him up into the acidic sunshine of his apartment. He was sure he'd closed his eyes for just moments, but in fact hours had passed. On the side table, his cell phone was ringing. Farah had never called him at this hour, and it was bizarre to hear her voice in daylight. His eyes ached, and he kept them closed through her words of concern and alarm. "Should I come down?" she asked, and wondered aloud about buses and flights. She was serious. The light behind Nasr's eyelids shifted from red to orange. He felt a spike of admiration for this bounty of spirit. It suited her. He knew he ought to acknowledge it, that it ought to be pleasant to think of how Farah might rise to be hardy and capable, that a few days ago he would have offered to call the airlines or find the bus schedules. But he hardly knew what to say. Fortunately, she mistook his silence for discretion. "Thank God they have you there to help them," she said, and he was grateful for the steadfastness of her faith in his abilities. But after he hung up, after he surveyed the almost comic wreckage of his apartment (mugs of tea scattered in corners, the hastily unplugged iron parked on the dining table, Jameela's gaping suitcase, her makeup bag wedged in the bathroom radiator), and especially when he was back in Jameela and Javaid's presence, he began to resent the role being assigned to him.

At the Khans', Nasr was greeted at the door by Malik, looking tense and concerned. He said that a cab had been called to take Javaid and Jameela to Javaid's apartment. He and Rashida hadn't been able to persuade them to stay another night. "At least I got him to postpone this driving back to Montreal tomorrow business," Malik whispered. In the living room, Javaid and Jameela were sitting beside each other on the sofa, poised and upright. Javaid already had his coat on; white bandages showed under his collar, and the white skullcap was back in place. Jameela's face under her headscarf was weary and meek. Her shirt fell off her shoulders, and she hardly looked like herself, though her expression lightened momentarily when she saw that Nasr had brought her suitcase. She immediately went off to change out of the oversized clothes she must have borrowed from Rashida.

The atmosphere in the room was somber—how could it be otherwise, with anxious hosts and ungrateful guests? Rashida and Malik made a few more attempts to persuade Javaid to stay a bit longer.

Javaid thanked them. He managed a smile, as though he'd remembered he probably should. His face was slightly more mobile now, though a big area around his right eye remained darkly bruised and stiff.

*I*n the cab to Javaid's apartment, Nasr offered to let Jameela and Javaid stay at his place, then to make flight arrangements, then to drive with them to Montreal. But the only help they wanted was with the packing, and the only items Javaid had decided to take were his books. The rest of the stuff Nasr was welcome to, or should get rid of in the easiest way possible.

Javaid lived in an old building, with grimy radiators in its cramped stairwell. He asked Jameela to please go ahead, up to his apartment, and when she finally did he began the slow climb, wincing around the turns, sweating with concentration, refusing to turn back or rest, accepting Nasr's help only when his balance was threatened.

At the landing to the apartment, Nasr nearly carried him to the futon, and Jameela promptly made him recline. The place was dark, with dusty windows. There were a couple of tall, unfinished wood bookcases lined with thick-spined math and physics textbooks and heavy black binders. In the middle of the room, planted across from the metallic-framed futon, was a large TV. The walls were empty, save for a calendar from a bank. The only colorful item in the whole place was a blue-and-yellow janamaaz spread on the floor of a blank corner, ever ready for prayer. In other corners, there were boxes, some taped and others gaping open, many marked with Jameela's big, blocky handwriting.

With Javaid on the futon, there was nowhere else to sit. Nasr and Jameela stood to discuss how many boxes might fit into the car and what was left to be done.

This is what she'd kept their conversation to all day, which was not so unexpected, Nasr supposed. When she said, "The boxes can be gotten at the post office," that's just what she meant—and not that she wished they could have a moment alone, to talk privately or openly, to forgive, or renew, or at least acknowledge what had happened between them. At first, Nasr tried to catch her eye: No, we must have it out. Fine, you love Javaid, but you cannot deny the kiss. But the more she spoke to him in this cooperatively impersonal manner, the more Nasr's natural inclination to follow the lead of others took hold. Now he heard himself agree that, yes, three boxes ought to do it.

"I think the rest of the stuff will fit into bags. Don't you?" she asked Javaid. His arm was flung over his eyes, but he gave a weak yes. Jameela nodded and returned her attention to counting books.

"Have you guys eaten?" Nasr asked.

Jameela shook her head but didn't look up.

"Let me at least get something. It'll be easy—"

"We're fasting," she replied. A moment later, and less sharply, she added, "We're fine. Thanks."

"Of course," Nasr said. "I meant for later." But this wasn't true. He'd forgotten it was Ramzaan, forgotten so thoroughly, in fact, that he failed to feel guilty for not having kept a fast himself.

He stood around for another several minutes, but neither Javaid nor Jameela invited him to stay, and soon the only thing to do was leave.

The next morning, Nasr woke to a tap on his bedroom door, or so he thought. The room was faintly lit. A pigeon was at his window, clawing the air-conditioning unit. Jameela was no more gone today than she had been yesterday morning, yet he found himself newly conscious of the emptiness on the other side of his door and of the long, dark length of his apartment. One summer day on that last trip to Lucknow, Nasr had returned to his family home only to be sent to find Jameela. After looking for her on the first two floors, he was told by a servant that Jameela Bibi had been seen going upstairs, to the rarely used rooftop. At each of the four corners of the roof, there was a pointed white dome, with black water stains running down its sides. Under each dome, there was a small room with blue double doors. The first two rooms, he discovered, were for storage—big black trunks were stacked to the ceilings—and the third had clearly served as someone's birdhouse, with empty cages and dried-up droppings.

He found Jameela in the fourth, sitting at a desk reading a book. "Hey," she said, cheerfully explaining that she'd escaped her relatives and had been hiding out here ever since. To enter the room, one stepped over the bottom edge of the door frame, a step so high that Nasr felt as though he were walking into a box. A whole posse of aunts and parents waited downstairs, he informed her—along with afternoon tea. "Oh, good. I'm starving," Jameela said, brushing dust from her hands and sleeves. This room, she told Nasr, had belonged to an aunt of his who'd died as a child. In addition to the desk and chair, there was a wardrobe at the back, and a string cot in the corner. A small high window let in some sun, but not a bit of breeze; and at this late-afternoon hour the stuffiness was nearly unbearable. Nevertheless, as they left, Jameela looked back and sighed. "That's all you need—a little place to yourself." Nasr had never seen anyone so happy and pleased to be alone. Maybe this was why when he saw her with Javaid in the hospital room, or yesterday in Javaid's apartment, or actually in any room Javaid was in, he thought of her as merely visiting—as being away from her true habitat, where someone like Javaid would surely not be found.

It was Monday, so Nasr rose to get ready for work, but his

mind remained open and exposed, and strange thoughts came to him. He wondered what Jameela was telling her parents about where she was staying. He spotted her sleeping bag in the hallway. He'd forgotten it yesterday when he collected her suitcase. Would she call today to ask for it? And where had she slept in Javaid's sparse apartment? Then, while riding the crowded subway, he couldn't help wondering if she'd risen early this morning, before the sun, to make Javaid tea.

During the course of the long, rainy day that followed, Nasr tried calling Javaid's cell phone several times, but no one answered. The next day, he got a call—they were ready to go, Jameela announced, like a secretary making an appointment with a courier. Would he mind coming by tomorrow?

Nasr took the next morning off from work, and with Jameela's help he brought the few pieces of furniture in Javaid's apartment down to a covered part of the sidewalk in front of the building. After an hour of heavy lifting and working together side by side, Jameela turned to him, while taping signs to various items ("1 yr old. Please take before it rains"). They were perfectly alone on the street, yet all she had to say was that Javaid's toaster was actually new—not a year old. It was then that Nasr began to feel as though he'd been made a fool, not just since the night in the hospital but from the moment Jameela arrived in New York. Those hours they'd spent touring the city—she had no right to act that way, to be so warm and willing. Not if she felt this way about Javaid. And this effort of hers to play down what had happened at the gala, to imply that it shouldn't be blown out of proportion or misconstrued, was not so much her taking the high road as being her usual risk-nothing self.

At noon, Nasr retrieved Javaid's car from the garage, then helped Javaid down the winding steps of five stories and into the passenger seat. Before getting into the driver's side, Jameela bid Nasr the formal goodbye that her fiancé used these days: "Allah-hafiz." God is the protector. May God protect you. May

He keep you safe, where you are and where you're going. It had many interpretations. She was firm and solemn, holding his eye. May He keep you where you should be. Away from me, her eyes seemed to add.

Then they were gone. As Nasr watched the little black car pause at the corner of the block, as if hesitating, then plunge into the stream of traffic, he felt a familiar sensation rising up in his chest. It was much like the one he'd experienced long ago in London while listening to Jameela's frantic messages—a feeling that he mistook for relief.

It was Leonard's opinion that Javaid was lucky in his injuries. Nasr saw the man a couple of days later on the street outside his apartment; the bulky figure sauntered over with smiling familiarity: "Hey, pal. You live round here?" Nasr's renewed wariness was immediately assuaged by Leonard's cough—he was clearly an ailing and weak man, not at all capable of inflicting serious injury on a person half his age. Leonard did, however, know what had happened to Javaid; the neighborhood was apparently abuzz with the news. "You know that guy?" he asked, in a disconcertingly penetrating way. Nasr said no, but Leonard didn't look convinced. The alley that night had been empty of cars but full of shadows. The men—there were three, Leonard said, without a note of uncertainty—had a baseball bat, and yet Nasr's "compatriot" had walked down the street as though he were in his own living room, hardly paid attention to anything around him, didn't notice that others had taken note of his cap. "That thing was so bright," Leonard said. "Like a big damn advertisement. Oh, thanks, man." He accepted Nasr's cigarettes almost absently. "I told you. I told you all to be careful, man. It's hunting season." All three of the men had been meaty and young. They'd taken turns punching Javaid, and when he fell to the ground, they kicked him in the stomach and used the bat across his back. Afterward, one had straddled him and pissed into his face.

*E*id was the following week. Nasr didn't go to the namaaz. In his office, the day was a non-event as usual, but the masjid experienced record crowds and security. Malik said that even the case for Rashida's sunglasses had been inspected on their way in. The Khans were throwing a party that night, a big event with visiting parents and extended family. Nasr declined the invitation. It was a busy time for him at the office, the final push before the holiday lull—busy enough that he'd decided it was fair to drop the fasting altogether. In truth, he relished the deadlines and hastily convened meetings and short tempers (his own and others'). And what a tremendous relief it was to rejoin his friends and spend long lunch hours talking too much and drinking just enough to simplify his thoughts.

Farah continued to call every day, and as Nasr could provide few updates on the Khans or on Shahida's wedding plans, she did much of the talking, but her focus was on Javaid's condition. A hairline fracture had been detected in his collarbone, and his shoulder would need a cast. The swelling in his face had gone down, and one set of his stitches would be coming out in a week. Jameela Baji was devoted to his recovery, and the two of them were inseparable, as they should be. Farah's concern struck Nasr as genuine and therefore noble—in fact, there was an almost grotesque contrast between her calls and his mother's, the content of which had already returned to the wedding, since it was merely a couple of weeks away.

Farah no doubt assumed that Nasr had continued to keep the fasts, but she didn't ask about his eating. He waited, in these phone calls, for her to mention Malik or the gang, and inquire why he hadn't seen them in so long, especially for Eid. But she didn't bring them up, either.

"You're not working too hard on purpose, are you?" she said one day with fascinating astuteness, and then observed that whenever something like this happened, it was easy to become angry or feel responsible, but such feelings were of no use to anyone.

"I'm sorry," Nasr blurted out in reply, without knowing exactly where he was headed.

"For what?" Farah's voice was as clear as a bell, not a ring of suspicion.

"I'm—" he began, then swerved away. "I'm sorry that you were not the first to meet the Khans."

"Don't be silly." She told him she was proud of him for having the foresight to call Malik. And besides, she added, letting out a laugh, Jameela Baji had confirmed to her what she'd guessed—that the Khans had excellent taste in all matters, and even their children were very pretty, like little dolls. Jameela Baji had also said that Rashida was rather beautiful in a Shabana Azmi sort of way. "But I fully excuse you for not telling me this."

Another day, she interrupted her own inquiries into Nasr's well-being and, with much hesitation, brought up the matter of the honeymoon. It seemed that people had been pressing her for details: When would they go? For how long? Would they come back to Montreal or go straight to New York? "I told them that you were surprising me. I hope it's okay," she said, filling the pause that had opened after her question, a silence during which Nasr was contemplating whether or not to admit that he hadn't given the matter any further thought.

Farah's charms all came through in her voice—the delicate hesitations, the boldly delivered admonishments, the shyly offered suggestions, the breathless enthusiasms, and now this strain of wise pragmatism. In each new conversation, he found her shifting rhythms both surprising and familiar, and the sounds served as guideposts back to the person he was just a few days before. When Farah's face finally came back into focus in Nasr's mind, it returned as a face he was acquainted with, one whose mysteries were available to him.

*T*he following week, the Khans invited Nasr to a post-Eid party, which turned out to be a sort of send-off. Rashida had a cake made—"Congrats Nasr and Farah (in absentia)." The party was supposed to be for friends only, but in the case of the ever-generous Khans, this meant there were more than thirty people in attendance. The conversation was just as it had been during earlier dinners—teasing, easy. Various people asked how Javaid was doing. The fact that Javaid had vague plans to return to Pakistan drew the most interest, though the general feeling was that one shouldn't retreat. That was something one's parents could have, might have, considered, but now, let's face it, our generation was just as American as anyone else; and being American was not about retreating—it was about establishing new settlements. This hunker-down-and-take-care-of-our-own mentality sent the wrong message, someone said. Yeah, why should we act as if there were something wrong with us? someone else demanded. It's only because we're beating them at their own system that they're so scared of us. How many hospitals have more Dr. Khans and Alis than Smiths and Joneses? Yes, but the one thing we don't do well is PR. And PR is what it's all about. Need more marketing whiz kids on the front lines. Working for whom—the office of Allah? Why not? Can't beat the benefits. No, but seriously, it's the imam situation—the more we keep hiring these Arab fellows from abroad, who can hardly speak a word of English, let alone formulate a media-savvy response, the more we look like self-contradicting idiots. Or just plain sneaky. As though we have nothing in common with anyone we live around—or, if we do, now it looks like infiltration. I mean, the Arabs are not *our* ruling élite. Yeah, aren't they only something like twenty percent of the world's Muslim population? What I mean is these maulana-wallahs are supposed to be educating my children, but I'm having to remind *them* that probably a press release is in order when something happens— like, for example, the attack on this poor guy Javaid. And that this official statement should probably not include a non-sequitur reference to the imam's own pet concerns—the Zionist control of Palestine, or how the Muslim Brotherhood is a misunderstood institution. It's true, very true—somebody should remind the Christians that we basically believe in what they believe in. We even give them the virgin birth, for God's sake! We do? Oh, but it's just the usual learning curve—all this stuff will get better sorted out when there are imams and such from our generation, home-growners. (Careful whom you say that around. Listen, that's the least of my worries—I'm sure my FBI record grows every day, what with all those trips to the halal grocery store I have to make, thanks to Rashida's extremely short-term memory. Hey, I'm not the one demanding a breaking of culinary frontiers with every meal.) Well, the parents didn't know what they were doing, bringing those guys over. They hardly ever do, someone said, sighing.

But the matter of Javaid was dropped just as effortlessly as it had been taken up. The new Pakistani dramas that had recently been released on DVD were more engaging. Arré, it's all coming to us, someone joked, why go back now?

There was nothing remarkable or new about this conversation, yet Nasr heard every word of it with impatience. What used to sound like sophistication now held the taint of shallowness and insulation. He heard intolerance in their easy dismissals, an intolerance for complexity and difficulty. They were like children: fickle, untested, whining; and in their jokes about the parents' ineptness, there wasn't, as Nasr had once thought, grudging affection or admiration, so much as renunciation and betrayal. They rode high above, on a splendidly paved road, yet they complained constantly about the view. Compared with those original adventurers of the first generation, who had come here bewildered and ill-equipped, faced wild thickets instead of well-worn paths and cut through them with difficult and perhaps bad decisions, these people were connoisseurs of mere taste and decorum, facile consumers and inheritors of spoils—shabby echoes. They would believe what they needed to believe; everything and everyone would be foreign to them, or familiar, depending on what was convenient. Had he become one of them? Nasr wondered with a strange, sudden pang, knowing the answer. Perhaps this was what Jameela had been trying to tell him, back in June.

PART *two*

23

*T*here are moments in life when one experiences exquisite and piercing clarity, and with it extreme calm. It would be surprising if the period leading up to one's wedding were to produce such a feeling in a person, but in Nasr's case it somehow did. Actually, his sense of calm had been building for a few weeks, but it crystallized at his bachelor party, which took place in New York a couple of days before he left for Canada. He had told his friends to do what they had to do to him now and then prepare to behave themselves, for there would be no time set aside for non-PG events in Montreal. The "party," such as it was, had begun as a four-hour dinner to which girlfriends and wives were invited. Afterward, Nasr and the guys went to a bar and from there to a new fashion strip club, where the dancers peeled off supposedly original haute-couture designs. By the time they arrived there, Nasr felt worn out. He sat at the back of the booth with Pete, trying to sober up and letting their other friends take turns telling each new dancer that he was the groom. From that short distance, just the length of the table, the whole thing seemed as if it were happening on television. The bodies of the women lost all the advantages of proximity—their skin was too evenly tanned and smooth, shiny like plastic, and their movements too effortless. They were about as interesting as gymnasts. He said as much to Pete, who didn't disagree but raised his glass and replied, "Welcome to the death of your imagination, my friend."

There are, of course, different varieties of calm. One that grows from within, radiates out of inner stillness, and is unresponsive to external stimuli. This calm is stable, unshakable, unimposed. And then there is the stillness of a heavy lid on a bubbling pot. Nasr was under no illusion that his equilibrium was of the former variety, but it didn't feel like that of the latter, either. His was a calm that required a policing of thoughts: he was obliged to find avenues to acceptable conclusions, yes, but his state of mind was not fragile or churning.

He confirmed this a few days later when he arrived in Montreal to a house in a frantic state, everyone caught up in preparations, with panicky errands and unforeseen shortages requiring immediate response. The more they bustled and fretted, the more he felt attuned to the nature of each person's needs: for attention, agreement, and sympathy. When viewed in this way, Montreal seemed circumscribed and ordered—pleasant enough that Nasr considered, for the first time in years, what it might be like to return and settle down here, to live among people whose motives were so transparent, and needs so simple.

The one person whose motives were still murky as a moat was Jameela, of course, whom Nasr had yet to see. For a while, it had been tempting to think that she had somehow bewitched him in New York, come up with a new way to interfere and throw him off course, but this logic wasn't ultimately satisfying. Nothing was. The kiss, he decided, was his mistake, an accident, a misguided consummation of the festive atmosphere, of champagne and curiosity. He and Jameela had finally experienced that long-awaited collision of their frank selves. He'd seen what was behind the brocaded curtain. Yes, at times the glimpse had been exciting, but the excitement, he saw now, was in the unveiling rather than what was unveiled, in the speculation of what could be there rather than what actually was. And, in the end, the encounter had, frankly, been disappointing (a secret interest in libraries?), but not disastrous. In fact, he and Farah were closer than ever. He would never understand Jameela, and it was best to stop trying. By the time Nasr arrived in Montreal, he was sure he'd sufficiently boarded himself up (again) from her confusing assaults. It was over—whatever it was.

This conviction sustained him even after he learned the news that had occupied the community's attention for the past few days: Javaid and Jameela had announced that after a small, simple wedding in March, they would move to Pakistan. Good, he thought, with all the defiance and challenge of a disbeliever. Go.

Nasr and Yasmine were on a quick run to the cake decorator's, waiting at a traffic light downtown, when she, gazing out her window, said, "They looked at some apartments down here. Jameela said they were even talking about buying a place." She turned to him now. "Don't you think you should talk to her?"

"About what?"

"About all this Karachi stuff."

"Why me?"

Yasmine opened her mouth to say something, clamped it shut, then finally said, "I don't know." She returned her attention to her legal pad, which had a master list, written in a meticulously neat hand, of all the errands that needed to be done before the various "big days." They drove in silence, but a few moments later she let out what seemed to Nasr an almost wistful sigh.

"I know Ammi pushed it hard," Nasr said, "but, you know, Javaid was never really right for you."

"Well, yeah, I know that," Yasmine replied. She seemed both embarrassed and surprised.

"But I mean, Ammi can be very—"

"All these parents are going to have to face the fact that people decide for themselves whom they're going to marry. It's just the way it's going to be. I mean, even you didn't exactly do what she wanted."

"What do you mean?"

"You decided on Farah without her consent. Jameela was always reminding me of that."

Nasr's first thought was: I did? What a funny interpretation of events, that his arranged marriage had nothing to do with his mother.

"What, exactly, happened in New York?" Yasmine asked.

"Happened?" The car jumped forward. He'd pressed the accelerator too hard.

"When Jameela left here, the plan was that Javaid was going to get another job. They were just going to move him out and come back."

"Guess he changed his mind after getting attacked," Nasr offered cautiously.

Yasmine shook her head. "I asked her about that. She said that wasn't it." There was a strange shrewdness to her face suddenly.

"What could it be, then?" he asked, letting an irritable note seep into his voice.

"She wouldn't say," Yasmine said. "Just clammed up."

Nasr shrugged. By the next traffic light, his sister was describing the sort of cake she and their mother had ordered: three creamy white tiers in a basket weave, real flower petals adorning each layer.

After some casual investigation, Nasr discovered that the community's attitude toward Javaid's plan to return to Pakistan had shifted radically in the past few weeks. Now everyone was brimming with encouragement. "What kind of place has this become when a boy is risking his life just to attend a namaaz?" Javaid's mother was known to have asked in a number of drawing rooms. Even Nasr's mother, perhaps now that Javaid's plans had no bearing on where Yasmine would live, thought returning to one's native land was an innovative idea. "Why not?" she mused airily. That these plans now included Jameela didn't seem to disturb her one bit.

Nasr's following afternoon was consumed by the inspection of garlands (to make sure the gardenias and roses were sufficiently plump) and with the search for candles that were the same linen-white shade as the centerpieces. Both tasks seemed not only tiresome but also the symptoms of a larger pettiness— a persistent fixation on things that couldn't possibly matter. And Nasr's irritation was further complicated by the fact that it was his "turn" with Masood Chacha—that is, to take him out of his mother's hair. In every shop, Nasr's uncle treated the person behind the counter like a cheat. "When were these flowers cut?" he asked of the devoutly cheerful florist, who had cooed over her own arrangements as she brought them out. "Last night? But why not this morning?"

At least Masood Chacha was useful in one respect. He seemed to know the inside story of Javaid's plans and was indiscriminate with gossip. He told Nasr how Javaid's grandfather, Saleem Ahmed, had amassed a small fortune in Karachi with a towel-manufacturing business; the man had no sons, and Masood Chacha suspected that Javaid would be groomed to take over. Although Masood Chacha could not have been more than two years old at the time, he claimed to remember the very day, in the fateful Partition year of 1947, that Saleem Sahib left for Pakistan. "You wouldn't think that man was capable of asking for an extra roti for himself, let alone building a business from less than nothing in an unknown land. When people started hearing that he had gained a fortune that doubled itself every few years—Arré, what a shock!" He smacked his forehead. "And all this based on the simple human need for a towel!"

Nasr also learned that while there had been no public objections from Hamid Uncle and Talat Auntie, Jameela's parents had originally withheld their blessing for the engagement on the condition that the plans to move to Pakistan be dropped. The recent change of mind had, therefore, led to considerable tension in the Farooqi home. "But they shouldn't have made such a demand in the first place," Masood Chacha said chidingly. "Wives go where their husbands are."

Nasr heard this—a previously innocuous fact of the lives and marriages he knew, a reality he'd never before questioned—and bristled. "Why does that have to be true?" he said. But to his further annoyance, Masood Chacha's eyes lit up with a connection.

"This is my feeling exactly, beta. The couple should be deciding together where to go—and that place should be Delhi, where there are prime markets in toilet linens." He went on at length about these prime markets, but concluded with a sigh: "Plus in Pakistan our Jameela is going to be smothered in nonsense."

Nasr didn't know quite what to make of this. His own experience of Pakistan was limited: a few days in a hot, humid climate where one stayed sequestered with one's relatives in the single room in the house that was air-conditioned. He certainly didn't trust Masood Chacha's impressions, but he couldn't help agreeing: Jameela no more belonged in Pakistan than she did in hijaab.

*F*or the rest of that afternoon, Nasr waited on the sidelines as the women of the house rushed to and fro between the first- and second-floor bathrooms, showers, and ironing boards. Treating the preparations like a spectator sport, Masood Chacha walked around pointing to his wristwatch and calling out to the women: "Be quick, be quick, ladies. Your final inspection is coming!" When he spotted Saira with a towel on her head, chasing after a half-dressed daughter, he said, "Your husband and I are just poor, blind men, Saira Begum—very easy to please. But the Nawab of Montreal has a most discerning eye." He had, in fact, developed many nicknames for Hamid Uncle, whose expertise on aesthetics was famous: the Sheikh of the Shalwar, the Badshah of the Gharara.

But once he arrived, Hamid Uncle didn't supply the usual commentary or suggestions for improvement. Beside him, Talat Auntie was decked out in a dark-green sari of shiny silk, her hair massively piled up and threaded with strings of pearls. But her expression was also strained and drawn, and she looked positively relieved when she was called upstairs to assist Yasmine with her new rupatta. The Farooqi family's odd demeanor was most dramatic in Jameela. She wore a shalwar suit of pale green with long sleeves. The kameez hung about her frame loosely and had a billowy waist, as though it were her mother's size. There was a thick white scarf covering her hair, and lightly wound over it was the suit's filmy green rupatta. There were no ears exposed that could have taken jewelry, no neckline to show off a chain—

even her fingers were bare of the blocky rings that could usually be found on them. Her lack of expression brought out the lines on her face.

After another half hour of preparations, the women finally assembled in the living room wearing, as was customary on such occasions in honor of the color of the henna, nine shades of green—from lime to seaweed. They inspected one another critically, the older ones putting the finishing touches on the young. Nasr's mother was disappointed in her daughters' timid sense of self-assembly. "Arré, what is this fashion of keeping to such a bare face?" she could be heard asking Saira as the group headed out. "At your ages, I was fighting with my mother for the smallest chance to wear lipstick."

*F*or the next two hours, it seemed as though three of the men gathered around the television were trying to ignore or endure the fourth: Masood Chacha. He spent half this time attempting to draw out Hamid Uncle (whose attention remained, just as tenaciously, glued to the screen) and the rest complaining to Nasr and his brother-in-law, Rizwan, about the country in which he was a guest. Its people were fat, its shops disappointing and overpriced, its monuments unmoving, and its news coverage of the terrorist attacks that had taken place on the Indian Parliament in mid-December atrocious, even insulting. "Arré, I had half a mind to call up Delhi directly just to ask someone to read me the newspaper!"

According to Masood Chacha, Canada's only redeeming feature was Niagara Falls. "The number-one honeymoon spot in the world," he told Nasr, as part of chiding his nephew's choice of Vancouver. "Number two if one is being fair and counting the Taj."

Hearing this, Nasr suspected that his uncle was behind the trouble he had in planning the honeymoon, which had become yet another issue to be negotiated with the parents. Italy was deemed by Nasr's mother as too far to be going "at a time like this," especially when "the top honeymoon spot in the world" (short of the Taj) was within Canada's own borders and "we" (his mother had actually, for once, lumped herself in with the Canadian masses) even had the good side of the Falls. If the happy couple wasn't interested in Niagara, Mr. Ansari had argued, well, there was also Quebec City to consider. But Nasr had managed to slip through all these recommendations. He'd found an exclusive country inn on Vancouver Island, an hour west of Victoria, in a town called Sooke, and he'd put down a non-refundable deposit. He and Farah would still be within the country, but as far away as possible. "How nice," Farah had said last week when he told her, and "It certainly sounds exotic" with enthusiasm or irony—he couldn't quite tell.

Presently Masood Chacha and Rizwan were debating which locale might be considered the world's number-three honeymoon spot.

"This isn't much of a bachelor's party for you, beta," Hamid Uncle whispered, leaning over with a rueful smile.

"Oh, it's okay," Nasr said.

Hamid Uncle had been silent for so long, and so intent upon the nature channel's offering (*Tide Pools: The Soup of Life*), that Nasr was surprised when he took the hookah from his lips and asked when Nasr's friends were arriving in town.

Nasr told him he was having brunch with them all tomorrow at their hotel, before the evening's festivities.

"They will have never seen a wedding like this before," Hamid Uncle said, and Nasr assured him that, yes, they were all very curious.

Then, all of a sudden, Hamid Uncle began to apologize. He

said that he had hoped to have a poet read at the Valima—in honor of the literary interest he shared with Nasr's father. But with the visa situation it was impossible. He shook his silvery head. "Those days are gone. Lucknow left with your father, and we are never to go back," he said in a thick voice. He pulled out a handkerchief, and Nasr looked away to let him wipe his eyes.

After a moment, Hamid Uncle leaned over again and patted his arm. "Beta, I know you are very busy. But may I ask one request? It is about Jameela, if you could speak to her about this—"

"Nasr is in agreement with me, Hamid Bhai," Masood Chacha said. "Your daughter should exchange these Pakistan plans for Hindustan."

Nasr shook his head in denial, and Hamid Uncle accepted this with a mild smile. "Of all people, Masood, my daughter has her own mind. She has made her choice."

"Still, as the father you must say something."

Hamid Uncle took a deliberate puff of the hookah, as though he were above the fray. But a little later, when Masood Chacha turned the conversation to bin Laden and began musing that nobody could know yet what effects his "victory" would have on the young people, that it had given many of them purpose, Hamid Uncle roared to life.

"Purpose?" he said with disgust. "Purpose is an illusion." He seemed all of a sudden to be addressing Nasr, as he had that evening back in October. "Islam knows the value of error. And if the mistake is genuine, beta, if it is a true misjudgment, then it can always be—" Hamid Uncle broke off, abruptly speechless, but his lips were trembling, as though vibrating with the words he hadn't been able to say. The room was quiet for a moment, then everyone's attention turned back to the TV.

All at once Nasr perceived the nature of Hamid Uncle's problem. He was a man whose hands were tied. He would support his Jameela publicly—how could he not, after his own past?—but when he spoke of intolerant people, he meant his future son-in-law, and when he spoke of people who wouldn't listen to reason, he meant his own daughter. So he was asking for help, for Nasr to speak to Jameela, and he was giving Nasr the words he might use to persuade her to stay. Even in desperation the only route available to his nature was this indirectness.

24

*N*asr supposed he wasn't the only man in the living room relieved to see the women troop in. One by one, they came up the steps, looking tired. All, that is, except Nasr's mother, who floated around the corner, pink with pleasure. Her eyes fixed on him with approval.

"I take it it went well?" Nasr said.

"Look at how they made these," she replied, holding up a small terra-cotta dish. It was decorated in green and pink satin, with silver sequins, and filled with mehendi, as the lush green odor that rose up confirmed. "Just like home—exactly."

"Ammi is so giddy, you'd think she were getting married," said Saira. Over the years, Nasr's older sister had grown stout, and she treated everyone with an almost professional motherliness. She stood in the hallway now, with her youngest daughter draped across her shoulders, and the middle one clinging to her leg. "Rizwan, could you please," she said, transferring the sleeping girl expertly in order to attend to the merely sleepy one.

Masood Chacha's wife, Asima Chachi, followed with her infant son. "Assalaam'alaikum," she sang to the room in a mild, lilting voice. She was a tiny woman with light-brown hair and pale skin and a face that you could already say, though she couldn't be much older than Nasr, had been striking once. Unlike Saira, she never asked or seemed to expect her husband to attend to their child.

"For us"—the sound of Talat Auntie's voice came from the stairwell—"this is the one you're allowed to enjoy." Being the roundest figure among the women, she was panting slightly by the time she appeared in the archway. She looked at Nasr and winked. "Especially when it's your son."

Nasr's eldest niece, Aisha, dashed past Talat Auntie. "Video!" she cried, and ran toward Nasr with a cassette raised in her hand like a souvenir from a victory.

Asima Chachi and Saira headed upstairs, and Yasmine collapsed on the sofa beside Hamid Uncle. When Jameela finally appeared, she stood in the archway with her coat on, as if she wasn't sure whether she would stay.

Rizwan began rounding up his daughters for bed. Nasr's nieces—ages three, five, and eight—all had dark tans and thick Texan drawls; they gasped whenever it snowed and persisted in calling Nasr's mother Nanny instead of Nani—just different enough that she never failed to notice.

"Can we please?" Aisha wailed, pleading with her father to see the video of the event she'd just attended. She was bent forward over the sofa, her knees on the carpet and the cassette pressed to her chest. "Can we, Naaw-nee?"

Nasr's mother looked startled at her granddaughter's almost perfect pronunciation. "Of course, meri jaan!"

Giving up, Rizwan scooped the middle girl into his arms and headed upstairs. The remaining adults rearranged themselves. Masood Chacha inquired into the "tea situation," and Nasr offered to make it, but, just as swiftly, his mother volunteered him to hook up the camcorder instead. Yasmine was sent to the kitchen, and Jameela followed her out.

Onscreen, the white sheet spread on the floor made the finished basement seem larger than it was. At one end, there was a divan with a curtained backdrop of tinsel mixed with red and white flowers. The professional videographer's spotlight thoroughly lit up the stage, but beyond its reach the room appeared dim, and the picture varied constantly in brightness and steadiness. Aisha's voice was often heard begging for a chance at the camcorder, and it was clear, by the low angles and close-ups of somebody's hair and another person's bangles, when she was indulged. Now Aisha sat tucked beside Nasr and commentated on the action. When Farah appeared, she whispered, "That's the bride. She's beautiful."

The crowd onscreen was quiet as Farah was led in, her sisters on either side—and the video's audience also became silent, as though Farah had entered the Siddiquis' living room as well. The three sisters sat down on the divan to pose for photographs, and the camera zoomed in on Farah's face. It was downcast and scrubbed clean. There was a bend to the neck that Nasr recognized from when he first saw the Ansari girls. There was Rafia's solemn brow on the left, and Suraiya's round and smiling features to the right. Farah's expression was glum, her lips pursed. By this time, Rizwan, Saira, and Asima Chachi had returned, and the attention of the entire room, its quiet, intense focus, was on the video—but also, Nasr suddenly sensed, on him and his reactions.

The camera was now traveling down to Farah's hands,

which were resting on her knees, palms up, and finally to her feet, which someone exposed by lifting the hemlines of her pajamas. Both the hands and feet were gloved in dark lacy patterns—paisleys, petals, and vines that were already bleeding red where the paste was drying and shrinking. The camera made its shaky way up to Farah's face again, zoomed out, then back in from a different angle. The tradition at the Mehendi was that while all the other women were dressed up, the bride wore plain clothes, in a color like solid yellow or pink, and avoided all ornamentation other than the mehendi. "Aha"; "Vaah-vaah-vaah. Very nice"; "Classic, exactly how a bride should look"—came from Masood Chacha and Hamid Uncle. Nasr felt such a rush of pride that its intensity surprised him.

"Come, come, beta," Masood Chacha called out when Jameela and Yasmine reappeared with teacups. He patted the seat beside him. "Now we can have a real discussion."

Jameela stayed busy distributing the tea, but Masood Chacha was undeterred: "So now, Miss Jameela, when are we hearing more about your settlement plans? You know, your Asima Chachi and I are here for two more weeks only."

"I appreciate your interest, Uncle," she replied in a respectful and friendly tone, but this—Nasr saw immediately—was a mistake.

Talat Auntie seized the opportunity to say, "Yes, do please talk to her, Masood Bhai. There is a proper way to go about planning such celebrations."

"Of course, and for you it should be big, beta," Masood Chacha said, casting an admiring glance in Jameela's direction. "The bigger the better!"

Jameela offered him a plate of sweets. "It's just not me," she said, but in a small voice that didn't sound convincing even to Nasr.

"Is me, is not me," Talat Auntie said, gesturing to Masood Chacha so that he could see the problem she had on her hands.

"Marriage is not only about oneself, after all. Others must be considered."

"Arré, Bhabi," Masood Chacha said in an indignant tone, as though Talat Auntie ought to be ashamed of herself, "you must do this one's shaadi back home—real Lucknawi style. Give me ten days' notice. None of this so-and-so is too expensive, hassling with these cooks and such who come here and get their heads turned. Ten days, and there will be a proper feast, sparing no expense. Mehendi, Mahnja we'll do at the house, and the Clark's Avadh can do the rest of the hosting. They are having beautiful grounds, the finest lawn, superb gardens, tents-wents, the whole dhamaka—even fireworks. And what is expense to you people with your dollars?" He had taken his time about selecting a piece of halva but didn't accept the dish to pass it on to others. Now he grimaced as he swallowed. "What do you say, beta?" he asked Jameela.

Jameela somehow made her turn to serve the rest of the room seem not as impolite a gesture as it could have been.

Talat Auntie looked hesitant now. This was clearly not the sort of advice she had in mind. "I was meaning that it is important to let one's elders participate and decide—March is just three months away," she said, glancing at Hamid Uncle for support, but his eyes were fixed on the screen. Talat Auntie's lips tightened. "These things take time, Masood."

"Time? What does time matter for a pair of mavericks such as these?"

Nasr looked for the signal—some word or indication from Jameela that he should create a need to run an errand, go out for milk. But even as she held the dish of halva for him and Aisha, she wouldn't meet his eye.

"Arré," Masood Chacha said, sitting up with new inspiration, "everyone is already assembled here—why not just take care of this business now? Grab the two of them and be done with the matter?"

As the unwelcome wedding planning continued, the maverick took her seat again. She actually looked a little sick now, eyes sliding tersely under their big flat lids.

Nasr turned the volume of the TV up, hoping it would distract. But the moment on the screen was a quiet one, in which the photographer was arranging Farah for a "candid" shot. The camera lingered as the bride was made to lift her arms out in front with her hands together, palms up, palms down, then it panned away to get the crowd's reaction. Jameela, who was sitting closest to the TV, turned her head, and now there were two profiles of her, nearly nose to nose, one in the room and the other onscreen. The expression in both was of unsmiling concentration, dark brows drawn. "This is a little too po-mo for me," Jameela said, rising. "You still want to practice those steps?" she asked Yasmine, who leaped up immediately.

The old Jameela—this was how Nasr was beginning to think of it—would have cut Talat Auntie off the minute she started in about proper ways. He felt sorry for this new one who simply left the room.

*F*or the next hour, as the video continued playing, the composition of the living room shifted constantly, but every time Nasr rose to leave or offered to fetch something, someone said, "No, you sit, beta. I'll get it." This was his wedding, and he was clearly expected to be interested in every single detail. Aisha's presence didn't help—she shrieked whenever anyone tried to fast-forward the action. "Maamo, watch this," she said, sometimes turning his chin with her small fingers. When Masood Chacha tried to distract her by describing how her Yasmine Khala and Jameela Khala were downstairs playing music and doing dances very much like those on the TV, Aisha put a finger to her lips to silence him.

By the time Jameela returned, Nasr's mother and aunts had gone to bed, and Hamid Uncle, too, was out of the room; possibly he'd gone home. Even though Aisha had finally drifted off to sleep, the video of the Mehendi still played. Saira and Rizwan, slumped on the couch against each other like teenagers, were tracking the onscreen appearances of a slim woman in a nearly transparent sari. Her blouse was not only sleeveless but cut high and almost as small as a bra. "So this is the rage now," Saira observed dryly when she spotted the offending figure's nearly bare back. Masood Chacha wondered how in the world the girl had been let in the door by the Ansaris. "What's wrong with it?" Rizwan asked, only to receive a fully expected punch in the arm from his wife.

Jameela listened to this exchange from the archway and then decisively sat down beside Masood Chacha. To Nasr's amazement, she then let herself be monopolized by his uncle, who launched into a discourse about how in India the washroom was about to be discovered by the wife of every well-to-do civil servant. No longer the hovel of the family home, it would soon, he assured Jameela, be having scents and soaps that nobody uses. "Just like you people here," he said. "And what will be the main feature of this upgrade? The humble towel, of course." After making this point, he was allowed to ramble on unchallenged about the advantages of Delhi over Karachi—the chief one being that he himself was available to serve as consultant and liaison. The more he spoke, the clearer it became that the motivation behind his ardent interest in changing Jameela and Javaid's minds was that he might benefit from a spillover of this downy wealth.

Because Jameela herself had opened the door, everybody's opinion on the matter of changing countries soon came spilling out. Rizwan, normally so laid-back, warmed to the task of explaining how Pakistan worked (and didn't work). His advice was that Jameela and Javaid should go for a trial period, six months tops. Saira, who claimed a measure of expertise from the trips her family took every other summer to see Rizwan's parents in Karachi, declared, "Visits back home, be they to India or Pakistan, are best when they are short and sweet. Always bring your own water, and don't stay after it runs out."

"But what are you going to do there, beta?" Saira suddenly asked.

"Arré, she is going to live the life of comfort and servants—what else?" Masood Chacha said, shaking his head in disgust. "You people are always needing such reasons."

"Well, we're not exactly going there to be rich," Jameela said. "But Javaid's family's resources were a consideration. They make you feel as if you have a chance to do something. I mean, Javaid says it better, but the focus here is so much on this or that ritual—personal piety. No one we know ever talks about social reform—or, if they do, they sound like they're out to convert everybody in sight. But social reform is a major part of Islam."

"But can't you do your social work here?" Saira said.

"It just seems better to commit yourself where you can make a difference."

To Nasr's ear, there was a ring of repetition and rehearsal to her words. He felt as though he was gazing upon an ailing person, and he wondered how long she'd been like this.

"Ah, Hamid Bhai," Masood Chacha said when Hamid Uncle appeared in the archway. "You will understand how it is the nature of woman to think critically." He patted the empty spot beside him on the couch, but Hamid Uncle took his usual place on the far end of the love seat. " 'A style of indifference will be her way,' " Masood Chacha called out. " 'A style of submission will be our creed.' "

Hamid Uncle smiled at the sound of the high Urdu.

"I believe that is your Faiz, Bhai sahib."

Hamid Uncle shook his head with reluctant admiration. " 'The expectation of houris in heaven,' " he rejoined with another couplet, " 'has fully trained the priest; / even that wise man seems naïve and tame.' "

"Vaah vaah vaah," Masood Chacha agreed.

"Iqbal," said Hamid Uncle, tipping his palm to his forehead to accept the praise.

"Fine," Saira declared. "I'll give them the poetry—but not the plumbing."

"You see!" Masood Chacha said to the men in the room. "Once they are set, nothing will change a woman's ideas. Why do you think the great armies of the world are composed of men only? We are simple and obedient."

"Maybe the reason we can't be pressed into duty so easily," Jameela suggested quietly, "is that we just don't have the same incentive awaiting us."

Saira let out a laugh. "No promise of heavenly beauties."

"Arré, Jameela beta," Masood Chacha said, "you are a Hindustani, through and through. You must not listen to these people. I can't speak for Karachi, but in Delhi society you would be a star, beta, toast of—"

"But the places *are* different, Uncle," Rizwan said. "Look, let's say there's a stop sign at an empty intersection, no one is in sight. What is an American who drives up to it going to do?"

In the brief silence that followed his question, he said with uncharacteristic animation, "Oh, sorry, sorry: *North* American. My wife would kill me if she heard."

Saira rolled her eyes.

"What would he do?" Rizwan asked again. "He would stop, of course. But our kebab-eating, Maruti-driving bhai sahib, what is his response? 'Stop here—arré, what for? What is the point when no one will catch you?' " Rizwan delivered these lines as if his character had a mouthful of paan. "Except the point," he continued, in his own voice, "is that stopping in that moment does matter. In fact, that's exactly where all this social contract business starts. *That's* the programming of democracy—but they're infants in it. They need to learn it. It needs to be taught like it's taught at Aisha's school. The American system may not be perfect, but at least it makes progress."

"But what kind of solution is it to Americanize the whole of the world, Rizwan beta?" Hamid Uncle suddenly said. "Why not leave the differences in place? These are complicated matters—"

"He just means there are real benefits to a certain kind of social and political change," Jameela said. "Why shouldn't those countries benefit—"

"Yes, but one cannot rush these things," Hamid Uncle replied, not quite addressing his daughter. "Old traditions and histories must be respected; you cannot be imposing new systems from the outside. And if making a difference is important to one, then perhaps it's best to stay where one has made one's life—"

"But there's no harm in trying at least," Jameela interrupted again. "Better than going around saying that everything you don't like is not part of Islam."

This time Hamid Uncle muzzled himself with the spout of his hookah. A silence fell across the room. Both father and daughter wore unreadable expressions. Nasr had never seen Hamid Uncle and Jameela disagree, not once. With Talat Auntie, one got the sense that there was always a disagreement threatening to break out, but the other two Farooqis' opinions were never far from each other.

The Mehendi video was now showing the inexplicably necessary shots of the food that had been served, heading into happy, gaping mouths.

Clicking off the TV, Rizwan said, "Well, the giant has awoken, as they say. Nothing anybody in the world can do about that now." A Texan drawl had seeped into his voice—perhaps available for making such statements.

Masood Chacha, for once, agreed with someone. "The one

thing to be remembering in all this is the faith of these Am-reekans. They are very chalaak. They are having faces like chil-dren, but the capability of these people is limitless."

Everyone in the room, Nasr noticed, was frowning by now, or nearly so. Nobody invited Masood Chacha to explain him-self, but he continued nevertheless: "Who else would be capable of the planning, the training, the organization. Does anyone ac-tually believe that a Saudi can pull off such a feat? Arré, even they themselves don't believe it! And why were the Jews warned to stay away from this thing here? Would *Saudi nationals* be warning them?"

"Those are just rumors," Saira said stiffly.

"They're not even rumors," Nasr said, "they're lies. Maybe wishful thinking."

"All I am asking, beta," Masood Chacha said, "is why this number? Nineteen? Why are there no questions about the nine-teen? Today, they say we were not expecting this thing; the next day, here are your villains. We've found them—all nineteen pro-files and faces and known intentions. Not one doubt."

"And so, what?" Nasr said. "The U.S. government is now supposed to have not just known, but gotten together with the Israelis to recruit some poor, unsuspecting Arabs, train them how to fly planes, and teach them how to breach their own secu-rity—making sure to send e-mails on the day of the attack to warn its own? And they're supposed to have done all this just to make Muslims look bad?"

Masood Chacha said, "Haven't we been hearing that half of these boys are still alive?"

"I don't believe this," Nasr said. Jameela's inexpressiveness suddenly struck him as revealing in a newly disturbing way; it was like a form of agreement, as though she, too, had fallen un-der the spell of these paranoid theories. "I just don't believe this," he repeated. "Do you?" he said, turning to Jameela.

At first he thought she wouldn't reply at all, but then she

shrugged and said, "I'm not going to go around ridiculing the people who do."

"And you both believe"—Nasr made a point of addressing Masood Chacha and Jameela together—"that the whole country, all its citizens, are now conspiring to look the other way? Or maybe they're just too stupid to see through it?"

"Not stupidity, beta," Masood Chacha said. "Faith. No religion has anything to match—"

Jameela cut him off. "I think that the feeling, at least, that we're living among people who believe we all somehow contributed to doing this thing to them is real."

"They don't believe that," Nasr said. "That's ridiculous—"

"Have you seen the interviews with the little kids at the mosques wondering why everybody blames the Muslims first?" Jameela said. "It's a good question, but it comes with a terrible answer—and a five-year-old is already asking."

She sat up now and suddenly she was sounding like herself again, which meant that she cut an incongruous figure: the head was still covered, but all traces of meekness had evaporated from the face. Nasr remembered the sensation, back in New York, of watching someone inhabit a costume.

"What question," Jameela continued, "is that kid—any of these kids his age—going to be asking when he's ten or fifteen? What's going to happen when he's twenty and boards a plane for the first time by himself?"

Nasr had seen the interview—the video, from Seattle, had been looping on the local news for days. "What about the policemen guarding those mosques?" he asked. He hadn't meant to pick a fight with her, and yet a small part of him felt a thrill in seeing her face fierce with argument. "They were American police, and the kid was within their protection. You don't find that incredible?"

"Sure, but that still doesn't mean the kid's whole life won't be lived under a cloud of suspicion." Her eyes fell on Aisha's sleeping form, but she quickly looked away. "I know I couldn't stand it."

"But this is precisely what I am saying!" Masood Chacha said, looking at Jameela with open admiration. "You were not meant for places with such restrictions, beta. In Delhi—"

"You don't have to stand it," Nasr said, feeling his voice grow loud. "If you'd just think for a second—"

"Come now, Masood," Hamid Uncle said, "you're upsetting the children."

Nasr was about to continue, but then he caught sight of Hamid Uncle's face. The older man looked miserable. This was clearly not the sort of help he wanted.

After the group broke for the night and everyone had finally gone to bed, Jameela caught Nasr's eye. "Still awake?" she asked, tentative again. Nasr felt himself nod as though his head were submerged in water. On the landing, as the two of them put on their coats, the silence of the dark house stretched out behind his back, for miles and miles. They had opened the front door when they heard a high-pitched voice: "I want to go. I want to go. I want to go." Aisha, refreshed from her nap, ran down and clamped her arms around Nasr's leg. Saira appeared at the top of the stairs, heavy-lidded and already in a nightgown. "Quiet, beta, please. Everyone is sleeping." But the child couldn't be bribed with bedtime stories or French toast for breakfast, much less quieted by her mother's impatient and sleepy threats.

"Do you guys mind?" Saira said finally. "She'll fall asleep in the car."

They hadn't planned on taking the car, but they said, "Sure" and "Of course."

A few minutes into the short drive to Jameela's house,

Aisha, who'd insisted on sitting in the front on Jameela's lap, did indeed fall asleep. Nasr pulled into the Farooqis' driveway. He supposed he should apologize, but before he could, Jameela turned to him. "Can I ask you for a favor?"

He said of course, and she asked if he might please talk to Javaid. "He's made all these plans to go, but it's happening too fast. Every time I suggest we think it through a little more, he thinks I'm trying to talk him out of it. Which I'm not," she added. "He just won't listen to anyone."

Nasr said he would try, but Jameela continued on, whispering above Aisha's curls. Could she ask one more thing? Could he also please ask Farah to back off?

"Back off?" he repeated.

"She keeps listening and encouraging him—her sisters, too. It's four against one."

He couldn't imagine Farah ganging up on anyone, on purpose or even inadvertently, but he agreed to talk to her as well.

"And also—" Jameela began again. Her voice dropped a pitch lower, thick with emotion. "Could you please make sure"—she hesitated, and her lips curled, as though she hated the taste of the words in her mouth—"could you make sure it doesn't sound like any of this came from me?" She was staring across the dark length of the car now. "I just need more time."

She turned to pull the seat belt around Aisha and slipped out of the car. As he had countless times before, Nasr watched the thin figure work the lock under the porch light, then disappear into the dark house. So she didn't want to go, he thought. Of course not. He had never believed she was actually going. It was so preposterous that it had to be impossible. But a few moments later Nasr felt his fingers finally loosening their grip on the steering wheel, and then came the sweeping and unmistakable rush of pure relief.

25

The next day, the lid on the pot began to rattle. Nasr discovered that for all Masood Chacha's inside information he perceived Jameela and Javaid to be a staunchly united front. Even Yasmine had no inkling of there being any reluctance on Jameela's part, which meant the reservations Jameela had expressed to Nasr were a true secret. In the morning, as soon as he could, Nasr called Javaid's cell phone, but there was no answer. He tried Javaid's house and learned from Shazia Phuphi that Javaid would be at the masjid for much of the day.

At the breakfast table, children of all ages were fed: aloo sabzi rounded up with fresh tikkias was being stuffed into various willing mouths. Asima Chachi was giving a bottle to Raza, the baby's large eyes staring dreamily at the chandelier. Yasmine rose with her clipboard and, speaking over the chatter like a camp counselor, began giving out her list of the day's assignments. While Nasr tried to find some activity for which he could solicit Javaid's help (he was still using a cane, so he could hardly be asked to set up chairs and tables), his phone rang.

He headed to the den to talk to Farah. She wondered whether Nasr had seen the video from last night and what he was doing today. He mentioned Yasmine's long list of errands. Too bad, she said, and what about the evening? Nasr replied that he had plans to see Javaid tonight.

"Isn't it exciting that Javaid Bhai and Jameela Baji finally made a decision?" Farah said cheerfully. "Javaid Bhai told me his grandfather had offered the two of them a whole wing of the family house. Imagine starting out in life with two floors and one's own courtyard!" She seemed to be so aware of the details that Nasr wondered how it was that she'd said nothing to him about Jameela and Javaid's plans in all their many recent conversations.

"Yes, but isn't leaving like this a bit sudden?" he asked. "Javaid's career is being thrown away—and is all this really fair to Jameela?"

"What do you mean?"

"Has he really considered what Jameela might do there?"

"Naturally, she wants to go where Javaid Bhai is going," Farah replied.

"Even if it would be uprooting her whole life?"

"How can it be uprooting her whole life when Javaid Bhai is now going to be the center of her life?" Farah returned.

"But Jameela's hardly the type to do something just because it's expected of her," he said. "I mean, she's not like other—she's accustomed to a certain amount of freedom."

"Such as?"

"Such as freedom in simple movement, in going where she

wants to go, doing what she wants to do. She's cultivated a life here, with friends and interests—"

"But friends can be made anywhere," Farah replied. "And these days friendships can be maintained from anywhere."

"That doesn't mean it's a fair sacrifice to ask of someone, does it?"

"But she knew from the beginning that Javaid Bhai might go," Farah said, quite rightly. "It was not as though he was surprising her. Marriage changes your perspective, after all—something that might have been viewed as a sacrifice isn't the same when you consider what you're getting in return."

Nasr had tried to keep the irritation out of his voice. All her replies were sound and sensible, and he knew that he himself would benefit from her faith in these principles of wifely devotion. But he couldn't help thinking that it was like talking to his mother. This is the way it would be from now on, he thought with a sigh. There would always be ideas that Farah would find so foreign to her being—or, rather, to the inherited logic of her parents—that trying to bring her over to his opinion would be pointless. Yet a part of him wished she would be offended with the sexism inherent in this thinking.

"Maybe you could come for a visit today?" Farah said suddenly. Then, as though she were pitching a daring proposition, she asked in a hushed voice if there wasn't anything that might need to be exchanged between the households—mehendi platters, garlands, something he could deliver to the Ansaris or bring back for his mother.

They were not scheduled to see each other for another two days, at the Nikaah, when they'd already be married. But instead of being flattered and thrilled, as he would have been just days ago, and instead of being impressed, as he might have been just moments ago, that she was scheming such a daring break with custom, Nasr felt a contrarian's spike of impatience at the girlish manner with which her voice had dropped. The Ansari house, he knew by now, was constantly full of the bustle of cousins and aunties dropping in for visits, and Nasr felt he was being made, with these lowered tones, to imagine the ears that might be listening: one of the relations leaning close at the bedroom door, or Mrs. Ansari herself coming down to the basement on the pretense of doing laundry.

"Cushions!" Farah said in a loud whisper. "Your mother had asked to borrow our floor cushions."

Why was such an elaborate excuse needed? Nasr wondered—especially for a proposal that would amount to very little intimacy, in any case. "I can't," he said. "I'm seeing Javaid," he reminded her.

"But does that have to be tonight?"

"We already made plans."

"Is Jameela Baji going to be there?" she asked.

Nasr said no.

After a pause, Farah exhibited, not for the first time, a strangely acute intuition. "Did she ask you to talk to him?"

"Sort of," he admitted.

"Is this about going away to Pakistan?"

"It's not that," he said, but in his confusion he'd hesitated just long enough.

"Why doesn't she just talk to him herself if she's changed her mind?"

"I have no idea," he said. His voice, he knew, contained a note of exasperation and reluctance. He let it linger there. After a moment, he seemed to have so successfully conveyed that he felt a sense of duty that Farah said, "Well, it's nice of you to help them."

• • •

317

A number of smiles passed across the table when Nasr returned to the dining room. Saira cocked her eyebrows and made a remark about the advantages of marrying in the cellphone age. "How about just the cordless-phone age?" Rizwan asked, laughing.

"I'm going to the cemetery," Nasr announced to the room. His mother froze, first with surprise, then emotion—perhaps she had expected to have to prompt him to make this visit on the eve of his marriage. Indeed, Masood Chacha, who complained indiscriminately about Nasr's unavailability, had already requested this trip to Nasr's father's gravesite several times, but Nasr had evaded him. "Would you like to come?" Nasr asked his uncle now, surprising him as well, into merciful silence. He also invited Rizwan, which immediately signaled to his mother and sisters, as he knew it would, that this excursion would be men only, and therefore somehow ceremonial, so no other errands or insistences were tied to it. Finally, Nasr called Javaid.

T he cemetery was empty, and there was just enough snow on the ground to hide the grass. The trip had lost all sense of its ceremony as soon as Masood Chacha inquired if they might, now that they were away from the "female factor," pick up a few of those Tim Hortons doughnuts. But now, before the modest gravestone, even Masood Chacha quieted, if you didn't count the deep sighs and the tongue-clicking.

"I've stood at too many of these," he said. "Your father, then Apa last year. Too many."

A blast of icy wind swept across the bare hill. The four men stood nearly shoulder to shoulder. Nobody reached down to sweep away the leaves, and after each man had finished his prayer, they turned toward the car by unspoken but mutually shivering consensus. Javaid made slow work down the slope, and Nasr let Rizwan and his uncle walk on ahead.

The bruises on Javaid's face had faded, or perhaps the beard he was growing covered up most of them, and he wore a light-weight sling on his shoulder. On the way to the cemetery, Nasr had decided that the best way to approach the matter would be to call attention to the loss that Javaid and Jameela's plans would impose on Javaid's own parents (and thus imply, by extension, the cost to Hamid Uncle and Talat Auntie).

But Javaid himself introduced the subject. "I guess we might not see you and Farah for a while."

"Well, we'll come to the wedding, of course," Nasr said, and Javaid nodded.

Nasr's words had been automatic, a courtesy that he felt he was programmed to perform, but, once uttered, the idea of this wedding seemed outlandish. He could no more imagine Jameela as a bride than himself as a guest. "What are you going to be doing in Karachi, anyway?" he asked Javaid, but this deepened his confusion, as he couldn't recall whether he was supposed to know this information or not.

"Didn't you hear?" Javaid asked with a wry smile. "I'm going to become a toilyah-wallah." He said his grandfather wanted him to join as the company's president, but he'd managed to convince the man that starting off as a lowly finance officer or something would be better. "That way, I can learn the ropes before I begin stepping on everyone's toes."

"But what if you get there and change your mind?" Nasr asked, though he had meant to build up to this question instead of blurting it out.

"I won't," Javaid said.

"And when do you go?"

"The sooner the better." Javaid was breathing fast, working hard down the slope.

Nasr pretended to tie his shoe, and when he rose he finally asked about Javaid's parents.

"We'll get them to visit," Javaid said.

"Isn't the journey too difficult for them to make as often as they would want to see you guys? I mean, you're both only children."

Javaid shrugged. "They can all come and stay there. It's a big house."

"I don't really see Hamid Uncle in Karachi," Nasr said. "No offense."

Javaid looked away and nodded thoughtfully, or else he was simply concentrating on his next step.

"What about Jameela?" Nasr asked, as though it were just occurring to him (or at least that's the effect he aimed for).

"What about her?" Javaid said gruffly, but of course he hadn't actually misunderstood the question. "She agrees with me. She'll like it there. Fortunately, she's very practical and capable."

"But you know she's got a whole life here—friends, job, school," Nasr said, perhaps going too far.

"She'll be able to visit. We can send her back every few months," Javaid said, adding, with what Nasr felt was a rather smug smile, "Jameela is a totally free person." Now the smugness crinkled into a secretive expression that suggested that there was something more Javaid could say but wouldn't. A moment later, Nasr found himself being treated like a member of an ancient tribe, teetering on irrelevancy. "It's just not the same for us," Javaid said, "as it was for you and Farah—perfect approvals, smooth sailing, the whole wedding works. Everything's changed now. How you go about these things is just not as big a deal."

26

*S*urprise," Farah said, as she sat gracefully beside Nasr at that evening's festivities. This party, invented to correspond to the bride's Mehendi, might not have taken place in India; and although it was tempting to refer to the affair as the groom's Mehendi, that would have been as ridiculous as calling it the groom's bridal shower. Perhaps for this reason, invitations had been sent rather indiscriminately, including to all the Ansaris—parents, sisters, men, women, in-laws—but under the assumption that only the parents and maybe one of the Ansari sisters would actually attend. In other words, the Ansaris would make sure the bride and groom were kept apart until the last possible minute. But now Farah was beside Nasr. He hadn't seen her in a month, and her presence, her face in full view, glowing out from a fringe of golden embroidery, had its usual unsettling effect.

Nasr had by now attended enough weddings and seen enough grooms to know what was expected of him: smiling obedience and acquiescence. A groom ought not to appear too eager or showily interested; a shy and amiably bewildered aspect was ideal. But Nasr had arrived at the hall distracted and brooding. He'd begun to suspect, when the Farooqis came to the house tonight, that Jameela was avoiding him. It would be just like her to avoid him after she herself had sought him out.

Then, on the drive to the hall, which was on the top floor of a tasteful hotel, Nasr heard his mother, in the back seat with Saira and Talat Auntie, comment that while an elementary school might have been less expensive, the difference in price was more than reflected in the setting. "Literally zameen asmaan," she'd said, laughingly tipping her head back to take in the height of the building—earth to heaven. It was true that the large room, with its wood paneling and panoramic views of the darkening city, was beyond the Ansaris' means and tastes, but calling attention to this struck Nasr as bad form on his mother's part.

Nasr's mood had been helped by the presence of his friends from New York, who were among the first guests to arrive. They appeared tentative and self-conscious, and he was glad for the opportunity to put them at ease by introducing them to his family. Pete congratulated his mother so heartily, in that exaggerated American way, that she looked both happy and nervous. When the Ansaris arrived, she and Nasr's sisters, along with Hamid Uncle, Talat Auntie, and Masood Chacha, took their places at the front of the room with garlands in hand to greet them. The rest of the assembled guests gathered behind. Nasr was at the very back. He rose from the couch, where he was expected to sit all night, and saw some eighty dark-haired buns, braids, and bald spots. Distant doors opened, and there was an immediate commotion. Nasr watched a series of whispers travel, via variously turned profiles, backward into the room, but he didn't learn the source of the excitement until a few murmur-filled moments later, when the crowd in front of him suddenly parted—at the none-too-gentle prodding of the videographer—and he saw, at the end of the lane, the gold-and-green-wrapped figure of his bride-to-be. Farah began walking—all by herself—toward Nasr. She seemed, in fact, to float, smiling broadly but not directly at him, and he felt himself doing the same, aiming his own smile somewhere past her ear. The stir she created was not simply due to her unexpected appearance at the party, nor to this unthinkably bold walk across the length of the room. In the heavy, dark-green shalwar suit with the gold accents, Farah's loveliness was vivid and undeniable. Her rupatta was arranged around her hair like the hood of a cloak, which meant there was nothing obscuring the gleam of her eyes and the fine molding of her lips. When she reached Nasr, she turned immediately and stood beside him to share the spotlights blazing from the umbrella-shaped lamps that the photographer had set up. Nasr had only the vaguest impression that they were being given instructions, yet he found himself looking up, down, turning this way, no, to the left. After dutifully applying themselves to a dozen more angles and endeavoring toward at least as many smiles, the bridal couple was permitted to sit, and it was then that Farah rested her expectant eyes on him to ask if he was surprised.

"You made it," Nasr said finally, snatching at his frayed wit.

"I knew you wouldn't actually be surprised," she replied. She held his eye and there was a private note of satisfaction in her voice.

Nasr felt thoroughly caught by her beauty. The whole picture was so impressive, and its effects so forceful at this proximity, that the Farah he had assembled in his mind—pieced together from their few unsatisfying encounters—felt like a shabby approximation of this vision. She was looking away now, back in the direction of the crowd. Maybe he *had* expected her, Nasr thought, gazing at the fine lines of her profile, or at least had expected her to be capable of engineering such a thing.

"But how did you know?" he asked, leaning in, whispering just as conspiratorially as she had.

Farah turned toward him, but her gaze fell to his shoulder, which was brushing hers, and a wrinkle formed on the smooth brow. She dipped forward, shifting slightly away from him. Nasr looked up and immediately saw the reason for the adjustment: a whole team of his future in-laws had made their way through the crowded room and were standing before him, and they didn't exactly look pleased.

The laddo is a meatball-size confection of sugar and chick-pea flour, often seasoned with cardamom or almond slivers. It is a sweetmeat that has starred as the main attraction of many a ritual and helped give shape to many an evening. Despite the confusion of its surprising launch, tonight's affair found its rhythm once the laddos were brought out. Along with the sweet-meat came the uppton and the mehendi, and soon the aunties and uncles began lining up, as if motivated by some elemental instinct, to come forward and give their blessings. The interactions fell into a comfortably choreographed and undemanding pattern. An unoriginal joke or two was made by an uncle, usually about how Nasr's wedding was evidence of one's own advancing age, and the aunties waggled their fingers and chided Farah for being such an "upstart." "Arré, what is the suspense now?" one asked. Or they noted the blood-redness of her mehendi. "Takes color well," they said. "Sign of a happy home." Nasr and Farah sat obediently, each with a palm held open, while Nasr's sisters stood on either side of them. Yasmine held the platter of laddos out and instructed that the feeding of the sweetmeat should be done first, then the swiping of the paste. Many of the older generation were tempted into defiance by her authoritative manner—*Since when has our little Yammo become such an expert?*—and soon fingers that featured an unpleasant mingling of sweet oil and gritty, green mehendi were shoved into Nasr's mouth. Saira placed a paan leaf on the bride's and groom's palms so the mehendi wouldn't stain their hands, but some of the aunties considered this cheating, at least in Nasr's case—*Why shouldn't the groom suffer a little marking here and there?* Catching their saris to their sides, they leaned in to take a swipe at Nasr's wrist or cheek. The more Westernized uncles bent over the platters cautiously, as though they'd never participated in such a strange custom. "I just spread it here? Oh, like icing, eh?" they asked, and fretted about coming away with a stain themselves. Other uncles, such as Masood Chacha, tried to insert the whole laddo into Nasr's mouth. "The privilege of a chacha, after all!" he said with a loud cackle, while Nasr tried to keep himself from gagging. At the end of the process, the adults would swirl a right hand containing a discreet and blessed fold of money above Nasr and Farah's heads, then pass the bills to Yasmine. For good measure, some of the aunties cracked their knuckles against their own temples, to avert bad luck from the bridal couple's future. Or they squeezed Nasr's chin, some Farah's, and said, "Cho chweet," as if they were admiring newborns.

"I have to *feed* him?" Pete said, his tall frame nearly bending in half to examine the tray of laddos. He and Laura were at the head of the small shy cluster of non-Indians in line.

"If you wish us well, you do," Farah said with a dazzlingly amiable smile.

As they waited in line, Nasr's friends were more courteous and meek than he had ever seen them. The guys had serious and interested faces, and the women had taken Mrs. Ansari's requests for modesty (which were actually intended for tomorrow's Nikaah) to heart. They wore long skirts or pants, blouses with long sleeves, and even jackets. Cynthia looked as though she were attending a conference, and both she and Laura had brought shawls in case more covering up was necessary. Nasr found himself awkward and hesitant. He had thought this introduction of Farah to his friends wouldn't take place until tomorrow or even Saturday at the Valima, where it might be hurried and short, and that the real acquaintance would begin when they were all back in New York, at a safe distance from the rituals and costumes. He clumsily blanked on relevant details, but luckily Pete was in top form. He asked Farah what he was supposed to do here, and as she explained the procedure for the giving of the blessing, he played the thick-headed brute, as if he found the instructions too complicated. Instead of feeding the groom, he chose the laddo that Nasr should eat by pointing to it—"Here you go, help yourself"—and when the donation was mentioned, he began haggling over the amount. "But Nasr doesn't need my money. He's loaded. My God, didn't he tell you?" he asked Farah.

Nasr laughed. "It's just for show. Just a dollar. We'll give it to charity if you want."

"Well, all right," Pete said to Farah, grudgingly holding his wallet open. "You guys want American or Canadian?"

"Either is fine," Farah said. "But no checks or money orders, please."

There was a pause—a nice fat one, during which you really couldn't be sure if this was a joke—and then Farah's cheeks dimpled, and Pete let out the booming laugh he saved for when he was really impressed.

Nasr felt a stab of contrition for his nervousness, for having underestimated her again. As the evening wore on, a wild idea began to take root, and he found himself struggling to concentrate on the conversations before him. If the purpose of the whole train of rituals to come tomorrow and the next day was to acquaint one with the stranger at one's side, in his and Farah's case the point was moot. Didn't this early contact render the showing of the bride's face to the groom in a mirror irrelevant? And what would be the purpose of going through those shoe-stealing negotiations after all the parties had witnessed the bride walk into a room and, of her own volition, sit beside the groom? Maybe now that they'd struck out this much, he and Farah could bypass the nonsense of all that manufactured emotion and silly playacting. He turned to see what she might think of this notion, but Farah was speaking with Laura and Cynthia at the moment: "I told him, 'Daddy, this is my day. A girl only does this once, and I want to see it all. When Rafia and Suraiya get married—those are my younger sisters—you can tell them to stay home.' " Everything she said sent Nasr's friends tripping with laughter—and he found himself laughing, too, but without entirely knowing why. It was not, however, until after dinner, when Jameela and Javaid came to visit, that he appreciated the full force of his bride-to-be's personality.

•

The visit was not entirely voluntary. Jameela and Javaid were brought forward by Javaid's mother, who was eager and apologetic. Could the photographer be persuaded to get some shots of the current happy couple with the future one? Shazia Phuphi asked. Of course, of course. While the lamps and tripods were moved, a small group of mothers, including Nasr's and Talat Auntie, gathered around to watch with pleased expressions and, naturally, to offer instructions and adjustments: the couples ought to stand side by side, then the two boys together on one side, girls on the other, now mix it up with girls in the center, boys on the outside.

Perhaps anyone would have paled beside Farah tonight, but Jameela looked particularly drab in the plain shalwar suit and headscarf. Having been recruited by Yasmine, she had spent much of the evening with some form of decoration in hand or a tray of food to be refreshed or rearranged. Now, as the mothers fussed over the photo-taking, she was compliant in a way that suggested practical urgency, as though she would do what was necessary in order to no longer be doing it. Both couples were visibly relieved when the photographer asked them to step aside so that she could take a few pictures of the older generation.

"Why don't they ever smile for photos?" Jameela asked as the mothers assembled.

Nasr immediately recognized his mother's way of arranging herself into a grim-faced statue. "Habit," he said.

"Yeah, but why?"

"Maybe because it makes them look more dignified," Farah ventured.

Jameela nodded, accepting this, but then said, "Or less double-chinned."

Nasr and Javaid laughed.

"We've decided that you two just can't go," Farah said suddenly. "Karachi is much too far, Javaid Bhai."

Still looking amused, Javaid asked what was behind this change of heart.

"Oh, selfishness," Farah said blithely. "Purely for our own sake." Jameela's smile was frozen in place as Farah went about explaining that she and Nasr couldn't help thinking how nice it would be for the four of them to be married couples together, and that it didn't seem right to be splitting up just when they were on the brink of this new arrangement.

Javaid shook his head indulgently. "Sorry, but I don't think we'll be changing our minds. You can come visit us, though."

Farah sighed, almost pouting. "At least we'll be keeping you here until the wedding," she said. "That should take a few years, with the plans Talat Auntie and Shazia Phuphi have in mind."

"We'll see," Javaid said, glancing at Jameela. "I think we're going to have to impose some limits on the mothers. Leave all this glamour stuff to you guys." Jameela nodded, still smiling, but in a distinctly mechanical way. Nasr could see what she'd meant about Farah not helping her. Even when Farah was arguing for Jameela's side, there was a distinct ring of endorsement in all her agreeable dissuasion.

Nasr's brooding mood returned. He tried to tell himself it was the effect of too many fake smiles, too much sugar coating the inside of his mouth, and too much heat from the lamps. But the true cause of his distraction was, ironically, Farah's continued ease in navigating the great range of people presented to her. The more Nasr watched her succeed, the more conscious he became of the parameters that defined this success. Instead of being impressed, he began to wonder about the liquid nature of her personality. She was at times totally impervious to her parents' disapproving stares, and at other times scrupulously observant—shifting as needed. And there was something in the way in which she broke the rules that had the odd effect of making Nasr even more aware of them. Every time she laughed or smiled, he was reminded that this was not what a proper Indian bride would do.

And there was Jameela, who now surely thought that Nasr had told Farah about her secret and maybe even asked for Farah's help with Javaid. She would never let him set the record straight; she would just believe that he was either stupid or incapable of any sort of loyalty. What puzzled him most, though, was that Jameela didn't seem upset, exactly. In fact, during the singing of the Mehendi songs, she sang and clapped as enthusiastically as Nasr's sisters—one might even say she saved the day. For the competition, the singers—all girls and women—gathered on white sheets in the center of the room, in front of Nasr and Farah, like subjects serenading a royal couple. Soon after the singing began, it became clear that the Ansari side was a commanding and synchronized force, while the Siddiqui side was full of embarrassed mumblers who appeared to be learning the lyrics as they were sung. But Jameela knew exactly what to do. For each song in which the Ansari girls lampooned Nasr or his relations, she, along with the other expert, Asima Chachi, retaliated, belting out the appropriately deriding and disparaging lyrics about Farah and the Ansaris.

After one round of competition finished, Jameela preempted the start of a second by popping up to announce that it was time for the dancing to begin. Following her lead, Yasmine prompted the audience and the singers to scoot back and make room in the center. Soon Nasr's nieces were performing the dance they had prepared in his honor: two of the girls twirled and spun, while the youngest collapsed in a heap and began sucking her thumb. Next, someone called for the lights to be dimmed in preparation for the dance that Yasmine and Jameela had practiced, first with Javaid, then with his replacement, Anjum Auntie's youngest son, Arif, a tall, skinny kid with gelled-back hair.

Yasmine, Arif, and Jameela took their positions on the white sheet, directly in front of Nasr and Farah. The three of them stood frozen and unsmiling until the music was cued. The dance number was from a recent Hindi film about a boy and girl from India who fall in love in Brooklyn but decide that the only life worth living is back in their village, where, as the song's lyrics explain, they were poor and inconvenienced but happy. Yasmine concentrated fiercely. She succeeded in smiling (or failed to frown) only when she remembered, and although she executed most of the bounces, slides, and spins accurately, she did so with stiff limbs, as if exercising rather than dancing. There was a big finish. Much applause. But then the music cycled back to the beginning of the disk. Arif cocked his head as if he were hearing a distant call, then playacted that the rhythm was traveling up his leg—a sort of Elvis-style quiver that ended with his lip-synching the male singer's cry, "Chalo na!" He sang the next line to Jameela, who looked back at him hesitatingly; then she turned to locate Yasmine, but Yasmine had slipped away as fast as humanly possible. She was stranded. "Chalo na!" Arif called out again, in mock desperation. He came down on one knee, pleading, and the audience gushed with laughter at his willingly pathetic display. The song's piercingly high female voice entered, and this time Jameela gave a slight pumping movement with one half of her body—it traveled down from her neck to her shoulders, then through her chest and hips. She turned to gaze over her shoulder, then looked away again, and began taking slow, pulsing steps toward Arif.

With just the two of them, the same dance became a scene: the upright and reluctant heroine who can't help being drawn to the wayward hero. The dancers circled each other, slowly this time, with milder versions of sly, purposeful eyes. Jameela's headscarf, which had already slid back over her hair, now spilled to the floor, and Arif, instead of returning it to her, tossed it into the audience with a cock of his chin and a licentious pump of his eyebrows. Jameela broke from her acting to laugh along with the onlookers, but she didn't drop her arms or fall out of step.

The crowd clapped to the music more energetically; eyes locked, Jameela and Arif revolved in tighter and tighter circles, their arms held up and out; Pete whistled when Jameela turned finally to face Arif, and there were more wolfish calls.

"No, I don't think this was planned," Nasr heard Farah say to someone, then agree in a whisper that Jameela was very good. "I'm so hopeless at such things."

Jameela had turned her back on Arif again and was gazing over her shoulder at him, and their movements, which had looked so different in the approach, were synchronized. They were not touching, but hovering nearly against each other in the

331

same motions. On the CD, the male and female singers took up the chorus, and Jameela danced a slow turn in the canopy of Arif's arms.

There was still some cheering, but much of the enthusiasm of the crowd had drained. Nasr caught sight of Masood Chacha clapping actively and scoffing at those around him who'd stopped. Javaid stood to the side with his arms crossed.

She's goading him, Nasr thought, with blinking surprise.

The song ended again, on the same quiet note, and Jameela held her final pose long enough that when she stepped out of it you could see how hard she was breathing. In the middle of the applause, more measured than before, the music started up again. Arif tried to pull Jameela back, but she slipped away and pushed Nasr's nieces forward, one of whom jumped up clutching Yasmine's hand. Yasmine insisted that Jameela return, no matter how tired she was. Arif drew out Saira, who gave in after lodging a halfhearted protest about being old and married; she pulled at her husband, who turned up both of his hands, as if he had nothing—no dancing skills; he soon relented, but not before drawing in Talat Auntie, which, considering her girth, was not easy to do. Talat Auntie invited Nasr's mother, who shook her head and looked appropriately mortified. Yasmine approached Nasr's friends, who didn't need much encouragement—"Can we? Are you sure?" "How do you do it?"—and their filling out the dance floor (for that's what it had become) was sufficient protection for other Indians to sneak on. Within a few minutes, there was a large group lesson taking place—with Jameela leading the women and Arif the men. Nasr's friends pressed him and Farah to join in, but nobody else did, of course.

The videographer turned the camera on the dancers, and Nasr enjoyed a cooling moment of relief from the lamp's hot ray. In the rare unobserved interval that followed, he couldn't help noticing the wrinkle of concern that had formed on the faces of his future in-laws—and when he turned to Farah he saw there was concern there, too. But the most perfect reflection of Mr. Ansari's disapproval and dismay could be found on Javaid's face.

The dancing, with all its mingling of male and female bodies, was no doubt a mistake, but it was clearly very innocent and awkward. The children bounced around between the adults, appalled but delighted. It was a harmless error of judgment—not even an error, just a lapse, or simply an unfortunate series of coincidences. Didn't Hamid Uncle say something about mistakes the other day? Nasr felt his ears tingle. Those objections of Hamid Uncle's—they were not merely to his daughter's plan to go to Karachi. Then Nasr thought: I know how to solve Jameela's problem. It was so obvious. Noble cause or not, Javaid was wrong for her. She had to see that.

27

*B*ack at the house, Nasr escaped and took his time packing his suitcase for the hotel, where he and Farah would stay from tomorrow night until their flight to Vancouver on Sunday afternoon. After a week in Victoria, they would come back to Montreal for a few days, collect the remainder of Farah's things, and finally head to New York. He'd confirmed the reservations just this morning, but it all felt like an itinerary for someone else.

By the time Nasr went downstairs, the older generation had, thankfully, gone to bed. Saira and Rizwan were settled deep in the sofa, Aisha asleep across their laps, and Yasmine stared groggily at the TV.

Squatting in the center of the room, Jameela was filling a

backpack with her various belongings. Although the pale-green headscarf was back in place, she had changed into jeans and a black V-necked sweater. There was a book by Nasr's feet with a painting of a reclining British lady on the cover.

"How do you find time to read?" Nasr asked, reaching down.

Jameela accepted the novel. "How do you not?"

He shrugged, handing her a brush and a couple of toothy plastic contraptions that he assumed were hair clips.

"I should go," she announced to the room, and shrugged on her coat.

"Here." Nasr reached for the backpack. "I'll walk you."

*T*he night was clear, moonlit, and still—so cold now that when Nasr saw Jameela put on gloves he felt the stiffness in his fingers and wished he'd brought his own. She walked ahead, past the front porch, and waited for him at the end of the driveway.

He felt her watching as he lit a cigarette. "Last I checked, tobacco wasn't on the haraam list. Not like Jell-O."

This earned him a smirk. Jameela quickly glanced at the house, then pulled off a glove and made a V with her fingers.

"The nice thing about when you Siddiquis are in town," she said, squinting through a long drag, "is that one never has to come up with an excuse for smelling like smoke."

Nasr lit another for himself, and they began to walk in the direction of her house.

"Maybe I shouldn't miss that," she said. "Probably healthier."

"Why miss anything?"

A silence fell between them, and as he didn't know quite what he'd meant, Nasr was glad when Jameela changed the subject. She said a friend of hers had been to Victoria. It was supposed to be very beautiful. Lots of amazing, tall trees. Would they have a chance to see Vancouver itself? No, he wished they could, but there wasn't time. Oh well, it was probably just a city like any other. When was he returning to New York? Was he keeping his apartment? He was for now, yes. All this until the turn for the park, and after taking it—the long way—they fell silent again as they walked through the band of trees separating Nasr's neighborhood from hers, and remained silent as they crossed the dark soccer field. At the end of the field was the small, sandy playground where he and Jameela used to linger sometimes. It was lit by two low streetlights. A slide, a merry-go-round, a swing set.

Nasr paused for another cigarette, and Jameela dropped into one of the swings, letting out a shivery sigh.

"I liked your dance tonight," he said.

She shrugged and looked away. "Another infamous lapse of self-restraint—tomorrow's headline." She drew herself back and pushed off, swinging gently. After a moment, she said, "Have you ever noticed how much they get wrong?"

"Who?" He took a seat beside her on the other swing. The chains were stiff and cold, like ropes of ice.

"All of them. My father. The Nawab of Montreal. In every story, there are these little mistakes, even some big ones. Take, for example, his tale of the Imambara." Nasr immediately knew the anecdote she was referring to. It was a familiar one from Hamid Uncle's repertoire about how a nawab of Lucknow saved his people from a famine by initiating a massive construction project, to build the Great Imambara, and how he ingeniously extended the relief program by hiring a crew to work at night to secretly undo each day's progress. Early this evening, Hamid Uncle had found a new audience among Nasr's friends.

"Yes," Jameela said, "there were people who worked 'under cover of darkness,' as Abba always puts it. But that's because they were from the noble families, who were also starving, and they hoped to keep their identities hidden. There was no *un*-building of the thing. Our nawab was not that kindhearted. It's just that these night workers were not used to menial labor, or any labor, so their progress was negligible." She swung forward and back, her eyes fixed on something in the dark field (a goal-post?), and soon she was gaining speed expertly: leaning flat, then swiftly pitching forward. From the top of each swing there came a tiny thrushing sound, a tinkle, as if she were wearing bells on her wrists.

Nasr was only half listening—he was, instead, formulating how he would say it: that Javaid's expecting her to pack up and leave the country was unfair, that she had reasonable grounds for breaking the engagement, that she ought to do it soon.

"You see?" she asked with an ironic curl to her mouth. "You track down one of their little stories about our fair city of origin, and you run into all kinds of actual facts that they never mentioned." She'd slowed down and was peeling off the strands of hair that stuck against her forehead. She tucked them behind her ears and brought the scarf forward.

It occurred to Nasr that Jameela had been on the far side of the room, setting up the appetizers, when Hamid Uncle was speaking to Pete and company.

"Oh, I can always tell when he's at it," she replied when he asked how she knew. "He shifts the hookah to his off hand. Happens when he's concentrating. Like when he wrote your peghaam. It sat there getting cold for hours." The curl was now a smile in the corner of her mouth. "You haven't heard it, have you? You should. It was really quite beautiful. He made two international calls to find the perfect synonym in Urdu for 'waiting.' " Her father, she continued, had written out the proposal on a scroll of parchment, but when the time came to present it to the Ansaris, he had risen up in their living room and recited the text from memory. "He pledged your nearly royal but humble devotion." She eyed Nasr, then looked away and began swinging again, more delicately now. "You know," she said, "at first when we all walked in we didn't—well, nobody actually knew whom you'd chosen. Who the bride was. Farah and her sisters were there in the room, but kind of in the background. They were sort of dressed alike, and they looked so—I guess we thought they were somebody's little cousins or something. And then there was a woman, very done up, a bit older-looking, older than the sisters at least, who stepped up to greet us— which should have been a sign, if you think about it: much too forward for a real bride. But even your mom hadn't met them, so everybody had the same thought." She shook her head. "Anyway, it turned out the woman was the cousin, married, had a couple of kids, which explained why she wasn't exactly shaped like a twig. Her name was Shirin or something. She was fine. But on the way back, in the car—you know how my mother is—they really laid into her. Began confessing how afraid they'd been when they first met her—'My God, what has he done?' and saying it had never occurred to them before that you were 'so willing to throw your life away' and 'What a face!' There was nothing wrong with the woman. A few little wrinkles maybe, a tan. She'd just come back from a vacation in Hawaii. Anyway, I'm still driving, and I hear them admit to each other that when she stepped forward both of them, *independently*, began praying—and as soon as we got back home they'd have to go straight in and do namaaz, because they owed ten, fifteen, twenty shukranas that she wasn't the one.

"That 'old hag,'" Jameela continued, "was my age, naturally. I sat beside her all evening, and in between the moments when one or the other party was overcome by the beauty of my father's words, she and I talked about resort vacations."

"You shouldn't worry about all that stuff," Nasr said with some force. His mother had never mentioned this confusion, but he could well imagine the scene.

Jameela slowed down again. "Can I get another one?" She

pulled off a glove, and as Nasr handed over his pack and lighter, he saw the source of the tinkling sound: three or four inches of dark-green and gold bangles.

"You're right," Jameela said. "Who knows—perhaps Karachi will be good for me. Toughen me up."

"I talked to Javaid," Nasr said, impatient himself now.

She nodded. "He told me." She started up again, gliding gently back and forth. With each swing, the thin, brittle churis slid out of her sleeve, then back across her wrist, separating and landing again in soft crashes of glass.

"Look, I'm sorry for the other night. We're still sorting out the timing—I think I just panicked a little. But we'll work it out."

"There's a big difference between living there and visiting," Nasr said.

She shrugged and looked almost bored when he proceeded to remind her that as a visitor you can ignore the difference— hole up in the family house, go where you're taken by relatives— but it's still there, in every aspect of life. Didn't she remember how annoyed she would get when the cousins said you were "spoiling" the servants every time you said "please" and "thank you"?

"People like us always think like that," she replied. "That there's a huge divide, and you can never go back. Maybe those pleases and thank-yous made those people uncomfortable—like they weren't part of the family, just doing a job somewhere. We don't know. It's like your uncle says. We immigrant types believe that just because we've left a certain kind of country we've made some sort of progress."

"But you've never been there."

"So I'll see something new."

"You've never lived outside the limits of the city you were born in."

"That's kind of a low blow," she observed.

"It's the truth, though, isn't it? There are realities to consider." Now that he'd warmed to the topic, Nasr found it easy to continue: Had she really thought about what it would be like to leave? What about simple basic freedoms—especially for a woman? Everything from getting into a car and going to the store to having a career was more complicated. Was she, of all people, ready to give all that up?

"What's so great about this place?" she asked. Her legs were pumping, as though she couldn't help picking up speed. "You make money, you spend money, you are constantly trying to 'improve' your life. But no matter what you do, that life is bound to be utterly thin, frivolous—"

"What about your parents?" Nasr asked.

"They won't say anything," she said. "They can't."

"Well, no. They won't, of course, for the sake of your happiness, but anybody can see that the prospect of your leaving is killing them."

She didn't reply at first. For a few moments, her profile pendulumed past him in a blur. "You know what Masood Uncle told Javaid?" she asked at the top of an arc. She hung there for a second before tucking her legs and sliding back. "My parents practically eloped. Abba's family had a different bride picked out, and he refused her. He'd seen my mother somewhere once. Once!" she said again, flinging open both of her arms, as if she were accepting applause. The cigarette in her hand slipped out, and she teetered as the swing twisted and fell back. "Careful," Nasr was tempted to say, but she made an athletic recovery, clutched the chain, and continued pumping her legs.

"He had hardly spoken to her, but apparently that was enough for this so-called *love* marriage." She shook her head. "This is exactly what I mean. They live in their own little world. And *we* live in their world. It's made up all around us. Romantic stories, imaginary versions of 'the way things used to be.' All that 'we are not the sort of people who' business. They get us early, and we cooperate—not every single rule, but the most important ones—we follow the spirit of them, thinking . . . I don't know, that we'll have a connection to a place that's interesting. Get to feel proud and different. But all these things they tell us, all these 'customs' and 'traditions' are just inventions. They're designed to get us to do what they want. And we're such suckers that we hardly notice that, when it's convenient, the way things used to be is adjusted and the old ways are cut loose."

"But if rules are what you're trying to avoid," Nasr asked, "isn't Pakistan entirely the wrong place to be going?"

"At least you can get away from all this propaganda over there. Things are what they are. There aren't any bygone days and sitting around thinking about how great life was or could have been. This half-and-half business doesn't work. You compromise and adjust—end up lying to yourself."

She was really going now, a rush of cold air each time she passed.

"What about your plan to come to New York?" Nasr asked. "You were supposed to come study at Columbia. That's what you really want, isn't it?"

She slid to a rough stop, her feet rutting the sand.

A long time ago, he continued, she had made all those plans, even won a scholarship, and then had set them aside for her parents' sake. Was it fair that she should have to give that up twice? When was she, for once, going to do what she wanted instead of sacrificing for other people?

He watched a tear form at the tip of an eyelash.

"You don't have to go. You shouldn't," he said. "Your life is here."

"What life?" she asked loudly. Her hand slapped against the chain of the swing and instantly retracted. "Shit."

Nasr leaped up and caught hold of the hand. There was a bright line of blood above her thumb. He could hear the glass rustling in the sleeve.

"Goddamn it."

"Wait," he said roughly, tightening his hold to keep her from pulling her arm away.

He knelt down and peeled back the fabric, trying to keep the sleeve from catching on the broken tips. Each roll shook out more glass, and on her arm there was a pileup of green and gold ribs angled haphazardly, hanging, stuck into her skin, sharp in every direction.

"Shit shit."

"Hold on," he said, stilling her arm. He began picking out the larger pieces. She submitted to the procedure, eventually slumping forward until her forehead was resting against the top of his.

"Look," he said, trying to keep his voice calm, "if Javaid feels he needs to go, then maybe you should let him." He hated to say it, he continued, but the truth was, engagements are broken all the time. Circumstances change. Nobody sensible would hold it against her. And, anyway, who cares what other people say? When did she ever live by all their stupid rules and conventions?

"You don't understand—"

But he did, he replied. He did understand. He understood that she was a loyal and supportive person. She always had been. She was kind and caring and brave. She had stood by Javaid through a very difficult time. She had helped him recover from his injuries, but also recover his desire to do something. "He was lucky to have had your help."

Her face was pinched and miserable. She let out a sigh, and then winced. The wreckage was worst at the wrist, and Nasr paused to decide whether to clear the inside or outside first. He chose the inside, where there was a maze of streaks. In the moonlight, it was hard to tell the glass from the glistening blood. He worked slowly and carefully. The intact bangles he snapped, so they wouldn't have to be slid off. The longer Nasr stared at the dark breaks in the delicate skin, the more strongly he felt the same sequence of surprise that he'd experienced in New York: first, at how small a person Jameela was, then that he'd hardly ever touched her, and finally that there were many ways in which he barely knew her at all.

"You feel sorry for him," he said gently. "That's understandable—we all do."

Embedded in the skin, too small to brush off, were tiny specks of glass. He dipped his head and blew across the top of her arm. A tear now spilled onto her wrist, mingling in swirls with the lines of blood, and it struck Nasr how dear this wrist was to him. He'd been around it his entire life, watched it gesture and articulate. But had he ever really noticed it? He knew the thrilling way her mind trampled along, knew its stubbornness and the humor with which it contradicted itself, but this wrist, with its delicate configuration of cords and its faint cover of down, was a mystery.

"You don't have to give up your whole life," he continued, "just because you feel bad about what happened to him."

She drew a shaky breath. There were more tears now, landing and mingling.

Just then Jameela came together for Nasr—the being whose thoughts he'd shared was also this flesh. He looked up, felt the soft chill of her cheek, then pressed his lips to hers. Here again was the sensation, cool and salty, of the familiar mingled with the new. What a fool he'd been to dismiss that kiss in the ballroom.

After a moment, she pulled back, but left her face resting again on his forehead. When she finally spoke, the words drained out from her, a warm and steady trickle of breath, sliding down the back of Nasr's neck and into his ear. "I kept him here," she whispered. "I changed his course. I convinced him that going to New York would be okay. I told him it was possible to avoid getting caught up in it. That you shouldn't overreact, or take things personally. That not everyone believed the stuff in the news. That it was still possible to steer clear, make a life around what's happened. But I was wrong." She took another breath, but the sob she was trying to smother broke free. It was the saddest sound Nasr had ever heard. "He would have been long gone—safe, if it weren't for me."

"That's crazy. You can't think like that. The only people responsible were those boys who actually committed the crime."

"What boys?" she said, lifting her head, but he tucked it into his shoulder.

She didn't have to pretend, he said. He knew everything—this guy had told him about the three boys, the bat—

"Oh, God."

There were fresh tears now, shuddering sobs—Nasr stopped immediately, realizing his information was new. Javaid hadn't told her. Her fingers began to pull away again, but he tightened his hold.

"Yes, it was terrible," he said. "No one can imagine what the poor guy must have gone through, but he's dealing with it." There was a stillness about her now, her fingers limp in his. Javaid, Nasr said, was doing what he needed to do, what he wanted to do. Maybe she should do the same. Return to the plan she'd made for herself, come to New York—try again to finish her degree, get away and do what she wanted for once.

Nasr lifted her chin. Her eyes were closed now, her lips a thin line.

"You can't go," he said. "You belong here, with me."

There was no change in the expression. He wasn't sure she'd heard him.

"I can help you," he continued. "Find a place. Get settled—whatever you need." He could even help her get a job if she didn't mind temp work. His company had openings all the time. "Then you can start the life you should have had all along."

"And then what?" she asked, eyes still closed. Her lashes cast a faint shadow on her cheeks.

Nasr paused. "And then"—well, he hadn't thought it all through yet. There were sure to be logistical troubles, he supposed, but really his mind went blank all of a sudden. He couldn't think of a thing to say. In a way, this was always how he found himself with Jameela: led out to a wide-open field with no paths running through it. You were exposed here, you felt your own self expanding, unbridled but uncertain. So why was it that these landscapes, though unfamiliar and indistinct, always felt more real to him than the cramped corridors that actually characterized his life? The other part of Nasr's brain recognized immediately that his hesitation was a mistake, and the body in his arms had stiffened.

"This is pathetic," she said, and pushed herself away from him. She examined her arm, turning it about as if she were just noticing the blood. "Every once in a while, you decide you don't know how you feel about the woman you're marrying, and you offer to get out of it. But you don't mean it. So what do you mean? Are you thinking I'd be up for an affair?" She lifted her face now. There weren't any tears—had he somehow imagined them? "God, you are such a coward." There was a fiercely drawn breath, a moment of sudden composure. "I'm married," she told him, and then the face crumpled. "It's done. All done. Get it?"

28

The face in crisis has a terrible hold. You can't look away. There is a sameness about the paroxysm: familiar muscles struggle with each other, the skin on the forehead folds, the eyebrows rear up and bunch together, clashing, before the entire structure collapses. Nasr couldn't say there hadn't been warnings. She was angry, perhaps more than anyone had ever been in his presence. But he wasn't prepared for the energy with which Jameela's words plowed through the empty, unresisting night air, his brain, the five hours he lay in bed failing to sleep, came out the other end, ripped through the middle of the next day's trivial panic and preparations, spilled into the evening, so that now, at the Nikaah, her revelations, insults, and accusations were still blasting through, puncturing holes in the ceremony's elaborate yet flimsy moments. In the moment Nasr happened to find himself, he was being led onto a stage. Through the curtain of roses and tinsel that hung over his face, the banquet hall appeared red and gold, tinkling indistinctly in dim light. It was a moment in which there was another sort of weeping—eyes too watery to meet his, tissues and solemn faces. This tearful display had first appeared back at the house when he'd sat obediently in the midst of his family as a sehra was tied to his head by Hamid Uncle and Masood Chacha. It had followed him on the long and quiet drive to Cornwall, and it enveloped him now as he took his seat. But this crying was neither remarkable nor unexpected, and it had nothing to do with the calamity in his head.

Aisha perched herself on the arm of Nasr's chair, her privilege as the oldest of the children closest in relation. To his left was an empty chair, also covered in red velvet and gold paint, where Farah would sit after the main portion of the ceremony. And in front was a sea of dining tables: the Ansaris to the left; Nasr's family and friends, a couple of hundred strong, to the right. Bright-colored saris encased all manner of women in tightly wound silken cylinders; children ran about in packs, boys in kurta-pajamas and dark vests went around demanding to be chased by the girls, who trailed sequined rupattas. Only near the edges of the room, where the painted cement brick of the walls still showed, was it possible to detect that this place was once actually an elementary-school cafeteria where children had laughed and squealed every day. Just off the stage, the maulana, in white robes and polished black shoes, stepped forward to manage the marriage contract. Nasr tried to gain focus—to feel part of it—but his vision began slipping, as if there was interference, and the faces blurred into a backdrop.

"The time for getting out of things is over," Jameela had said the night before. "You'd know that if you could for once stop thinking about yourself." Married—how had this happened? Nasr had asked her. When? At the courthouse, she said, a week after she and Javaid came back from New York. In front of a lady judge and two witnesses solicited from among the government staff. While wearing their winter coats it had happened. "You love him?" he said. "You have no right to ask me that," she said.

The maulana was now tapping the microphone on the podium. "Brothers and sisters," he said in deep-voiced English, "if I may have silence, a little attention—especially from the young people in the audience. Brother and Sister Ansari have kindly allowed for a few words to be said before we proceed." He drew very little of the crowd's attention, but began anyway: "The Prophet Muhammad, sallallaahu 'alayhi wa sallam, tells us that Islam is a religion of peace. It is a religion of duty and goodwill. At no time, brothers and sisters, is it more important to maintain one's faith than when that goodwill and sense of duty are tested. You may think that the past few months have been the darkest of our faith. But that is not true. We have survived much darker days. History has subjected us to countless injustices and interferences. But we will not dwell on such matters today, on this happy occasion, for the very way such troubles are overcome is by living in the faith of the Prophet, peace be upon him, which means having the strength and the courage to keep to the straight path, the guided path, the path that has been lighted for us and us alone. Where, you might be wondering, do such courage and strength come from? The number-one source, brothers and sisters, is the family. And this is what Sister Siddiqui's son and Brother and Sister Ansari's daughter have entered into this marriage to do, to create a family in the faith."

What do you mean, married? Nasr had asked. There'd been no sex yet, Jameela said, if that's what he wanted to know. She strode out of the park, and Nasr followed. No, I mean, why? he said. How are you married? Was it really so surprising? she asked. Did he find it inconceivable that someone would want to marry her? Treat her with a little dignity and respect, instead

of this weird and convenient obliviousness? At first, Jameela
headed home, but when she saw that Nasr was willing to have
this conversation anywhere, talk in plain view of her house and
the neighbors, that he wouldn't leave and didn't care if their
voices carried, she circled back, past streetlamps and pavement,
into the woods between their subdivisions. That's not what I
meant, either, he said. Well, should she start at the beginning,
then? she asked, her brisk pace matching the angry words, and
Nasr soon learned more than he cared to know: how Javaid's
voice and hands shook, back in October, when he'd first proposed; how politely he'd worded the question—that he knew his
proposal might seem sudden, but in a few weeks he felt he'd become closer to her than to anyone else in his life; how sweetly
pleased he had been when Jameela asked for a day to think
about it, as though he hadn't expected even that much kindness;
how shocked he'd sounded when she called back an hour later.
What else? Jameela demanded. After the engagement party, she
continued—now they were on a dark trail, making their way
around damp stones and slick roots—when she and Javaid had
started talking about the configurations of their lives together,
she told him that she hoped graduate school was still in her future and he confessed that he'd been sick of his work for a long
time, wanted to try something new. It was ridiculous, but she
had started feeling hopeful. It had been so nice to have someone
to go places with—marches and protests; she'd even enjoyed ac-
companying him to the masjid, but also they'd just run errands
together or go to dinner. "I was actually happy," Jameela said,
"for about twenty minutes." Her parents hadn't liked the idea of
Pakistan, but Javaid was so easily dissuaded from going that she
didn't think it was a big deal. She assumed his interest in the
idea had been academic, that he'd been satisfied to talk about
going and think about it, and the thought had served its purpose
by extracting him from his job.

The maulana said, "In our marriages, there is order and

serenity and balance. Yes, balance. They will tell you different because they don't know us, but the balance is there. It is built-in: the husband providing for the family, the wife helping her husband and children stay true to the tenets of the faith and steer the family through the obstacles of this world. The cooperation of both partners is essential. Those who are not of our faith will insist that we are not like this, that our marriages have no partnerships, that they promote oppression and division—but secretly they know this is not true. Why else do they look to us and say, How is it that your people have so few divorces and unpleasant disruptions? Why are your children so content and successful? How do you do it? It's not a question of how, brothers and sisters—but why. Why do we do it? Why do we work so hard, face such trials, to preserve our way of life? We do it because we believe—we do it because we know our path is the right path, the final word. But these days our families, as you all are knowing, are under constant attack. Not simply by the West. The West, in fact, has given up on the family. What was once thought to be a unit has been broken down into individuals. The Prophet, alayhis-salaam, foresaw this type of decline. He foresaw that the greatest test of faith would *not* occur in the fighting on a battlefield. It would be fought on the grounds of the home, and it would be a test of the foundations of that home. A test of whether women can be led away from the concerns of their children, whether men can be distracted from the duties of providing for their families. This battle is not only being waged within our families, but within ourselves. It is fueled by self-doubt and needless questioning. Temptation, distraction, instant gratification—these are the real enemies of peace, of a peaceful, pure, and dedicated life. Which is why the Prophet, sallallaahu 'alayhi wa sallam, lived by example, why his life is the one we look to for guidance in domestic matters. This is why marriage is the sanctuary, brothers and sisters. It is a vital action. The first step in building a boundary between the forces that will erode one's faith and the true content of our hearts . . ."

At the hospital that night, Javaid wouldn't tell her what had happened, not the whole truth. Eventually, she got him to admit that it hadn't been a simple mugging, but that was all he was going to say. She'd been left to imagine the rest from the bruising, or, rather, from as much of that as he'd let her see. And no matter how much she urged, he refused to file a report with the police. Who would really care, he said, that a Muslim was beaten up on the streets of New York these days—if they ever had? The only thing Javaid would talk to Jameela about was the decision he'd made: he would be leaving for sure—as soon as possible. There was nothing here for him, for any of them, except more of the same—the same misunderstandings, ignorance, humiliations. She tried to assure him that they would get past this, but nothing she said sounded believable to her own ears. She wanted to help him, and the only way that seemed right, made sense that night, was to agree—to say of course they would try Pakistan. It was where he still felt most at home, so naturally she was interested in seeing it. Not just seeing it, he said. He wanted to be clear—he would be going there to stay. No changing his mind this time. He wanted something in his life to be decided and settled once and for all. Was sick of all the going back and forth and having such an important matter up in the air. Yes, she said. She could understand that feeling. Well, then, maybe she'd understand why he needed a commitment, he said. Couldn't she just marry him now—as soon as possible? Wouldn't it be nice to have one thing set and secure? Though his voice didn't shake this time, he could hardly look at her—who knew how much they'd hurt him, she thought. Before she could reply, he said that he would release her if she liked. He'd be sorry to do it, but he'd understand. He seemed so angry and alone to her, and yet he was making this gesture. No, no, she said; she didn't want to be released from anything, but she wondered if they might wait just a bit. She couldn't deprive her mother of the chance to arrange a wedding. Of all people, Javaid replied, her parents might understand. He told her the truth then about her own life—what he'd learned from Masood Chacha about how her mother and father had met and the scandal of their early years. She was born of rebels, Javaid said, didn't she know? That's when it finally became clear to her why there was no longer any place for them here: living in this half-and-half way turned people into liars and hypocrites. She agreed—they would go, they would make a new life, away from all this. It was she who suggested the courthouse, as it would be the fastest way.

"You decided all this that night?" Nasr asked, grabbing her arm to stop her. "The night of the party?"

She shrugged herself free. "I'd already decided—it was a moot point by then."

"Who knows you're married?"

"No one."

"What about the wedding—what, exactly, is everyone planning?"

After the ceremony in the courthouse, she'd had a weak moment and asked Javaid if they could indulge the parents: announce their decision to go to Karachi, but not the marriage; wait a few months and let their mothers arrange a small, simple wedding. "After all their lies, I still tried to do something for them," she said to Nasr, disgusted.

"But why did you need my help two days ago?"

"Time—Talat's plans are getting so elaborate, Javaid's afraid we won't be able to leave until the end of next year. All I wanted was a little time."

Nasr felt a tap on his shoulder—the maulana was waiting. He was surprisingly young, an Arab with candid eyes and a trim reddish-brown beard. There was a flush in each of his cheeks. He prompted Nasr to confirm the amount of the meher, the three months of financial subsistence to be set aside for a wife in case of death or divorce. Nasr nodded, but the man still waited. He lifted an arm to part the curtain of flowers in front of his face. After receiving this confirmation, the maulana stood up and slipped through a door behind the stage. Nasr dropped his arm, and was again enclosed in roses. Mr. Ansari had looked surprised by the amount. It had been Nasr's suggestion (made just weeks ago in a moment whose sense of triumph now seemed grotesque) that the money should be in American dollars.

"What about us?" he'd asked Jameela, amid trees and shadows. "There is no us," she said matter-of-factly. "That's not true. You kissed me," Nasr said. "I didn't—" Jameela began. "Fine, you let me kiss you—what was that?" "Too much champagne," she replied, echoing his own use of this excuse. "Which I shouldn't have been drinking in the first place."

The maulana emerged a few minutes later. He was quickly surrounded by a tight circle of men. A quiet had settled across the hall. There was shuffling, a child's whine, someone ordering tea.

Then Nasr heard congratulations being exchanged, and felt the crowd released into motion; the music was cued, the single note of the shehnai rising up woefully—he had become a married man. Someone bent down and pressed his head to Nasr's, shuddering, and the fat flowers of the sehra bounced soft and cool against his face. The more the activity pressed in around him, the farther Nasr felt from it, catching glimpses as from the back of a dim cave. At the entrance of the cave were his uncles, his brother-in-law, his mother and sisters, in tears. And beyond his family, the same face appeared in every slice of his view: openly stricken by the sight of him.

"He tricked you," Nasr had told Jameela.

They had reached a clearing, spacious with moonlight.

There was a bench and a water fountain. Jameela walked ahead and sank down on the seat. "Why don't you go home?" she replied.

Nasr joined her on the bench. She stared ahead, a mute profile, as he tried to make her see how Javaid had guilted her into doing what he wanted. When she finally spoke, her voice was dull and low. "You get to a point and you realize that the time for fantasies is over and what matters now are the realities. To have lived by it, to have seen what it can do, on TV, on the world's stage, put in action on those planes—that's the reality."

"What are you talking about?"

Jameela looked at him now, but as though he were simpleminded. In a tone that was almost kind, she asked, "Don't you ever wonder what it is that makes us do these things?"

"What things?" he said. Nasr's brain lurched forward, caught up to the meaning of her words. "We don't do these things. There's no connection there."

"You know what these people believe is promised to them?" There was a grim smile on her thin lips. "What kind of heaven is described in the pages of our holy Qur'an?"

The question hung between them for a moment. How did they get to be talking about this? he wondered.

"They imagine it's all about sex up there. The afterlife is a place filled with virgins, attending to our true believers' every need. A paradise of women and wine. *Wine*. The planning, the execution, the timing just right so that it can appear live on CNN—it was all a sick little mating dance for drunken sex. Maybe this shouldn't be so surprising. Maybe we should sympathize. They were just lonely, pathetic men, after all, living by the same—"

"It's not the same," Nasr insisted. "What they believe has nothing to do with us."

"Which of us is us?" she asked.

He thought she was being flippant, but she wasn't. It was a

genuine question, and she seemed to be waiting to hear what he would say. He felt, all of a sudden, embarrassed by her seriousness—this sort of confusion was beneath her. "They're criminals," he replied. "We're not."

She shook her head, not so much a signal that this was the wrong answer as that he'd missed her point entirely. "There is a despicable echo in it that people like us ignore—for everything good, fair, and flexible, there is a sexist part, a bigoted part, a part that can't take a word of criticism. This is the Islam that we don't know what to do with, so we don't do anything. We just keep our distance, pick and choose what we want to believe in, and hope that nobody will take the other stuff seriously. But it is taken seriously. The echo is heard all the time—for some people, this is the only part of Islam that makes sense to them. You feel lonely and angry, ignored, disappointed. You wonder if there's a reason why you've been alone for so long; you wonder if you're waiting for something special. You hope there will be a reward for your patience. You keep to yourself, intentionally now, just to preserve this perfect state you're in—of waiting. But in the meantime friends have moved on, parents age, people treat you as though you are immature or stubborn, that your feelings are too strong and you should outgrow them. And soon in your mind there's a divide—one side you compromise and betray yourself; the other side you remain alone. This is when the echo slips in—it assures you that your years of loneliness will eventually come to mean something, that yes, there is a reward awaiting you. The only thing is, you don't collect it in this life but when you're dead.

"My father sits around every evening asking, 'What are these people after?' He can't imagine. He claims to have no idea what is wrong. But it's so obvious. They want to believe in something, to belong to it. They need to—more purely than the rest of us. But what they long for is poisoned at the core."

Through the corner of his vision, Nasr saw a grown man

holding his hands up to cover his eyes. It ought to have been humbling or moving—that so many people felt such emotion on his behalf—but instead it was appalling.

A murmur arose. Farah was being led in. Her small figure advanced slowly to the stage, supported on one side by her mother and on the other by a sister. Her gharara was dark red, with a thick net of silver embroidery. The rupatta that covered her head and face was of the same color, and it had a border of heavy silver fringe that swung faintly with each step. She was made to pause for the photographer, but she didn't pull aside the rupatta as instructed, even seemed to turn away to avoid the camera.

"You don't love him," Nasr said, and Jameela deflected him again with the same maddeningly casual denial. "You have no idea what I feel."

"What about those messages you left?"

She grew quiet then as he reminded her of the phone calls she'd made in September. He told her how he'd listened to her messages on the balcony of his hotel room, on that cold wet day when nothing made sense. He knew all the things she'd done. She'd tried to help him, save him from making a mistake, but at the time he'd been too stupid and blind—he'd gotten it all wrong. But he could see now that she knew him, understood him, better than he knew himself, and that the two of them were meant to be together. The more Nasr said such things, the more he felt he was grasping the truth of them—seeing how uniquely he and Jameela were suited to each other, how they were forged from the same experiences, and had grown something real and actual, something to build a life on. The nature of this life suddenly grew so vivid to him that he was compelled to describe it. He extrapolated from those mornings that he and Jameela had shared in the intimate dark of his kitchen. Each morning of their lives, he declared, would be exactly like that: warm toast, strong tea, and hushed conversation. After this, the two of them would head out together, bustle into the subway. On weekdays, they would have to separate, of course: she to go to her classes, he to work, but they would meet for lunch. Sometimes he'd take a half day and they'd languish in a museum or two—she'd lecture him on abstract painting or classical Indian dance. On weekends, they'd drive up to Long Island or Boston or Maine. Explore coastlines, rent cottages, try sailing. She sat still, gazing into the distance as though his words were projecting a film of their future on the far canopy of trees, a future she seemed to find as engrossing as he did. Or, he continued, if she didn't want to live in New York, they would go far away, discover a new city, make it theirs.

"Do you know how many times I could have said something?" she asked in a wry, defeated tone. "Done something? But I just watched. I *talked* to you. I thought by talking to you there would be opportunities. But apparently it was not that kind of talk."

He caught her up in his arms. Her hair was cold, smooth, faintly perfumed under his lips. He felt her lean into him. "How could you wait so long?" Nasr said, groaning. "All those years—all those ridiculous conversations . . ."

"I was hardly subtle," she said, her voice mumbling but incredulous.

"No, but you were," he said. "You were very Lucknawi about it, never said the thing straight."

Now there was a laugh—a laugh after all those tears!—and he felt a spike of hope. "And I was stupid," he rushed on. "Stupid about you, us. Stupid about that damn search."

She drew herself back. "But I didn't think you were," she said. There was a somber light in her eyes. The quality of its attention wasn't at all disconcerting and overly serious (as his mother often intimated), but full of deep consideration and complicated interest. "I may not have liked it, or thought it would work, but I always admired that it was a choice you made

357

after giving other things a try. And that you waited and tried to find someone who'd struck out and done something with her life. That's what you always used to say you were looking for, and I—I was never that person."

"Of course you were. You are! More than anyone. You don't have to actually do things to be adventurous." But she was unwilling to accept these compliments, and the moment became so unfamiliar and awkward for them both that Nasr wondered if he'd ever complimented her before. "Why didn't you just tell me?" he said, chiding now, though as gently as possible.

Her gaze remained one of extreme composure, but the voice wavered, the sound half-swallowed and small. Yet there was just enough breath that he could make out the words: "I didn't want to have to."

"And you shouldn't ever have to," he said, "not a person like you." But at this she looked even more miserable.

Now that it was before him, the nature of love's arrival seemed appropriately chaotic. Wasn't it supposed to be something that overtook people, caught them off guard, even those who were much more experienced in such matters, who went about expecting to find themselves in love? Whenever he had heard reports from friends, Nasr had always regarded the trouble of being in love as just that: trouble. The heartache, confusion, awkward breakups, and insufficiently satisfying reconciliations that people complained about had always sounded exaggerated and unnecessary—an overly complicated drama that one accepted with surprising submissiveness or even welcomed as though it were a point of pride. But now—with Jameela's face before him, stricken and caught—it seemed so right to Nasr that love should entail such explosive recognition, disarray, and turmoil. This feeling was such a prize that there ought to be a price for finding it.

"Look," he said, "I can't marry her now. It's not too late." He grabbed her hand, but she slipped it out. A restlessness had overtaken him. They had wasted so much time; they were wasting time now, lingering in these woods, in the cold, when they should be having difficult but necessary conversations, explaining, apologizing, canceling reservations, asking for forgiveness. Or they could just go—drive away right now, do it all from a distance. "We'll get you out of it. Javaid is a reasonable guy."

Her eyes filled, but then she blinked. "Don't say that," she said, blinking again.

"It won't be easy," he admitted. "But it's not impossible."

She shook her head. "It doesn't work that way."

"Shouldn't we at least try?" he asked. Why should the two of them be bound by the conventions they both had always known were artificial and trivial? he asked her. What they had between them didn't need—had never needed—the approval of others. Didn't the mere fact of this mean they were free? "We'll tell them together. They'll get over it."

"No," she said. "I don't want to."

Of all the surprises of the evening, this one caught Nasr most off guard. "What do you mean?"

"Don't you get it?" she said. "I thought you'd *died*. I thought they'd killed you. I was sure of it. Before that day, I was so angry with you, and then suddenly you weren't there to be angry at. I tried to pray, but the only prayers I knew were the ones those people probably recited—" She drew a quick breath. "I spent that whole day saying them, probably not in the right order, but as many as I could remember, over and over again, and soon a strange thing happened—they worked. I heard that you were safe, and it was enough."

Wasn't this all the more reason why they had to try to be together, no matter what the cost? Nasr asked.

"No, it's exactly why we should do what we promised we would." She stood up suddenly, and Nasr followed, afraid that she was headed back into the trails, but she merely walked around to the fountain.

"But wouldn't that be living a lie?"

"This isn't about you and me or what we want anymore," she said. An annoyingly reasonable tone entered her voice again. "That's the way we used to think. But it's not enough anymore to sit around saying that they're not like us, when everybody else thinks they are. Not when it's come to our door like this."

"You keep changing the subject," he said. He let himself sound accusing—anything to get her to admit that she loved him. But when he reached, she pulled away. "I don't understand you," he said.

She nodded now, as if this wasn't surprising to her at all. "Because you don't know how it can help. How it helped me. When you stop tuning into the echo, when you get to know it, it's a good thing—it has lightness and clarity. It's generous, beautiful even. And what's worthy about it is not what it promises in the afterlife but what it says about how you should conduct yourself now, in your actual life." The moonlight caught her features, pale eyes floating in a strangely serene white face. "But it's in trouble. To believe in it these days, you have to reconcile, explain, and apologize. It shouldn't be that way. If we really want to get rid of the echo, then we should offer something in its place. And the only way to do that is to be honest with it and yourself, to practice being a different kind of Muslim. But you can't do that here anymore—it's too late."

"Maybe it's easy to think that when you also want to run away, to punish your parents," Nasr said. "But they just made a mistake. They were young. They don't want you to make one, too."

Her eyes snapped in his direction and she stared.

He changed tactics. "Or maybe you're running away from me again, or still. But why? You yourself said it's so hard to find one's equivalent—"

"You knew about them?" she said.

Nasr admitted that his mother had told him her parents' story.

"When?"

"What does it matter?"

"Before New York?" she demanded.

"This summer."

Her lips tightened, and she nodded. "You should go with Farah," she said. Nasr had heard this voice before—back in the hospital room. "She's the one for you."

She collected her bag from where he'd left it, at the base of the fountain.

Nasr felt a choking bitterness rise up. "So this is all about some principle?" When she didn't reply, he said, "You won't be happy there."

"I'm not going there to be happy," she said, and turned to leave.

The flower ropes of Nasr's sehra jostled and parted, and there was yet another face in crisis, eyebrows rearing up.

He had called after her. "Maybe you're the coward, not telling me all that time and then walking away like this when we could still do something about it." Just when he thought she would keep walking, she turned to him a face that hardly looked like a face at all. It was turbulent and distorted, like a balloon tearing away from its tethers. The eyes weren't crying tears so much as leaking them; the mouth was open and moving but, for a long moment, utterly soundless. Then: What had taken him so long? Had he ever thought about how she might have spent years wondering what was wrong with her? And why the fuck didn't he call her back?

Wake up. Are you listening? Have I got your attention?

The photographer was snapping her fingers at someone who had stepped into her frame. Nasr felt a warm splash on his hands—his own face, as wet as theirs. He rose to his feet, as if to leave—but why was he leaving? Was he allowed to leave? No. It was just a response to the photographer's signaling.

"Behind your wife's chair," she commanded, smiling but not kindly. Someone pulled the flowers of Nasr's sehra over onto his shoulder. The light of the room flooded into his eyes. "Arm around the back and lean in." There was much milling about; mubaraks were being exchanged. "Big smile, groom." The photographer dipped back behind her lens, reappeared with a stern look. "Bigger." Nasr complied, though it felt as if he were baring his teeth.

On one side of the room were fine wool sherwanis; on the other, business suits of all colors. Vice presidents, surgeons, engineers, lawyers to his right; on his left, the merchants who ran motels, convenience marts, small shops in strip malls. Nasr felt alert now to a second contrast: every single face in crisis, every set of wrecked and swollen features, belonged to someone from *his* side. He located Mrs. Ansari, solemn but smiling, collecting congratulations, and Mr. Ansari directing guests to line up along the stage for the picture-taking. Nasr's mother shuddered against someone's shoulder.

"Darling, you have such a beautiful smile," the photographer called to Farah. She was a tall, middle-aged French woman. "Come, make her smile," she said, catching Nasr's eye.

Why didn't he call her back? Nasr had told Jameela he didn't understand her, but late in the night, back at home, in bed, he found himself imagining her view of the past years: the parade of women he'd brought before her; and the suspicions he'd conveniently developed when she had come closest to convincing him of what a failure the past three years had been. He remembered their conversation in June—how it had been full of strange convolutions and exposures. How disgusted she'd been with him at the end, and how he'd told himself she was being self-righteous, interfering, uncouth, judgmental, a poisonous influence, whatever excuse was easiest to believe. He tried now to recall if Jameela had ever said a word against a prospective bride, an actual person. He wondered how many other times he'd been that despicably quick to assume the worst about her. And what had been Jameela's reward for showing such discretion? Conversation after conversation focused on the most trifling details—insufficiencies in beauty, or this or that attribute. He saw how those discussions must have seemed to someone who was waiting, who herself was never too young, too religious, too dependent, too quiet, too dowdy . . . What a mess he'd made of it. Relying on a creaky old system, thinking he could make it work to his advantage, thinking he would be getting the best of both worlds. Now he was stuck with the worst: the one woman who had loved him had been beside him all along, and he had chosen a stranger instead. But how could he have known? Nasr wondered. He had no experience in recognizing love. His past relationships, which he'd secretly been so proud of even when they failed, experiences which had felt so real and dangerous, which he'd thought had "grown" him and set him apart from his peers, now seemed desiccated: formulaic experiments in which he'd hardly risked anything. With Jameela, there had never been any need for concealments or deceptions; the rapport between them required no translations or accommodation because, Nasr realized now, it was conditional, specific to him, suited to his whole self. There were ways out, he thought—not pleasant but possible. It was not too late. He knew he didn't deserve this chance, but the bigger mistake would be to deny what was between them and stay with these other people.

There was a pale light behind the blinds at the window. He

would tell Farah first—or no, maybe his mother. Perhaps the Ansaris would appreciate—after things settled down—that he'd kept his distance from their daughter under such circumstances. He tried to formulate what he would say. A few moments later, or perhaps some hours, there was a soft knock at his door. He heard his mother pad into the room and place a cup of tea (its saucer would be on top and turned over) on his nightstand. "Beta, we will be leaving soon," she whispered, girlish and excited. Yasmine had scheduled a long day at the salon, assigned the women of the house to go in shifts. Nasr pretended to sleep. There were three soft claps, then he felt her breath blown across his face and form, spreading the protection of the prayer as she had so many times before. Soon she had left, and he had said nothing.

*D*inner was served to the guests, and brought, in heavily mounded plates, to him and Farah. Suraiya and Rafia held Farah's rupatta away from her face, while an auntie attempted to feed her spoonfuls of rice.

"I do not," Suraiya was saying in a scandalized voice.

"Your feet are twice as big as Apa's," Rafia said, "and one and a half times mine. Look."

"They are not!" Suraiya raised the hem of her gharara and gave her sandal to her sister to compare.

"See, you could wear a man's size. Here, just look." Rafia asked to borrow Nasr's shoes, while Suraiya cried out in protest.

Nasr heard the false note in Suraiya's voice a moment too late—their trick had worked. Soon, Yasmine was standing on the stage in front of him, frowning. "You just handed them to her. We saw you." "Yeah, mister, whose side are you on, anyway?" Saira asked, her hands on her hips, a joke that made her daughters laugh. A crowd began gathering behind Suraiya and Rafia, who had wedged themselves into the narrow space between Nasr's and Farah's chairs. Each girl held a black shoe triumphantly in the air.

Farah's side started with preposterous amounts, demanding thousands of dollars for the return of the footwear. Yasmine tried to work them down by saying she was not going to pay more than the shoes were actually worth, and she even held out the money up front—one hundred and fifty dollars for a quick resolution. Suraiya and Rafia closed their eyes and shook their heads to the cheering delight of their legion of cousins, a mass of girls who made outraged faces on cue. Yasmine added one more fifty-dollar bill and then another, and each time there were screeching refusals. Behind the wall of girls was a row of boys, who began chanting: "Cheap, cheap, cheap, cheap." Boys were not normally involved in the shoe-stealing game, but Nasr knew immediately that their tactic would work. Yasmine wouldn't be able to bear such an accusation, and indeed she held all the money she had in one hand and her cell phone in the other, as if she were offering to wire funds into accounts if need be. Saira looked puzzled and a little put out, and her daughters were just as bewildered. "We have no more," she said, shaking her head, then she turned back to the aunties on the outer rim and said the same thing to them. Nasr opened his wallet, which elicited a roar of applause from Farah's side. He gave Yasmine another couple of fifties. But the shoes weren't turned over, and the chanting continued.

Some of the boys had slipped in front and were drumming on the stage with their fists—"Cheap, cheap, cheap"—like birds of the next generation, eager and greedy, capable of demanding more than he ever could. "You think you can take her for a measly four hundred dollars?" one of them said, laughing. "Yes, am I worth only this much?" Farah asked. Now that she was surrounded by her family, she seemed revived, had shed the traditional bridal gravity, and the sound of her voice spurred on the drumming.

As Saira and Yasmine went about collecting bills from aunties and uncles, Masood Chacha came forward, drawing Javaid with him. He clapped the groom's "brother" about the shoulders and declared that it was time for the men of the family to get involved. It was immediately clear that Masood Chacha was an accomplished practitioner in the ritual. He pulled out a few loonies and joked at length about exchange rates, then emphasized their own side's willingness, if a reasonable settlement couldn't be reached, to carry the groom and bride out on their shoulders—canceling altogether the need for shoes. Javaid also seemed capable of playing his part. A wicked smile in place, he wondered loudly and pointedly when it would occur to Farah's sisters that Nasr's family might have brought backup footwear for the groom. "Aha, yes!" Masood Chacha said, impressed and approving. "One should not be forgetting the B Plan." In response, there were scandalized squeals from Farah's side and accusations of cheating. Righted, the ritual proceeded through its programmatic lines of barter and exchange.

Where was Jameela? Nasr wondered. She wouldn't, of course, have any part of this game. For a second, he thought he had spotted her profile, but she had disappeared, blended into the crowd.

During the Rukhsati, he and Farah were walked out of the hall. The procession was slow. There was the train of Farah's gharara to contend with, as well as the videographer, who drew his camera backward in front of them and kept getting his feet caught in its cables. Farah was solemn again, a tiny figure at Nasr's side, hunched and covered. She leaned heavily against her mother since he, of course, wasn't allowed to offer her an arm. Nasr's own mother was on his other side, and the rest of the family members and guests followed. Nasr was grateful his sehra had been dropped over his face for the walk, but the curtain parted when he climbed into the awaiting car, and he caught sight of the weeping faces. Now the Ansaris had broken down as well; each looked disconsolate and defeated. He wished it were possible to do something to break the spell, to reassure them, to show that he was fully sympathetic, that once he'd been on the other side of this terrible moment. But it was not his role, hardly his place, to diminish their sorrow. Farah was at the other end of the back seat now, a foot away. Her head was bent and her hands were cupped in her lap. Possibly she was reciting a prayer. Beyond her, people reached in to bid farewell, and others shouted instructions to each other or readied themselves to leave. After some time, Rizwan slipped into the driver's seat, and Hamid Uncle into the passenger's. The drive home was long and quiet.

A̲t the door to the house, it was Nasr's nieces' turn to extract payment from him by barring the entry of the new bride. "You can't come in," they wailed, sounding like alien creatures with their Texan drawls. Behind them stood Yasmine and Saira, reluctant and apologetic; and at the back were the aunties, urging the girls to stand firm. Behind all of them, the foyer was warm and yellow. Nasr tried to smile and play along. He took out all his remaining cash and held the money up. His fingers were stiff, and he saw his breath. At the sight of the bills, the nieces looked willing to yield, but the older women demanded more. Nasr felt the icy slide of satin against the back of his wrist. "She's cold," he said, and all of a sudden the door was yanked open, to cheers and cries of protest. "Oof-oh, that's all you girls can manage?" Talat Auntie called out. "In our day, we would settle for no less than a thousand from our brothers." "That was rupees, for God's sake," Jameela said. There she was, at the back of the foyer: a thin figure in a dark-blue gharara with a pinched face and haunted eyes. He tried to seek out those eyes, in sympathy, but she failed to look at him.

The newlyweds were made to sit on a divan in the living room, yet another flowered and decorated stage. Farah's rupatta was pulled aside and a mirror was brought in for the "first" showing. He was supposed to feel pleased with the silly, shaky glimpse of her cheek. The two of them were made to feed each other tepid spoonfuls of kheer. Then the room was reshuffled for the next ritual.

Hamid Uncle came to sit beside Nasr, putting a hand on his shoulder. His broad chest was tightly encased in a white silk sherwani that had been made to match Nasr's and that set off his neat silver hair.

"I must confess a failure on my part, beta," Hamid Uncle said, with a heavy breath. "They are fine people. If I may have said things recently, please"—he brought a handkerchief to his eyes—"rantings of an old man putting on airs."

A moment later, Nasr was prompted to kneel beside Farah, but when he washed her feet, they were just feet to him. The color of the mehendi pattern on the toes was brown, but the leaves, dots, and paisleys grew redder as they traveled up to the ankle. The rough-skinned hands of several aunties mixed in, large and bare against Farah's stained skin. But he felt nothing, even though the feet were cold and small, dangling like a child's.

Nasr sensed then a silence gathering at his back, yet he knew they were all there, his family collected behind him, looking over his shoulder. His face grew warm. He began to have the strangest sensation that everyone in this room thought he was a fool, that they felt sorry for him. Was that why, after all those years of searching and debates, no one had ever asked him, "Why this girl?" A sweet, rotting smell rose up. The flowers of his sehra were wilting. Had he just entered an arranged marriage that nobody approved of? Could such a thing even exist?

The foot in Nasr's hand wriggled. He looked up and Farah smiled at him with recognition, as she had smiled yesterday, as she had smiled at the boys during the negotiations for his shoes, a suppressed smile meant to assure him that behind the suppression she was indeed herself. But what could such an assurance mean to him?

Her cheeks were composed of pure and sweet lines, as was her brow. Her skin was as smooth as plastic. He could tell her anything, and she would believe it. Nasr took his seat. He accepted a towel to dry his hands. He didn't dare turn his eyes in Farah's direction. On the back of his neck was the cold, damp press of flowers. Someone signaled that it was time to leave for the hotel. Nasr's leg began to shake. He'd been tricked. This wasn't his choice. He'd made a mistake. Love had been right there, authentic and immoderate. And, instead, he'd put his faith in an ancient and obsolete custom.

Hamid Uncle led Farah ahead, down the hall. Jameela was nowhere to be seen. She was the only person who had ever given him a pure choice. Her staying away now was just like her refusing to interfere with the search: admirable and even endearing, but stubborn, too. At the front door, Nasr's mother clutched his arm, red-eyed and unable to speak, then let him go. What was her role in all this? he wondered. How long ago did gossip and complaint become the only way she talked about Jameela? He stepped out from the house and drank the cold night air deep into his lungs. He'd heard somewhere that in Islam all a man had to do was say "I divorce you" three times to separate himself from a wife. Jameela was right—the system could be wise and sensible, accommodating of mistakes. Forgiving, even.

29

*I*n the lobby of the hotel, after saying goodbye to his family, while making their way across the marble-floored reception area, Nasr heard an intimate, crunching sound. Farah bent to lift a panel of her gharara, but the beads on the hem still caught under her sandals, and each slow, careful step produced the snap and pop of embroidery being pulverized. Probably a man who was alone with his wife for the first time would do something to help, but now they were in the carpeted elevator and it didn't matter.

The bridal suite consisted of two rooms. The first had red armchairs and dark, heavy furniture. White candles of varying heights created a trail of light from the coffee table to the desk, into the bedroom, where a cluster of them sat on the dressing table, glowing before a long mirror. On the massive bed, rose petals were strewn on the wedding quilt his mother had commissioned, and strings of white carnations hung along the canopy (the hotel staff had been left instructions). In the bathroom, there was a large pink tub.

Farah went to the mirror and began unpinning her rupatta. She pulled the fabric off, then gave it a shake. Her shirt was plain and simple, with long sleeves and a round neckline. It was shiny and of the same dark red as the rest of the suit.

After folding her rupatta, she sat down and bent toward her reflection, touching the necklaces she wore. "Your mother has such beautiful pieces."

Nasr nodded. He sat behind her, on the bed, unwinding his turban. He had a vague impulse to say something like "She got them for you," but this was a lie of sorts, as his mother had bought most of this jewelry over the course of many years, well in advance of the bride.

He went to the closet to hang his sherwani. "I might just take a shower," he said when he saw that she was waiting.

He lingered under the steam and noise until the skin on his fingers puckered, and when he emerged, she was sitting on the bed, her knees drawn up to her chest—or so he thought. Actually, she was asleep. She had removed her jewelry and undone her hair, but she was still wearing the rest of the gharara. Nasr blew out the candles that hadn't burned themselves out and turned off the lights. He went to the other side of the bed and slipped under the covers. She stirred and woke—it was clear from her breathing. But he kept his back turned. There were faint dips in the bed, rustles of fabric. Perhaps the gharara coming off now? He forced his own breathing to slow, and lay there—for hours, it seemed—willing her to sleep.

30

*T*he hall Yasmine had chosen for the Valima was not in the least bit makeshift. It was a ballroom properly suited to a large party. It had a high ornate ceiling, creamy wainscoting, and a spacious parquet dance floor in the center, around which were dinner tables decorated with carefully coordinated linens and centerpieces, tasteful party favors, and scented candles. The scene perfectly resembled the cover of the wedding planner's catalog. Nasr posed for pictures, listened to tearful and teasing speeches by his sisters and uncles, accepted congratulations—all with the obedience of a man planning an escape.

The newlyweds had been fetched this morning from the hotel for a breakfast hosted by Nasr's mother. Mr. Ansari had seemed as shy and cowed as the first time Nasr met him, and he could hardly shake his son-in-law's hand. Mrs. Ansari made a point of being the one to serve and refresh Nasr's tea all throughout the meal. Nasr had tried not to notice the smiles the mothers exchanged above Farah's head, as though they thought her warm and unchanged manner on a morning such as this was a feat of heroic effort. After breakfast, Farah was whisked off by Nasr's sisters to be treated to a day at the salon, and Nasr spent the afternoon at home with the uncles in a grateful stupor.

This evening, he endured another endless stream of congratulations, though by now people seemed more interested in each other than in the bridal couple. Nasr shook limp hands and accepted pats on the cheek, but all the while a broken speech ran through his head—or, rather, there were several speeches. Each one was to be delivered from some safe point in the future. The wording would automatically adjust, depending on whom he'd be addressing. So-and-so auntie and uncle came forward, and Nasr responded as any new groom should, but what he secretly rehearsed was "Well, Seema Auntie, it just didn't feel right. The Ansaris are fine people, and I am most sorry about having made the discovery so late, but when you know you belong with someone else, isn't it better to have wasted a few months of people's time rather than ruin another girl's entire life?" Although Nasr was desperate to see Jameela, he did not rehearse the speech to be made to her. The two of them had said all that was needed. It was true that they hadn't exactly reached an understanding or made any actual plans. But that didn't matter. They were beyond words now. She had a right to be angry, sure, and she wouldn't be Jameela if she didn't mulishly cling to all those principled excuses. But doing the right thing now would be a lie—and if there was anyone who couldn't live with a lie, it was her. Once the anger wore off, she would see that. This time it was Nasr's turn to wait, and he would do it. If all he got tonight was a look, that would be enough.

But when Jameela finally came to greet him, it was with

Javaid. As the two of them approached the stage, where throne-like chairs had again been placed for him and Farah to sit on, Jameela split off to speak to Farah. Nasr was then required to listen to Javaid go on about how much he had enjoyed the wedding, how last night's negotiations had gotten a bit hairy, and what a character that Masood Chacha was. "Good fun," he said, smiling with strange ease.

To an unmoved heart, Javaid's cheeriness grated, and Nasr couldn't keep from glancing over at Jameela and Farah, who seemed to be talking intently, their heads dipped and close. Tonight, Jameela had abandoned her uniform for a white, form-fitting lehenga, and her hair was artful and arranged as fancily as the salon had rendered Farah's.

"Well, we're off," Javaid said. "Next week."

"Where's that?" Nasr asked. He had immediately recognized the secretive tone in Javaid's voice, and the hair on his neck had risen.

The answer, of course, was Karachi. Javaid said he'd spent the day calling travel agents, but since it was the high season, they claimed to have run out of specials. Did Nasr happen to know of any agents in New York that he might try?

To Nasr, the conversation had taken on a peculiar, imbecilic quality, but eventually he managed to ask: "So soon?"

Javaid shrugged, smiling. "Jameela's settled about it. And I thinks she's right. Why wait?"

"What about the wedding?"

Javaid glanced around the room, leaned in. There was in his eye the excited gleam of someone who possessed secret, explosive knowledge. "All that's taken care of," he whispered to Nasr. "You'll see."

Jameela was now pulling at Javaid's sleeves. "Here she comes," she said, interrupting the men with brisk courtesy.

"She" was the photographer, who had, Nasr soon learned, been invited over at Jameela's request. The four of them arranged

374

themselves in the same configurations as they had last night—or was it two nights ago?—but then Jameela turned to Farah. "You're sure?" she asked, and Farah replied, "Of course. Please." Drawing Javaid to the side of the stage, Jameela asked the photographer if some shots could be taken of just the two of them.

"I wish we could run away together," Farah whispered to Nasr, sighing as they watched the other couple submit to the photographer's instructions.

"Do you?" Nasr asked. Jameela looped an arm through Javaid's gray suit. Nasr felt Farah hovering beside him—had she inched closer? "Where would we go?" he added, taking a step back so he could turn to her.

"Wherever," Farah replied whimsically, displaying again what Nasr had decided was an impressive imperviousness to the moods of others. "Now that we're married, we can do what we want, right?"

The photographer had left, and Jameela, her arm still through Javaid's, turned to thank Farah. Then, to Nasr, she said, "Congratulations to you both," with a convincingly cool and undisturbed smile.

D inner was signaled, and Nasr's confusion thickened. Their going to Pakistan next week was ludicrous, but perhaps the information was not surprising, coming from Javaid. He hardly seemed to know Jameela at all. Or maybe he suspected something and had told Nasr a lie to test him? Or maybe Jameela felt she ought to go to Karachi and get Javaid settled before she broke the news.

Nasr's mounting speculations occupied him through the long meal, but he was also struck by how his thoughts had no bearing on the workings of the evening. His disorientation was compounded by the fact that the night's rituals were only half familiar. Instead of the turbaned bearers and manservants who had stood at the edges of Saira's wedding, there were crisply dressed, white college students fetching extra naan. And so, despite his treacherous thoughts, his wedding, by all accounts—and as evidenced by the happy smiles finally appearing on his mother's face—was being hailed a success. Even Masood Chacha declared the festivities to be entirely befitting the long tradition of the Siddiqui line. As if to serve as further proof that the event was already receding into the creases of family history, the amity of the past few days of cooperation was beginning to fray. Nasr overheard his sisters talking: "You're next!" Saira declared affectionately. "No way," replied Yasmine. "We've already got someone picked out in Houston," Saira said. "Nice guy, tall, just finishing his residency. I told Ammi it's about time we had a doctor—" "You talked to her first? God, Apa, why did you do that?" "What—where are you going?" Hearing the bewilderment in Saira's voice, Nasr remembered the concerns he'd had, back in the summer, about Yasmine's prospects, and he had the sensation that his thoughts about his younger sister had been patronizing and misguided for quite some time, that Yasmine's silences on certain matters contained a knowledge he'd never credited her with.

As the evening progressed, Nasr entered conversations poorly—he could hear himself. His listeners generously stowed away their confusion and spoke around him. He failed to maintain a smile, and he was often left alone. While eating dessert, he caught sight of his bride—tonight in a broad-striped concoction of creamy white and turquoise—and realized that he had not looked at her in perhaps an hour. That no one saw anything amiss only confirmed to Nasr that he was simply holding a place. And from this there seemed only one conclusion to be drawn: he might as well not be here. This was not a wedding for him. It had no connection to his actual life, the one that had taken root in his imagination and become more vivid and invit-

376

ing the more he thought about it—that life was still somewhere far off, waiting for him.

"Lost control of the little woman so soon?" Pete asked late in the evening. He and Ramesh had appeared beside Nasr during a moment when he found himself standing alone on the stage. Their smiling, joking presence only contributed to Nasr's sense of incongruity. He felt as if an age had passed since he'd last seen familiar faces.

"Quite a show you guys put on," Pete said.

Nasr nodded, but then replied, "Not me."

Arif approached and fell into an easy banter with Pete and Ramesh, as if the three of them were old friends. Nasr stood up, feeling ridiculous in his high-backed chair, but he found he had nothing to contribute to the discussion. The dj's station was at the far end of the hall, and the music had been going for hours. But the Ansaris had asked for the volume to be turned down for the namaaz break, and since then the dj's efforts had largely been ignored by the crowd, with the possible exception of the few people (children and non-Indians) shuffling about on the dance floor. Hiring him had clearly been a waste, Nasr thought. But perhaps that was just as well.

Farah drifted back to her spot beside him, smiling in the same warm and responsive manner she had exhibited all night. Another girl might have demanded an explanation or sulked, but she'd been remarkably uninsistent. A part of Nasr wished for the confrontation—if only because it would hasten a resolution—but mostly he felt he must speak to Jameela first. They were the two people who must decide what to do next.

"What was that?" Nasr asked, turning to see that his friends were watching him expectantly.

"I said how long do you have to keep frowning?" Pete asked. "I'm just asking because you look like a serial killer."

Nasr ventured an effort.

"Fine, fine," Pete said, rolling his eyes. "Too much." He

leaned in then and whispered, "But, seriously, do you even know your fly is open?"

The moment Nasr looked down, he felt himself being lifted up, their hands sliding under his thighs, tipping him forward until he was aloft on their shoulders.

"Sorry, no, I can't," he said. The dance floor darkened and began flashing with multicolored strobe lights. Over his shoulder, he saw Farah watching him. This was the last thing she needed. He tried to climb down. "Really, thanks—"

"Easy there, killer," Pete said, roughly hoisting Nasr higher. "Whose idea did you think it was?"

Glancing back again, Nasr saw Farah wink.

They carried him out onto the dance floor, and immediately the music picked up. It was a bhangra sampled with the theme from *Knight Rider*, a little toggle of high notes, then a hard, driving beat. All at once, as if he'd given some sort of signal, people swarmed around Nasr. He felt his arms rise, his chest uncurl, his whole body lifting and lightening. There was a shadow on the wall opposite the stage. In it, the groom was a tall spidery creature, the head and shoulders riding above the crowd's black arms. The creature's limbs were elongated, stretching and floating as though he was trying to steady himself. When they set him down, the walls of the room retreated—as if the tables, with their unsmiling occupants, were miles away—and Nasr felt the heavy bass climb into his shoulders. He thrust his arms up and began stamping his feet. He was the groom, after all, he thought, with a queer jolt of elation. The crowd gave slightly, and Nasr saw Jameela whirl toward him through a corridor of people. Her arms, thin and nearly bare in her short white sleeves, were pumping above her head as she approached. She stopped less than a foot away, and with a quick sidestep began circling him, staring over her shoulder with a frown of concentration. Her bare feet pounded into the floor in time to the music, and with each stomp her jewelry shook and jingled, the heavy silver earrings swinging in arcs. You could almost mistake that frown as one meant for the dance, like the frown of a tango, but in fact it was a genuine grimace. Nasr's eyes followed the right arm and detected, above a long stack of bangles, the faint outline of bandaging. He allowed her to revolve around him once, then raised his arms and turned his shoulder to circle with her. There was more cheering, some whistles, and the crowd parted to give the two of them extra room.

Jameela winced again. It was too much, but Nasr made himself meet her gaze. Her eyes were darkly lined, making their color all the more pale and gold. They executed one turn and then another, continued looking and looking, and Nasr felt as though they had never before communicated so clearly and directly. She would indeed be leaving within a week, she seemed to say. Trailing behind her departure with Javaid would be a scandal the likes of which the community had not yet seen, though since this was Jameela it couldn't be entirely surprising. Her parents would be obliged to break all contact with her, but even in this their styles would contrast. For several months, Talat Auntie would declare that she didn't have a daughter, but would soon become contrite and lonely, be the first to call Jameela in Karachi. Hamid Uncle would maintain his disapproval more firmly, hold out for more than a year—that is, until his first grandchild was born. The girl would be small, serious, and talkative, with her mother's fierce scowl but not her easy laugh. Jameela herself, on visits back to Canada, would be somber and reserved. She would speak of projects (a lending library to be installed in her and Javaid's portion of the family compound) and the ornate logistics involved in trying to get anything done in a developing country, and she would talk about the cousins and in-laws she lived among with familiar affection, as if becoming a member of a large joint family were the most natural thing in the world. The hijaab would no longer seem like an incongruous accessory, though you could almost say she didn't need it any longer, that something in her face had begun to set her apart. With Nasr, she would never again share a word of knowingness or joke about a past. She would talk to him, efficiently and politely, as the cousin of her husband. This difference in their relationship would hardly be detectable to anyone else, though people would find Jameela changed in other ways. To them, she would seem to have acquired focus and a propensity to use more Urdu in her speech. Some would say there was a new inflexibility there, as though one eye was always out to judge, but perhaps that, they would concede, was simply the usual consequence of living a suitably Islamic life.

Nasr couldn't, of course, know any of this at the Valima, but what he believed (and continued always to believe) he had detected in this long moment was that Jameela was saying goodbye. She was distancing herself from any recognition of their night in the park, any intimation that something might exist between them, and any possibility of reconciliation or future overture. Dancing together this openly would, in their world, be acceptable only between people who were completely unavailable to each other—he knew it as well as she did. But in the years to come, as this moment returned to Nasr's mind through a longer and longer corridor of memory and new experience, he would eventually decide that the farewell had not simply been directed at him. It was aimed at the people in the hall, the individuals but also all the timidity and compromise the group represented, and perhaps even at the act of dancing itself, the free movement of limbs and the flashing of skin—at this entire life and the Jameela they had known here.

The rhythms of the song oscillated into a frenzy. Nasr missed his footing, bumped into someone, lurched back into balance. An unknown expression scurried across Jameela's face. She held his gaze through another turn, but then, all in one motion, she lifted her chin and broke off, twirling away as if this gesture were part of the dance.

Nasr watched her white figure disappear into the crowd, in the direction of the far wall, where his shadow had been. This was the most passionate anyone would ever feel about him—he recognized this immediately, and it became one aspect of the moment that he never revised. But he also recognized that what he'd encountered in the park and now on the dance floor was not love. Or, rather, that it was the end of love—how love burned itself out before fading away.

31

*B*ack in the hotel room after the Valima—no candles this time, and a maid had clearly tidied up—Farah was settled in front of the dressing table again. Nasr was in the other room, at the window. It had begun snowing, and the view lightened as the buildings became covered. After a while, he heard: "Could you?"

As she had last night, Farah had taken off her rupatta first, and sat in just her kurta and gharara. When he walked in, she bent forward with a languid dip of her head, exposing the back of a long, pale neck.

He reached for one of the many necklaces, but the skin under his fingers leaped. "Let me warm them," he said. In the bathroom mirror, as he ran his hands under the hot water, he saw that her head was still dipped forward but that she was watching him.

"It's been such a week of asking for things you could do yourself," she said, after he had managed to get the first tiny clasp open. The body still twitched when he grazed it.

"Yes," he replied belatedly, seeing that she expected him to agree.

"It will all vanish soon," she said. "As it ought to."

"What will?"

"The privilege of being waited on, hand and foot."

He felt he ought to make some oath, as a proper groom might, never to let this happen. But another moment passed.

When he finished with the necklaces, Nasr noticed a stray pin dangling at the side of her head. Just as he plucked it out, Farah's arms swept up, and her elbows began moving like wings, taking her hands from one spot to another in the dark nest of hair. He watched her fingers pry through the thicket, the bangles on her wrists thrushing against each other as she retrieved pin upon pin where Nasr saw only hair.

He began to help, and the two of them worked together in silence until Farah's arms dropped to her sides, and she let out a tired sigh.

"There are hundreds," he said.

"It took them hours."

"Who?" Nasr asked. He continued to search for pins while she explained how the women at the beauty salon had never seen Indian jewelry before and had spent much of the afternoon devising ways to make sure her hair stayed up and out of the way.

"They thought I would be moving around a lot," she said with a faintly sardonic smile, "so they made something special to hold the teeka."

She tipped her head back, and Nasr saw an intricate structure installed in her part. On both sides of the white line of skin, there were six pins angled away and parallel like ribs, and one pin at the top that was directed backward. Hooked to the final pin was the teeka, and its string fit snugly between the ribs to ensure that the gold disk at the other end was centered and flat against Farah's forehead.

Nasr pulled out the teeka and dismantled the construction. He then pushed his fingers through the curls and felt along the scalp. She was quiet, and in the mirror her eyes were closed. He thought she might have drifted to sleep, but then she asked, "How did you know it was me?" She added, "Back then?" but she needn't have. Nasr knew exactly when she meant. He remembered the composition, three turned-down faces—the lines of each agreeable and sweet in their own way.

"You were the one who let your tea get cold," he said.

"But I always do that." Her eyes were still closed, but there was a faint smile now on her lips, as though she thought he was teasing her.

How *had* he picked her out correctly? Nasr wondered. Yet, instead of the Ansaris' living room, myriad other rooms came into his mind. He remembered the sensation of crossing the threshold into them—feeling like a prized client, a bringer of good fortune and promise.

"I was afraid we wouldn't get here," Farah said.

Nasr nodded dumbly, though her eyes were still closed. He caught sight of his own features in the mirror—he was a thin figure in shadow. His white shirt was crushed and hung loose on his body.

She seemed to be waiting for him to say more, but then she herself said, "Jameela Baji told me something about you once." Nasr's fingers stopped at the sound of Jameela's name, but he swiftly applied more energy to them, as though he were digging out a stray pin. He wasn't sure if this would incite her to continue or to stop, nor was he sure which he preferred. She began again, timidly but with clear determination to finish: "She said that you took so long to decide not because you knew too little about those other girls, but because you knew too much. That you'd figure out the whole story when you went to see them—at least, you thought you could." Now there was a plainly nervous laugh. Under his kneading, the hair was breaking loose and spilling down her back. "Suraiya said to be myself. Rafia thought I should put you through tests, and if you broke the engagement, then—I didn't know who you expected me to be."

Nasr remembered the strain of their early conversations, when she would be warm one minute and distant the next. So those mixed signals were simply a reaction to what she'd learned of his fickleness. He suppressed a pitying sigh, and his mind drifted farther back, to the intriguing line-up of profiles and the constantly refreshed samosas and hot tea. He recalled not being able to keep his eyes from returning to the face closest to him, noticing again and again the dazzle of its smile, then feeling disappointed for some reason . . . "You're right. I'm Farah." Yes, she had said that, and if she hadn't—in the mirror, his own face was utterly devoid of expression—then he would have left that room none the wiser. He would have left it like all the other men who'd come to see her, whether or not—again, he felt his surprise grow, although the features in the reflection remained blank—*whether or not* he'd guessed correctly.

Nasr pulled his fingers from Farah's hair and took a step back. She had revealed herself to him. If anyone had made a choice, it was her.

After a moment, Farah crossed her arms down to the ends of her shirt and began to lift it up. Nasr cleared his throat. She froze in the gesture, but then she stood up and turned to him. With downcast eyes, she held out the two corners of her shirt for him to take. "You can help me," she said. Still not looking at him, she raised her arms up above her head. Her churis slid down and landed against her sleeves.

Nasr felt his breath catch, as if a rose were blooming in his chest. Her choice, a decision she had made—on that day, not to marry just anyone, but to marry him.

He brought her arms down. Her hands were gloved in the red stain of mehendi, a lacy pattern that came to a point on both the insides and outsides of her wrists. Taking a hand in his, he pulled a few bangles forward. They slid easily over the wrist, but got stuck over the thumb. He squeezed the palm, trying to work the bangles around, but they remained stranded, and the skin on either side began to darken. Nasr dipped his head and licked the raised pad at the head of her thumb, then turned the churis like a knob until they came off. He pulled six more bangles forward, tasted again the salt in the soft V between her thumb and finger. Her pulse was visible under his fingertips, and there was a trace of perfume. Another set of six, then one more. Just as he was lifting her other wrist, he remembered that this was the second time he had done such a thing in two days, though in this case the skin on the wrists was unmarred and the glass of the woman's bangles was deep red, for a bride. Why had he been chosen? Nasr wondered. On what basis? And what did she hope to make of this?

The spikes in Farah's breathing settled into a brisk but steady rise and fall, and she was watching him now, unwary and expectant. A choice, he thought, requires trust. Trust in oneself, and trust in others. It requires faith and mutual goodwill. All those things. But did he deserve this trust? Those rooms that he had always thought were so dismal and bare—they'd been brimming with fear. Fear had been in every overcourteous welcome, fear behind each elaborately offered sweet dish, fear in each departure. Fear in the face of an equally abiding hopefulness. Desperation, really. A desperation, Nasr suddenly recognized, that he himself shared. Jameela's broken-up face came before him now, and the shudder of her body against his. He was worse than a fool. He had gained entry into all those rooms—now an innocent girl's hopes—all on a pretense.

He drew Farah over to the bed and kissed her forehead. He took off her shirt, then undid her gharara and let it slip to the floor. He laid her down, looking away from the red wrinkles left around her waist by the cummerbund's tie, and pulled a sheet over her body. She would have to be told everything, even still. Wasn't it unfair not to? He turned off the lights and lay beside her on the covers, rubbed her head until her eyes finally closed.

When Nasr woke some time later, the room was still dark, but there was a thin line of light on the carpet under the curtains. Farah stirred and, once she was awake, turned toward him. Her eyes dropped to his collar. The beautiful brow knotted. "It'll be morning soon," she said, and the note in her voice, Nasr would often think later, was unmistakable. It was a clear signal for what must happen, for what she, like him, needed to indicate had happened successfully. A reminder that the success of everything that might form between them, her choice and his, depended on it.

She had full, pink-tipped breasts, a narrow waist that cut deeply into a delicate belly, and creamy skin that blushed or tightened or quivered wherever it was touched. He didn't rush anything. He applied all his experience to allow her body to adjust to his, kept careful track of what was to be done: where to kiss her, how long to linger. This is how he would earn this, he thought, sliding her legs open with his knee. He would persuade her. He would make sure that everything in her path was pleasing and easy, and she would catch up, and the differences between them would be banished.

But it was not easy. It took several hours, through the dawn light, and when he felt her body finally take him all in, it seemed to come as a relief to both of them. Just before the moment, he saw her forehead clench, and he heard the words, or felt the

whisper, or sensed himself thinking: "Bismillahir rahmanir ra-
heem." And then her body gave; he felt it flinch, clutch him, and
there was a muffled sound of pain.

"It won't always be like this," he suggested. She hastily
agreed, nodding; there was a faint sniffle, and a corner of her
lower lip was in her teeth. "With me on top," he said.

Her eyes flashed open, two dark marbles glistening in pools
of white, and he saw it happen there, frame by frame, the slow,
dawning seduction: a shock of comprehension followed by a
deep blush, the lovely bloom of color traveling from heart to
head, signaling a shift in sympathies, perhaps a kind of conver-
sion. He felt a tremor begin in his leg, also travel upward, felt his
body finally move of its own accord, dip thoroughly into hers.
Yes, why not, in the name of God?

*B*y the time they had moved her possessions to New York,
Nasr and Farah discovered, with mutual surprise and satisfaction, that they had already lived through ("survived," as one
still said too casually) a great deal of experience as a couple: the
multi-event initiation of the wedding itself; complicated honeymoon travel involving flights, ferries, rental cars—and thus, in-
evitably, a number of delays; the return from Vancouver to yet
more demanding (though manageable) parties, each of which
was abuzz with shock and gossipy theories about Jameela and
Javaid's sudden departure; the packing of a moving van with
Farah's boxes and wedding presents; the occasionally harrowing
drive on what turned out to be the coldest and snowiest day of
that winter; a painstakingly thorough inspection at the border.
One by one, these small trials began to fill in the absence of the
very first night of their marriage—and Nasr ventured to hope
that the moment wouldn't live between them forever. But the

residue of it lingered long enough in their marriage that he felt the need to exert himself, to attune his desires to Farah's, to be patient as he searched for new ways to erase that night from the record.

Fortunately, their early years as a couple brought on many distracting and involving changes, even some meaningful shifts in alliance. Farah had an eye for fashionable clothes, and Nasr soon discovered he could persuade her away from styles that were too blocky or bulky, selections her mother had imposed in girlhood, by simply observing how good she looked when she didn't hide herself away. More significantly, Farah began to not always agree with her parents' views, and Nasr liked to think it was his influence showing when she backed her sister Rafia up when the girl announced that she wanted to get a master's degree before becoming engaged. As a couple, the two of them made efforts to observe Ramzaans and Eids and eat halal when possible; and, save for the occasional beer at lunch, Nasr found that he hardly missed drinking. In New York, Rashida and Malik and the rest of that set did become friends, but Farah didn't seem to mind when Nasr found them overbearing and needed a break. They waited a bit to have children—it seemed only right that she finish her degree, and they did some of the traveling he'd envisioned. Eventually, they declared that they loved each other, but the words sounded like other people's. This was less true a few months further on, when they briefly thought she was pregnant. Still later, by the time their son was born, they found their own way of expressing the affection between them.

Nasr never forgot that as little as a few days before his wedding, he was on course to becoming another kind of groom. At first, he believed that this bypassed trajectory was one that would have involved Jameela and thus required demanding breaks and strong stands—all the rare high drama of life. But actually, when he was honest, he realized that that path had never been a real possibility for him—that, as strongly as he had felt during the Nikaah that he and Jameela belonged together, the instincts working against this impulse were just as strong. No, the more likely danger for him was that he would have become a man who slipped into a reluctant obedience that left him bored and resentful—a man who secretly pined for a different life, constantly went in search of distraction and escape, was prone to belittling and scorn. There were, of course, times in his and Farah's years together when Nasr caught himself reformulating or avoiding a certain opinion or confidence. Implicit in their sort of marriage was that Farah would love him without needing to know him thoroughly. But this, he discovered, turned out to be a curious kind of loving. Its conditions ought to have been the easiest to satisfy, but in fact they provoked an altogether unexpected response: you began to feel as though you wanted to live up to it, earn what was being freely offered.

Eventually, Nasr became convinced that there was an obvious reason why he hadn't seen what was between him and Jameela all those years (why he had, as someone else might see it, "failed" her), and the reason was that there hadn't actually been anything there, aside from a mess of confusing signals and circumstances. He came to believe that this was the very sort of thing that happened when you let yourself get caught in one culture's insistence that love ought to be like this or that. The key for people like him, he ultimately concluded, in this as in most matters, was to be nimble. Your privilege as an immigrant was to pick and choose your inheritance, maintain what suited you and participate merely to the extent of your patience and interest. It was not in your nature to align with one side fully, and so you couldn't help but make a life that was both apart and among. You didn't make one choice and stick with it but, rather, hundreds of minor choices with which you created a unique path through the corridors of old traditions and the avenues of the new. And you cultivated this dividedness because you carried always the imprint of that first move—the decision to leave home. Indeed, this initiating choice, more than anything, was your true inheritance.

As time went on, it sometimes became less clear to Nasr who had actually altered the trajectory of events—which woman, and when, and occasionally even what, exactly, the original trajectory had been. But for a long time he believed that Jameela was the person responsible for knocking him off course. On those rare occasions when he encountered her (every few years, when their visits to Montreal overlapped), and she seemed defensive and diminished or simply dissatisfied, he wondered if she knew what she'd done for him—the gift of it—and he hoped for her sake that she had no idea.

*T*hat morning in the still dim hotel room, however, as the world seemed to close in around Farah's face, Nasr had been struck by an entirely different vision. Amid the angles of light, he saw in the purity of his wife's cheeks, lips, and smile the flowering of a straight and clearly marked path. Only she could do this, he thought—trust him this much and with this trust furnish him with a tremendous feeling of wondering why he, of all people, had been chosen. This was the spark that had drawn his initial interest. There was an allure here, he told himself, that people like Jameela didn't understand, of submitting, of trusting in something greater and larger without wanting to change it. And also, there was the sheer glamour of reaching back and finally doing something his father had done: taking a woman across a divide, to another country even, some place where she had never expected she could be happy.

Did it matter, after all, where the desire to be this kind of man came from? Wasn't being able to feel this way—wasn't that the point?

acknowledgments

First and foremost, I would like to thank my parents, Manzoor and Nuzhat Alam, for their many years of remarkable sacrifice, patience, and love. Thanks also to Ahmer Alam for his steadfast encouragement.

Grateful acknowledgment is made to Emory University and the Creative Writing Program at Boston University, especially my teachers Susanna Kaysen and Leslie Epstein.

Thanks also to Eleanor Jackson and Anton DiSclafani for vital support during the writing process. Many thanks to Michael Mezzo for his keen eye and deep commitment. And special thanks to Kim Witherspoon for her long enthusiasm and faith.

My deepest gratitude to Ronica Bhattacharya, bachpan ki dost, for her matchless insights and foresights, especially for knowing before everyone else that this was a novel.

And finally, thanks to my dear ones, Marshall and Aziz, who are essential in every way.

about the author

SAHER ALAM was born in Lucknow,
India, in 1973 and moved to the United
States when she was five. She is a graduate of Princeton University, where she
majored in chemical engineering, and the
Creative Writing Program at Boston University. She was a fiction fellow at Emory
University, and her stories have appeared
in *Best of the Fiction Workshops* and the
journal *Literary Imagination*. She lives in
St. Louis, Missouri.

READERS' GUIDE

I.   How does the alternative life that Nasr imagines for himself affect his relationship with Farah? In your experience, has the ability to imagine a path not taken haunted your life?

2.   What do you think of Nasr's mother's generation's desire to push their children into arranged marriages?

3.   In a love marriage, the desire to commit to someone for life comes after falling in love. In an arranged marriage, the opposite is true: with the commitment of marriage comes love. Given this difference, would a love marriage between Nasr and Jameela have been more successful than the arranged marriage he has with Farah? Can Nasr ever hope to develop feelings for Farah that are as strong as the feelings he has for Jameela?

4. In Chapter 13, while talking to Jameela, why does Nasr recall the awkwardness of his exchange with Lillian on the plane home from London? How do the emotions lingering from that encounter affect his conversation with Jameela? He has been angry with Jameela for weeks, so why doesn't he finally confront her?

5. If first-generation Americans often feel that they straddle two cultures, for many of the main characters in this novel, September 11 exacerbates their sense of being culturally marooned. They resist both of the communities that make claims on their allegiance: the Americans they live among and, despite themselves, have come to resemble, and the terrorists, who share their religious beliefs and customs and who, to a certain extent, claim to have acted in their name. At the end of Book One, why does Nasr conflate the memory of his sister Saira's wedding with his behavior at Heathrow airport when he ignores the Arab passenger's imploring calls for help? How are the emotions that these two events stir up similar?

6. Along the same lines, why do Nasr's feelings about the people he meets at the masjid (Malik, Rashida, etc.) shift so dramatically after Javaid and Jameela leave New York? And what does this mean for him and his future with Farah?

7. What does Javaid tell Jameela that makes her finally decide to elope with him? Why is this piece of information particularly effective in persuading her?

8. *The Groom to Have Been* is preceded by two epigraphs—one from Edith Wharton's novel *The Age of Innocence* and the other from the Qur'an. Why do you think these epigraphs were chosen?

9. Late in the novel, Nasr thinks the following of his and Farah's relationship: "Implicit in their sort of marriage was that

Farah would love him without needing to know him thoroughly." What does Nasr mean by this? Discuss this notion of marriage. Can anyone in a marriage know the other person thoroughly?

10.   Is Nasr an admirable figure? Do you find his way of being in a world changed by the attacks on September 11 reasonable and practical, or cowardly and insufficient?

11.   Do you think the novel has a happy ending?